THE FIRST LADY

THE FIRST LADY

CARL WEBER

KENSINGTON PUBLISHING CORP.
http://www.kensingtonbooks.com

DAFINA BOOKS are published by

Kensington Publishing Corp.
850 Third Avenue
New York, NY 10022

All Kensington titles, imprints and distributed lines are available at special quantity discounts for bulk purchases for sales promotion, premiums, fund-raising, educational or institutional use.

Special book excerpts or customized printings can also be created to fit specific needs. For details, write or phone the office of the Kensington Special Sales Manager: Kensington Publishing Corp., 850 Third Avenue, New York, NY 10022, Attn. Special Sales Department. Phone: 1-800-221-2647.

ISBN-13: 978-0-7582-1576-5
ISBN-10: 0-7582-1576-2

First Hardcover Printing: January 2007
First Trade Paperback Printing: January 2008
10 9 8 7 6 5 4 3 2

Printed in the United States of America

This book is dedicated to the Reverend Joseph Simmons, Minister Tyrone Thompson, Pastor Jerry Cannon, and Reverend Stanley Wright. Each of you has taught me a respect for the ministry in a different way. I'll always appreciate it. God bless.

Acknowledgments

I'd like to thank my editor, Karen Thomas, for all the things she's done for me and my career. Not only have you been a great editor and colleague, but you've been a terrific friend.

PROLOGUE

"Hey, Charlene, you ready to get started?"

My good friend and confidante, Alison Williams, smiled as she walked into my hospital room. I tried to smile back when she kissed my forehead, but the abdominal pains I was experiencing wouldn't allow it. So, I lay there in my bed, grappling through the pain as I watched her sit in the chair next to my bed and pull out some of my personal stationery and a pen. I pressed the button that controlled the morphine drip in my arm, and Alison waited patiently for my pain reliever to kick in. Six months ago, I refused to use any type of pain medication, but now I understood why the Lord invented addictive drugs like morphine and Demerol. Without them, I probably would have died from the pain of my pancreatic cancer weeks ago. As it was now, I was pushing the darn drip button every fifteen minutes. I was on the highest dose there was, which meant I didn't have long to live, probably a few weeks at best.

I wasn't afraid of dying, though. I'd lived a good life, married a wonderful man in Bishop T.K. Wilson, raised two fantastic children, and had the honor of being the first lady of absolutely the best church in New York—First Jamaica Ministries. So, if the Lord was ready to call me home, although I considered myself young at forty-four, I was ready to go. The only thing I was afraid of was what would happen to my family—more importantly, my husband—after I was gone. I was now making preparations to be sure my man was taken care of after my death.

You see, as good and honorable a man of God as T.K. was, he was still just a man with desires and needs; and men, no matter how bright they may appear to be, are very naive when it comes to women, *especially* slick-ass churchwomen. I could see it now.

Fifteen minutes after they put me in the ground, those church heifers would be in my house trying to figure out the best way to redecorate and move my shit out. Say what you might about my choice of words, but I'd seen these so-called churchwomen in action too many times in the past.

Last year when Sister Betty Jean White passed away, within six months, her worst enemy, Jeannette Wilcox, had weaseled her way into Sister Betty's house and was sleeping with her husband. A few months after that, they were married. If you walk in that house today, there's not one sign that Sister Betty even lived there. So, I could envision T.K., in his moment of grief and loneliness, letting some church heifer manipulate him into doing just about anything she wanted, and I was not about to allow that.

Don't get me wrong. I wasn't trying to stop my husband from moving on with his life after I was gone. On the contrary, I wanted him to find someone to spend the rest of his days with and be happy. I just wanted to make sure that that someone had his best interests at heart and wasn't just some ambitious, Bible-carrying gold digger with her own agenda. That's why, with the help of Alison, I was planning on helping my husband pick my successor from the grave.

I felt some relief when the pain medication finally kicked in, and Alison helped me as I struggled to sit up. She placed a pillow behind my head, then sat back in her seat to take notes as I began to dictate the fourth of several letters to be given out after my death. One would be for T.K., to let him know how much I loved him and that I wanted him to move on with his life. The next letters would be to the four women I thought were the top candidates to vie for my husband's heart and become the next first lady of First Jamaica Ministries. In my opinion, not every one of these women was a suitable candidate, which was even more reason for me to be writing these letters. I had to steer the course of events so that T.K. would not end up with the wrong woman.

I started this day's dictation with a letter for T.K.'s first love, Marlene, the mother of his illegitimate daughter, Tanisha. I never really told anyone this, but I liked Marlene, even if she was extremely rough around the edges. She had spunk, and from what I was told, a loyalty to T.K. that almost rivaled my own. I know it might sound strange for a woman, any woman, to have kind words about her husband's ex-lover, but their relationship happened long before I met T.K. and before he found the Lord.

I will admit, though, that at one time I had been glad that Marlene had moved to D.C. But that was before I was diagnosed with cancer, when I made it a point to keep any woman who might tempt T.K. as far away as possible. Now I was happy to hear that she had recently moved back to Queens and had even shown up at a few church services. She, unlike any of the other candidates, had a connection to my family, which made her a very favorable competitor in the race for T.K.'s heart. Her only flaw in my eyes was that she was a recovering drug abuser . . . but then again, so was my husband.

The next letter was to be written to Savannah Dickens. Savannah was the church's new choir soloist. She was a quiet, attractive woman in her mid-thirties who kept to herself. She'd grown up in our church but had been living in California for the past fifteen years. I didn't know much about her except that she had a phenomenal voice and had just recently returned to the church and the community. I will admit I'm not much for quiet folks because they're usually trying to hide something. She was, however, the daughter of Deacon Joe Dickens, so there was no denying that she would be at least considered for the position of first lady after my death. Her father was one of the more prominent older members of our church, and he was looking to become the chairman of the Deacons Board, so I was sure that after my death he would be trying his best to push T.K. and Savannah together in an effort to consolidate power. It was a move I wasn't against, because it would probably benefit T.K. in the long run. The more people he had watching his back the better. What I didn't like was the fact that Savannah was only thirty-five years old. I wasn't objecting to her age so much; she was only ten years younger than T.K. I was worried that she was thirty-five and didn't have any children. A woman under forty who hadn't had a child probably wanted kids of her own, and that was out. The last thing T.K. needed after raising my son, Dante, and my daughter, Donna, and then putting them through college was another baby to support. Besides, he was now a grandfather. How would he look having a child that was younger than his grandchildren?

The next letter was to my very good friend Sister Lisa Mae Jones. Lisa and I had been friends for years. She was the widow of Pastor Lee Jones, who passed away suddenly four years ago. She joined our church a year after her husband's church hired a new pastor, and his wife replaced her as first lady. Lisa had everything it took to be a first lady. She was smart, attractive, had plenty of connections, and, most importantly, Lisa had enough attitude that she wouldn't let these church heifers run over her or T.K. She also had a true loyalty to me. I didn't know if she'd want the job, but one could always hope.

Next in line was Ms. Monique Johnson, the first lady of plastic surgery and implants. Oh, she would swear she'd never been touched cosmetically except for the blessings the Lord had given her, but I'm sorry, there was no way a forty-year-old woman who'd given birth could have a body like hers without having something nipped and tucked. The way she walked around the church showing off her fake cleavage and that humongous booty of hers in those tight dresses was disgraceful. And not only was her body fake, but so was her personality. I'd never met a phonier woman in my entire life. She was always smiling in my face like she was my best friend, then grinning at T.K. like he was the last man on earth and she had to have him.

Monique knew I was aware that she wanted my husband, but that didn't stop her from disrespecting me by always trying to get in his face. I had a thought to slap her a few times over the past few years. The sad thing was that T.K. just couldn't see it. I brought it up to him several times before I got sick, but he just dismissed it as me being paranoid. He might have been right to an extent, because I was paranoid. My husband was a powerful and handsome man in a position that put him in contact with many lonely, single women with low self-esteem. But paranoid or not, my watchfulness had served me well over twenty-plus years of marriage, and I never had a reason to think my man had strayed. I trusted my husband, but I wasn't taking any chances with Monique or any other woman with her reputation.

Rumor had it that she had had extramarital affairs with at least two high-profile members of the church. So, for years, I'd kept that wench as far away from my husband as possible. I planned to try to continue doing that even after my death. Some of my girlfriends from the church confirmed that Monique's overtures toward T.K. had become even bolder since I was hospitalized. I was sure T.K. hadn't even given the woman a second thought with me being sick and all, but a question still remained: Would he be strong-willed enough to stay away from her after my death? I could only hope.

By the time we'd written Monique's first letter, the pain was starting to return. I wanted to push the drip, but the machine only allowed me medication every fifteen minutes, and I'd just pushed it for the third time five minutes earlier. Being the concerned friend she was, Alison insisted that we'd done enough for the day. God willing, we'd finish the rest of the letters in the next few days. Although I'm not going to reveal their content, I can assure you that they would shake up a whole lot of people. Six months from now, I'd be dead, but I could guarantee that my presence would still be felt.

Can you dictate the lives of your family, friends, and enemies from the grave? Those were the thoughts I contemplated as I waited for the new dose of pain medication to take effect. I could picture the scenario now: *The first lady of First Jamaica Ministries is dead. Who will win the bishop's heart and become the next first lady? Only time will tell.*

1

BISHOP

Six months later

I leaned forward in my chair and opened my desk drawer, taking out two glasses and a bottle of cognac that I saved for special occasions. I poured myself a drink and one for my best friend, James Black. There was nothing like drinking some good old-fashioned cognac with James, especially after a day when the fish weren't biting worth a darn. James and I spent a great deal of time together when it came to both business and pleasure. He was a loyal friend, a former deacon, and now the chairman of the board of trustees of our church. He was also my eyes and ears among the members of the church since my wife, Charlene, passed away, God bless her soul, six months ago.

Lately, James seemed to be seeing and hearing more things that I was oblivious to in the church. I hated that because I tried to remain close to all the members of the congregation, but there are some things that church folks just won't tell their pastor. That's where my wife, and now James, had come in handy. They both had a knack for discovering things before they blew up in my face—my wife, because she was very nosy and intimidating, and James because . . . well, let's just say he was a ladies' man, and I had to turn my head every once in a while from his lustful behavior. Nonetheless, they both got the job done in their own way, and I was appreciative.

"T.K.," James said, swirling his cognac before taking a sip. He stared at me long and hard, as if he were trying to find the proper words to express himself. Normally, this was something James didn't seem to have a problem with. I also noted that he'd called me T.K. instead of Bishop. He did that only when he wanted us to step aside from our roles as church heads and deal with each other as men of flesh.

"What's on your mind, James? You got something to tell me? You haven't been yourself all day."

James took another sip of his drink. It was obvious he was stalling. "Well, yes, I do," he finally said.

"All right, then, man. Spit it out," I encouraged.

"All right. T.K., I've been talking to some of the sisters of the church, and well . . . they think it's time." He leaned back patiently in his chair, obviously relieved to get this off his chest. I just wished I knew what he was so relieved about. I didn't have a clue what he thought it was time for.

"Time? Time for what?" I stared at him as I lifted my glass and took a swallow.

"Time for you to make a choice. So, I hope you're ready because life around here isn't going to be easy until you've made your choice."

"And what choice do I have to make?" I asked calmly, still not sure where he was going.

"Whether we're going to have Armageddon or peace around here," he replied between sips, staring back at me with so little emotion, he could have been a professional poker player.

I sat up straight in my chair, trying my best to read my friend's face because Armageddon was not a word to be used lightly. "What are you talking about, James?"

"T.K., there is about to be Armageddon in this church, and you're about to be right in the middle of it."

There was that word again. James's face still showed no emotion, but now his voice had a chill that had me concerned. Had James been given some divine message from God that I had been left out of? Was there dissention in the congregation? Were they about to try to vote me out as pastor? I wasn't sure what was going on, but before he left my office, my good friend James Black was going to explain himself.

"James, you of all people know I do not like to play games. So, will you please stop beating around the bush and get to the point?" My voice was firm, and I'm sure he knew I was serious.

"Look, I'm sorry about that, T.K. I just figured you'd want to hear this subtly." He took a breath before he spoke. "The women of the church are about to tear this place apart, and it's all because of you."

I searched my mind for reasons I might have upset the women of my congregation. "What have I supposedly done this time?"

"It's what you haven't done, Bishop. These women are losing their minds. Haven't you noticed what's going on around here? The women are arriving at church a half hour early just to assure themselves a spot in the front. I'm not just talking about two or three women. There had to be fifty or sixty of them this past Sunday. And I bet you a hundred dollars there'll be even more this week. It's crazy."

I smiled at my friend with pride. "That's not necessarily a bad thing, James. The word must be getting around that I give one heck of a sermon."

He laughed. "Are you really that naive? These women don't give a damn about your sermons. They only—"

I shot him a look, and he tried to clean up his words. "What I mean is, all they care about is you." He pointed a finger at me. "They are all bound and determined by any means necessary to be the one to become your wife, the next first lady of the church."

For the first time, I understood what he was talking about, and I dismissed it immediately. Yes, I knew that every congregation wanted their pastor to be married. It just made sense, if you really thought about it. But my Charlene had been gone only six months. That was way too soon for me to even be entertaining the thought of dating, let alone remarrying.

I looked at the picture of Charlene I kept on my desk. Oh, how I missed her. My wife was a spitfire who had loved me, my family, and this church more than life itself, and to be honest, I wasn't ready to let her go yet. And I didn't think the church was, either.

"That's ridiculous, James. Let me assure you, that's got to be the last thing on these women's minds. Trust me. Like I told you, I know these things. I know the hearts of the women of this church. It's just in their nature to be caring. You can't go taking it the wrong way, James. I sure don't."

"Are you kidding?" He chuckled, but there was a twinge of disdain in his voice. "No offense to your sermons, Bishop, but there's not a hat shop in Queens with a single fancy brim left on its shelves. There are women in this borough who have wiped out their entire savings, and others who have taken out loans just to buy enough hats for as many Sundays as it's going to take to catch the bishop's eye. And how better to catch the bishop's eye than to reserve a place right across from the pulpit every Sunday?"

"James, stop exaggerating," I chortled. "These are good churchwomen who just want to hear the word."

"You can play dumb all you want, T.K.," James said as he poured the last of the liquor into our glasses. "But you can't say that I didn't warn you."

"Well, thanks for the warning, but I'm sure you're wrong."

He held up his glass, a sign for me to toast. I hesitantly followed suit and lifted my glass in the air.

"Here's to me being wrong," James said. Before either one of us could put our glasses to our lips, we were startled by a knock on the door. The concern in James's eyes mirrored my own. The last thing we needed as prominent men of the church was to get caught sipping liquor. Jesus might have turned water to wine, and even taken a sip or two himself with every meal, but God forbid I was caught having an innocent drink with a friend. They'd swear I was a drunk. So, without having to say a word, we simultaneously downed the contents of our glasses. I held out my hand for James to give me his empty glass.

"Come in," I said as I quickly placed the empty bottle and two glasses in my bottom desk drawer. I did so just in the nick of time, because as soon as I closed the drawer, the office door opened.

"Gentlemen," Deacon Joe Dickens said as he entered the office.

"How you doin', Deacon?" I asked as James replied with a courteous nod.

"Fine, Bishop. I'm doin' just fine. Heard you two went fishin'. Hope they were biting"—the deacon smiled—"'cause I'd love to have a few porgies."

"Put it this way, Deacon," I told him. "If you or anyone else ever had to depend upon Trustee Black's and my ability to catch fish, we'd all starve. The only thing we got in that cooler over there is ice."

Laughter filled the room momentarily before Deacon Dickens cleared his throat so that he could speak on what he'd really come for. "Speaking of food and eating, Bishop, my daughter, Savannah, is going to be doing a little cooking this weekend. You know that cobbler you were so fond of at the deacons' banquet last month?"

I smiled at the memory of that cobbler. It was quite possibly the best I'd ever had. "How could I forget? The darn thing was so good I must have gone back for seconds three times." I patted my belly as I grinned.

"Well, that was Savannah's doing. She made that cobbler."

"Sister Savannah is responsible for that cobbler? Well, I may have to stop by your house a little more often, Deacon, 'cause your daughter sure can burn."

"You're always welcome, Bishop. Matter of fact, along with that cobbler, she's cooking smothered pork chops and collard greens for dinner tomorrow. If I remember correctly, you're rather fond of pork chops, aren't you?"

"Could eat them every day," I said with a nod.

"Well, then you're going to have to come over for dinner tomorrow night. I insist."

I let out a disappointed sigh. "I wish I could, Deacon, but I already have dinner plans to meet with the bookstore committee tomorrow night. How about a rain check?"

The deacon looked truly disappointed. "All right. How's next Sunday sound? I can't promise pork chops, but I'm sure Savannah will make another cobbler."

I glanced down at my weekly planner, then looked up at the deacon with a smile. "Deacon, it's a date. And whether it's pork chops or not, I'll be looking forward to it."

"Good, good," he replied. "How's seven o'clock sound to you?"

"Seven o'clock next Sunday is fine." I wrote it in my planner, then made a mental note to tell my secretary, Alison, to put it in hers.

"Well, gentlemen, I guess it's time I got home. I'll see you at service on Sunday." The deacon shook our hands and left, closing the door behind him.

It was obvious that James could barely wait until Deacon's footsteps faded down the hall before he exploded with laughter. "Oh, my Lord, that guy is hilarious."

"Why? What's so funny?" I asked.

"What's so funny? You're what's so funny. Can't you see a setup when it's right in front of your face?" James stood up, shaking his head. "Like I told you before the deacon came in, it's starting, my friend. The battle for who's going to be the next first lady has started, and it looks like the first woman in the ring is Savannah Dickens. And her father's the one who's throwing her in."

"James, my man, you're reading far too much into this."

"Am I, T.K.? Since when does a prominent member of the church invite the pastor to dinner and not at least extend an invitation to any other prominent member of the church who's in the room? I might as well have been invisible."

I sat back in my chair and thought about what he was saying. I didn't reply at first because the more I thought about it, the more his words started to make sense. He did have an intriguing point. Why didn't the deacon invite him to dinner? He could have at least invited him when I declined. Was the deacon trying to orchestrate a relationship between me and his daughter? It was possible. The real question was whether I was willing to be a participant in his plan.

Savannah was single, and she was also a very attractive woman. She had some of the prettiest black hair I'd ever seen. For the first time, I began to imagine her as a woman and not just a member of the church. The image brought a slight grin to my face, which quickly morphed into a guilty frown as Savannah's image was replaced by Charlene's.

"You might be right about the deacon, James, but then again, maybe your dinner invitation just slipped the deacon's mind."

James chuckled. "If you believe that, I got a bridge to sell you out back."

I rose from my chair, reached in my pocket, and pulled out some money. "How much?"

James's chuckle became a full-fledged laugh. "You crazy, you know that, Bishop?"

"That's what they tell me." I laughed with him.

"So, T.K., what do you think?"

"Think about what, James?" I said flatly, knowing from the look on his face what he was referring to.

"Savannah. What do you think about Savannah? Old girl

does have some hips on her, doesn't she?" James traced his fingers in the air like he was outlining a shapely woman's figure.

"I hadn't noticed," I lied.

"Yeah, right. Sure you haven't." James waved his hand at me. "Look, T.K., you may have the title of bishop, but you're still a man. Don't think I forgot about what happened in the Bahamas."

Blood rushed to my face. "You're never gonna let me forget that, are you?"

"Nope. Never."

"Okay, hold it over my head. Just don't forget I've seen you in a few compromising positions too. You seem to have forgotten about Las Vegas."

He laughed. "Hey, whatever happened to what goes on in Vegas stays in Vegas?"

"Same thing that happened to what goes on in the Bahamas stays in the Bahamas. At least I was with my wife."

"Aw'ight, I get your point. Look, I gotta get outta here. I got a big date tonight with Sister Renée Wilcox."

I shook my head. "I don't know why these sisters let you get away with your foolishness, James."

"Same reason they're filling the front rows of the church these past few Sundays, Bishop."

"And why's that?" I asked.

" 'Cause a good man is hard to find." James smiled as he opened my office door. "Remember, Bishop," he called as he gave me one last warning. "Deacon Dickens and Savannah are just the first."

I smiled, nodded, and waved as James exited the room, halfway closing the door behind him. I proceeded to remove the empty liquor bottle from my desk drawer and stuffed it down in my leather briefcase with the intent of disposing of it in the Dumpster in the back parking lot. I carried the two glasses we'd been drinking from down the hall to the church kitchen to rinse them out.

As I turned the corner to return to my office, I spotted an envelope taped to my door. It actually gave me déjà vu because for years, Charlene would leave me messages in the same exact fashion. By the time I got to the door, my hands were shaking and my heart felt like it was going to beat out of my chest, I was so nervous and confused. She'd been dead for six months, but the envelope taped to the door was from my wife's personal stationery.

Somehow, I managed to remove the envelope from the door, make my way into my office and into my chair. I stared at the envelope for the better part of five minutes before I opened it and began to read. The note was indeed from Charlene. Although it wasn't in her handwriting, the words were definitely hers. James was right about one thing: Armageddon was about to start in our church, but what he probably never suspected was that its creator was going to be my deceased wife, Charlene Wilson.

2

MARLENE

For almost three years I'd asked God to bless me with a job so I could get off public assistance and not have to look for handouts from my son-in-law, Dante, and my daughter, Tanisha, to take care of my teenage son, Aubrey. But perhaps I should have been a little bit more specific when I put in my request. Shopping at Key Food is one thing, but working there is a completely different story, with all the rude customers and sexual harassment I had to put up with from my pain-in-the-ass manager. Every day when I left that place, I felt like I needed a drink. Don't get me wrong, I was grateful for the job in these troubled times, but how was I supposed to support a teenage boy on $320 a week in New York City?

Aubrey's birthday was in two weeks, and the only thing he asked for was one of those new PlayStation 3 video game consoles, but those things cost $400, and that doesn't include the games he wanted. How can a kid's video game console cost more than what a parent makes in a week?

Oh, well, I guess the landlord's wife isn't gonna be shopping at Lord and Taylor on my money next week, I thought. My son was going to get that gaming unit if I had to be late on my rent to get it. Just thinking about it made me depressed and ready to give up, but instead I decided to take my butt home to shower and go to a Narcotics Anonymous meeting.

"Whatchu need?" the young drug boys hollered, interrupting my thoughts. I was only two blocks from home.

Every day, for as long as I could remember, the drug boys had manned the corner of 109th and Guy Brewer Boulevard, selling almost any junkie's drug of choice: weed, heroin, Ecstasy, and my personal favorite, crack cocaine. Back when I was smoking crack, they were like my own personal Walgreen's pharmacy, open twenty-four hours a day for my convenience. Thank God, those days were long behind me, but even so, that still didn't stop the drug boys from asking me that same question.

"Whatchu need, Ma?" Reggie, a dealer in his late twenties, asked as he ran up to me. I used to cop from him, and I'm sure he missed me as a customer, for various reasons. When he was close enough, he opened his hands to reveal two nickel bags of crack. "I got a two-for-one special just for you, Ma. Guaranteed to solve all your problems." He smiled, showing me a mouth full of gold teeth.

"Fool, now you know got-damn well I don't fuck with that shit no more," I replied, and kept walking toward my building.

"You may be clean now, Ma," he shouted out behind me, "but it's all just a matter of time. Sooner or later you gonna need to get that monkey off your back. But don't worry. I'll be right here waiting for you with your only real friend."

The scary thing about what Reggie had just said was that I had considered getting that monkey off my back. I thought about it every day, but as a recovering addict, I had to constantly fight through that temptation. For two years, I'd been winning the battle over crack cocaine and the Reggies of the world, but the war, the war over my sobriety, continued daily.

Once I reached the stoop, I reached in my bag and dug out the key that unlocked the security door. I entered the building and headed straight for the elevator, though I don't know why. I guess I hoped that today it would actually be working, but that same tired OUT OF SERVICE sign was still taped to the doors.

"Thank goodness I didn't take the apartment on the seventh floor," I said to myself as I finished off the last of three flights of steps. As I headed down the hall, now immune to the odor that was a combination of piss and shit, I noticed an envelope taped to my door. Immediately, my heart dropped.

"Dammit, what's cut off now?" I asked myself. My rent wasn't due until next week, so that wasn't it. I paid my electric bill with my check on Friday, so what the hell could it be? The gas, maybe, or the cable? Damn, I bet they shut my cable off. Oh, God, Aubrey would kill me.

As I continued my slow steps toward the door, my brain raced to figure out what bill I had neglected to pay. The more steps I took, the farther away the door seemed to be and the more labored my breathing became. Three flights of stairs always had me breathing heavy, but the anxiety I was feeling had me about ready to pass out. Nonetheless, I finally made it to the door, where I removed the envelope that had my name handwritten across it.

Entering my apartment, I locked the door behind me, went straight to my bedroom without even saying hello to Aubrey, and sat down on my bed with the envelope in hand. I held it, still trying to guess what could be inside before actually opening it.

When I gathered my nerve and slid out the paper contained inside, I was surprised to see that it was a handwritten note on paper with First Lady Charlene Wilson's letterhead on it. This confused me, because she had been dead for a while now. How could this letter have gotten here, and who was using her stationery? I wondered. As I kicked off my shoes, I began reading it aloud:

Dearest Marlene,

If you are reading this letter, it means that I have been dead for at least six months now. As the stepmother of your daughter, I've seen both you and her grow with Christ. Although you and I weren't that close while I was alive, I must say that I truly admired you. You made strides in your life that most people only dream of. When I think of where God brought you from, I can't help but think back to where God brought T.K. from as well . . . where he brought you two from 'together,' in a sense.

At that point, the letter really had my attention. Even with the envelope open and the letter in my hand, I was more curious now than when it was sealed, taped to my door. I got into a comfortable position on the bed as I continued to read:

Now that I'm gone, I know that right about now the issue of who will marry T.K. is probably the main topic of discussion among the members of First Jamaica Ministries. That's why I'm writing you this letter, Marlene. It's no secret to anyone about the life—and love—you shared with my husband before he moved to New York and became one of the most respected men of God in the city. So, it wouldn't be a huge shock if somehow you were to become the woman at his side.

If anything, it might be more of a shock to you to be reading these words from me. Nonetheless, I can't help but think that God had a reason for putting you back into T.K.'s life after all of your years apart from him. And if it's the Lord's desire for you and T.K. to become one, then I find comfort in that because God doesn't make mistakes. And since God put it in my heart to write you this letter, I only ask that if the day does come to pass that you become the wife of my T.K., take care of him like I would, because he is a good man.

All the best,
Charlene

I placed the letter down on the nightstand next to my bed, almost afraid to look at it again. I stared off into space, actually wondering for a moment if I was dreaming or awake. I pinched myself, and the pain that shot through my arm told me I was indeed awake. Suddenly, I had so many questions. Was the note real? And if it was, who had left it on my door? Was it one of his kids, or was it T.K. himself? I went to Charlene's funeral and watched them put her casket in the ground, so she obviously didn't leave this envelope on my door.

The bigger question, of course, was, Who had written the letter? Had Charlene, before her death, really given me her blessing to be with T.K.? I guess it was possible, but if so, why? And even more importantly, was I going to act on her request? I closed my eyes and buried my face into the palms of my hands.

I'd been in love with Thomas Kelly—T.K., as they called him now—since I was sixteen years old. He was the captain of the football and basketball teams, and I was the head cheerleader when we were in high school in Richmond, Virginia. I let him take my virginity the last day of my sophomore year, and I never regretted it once. He had always treated me with respect. We both attended Virginia State University, and he even asked me to marry him during our freshman year.

I messed that all up a few days after school let out for summer break, when some guys from New York introduced me to crack cocaine, or as we in the South called it back then, cook-'em-up.

Hell, they were giving it away back when it first came out, just to get you hooked.

Thomas Kelly tried to warn me about messing with that stuff from the start, but I didn't listen, and he didn't press the issue because I had him under control. The power of pussy is a dangerous thing when it comes to men, young and old, and Thomas Kelly was no different from the rest. The last thing he wanted was for me to cut him off from the poontang.

Nobody knew how cook-'em-up really was back then, so I was oblivious to the danger I was putting myself in, until it was too late for both me and Thomas Kelly. I tricked him into smoking some crack about two weeks after I started. We'd gone to a cheap motel on Jeff Davis Highway that night, like we always did on Friday nights. I'd already smoked up my check from working at Church's Fried Chicken before we got there. I wanted some more of that rock so bad that I flat out refused to have sex with him unless he gave me twenty dollars to buy some more. Well, he was a horny nineteen-year-old boy, so you know he gave me what I wanted. By the time we got back to the room, I'd promised to give him his first blow job if he'd try smoking with me. Well, to make a long story short, we ended up smoking up his check from Home Depot by the end of that night.

Within six months, everyone on our side of town referred to us as "Mr. and Mrs. Crackhead." The community joke about us was, "The couple that smokes together stays together." And I guess they were right to an extent because we were crackheads, and we did smoke together. What most people didn't understand was that despite our addiction and the foul shit we did to our bodies, we still really loved each other.

Unfortunately, that love we shared wasn't strong enough to overcome the love I had for crack. At some point, Thomas Kelly found God and cleaned himself up. When he asked me to get clean with him, I refused. He ended up moving to New York with his new mentor, a man named Reverend Jackson. He never knew that I was pregnant when he left me, and I never blamed him for going. It wasn't until many years later, by the strangest coincidence you could ever imagine, that Thomas Kelly and I reconnected. I had moved to New York but was still too strung out on crack to go looking for him, even if I had wanted to. Anyway, by that time he had his church, a son and a daughter, and his wife, Charlene. Our paths probably never would have crossed if it weren't for Tanisha.

Thomas Kelly didn't know it at the time, but Tanisha, the woman his son Dante was about to marry, was his child, the daughter I gave birth to after he had cleaned himself up and left Virginia. Now, you know all hell broke loose when the truth was revealed at Dante and Tanisha's wedding, but it's not really as bad as it sounds. It turned out that Charlene was already pregnant when she met Thomas Kelly, so he was not Dante's biological father. Things were crazy for a while until all the facts were pieced together, but Dante and Tanisha were eventually married, and I became a part of the bishop's extended family. After some initial strained feelings, they accepted me into their family and even helped me finally get clean, but I had no idea that Charlene had felt the way this letter said she did.

I glanced at the letter one more time, then reached for my phone, dialing my daughter's cell number. Tanisha and I never really had a mother/daughter relationship, mostly because my addiction made me incapable of properly mothering her. By the time she was able to take care of herself, Tanisha was trying to be the mother to me. She was a good kid and made a lot of sacrifices for me over the years. I was so happy she'd found happiness with Dante.

"Hey, Momma, whatchu doing?"

"Nothing. Um, just wanted to ask you something." I picked up a cigarette and lit it.

"What, Momma? Everything all right? Is Aubrey okay?" That girl sure knew how to worry. She must have got that trait from her father.

"Everything's fine, Tanisha. I was just thinking about asking a male friend of mine out to dinner. What do you think?"

There was silence for a second, then my daughter said sadly, "Did you say somebody asked you to dinner, or you're gonna ask somebody to dinner?"

Now, I know she wasn't hard of hearing, but I repeated myself anyway. "I was thinking about asking somebody."

Again there was a brief silence, then that sadness to her voice when she finally spoke. "Whatever you wanna do, Momma."

"You mad at me or something?"

"No, Momma I just—" She stopped herself. "If it's gonna make you happy, Momma, ask him out. You deserve all the happiness you can get." She could play like she was happy for me, but she wasn't. I knew my child.

"Tanisha, what's bothering you? And don't tell me nothin'. I know you, girl."

She took an audible breath. "I don't know. I guess I was just hoping that you and the bishop might get back together now that Ms. Charlene is gone."

A smile came to my face, but I didn't know if I should tell her about the letter, because I didn't know if she'd believe me. I wasn't sure if the letter was authentic myself, but it had me thinking. "Why? Do you think your father's interested? Or are you acting like every other child who wants to see their parents get back together?"

"Of course I wanna see my parents together. I love you both. No disrespect to Ms. Charlene, but I think she'd wanna see the bishop happy."

"Well, I'm gonna tell you a secret, and I don't want you to tell your husband. I'm going down to the church, and I'm planning to ask Thomas Kelly out to dinner."

"Really, Momma?" I could hear the glee in her voice. "Are you serious?"

"Yes, I'm serious, but I don't want you to tell Dante because he'll tell Donna. I don't know how she'd feel about the idea of her father moving on so soon after her mother's death. And you know since they're Thomas Kelly's kids, they may not think he's ready."

"I know Dante doesn't, but you know he was a momma's boy anyway. Hey, Momma . . ."

"What is it, Tanisha?"

"Do you . . . do you still love the bishop?"

This time I hesitated before answering. "I never stopped loving him, baby. I just accepted that he loved someone else."

I swear I could hear Tanisha smile through the phone. "Do me a favor, Momma. Don't ask the bishop to dinner until tomorrow night."

"Why?" I asked quickly.

"Because I wanna send you some money so you can get your hair done and buy a new outfit. I'm so excited!"

"Don't get excited yet," I cautioned. "I haven't asked him, and he hasn't said yes."

"He's gonna say yes. Every time I talk to him, he always asks about you."

"Well, that's good to know."

"Well, look, Momma, I gotta go. The baby's crying. But I'm going down to Western Union to send you that money this evening, so make sure you call Nu-Tribe to make an appointment, and tell Niecy I said to hook you up."

I hung up the phone, then picked up the letter, reading it aloud one more time. When I finished, I called the hair salon and made an appointment with Tanisha's girl, Niecy. After throwing something together for dinner and helping Aubrey with his homework, I took a long, hot shower, then climbed into bed, hoping that I'd dream of the future when I'd be the wife of Thomas Kelly Wilson. Charlene wouldn't have to worry the least bit about me taking real good care of him. I owed him that much. Hell, I owed us both that much.

3

MONIQUE

"Mmm, mmm, mmm, girl, you look good," I told myself as I stared in the full-length mirror hanging on the back of my bedroom door. I ran my hands down my very round hips, my freshly manicured nails raking over my charcoal-colored wool pants. I had scoured every shop on the Avenue to find a pair of wool slacks just the right shade of black to complement my favorite sweater that zipped up the neck, or rather down the cleavage, which is how I preferred to wear it. I knew other women, especially the women at church, hated me and talked about me because of my large, firm breasts and how I showed them off every chance I got, but the Lord had given them to me for a reason, so covering them up completely would be a sin. I glanced at the mirror one last time. I knew I liked what I saw staring back at me. I just hoped the bishop would like it too.

It was still hard for me to believe that after all these years the bishop was actually coming to my house for Sunday dinner. And even more unbelievable was the fact that he was coming alone. Ever since the first lady died, he'd been traveling with an entourage of blockers who made it impossible for me to get any alone time with him, but tonight I was going to have him all to myself, in my house. Of course, he thought he was only coming over to discuss my proposal to open a Christian bookstore at the church. He had no idea that the other two members of my committee weren't coming, because they didn't exist. I know it was sneaky, but I got nervous with all the talk among the congregation that it was time to find the bishop a new wife. If he were going to have a new wife, it was going to be me. But those haters weren't about to help me, so I had to help myself. If I were to get my way, this would only be the first of many candlelit dinners between me and Bishop T.K. Wilson.

I took a deep breath, pulling in what little stomach I had. I couldn't help but smile as my breasts and butt just seemed to look a little larger. Yes, the bishop was going to like what he saw tonight. What man could resist a body like mine?

No sooner had I reached the kitchen and laid the pork chops on the cooling rack than the doorbell rang. "It's him," I said to myself in a singsong tone, my heart racing like a young girl on her first date. I quickly removed the oven mitts from my hands, placed them on the counter, and headed straight for the door. "Coming!" I yelled as the doorbell rang again. "Coming!"

When I opened the door, there he stood, Bishop T.K. Wilson, six feet tall with deep chocolate-colored skin and a perfectly groomed salt-and-pepper beard all wrapped up in a London Fog overcoat. He was quite possibly the most handsome man I'd ever seen, and the sudden heat between my legs emphasized the point. As much as I wanted to be a good Christian, the woman inside me felt like taking his hand and leading him straight to my bedroom to show him what he'd been missing all these years.

"Bishop," I said, pulling the door open wide and stepping aside so that he could come in. His cologne made my knees weak.

"Sister Johnson," he replied in his soothing baritone voice, checking his watch. "Am I early? I thought we were going to have dinner with your entire committee."

"Bishop, would you believe they both canceled on me at the last minute? I think their kids have the flu. You know how bad that's running around these days."

The bishop nodded, but I'm not sure if he believed me. I was thankful that he'd come alone but was a little worried when he peered suspiciously into the candlelit dining room. I knew I should have waited to light the candles until dinner was served.

"Well, let me know when they reschedule." He turned to the door.

"Don't be silly, Bishop. We don't need them to have a bookstore meeting. Besides, I've already made dinner. You haven't eaten yet, have you?"

"No, I haven't, but I don't want to impose."

"Nonsense. You're not imposing. Both my boys live with their father now. It'll be nice to have a dinner companion for once. Here, let me take your coat," I insisted as I slowly slid his coat down his back and hung it on the coatrack next to the door. "Please, have a seat on the couch. I just took the pork chops out of the oven, so they need to cool a little bit."

"Pork chops? I love pork chops." As he moved to place his keys in his pocket, they dropped, and when he bent over to pick them up, I had to catch my breath, because the tingle between my legs was intensifying. Mmm, mmm, mmm, the man had a butt like two halves of a honeydew melon, and all I wanted to do was take a bite.

"So, Sister Johnson," Bishop said, sitting on the couch and getting right to business. "I think your idea of opening up a Christian bookstore is awesome."

"Bishop," I said, sitting next to him, "it just came to me one day while I was out looking for an NIV Bible. There just aren't any places to find good Christian books in this borough."

We talked about the bookstore for ten minutes, but the bishop wasn't looking at me—at least not in the way I felt he should've been. I sighed, repositioned myself, and did whatever else I could do so that he would notice my cleavage, but the man would not take his eyes off my face. I know my brown, saucer-shaped eyes were mesmerizing, but with a zip-down sweater on, I thought the bishop's eyes would wander south at least once. I'm not about to lie; it was frustrating. How could he not want to look at them? They were beautiful.

The thought crossed my mind that he could possibly be gay. I mean, there were plenty of gay men in the church. Heck, some might even call our church Down Low City. But I knew he wasn't gay. He had two children and was married for at least twenty years. Besides, before his wife died, I'd caught him sneaking a peek more than once. No, he wasn't gay. He was careful, and I couldn't blame him. After all, he was the pastor of the biggest church in Queens. It had to be my approach. There was something I wasn't doing right. But what? My momma always told me the key to any man's heart lies between your thighs. And up until now, she ain't never lied.

"Do you have any idea where you'd like to have the store?" he asked.

"Yep, I sure do." Now was my opportunity to show off my hips and firm, round ass. Maybe he wasn't a breast man. Maybe he was an ass man. "There's a vacant store right across the street from the church. I took a picture of it this morning with my camera phone." I got up and walked across the room, taking my time as I bent over to retrieve my phone from my bag. When I stood up and turned to him, he had to sit back and look up in the air for a second 'cause he was busted!

Gotcha, I told myself as I smiled. *So, you're an ass man, huh? Well, I can do tricks like those video dancers.*

"What do you think of this?" I sat down next to him, showing him the pictures on my phone.

"Perfect," he said with a smile. "Absolutely perfect. I've looked at that vacant store a thousand times over the past year and never even thought about its potential. And you would be the perfect woman to spearhead the church's Christian bookstore if it were to come to fruition."

"I don't know about the perfect woman . . ." I blushed, playfully putting my hand on the bishop's hand, which was resting on his knee. "After all, I think Ms. Charlene was the perfect woman."

"Oh, thank you," he said genuinely, sliding his hand from underneath mine, patting it gently before folding his on his lap. "What a great compliment for the first la—"

The bishop caught himself. I guess he realized, just like I did, that she was the late first lady, and never being one to bite my tongue, I decided to speak on that.

"You miss her, don't you?"

"Yes." He nodded. "More than anyone can ever imagine."

"Look, I didn't mean to sour the mood. Dinner should be cooled off by now. What do you say we eat?" I said, changing the subject . . . for now.

Over dinner, the bishop listened attentively while I discussed some of my ideas about the bookstore. After dinner, over two cups of coffee, I listened attentively while he discussed some of his ideas about the bookstore. After the second cup, unfortunately, he was ready to call it a night.

"Well, Sister Johnson," he said as he rose from the dinner table.

"Oh, please, Bishop," I said, cutting him off as I stood up and placed my hand on his shoulder. "We just spent the evening together. Call me Monique."

"Well, Sister Monique," the Bishop continued, "I must say that this idea of a Christian bookstore is definitely an ordained vision that I'm certain God will manifest if He's in agreement. It will be hard work at first, I'm sure. But the fruits of your labor will be so rewarding."

"Oh, Bishop," I said, slowly sliding my hand down his shoulder and to his slightly crooked tie. Being the perfectionist that I am, the slant of his tie was driving me crazy, so I had to take the initiative to straighten it out. "I love hard work. And like the Bible says, "To whom much is given, much is required." Well, I'm willing to give it my all." At that point, I felt a little piece of hair sticking to my cotton-candy lipstick, which matched my polish, so I licked my lips, then slowly ran my index finger across my bottom lip until I removed the piece of hair.

How embarrassing, I thought. *No telling how long that stupid piece of hair has been on my lip.*

"Oh, I don't doubt at all, Sister Monique, that you'll put your everything into the bookstore," he said, finally taking his eyes away from my luscious mouth. "But as you know, I have to take it to the trustee board first." He turned and headed for the door.

"Oh, of course, Bishop," I said, close on his heels.

"But I think they will see the benefits of having the bookstore."

"Bishop, you have no idea just how endless the benefits are going to be." I removed his coat from the rack and helped him into it.

"Oh, I think I do," the bishop said, taking my hand off his lapel and patting it like I was a cute little puppy. "So, you'll definitely be hearing from me again regarding this matter. Matter of fact, I'll have my secretary set up a meeting for sometime next week, but in the meantime, thank you for a lovely evening."

"No, Bishop, thank you."

I wasn't about to let him end our evening with just a pat on the hand, so I leaned in to plant a kiss on his lips. Just as my lips were about to touch his, he turned his right cheek, but I gently raised my hand, stopping his head. Our lips met in a soft kiss. Less than a second later, he stepped away with a confused look. I smiled as I noticed he was now wearing a fresh coat of cotton-candy lipstick.

"I hope I wasn't too forward, Bishop, but I just wanted to thank you properly—my way."

"Well, you were a little more forward than I'm used to, Sister Monique." It was not exactly the response I'd hoped for, but at least he didn't sound angry; just surprised.

"I just wanted to let you know how I feel."

He didn't comment either way about the kiss. He just made it known it was time for him to leave.

"Have a good evening, Sister Monique," he said as he turned the doorknob to let himself out. "Oh, Sister Monique," he said right before exiting.

I knew he couldn't leave without just one more little peck, so I subtly leaned my head toward him. "Yes, Bishop?" I said eagerly.

"I'll see you at Bible study this Wednesday?"

"Huh?" He caught me off guard.

"Bible study. You'll be there this week?"

"Oh, yes," I said, trying to hide my disappointment. "Bible study. Wednesday. I'll be there." On that note, he winked, nodded his head, and was on his way.

"He winked," I said to reassure myself as I closed the door behind him and leaned my back against it.

That Bishop T.K. Wilson is some kind of fine, I thought. *He's got it all, the full package. He's only missing one thing—me.*

Although the evening didn't end with as much romantic promise as I'd hoped, I thought he might have at least gotten some kind of sign that he could definitely find the qualities of a first lady in me. He did say that I was perfect, and he did let me kiss him. It wasn't a French kiss, but it was a start. The evening wasn't totally in vain. In fact, while I might have used it as a ploy to get the bishop into my house, I was serious about the bookstore. Running the store would mean spending lots of time at the church. And who spends more time at church than anybody? The headlining man of God, of course. Yes, this would all work out just fine.

4

BISHOP

I left Monique's house and drove home feeling a little vulnerable. I don't know who I'm fooling—I felt a lot vulnerable. Monique had awakened feelings in me that I thought I'd suppressed over a year ago when Charlene went into the hospital. Monique brought out the weakness in me, the one part of being a Christian that I found the hardest to control. She brought out the lust in me. I could still feel the soft tenderness of the kiss she gave me. My mind couldn't block the images of Monique's beautiful body or the way her backside looked in those tight pants as she bent over to retrieve her cell phone. And I wondered if she'd felt the chemistry I'd been feeling throughout the evening, or if I had just become paranoid because of the seeds planted by James's words.

I picked up my cell phone and plugged in my hands-free device, then dialed James's number. He answered on the second ring, sounding out of breath. "Hel . . . lo?"

"James, it's T.K."

"What's up, Bishop?" he huffed. "You think I can call you tomorrow? I'm a little busy here, if you know what I mean." There was no doubt in my mind James had a woman at his place.

"Look, I'm sorry to call you so late, but I really just need a minute. This is important."

"Aw'ight, Bishop. Hold on a second." I knew he'd covered up the phone because the background noise disappeared. But he came back right away. "What's on your mind, Bishop?"

Now that I was on the spot, I was at a loss for words. Having lustful thoughts was one thing, but expressing them to someone else, whether he's your best friend or not, was another.

"Bishop, you there?"

"Yes, James, I'm here." I took a deep breath before I spoke. "What do you think about me seeing Monique Johnson?"

His answer did not come as quickly as I thought it would.

"Are you talking about big-tittie Monique Johnson?" James finally asked.

"That's not very nice, James. And I think you know who I'm talking about. There's only one Monique Johnson that we both know."

I could hear him sigh into the phone, and I knew his answer before he spoke. "Are we talking about seeing her behind closed doors or publicly?"

I did not like the way he asked his question, nor did I like his tone.

"Publicly, of course."

"What are you, crazy?" he hollered into the phone. "Do you have any idea what that woman could do to your career as bishop of our church? If you have a death wish, Bishop, why don't you just put a fucking gun to your head? It'd be a lot quicker." I had to hold the phone away from my ear. I'd never heard him speak to me like this.

"What exactly is that supposed to mean? She's a good Christian woman, James."

"Yeah, she's a good Christian woman, all right—with a reputation for screwing every man with *Deacon* or *Trustee* in front of his name. And now it looks like she's set her sights on one with *Bishop* in front of his name."

"Oh, really?" I snapped. "Have you slept with her? 'Cause everyone knows you're the biggest male whore in our church." I regretted the words as soon as I uttered them. What was it about this woman, whose reputation was every bit as bad as James said it was, that made me jump to her defense so quickly? True, as a man of God, I would defend any member of my congregation against unproven rumors, but perhaps not as vigorously as I was defending Sister Monique. Something about her intrigued me, and it was more than just her shapely figure. I would need some time to sort out these feelings.

There was silence on the line for a few seconds. I knew I'd hurt James's feelings.

"I resent that, Bishop," James finally replied. "And no, I haven't slept with her."

"My point exactly. So what makes you think everyone else has?"

"I hear things, Bishop. People talk."

This time I chuckled. "They talk about you, James, but that doesn't stop me from hanging around you. What did I tell you about listening to unfounded rumors? Even if they did sleep with her, what self-respecting deacon or trustee would go around bragging he'd slept with Sister Johnson? I hate to say this, James, but I'm pretty sure this rumor was started by my wife . . . God rest her soul. Sister Johnson and Charlene never got along. Matter of fact, Charlene hated her."

"Nonetheless, Bishop, the rumors are still planted inside the heads of the women in the church. Showing up with her at church one Sunday would be like dropping an atom bomb on Manhattan. Nothing will ever be the same."

"Well, then I guess I've got something to think about, don't I?"

"T.K., as your friend, I'm telling you right now, don't do anything stupid. If you wanna roll in the hay with Monique for a little while, I'll point everyone in the opposite direction. But you can't take that woman out in public."

"Can't—" I stopped myself before I spoke to my friend more harshly than I wanted. "You know what, James? I'm gonna say good evening. And in the future, don't tell me what I can or cannot do!" I hung up the phone angrily.

I was tempted to call him back. I shouldn't have yelled at him that way. I just hated the judgmental attitudes of some of the more vocal members of my church. I hadn't even made a decision to move on after my wife's death, and already tongues were wagging—or at least James's was—about my taste in women. I know James thought he was protecting my reputation and my career from the churchpeople who would be scrutinizing my every move, but who were they to tell me who I could or couldn't see? I knew Monique Johnson had a bad reputation. My own wife helped create it because of her jealousy. What James, Charlene, and the rest of the church needed to recognize was that despite her faults, Monique was a good Christian woman who participated in every church function she could, unlike others in our congregation.

I pulled into my driveway. Just as I got out of the car, my

phone rang. I quickly answered, thinking it was James. I was glad to have the opportunity to apologize and explain myself.

"James?"

"No, Thomas Kelly, it's not James. This is Marlene. How're you doing?"

"I'm good, Marlene. How are you doing?" I was happy to hear from her. I could talk to Marlene about almost anything. "I saw you in church last Sunday. Why didn't you stick around and say hello?"

"Oh, I left Aubrey at home alone, and I had promised him we could go buy some sneakers on the Avenue."

"Okay. So, to what do I owe the pleasure of this call?" I checked my watch. "It's pretty late. Is everything all right?"

"Everything's fine. I was just thinking about you, and I was hoping we could get together for dinner. I'd love to sit around and chat. I miss talking to you, Thomas Kelly."

"I miss talking to you, too, Marlene. With Charlene gone, I miss having a woman to talk to about something other than church business."

"That's exactly why I thought we should talk. So, when are you free?"

With the seeds of change planted in my head by James's words, I could use someone to talk to. Marlene and I had a history together, and she knew me before I was Bishop T.K. Wilson. She knew me when I was just a man, and she accepted me with all my habits and flaws. Maybe she would be able to advise me on how I should proceed if I decided I was ready to start dating. At least I knew Marlene wouldn't be concerned like others in the church about the reputation of whichever woman I chose. If anyone understood the ability of the human spirit to redeem itself after past mistakes, Marlene did. I knew she wouldn't judge Monique as harshly as James had.

"The only day I've got free is this Wednesday night after Bible study," I told her. "How about we take a ride over to City Island and get us some crab legs and shrimp?"

"Mmmm, that sounds good. I love crab legs."

"You sure do. Remember the time we went to Captain George's in Richmond and you ate so many crabs from the buffet they wouldn't bring any more out?" We both laughed.

"Uh-huh, that's when I started to eat all the shrimp they had."

"Girl, you sure could eat back then. I still don't know how you could eat so much and stay so skinny."

"I wish I could do it now, 'cause everything I eat goes right to my hips."

"Trust me. That's not necessarily a bad thing. I think you have nice hips." *Now why did I just say that?* I wondered. *Because it's true.*

"Thomas Kelly, have you been looking at my hips?"

I was silent for a while; then I decided to tell the truth like you can do only with a woman you've had a child with. "Marlene, I hope you don't take offense to this, but I've always looked at your hips. It's been a very bad habit since we were kids. Please forgive me." For the last sentence, I put on my most sarcastic voice.

"Please forgive you, huh? Negro, please." She burst out laughing, and I joined in. "Thomas Kelly Wilson, you are a trip. I'm glad to see you haven't lost your sense of humor and let this bishop stuff go to your head."

"I'm still the same man inside that I've always been, Marlene. I just let the Lord guide my heart," I said sincerely. "Look, why don't you meet me at the church on Wednesday just in case I'm running late? I really can't wait to see you."

"Wednesday night after Bible study. It's a date."

We said our good-byes, then I hung up the phone. For a second there, I had to admit I got a little nervous when I heard the word *date*. James had me paranoid, I guess. Then I realized it was my good friend Marlene, and there was no way she would be caught up in this church nonsense about finding a new first lady.

5

SAVANNAH

I was standing in the kitchen thumbing down the dough of the crust that would hold the best peach cobbler I'd ever made. Before pouring in the filling, I scooped up a little with the tip of my index finger, just to confirm what I already knew.

"Delicious," I said as I licked every drop off my fingertip. I had used just the right amount of each ingredient, although in doing so I went against the way my mama had taught me to prepare the family's favorite recipe. I used measuring cups for this one. No way was I chancing too much of a pinch of this and too little of a hint of that. After all, this cobbler was for the head of the church himself.

I still could hardly believe that my daddy had set it up for me to have dinner with Bishop T.K. Wilson. It wasn't that I didn't think Bishop Wilson was a fine man. It was just that I had no interest in him in the way Daddy wanted me to—at least not yet anyway.

"Umm, umm, umm," my daddy said as he entered the kitchen, nostrils flared, inhaling the aroma of the splendid meal I had prepared. "If you ain't good for nothing else to a man, you going to be good for taking care of his appetite. The bishop is going to be back every Sunday after he gets some of your cooking, little girl."

"If there's any left by the time he gets here," I said, stepping away from the cobbler and smacking the back of Daddy's hand, which held the ladle that had just fed him a mouthful of my homemade chicken and dumplings. "Mama never liked it when you ate out of the pots while she was cooking, so what makes you think I wouldn't mind?"

"Oh, you can hardly compare your cooking to your mama's," Daddy said as he stared off, thinking back to when my mother was alive and how she'd start preparing Sunday dinner at six in the morning. "Now, you might have her on that cobbler of yours, but as far as everything else? Humph. Not even close. You got some years of practice before you'll even be fit to lick the bowls she cooked in. That's why you need to work on getting you a husband. What better practice than cooking for your husband every day? Your mama loved cooking for me. That woman gave me everything I needed."

"Everything," I said sarcastically, rolling my eyes as I put the top dough across the filling and placed the cobbler in the oven.

I must admit, it was good to see a smile on Daddy's face as he reminisced about him and Mama. I just wish he didn't always have to put me down in the process. But that was Daddy for you. I think the only time he ever spared me a compliment was when it came to my peach cobbler.

"Girl, you put your foot in this one," Daddy said as he licked the bowl that had held the filling for the cobbler. He headed toward the kitchen door, but not before stopping to steal one more bite from the pot of chicken and dumplings.

"Daddy, what did I just say about eating out of the pot?" I playfully scolded.

"Is that the real reason, or you just don't want nobody else besides the bishop getting any of your cooking?" Daddy asked.

"Cut it out and give me that," I said, smiling at him and taking the ladle from his hand. As I stirred the chicken and dumplings, I couldn't help but start having doubts about the bishop's reasons for wanting to share a meal with me. "Daddy, you sure this was all the bishop's idea, wanting me to prepare a dinner for him?"

"He said himself that he just loves that peach cobbler of yours," Daddy said, nodding toward the oven.

"Oh, yes, the cobbler. Thanks for reminding me," I said as I hurried over to set the timer.

"Timer? Your mama never cooked with no timer. She could wake up out of a deep sleep and know that it was time to take the food out of the oven." He shooed with his hand. "But anyway, why wouldn't the bishop want to have dinner with you, Savannah?"

I shrugged. I mean, certainly I could think of a few reasons, but if I dare got started, the list would certainly take us into

Monday morning's breakfast. Of course, there was my age to consider. Being thirty-five years old didn't make me a spring chicken, but with the bishop being ten years my senior, it still pushed me into the "younger woman" stereotype that most men try to avoid after a divorce or the death of their spouse. Oh, that would definitely give the church gossipers something to talk about. Some of the other folks in the choir already commented about all the solos I did, solos of which I felt I was most deserving. I might not be able to reach five octaves like that Mariah Carey, but I knew that God had indeed anointed me with the vocals to minister His word. But just imagine if the bishop were to show me any special kind of attention. Oooh, them heifers would sure enough have something to say then.

And there was the fact that I was not nearly as outgoing and aggressive as some of those other women at the church. Of course, the bishop appeared to be oblivious to the fact that ever since the first lady passed away, the dresses had been getting shorter and the slits in the skirts had been getting higher. I've always been a quiet girl, though, and I didn't plan on changing to get no man, either. But then again, we weren't talking about just any man; we were talking about the bishop.

"I can't think of a reason why the bishop wouldn't want to have dinner with you, either," Daddy said with conviction. "Savannah, sweetheart." Daddy walked over to me and took my hands. "Don't doubt who you are. You are worthy. Look what all you've been through. The Bible says the suffering can't be compared to the glory. Well, now it's time for you to partake in the glory. You deserve this."

I couldn't believe this was actually my father holding my hands and speaking to me with such heartfelt sincerity. I had almost forgotten just how critical of me he could be. But it didn't take long for him to remind me.

"I mean, sure, every now and then you hit a bad note during your solos, and you could stand to change that hairdo of yours every once in a while, but overall, you're a good girl, Savannah. A good woman. And you're gonna make a good wife someday, too, with a little hard work. I mean, ya gotta start doing more with yourself. You know what I mean. A woman's gotta use her body to get what she wants sometimes." He slugged me on the shoulder as if I were one of his pals.

"Yeah, well"—I sighed—"you know the Lord gives us a spirit of discernment, and something just tells me that—" Before I could finish my sentence, the doorbell rang.

"It's him!" Daddy said, sounding more excited than I felt that the bishop was coming for dinner. Come to think of it, he probably *was* more excited, because *nervous* more accurately described the emotion I was overcome by. "You go on to your room and get dressed. I'll keep the bishop company."

I looked down at the outfit I had picked out for dinner with the bishop. Before I could tell Daddy that I was, in fact, already dressed, he raced out of the kitchen, straightening his tie. I quickly followed him out of the kitchen and headed to the back bedroom while he answered the door.

The back bedroom used to be the bedroom my mother and father had shared during their forty-two years of marriage. But once the female cancer ate Mama to her grave, Daddy couldn't bear the memories that bedroom held, so he moved into the bedroom that I had grown up in. I didn't mind having the bigger bedroom at all. And staring at that flowered wallpaper Mama had fallen in love with at Kmart reminded me of her every day—the only good memory I had in my life.

Once I got to my room, I immediately kicked off my house shoes and replaced them with my black pumps to match my black knee-length skirt. Perhaps I shouldn't wear a black skirt, or a white blouse, for that matter. Seeing as how these were the required wardrobe colors that we wore in the church choir, it almost made it seem like I hadn't bothered to change clothes after services. I did change, though. This white blouse had ruffles along the neckline and down the front, and the skirt I wore to church earlier was longer, ankle-length. But I was certain the bishop wouldn't notice. No one besides the hens paid such close attention to me.

After tightening the bun in my hair, Daddy's words set in, and I wish I had also decided to change my hairstyle too. Daddy was right; I always wore my hair in its same old bun. Nobody knew that I had hair dang near down to my butt.

"What's taking you so long?" my eager father, sticking his head in my door, asked. "Come barefoot and naked if you got to . . . dang! You don't keep a man waiting this long." Daddy signaled with his hand for me to follow him out. He then led the way to the living room where the bishop sat waiting on the couch.

"Here she is, Bishop," Daddy said, introducing me like I was Miss America. He then plucked and brushed a couple of pieces of lint off my shoulder.

"Sister Savannah," the bishop said, rising off the couch and extending his hands to me.

After a nudge from Daddy, I walked over and placed my hands in the bishop's. "Good to see you again today, Bishop," I said as we shook hands and then released. I turned and walked back toward Daddy, who had a very displeased look on his face. If he could have, he would have pushed me a little harder, right into the bishop's arms.

"It certainly smells good," the bishop said with a smile. Funny thing was, I had never noticed before just how nice a smile the bishop had.

"Savannah's been slaving all afternoon over this meal, Bishop," Daddy bragged. "She wanted to make sure everything was just right for you. And I took the liberty of tasting it. Girl cooks better than her mama, and you know how well Sister Doreen could cook."

I stood there staring at Daddy for a moment, ready to perform the Heimlich maneuver on him, just in case he started to choke on that lie he just told. Not five minutes ago he was telling me how inferior my cooking was, and now he was raving as if I were the black Julia Child. I figured I had to get Daddy away from the spot he was standing in before the lightning struck, so I suggested we go sit down for dinner.

"Dinner's all ready, so why don't we go eat?" I said, bound and determined to stuff something into Daddy's mouth before he could say another word.

Daddy asked the bishop to bless the food, but Bishop Wilson insisted that the man of the house have the honor as the head of the table. During dinner, I could barely get a word in edgewise. Seems as though Daddy was set on doing all the talking.

"So, Bishop," Daddy asked, "what do you think about Savannah's outfit? She picked it out just for this evening."

"Nice," the bishop managed to say before placing one of my homemade dumplings in his mouth. If it were up to my daddy, he wouldn't have even managed to get that bite down. "But you didn't have to do that, Sister Savannah. The skirt you had on earlier today would have been just fine."

He noticed? I took a bite of chicken. It wasn't until after dessert that I could squeeze in a word or two.

"Did you enjoy that cobbler?" I asked the bishop.

"Oh, did I," the bishop said after taking his last forkful and pushing the saucer away. "I swear you make the best peach cobbler in the State of New York."

"She used measuring cups and all this time, Bishop." Daddy winked at me. "She wanted to make sure it was just perfect for you."

"Daddy!" I silently mouthed.

"Well, then, measuring cups must be the secret to why your cobbler always tastes just perfect," the bishop complimented me.

"Thank you, Bishop." I blushed. I didn't mean to blush. I didn't want to blush. I just did.

I had been eyeball-to-eyeball with the bishop during Bible study, but he had never made me blush before. Maybe it was because I had never noticed just how creamy his chocolate skin was or how becoming his salt-and-pepper beard was. I hadn't noticed a lot of things, so maybe I hadn't noticed the bishop noticing me.

No, how silly is that? I thought, and quickly disposed of the idea.

"Bishop, can I ask a favor of you?" Daddy said, then continued without giving him enough time to respond. "I just put some money down for Savannah to go to that revival next week in the Poconos. I was going to go as well, but when I remembered that that's the weekend of my wedding anniversary, I didn't think I'd be up to it. Not saying that I'm allowing the spirit of grief to take over me, but it's just that . . . you know."

"Oh, I understand, Deacon," Bishop said, putting his hand on his shoulder.

"Since I can't go," Daddy continued, "I was wondering if you could keep an eye on Savannah for me."

"I don't see why not," the bishop said. "And if I can't, God watches over all of His children. But I'll make sure I say a special prayer that He watches over this one."

The bishop looked over at me and smiled. I know that I usually only see the bishop when he is in serious mode at the pulpit, but I swear I had never seen him smile so many times in my life. Not only had he looked over and smiled at me, but even though it was at Daddy's request, he was going to say a prayer for me as well. Not just any prayer, like he had probably done for many people, but mine was going to be special. Maybe that was the bishop's way of telling me that I was special.

Suddenly, an uneasy feeling came over me. Daddy used to say I was special once upon a time too. But he had a funny way of showing it.

"Well, it's getting late, and I promised Sister Alberta that I'd stop by this evening and have a talk with that son of hers," the bishop said, rising from the dining room table. "You know the youth today."

"Don't I?" Daddy said as he stood up along with the bishop. "Savannah, why don't you go on and walk the bishop to the door while I clear the table?"

"What?" I said with a puzzled look on my face, as if I had spotted an alien. Daddy would rather cut off both his hands than have to lift a dish to clear the table. He always said that was a woman's duty. This had to be a test. I wasn't about to let him clear that table so I could hear him rant and rave later about how he had to do a woman's job because I wasn't woman enough to do it. No way!

"Oh, no, Daddy," I insisted. "You go on and relax. I'll clear the table after I see the bishop out."

"Great idea," Daddy said, winking at me as he retired to his bedroom.

Whew! I had passed the test.

Seeing the bishop out was uneventful, according to what Daddy probably had in mind for us. He thanked me for a wonderful evening, and I sent him on his way with something to remember me by—a slice of peach cobbler to go.

As I was clearing off the dinner table, the doorbell rang.

"I'll get it," I called out to Daddy, who I knew wouldn't get up to answer the door anyway.

"You Savannah?" a young man asked when I opened the door.

"Who wants to know?" I replied.

"Are you Savannah Dickens?" he said more sternly.

"Well, yes, but—"

"Here," he said, handing me a lavender envelope addressed to me. "This is for you."

After the young man walked away, I closed the door and walked over to the couch, puzzled about the letter he had just given me. I slowly sat down and eyeballed the envelope before opening it. I pulled out a handwritten letter.

What is this? I wondered. *And who in the world could it be from?*

ALISON AND THE FIRST LADY

I stepped out of my car and opened the back door, picking up the vase that held the lavender-colored lilies I'd placed on the floor behind my seat. Stepping onto the grass, I walked about thirty yards, until I was in front of the four-foot-wide, three-and-a-half-foot-tall headstone, where I placed the flowers, very pleased with myself. Charlene had loved fresh-cut flowers, and I had made it my business to see that she had some at least once a month since her death. I kneeled down and pulled up the few weeds that had sprouted since my last visit. Then I read the headstone inscription with tears in my eyes:

HERE LIES CHARLENE WILSON, WIFE, MOTHER, AND FIRST LADY OF FIRST JAMAICA MINISTRIES. EVEN IN DEATH HER PRESENCE WILL ALWAYS BE FELT.
1962–2006.

I don't think I'd ever read truer words. Charlene's presence was going to be felt for a long, long, long time when we got finished.

I stared at the gravesite and could almost see my best friend in her favorite cream-colored church dress, leaning against her own headstone, waiting to hear the latest news about her husband and his pursuers. When she was alive, Charlene would never admit it, but she loved gossip as much as anyone. She knew every rumor, theory, and secret about anybody who attended First Jamaica Ministries. She just never spread any of it unless it benefited her, her family, or the church.

I wiped the tears from my eyes, then spoke to my friend. "Hey, Charlene, I gave them all their first letters. All in all, so far everything is working out exactly the way you planned. Marlene and the bishop are supposed to go to dinner tomorrow night. Gurrrl, she is walking around Forty Projects with her hair all done up like she's about to go on *America's Next Top Model.*" I laughed, and I swear I could hear Charlene laughing with me.

"And from what I hear through the church grapevine, Lisa Mae's about to make her presence felt in the next few days. From what her best friend, Loretta, has told me, she's had her eye on the bishop for a few weeks now and feels the church is ready for a new first lady." The thought of Lisa Mae being the next first lady brought a smile to my face because she was my personal favorite of all the candidates.

"Oh, and once again, I have to give you credit for thinking of everything. If I hadn't taken the job as the bishop's new secretary right before you passed, I wouldn't have known any of this. Fast-ass Monique Johnson tricked the bishop into dinner at her house the other night, saying she was having some bogus meeting with the bookstore committee. I did some checking, and get this—I couldn't find one person who was even on this supposed bookstore committee. No need to worry, though. He was only there for about two hours, and you know if he was there any longer, I would have walked my behind right up to her door and said, 'Sorry I'm late for the meeting.' If I have anything to say about scheduling them, you can bet that from now on, any meetings with her will be held at the church.

"I guess you're wondering what's going on with Savannah Dickens, but I don't have much to say except that the bishop's had dinner with Deacon Dickens this past Sunday. The bishop didn't even mention her, other than to say she cooked the food. One thing's for sure, I'm going to keep my eye on the deacon because he's been hanging around the administration wing of the church a lot lately, and I'm sure he's up to something. I just haven't figured it out yet." I knelt down and straightened up the vase and flowers.

"Well, Charlene, I gotta go to work before I'm late, but I love you, and I'll keep you posted." I started to walk away, then turned back toward the gravesite to take one more look. I still missed Charlene so much, but I knew she was in a good place now. If she couldn't be at the bishop's side, then I must play my part to be sure that a worthy woman filled her shoes. I knew what I had to do to help my friend rest in peace.

6

MARLENE

I arrived early at First Jamaica Ministries for my date with Thomas Kelly. Tanisha's friend Niecy had truly done her thing. My hair was hooked up, and I knew I looked good, so I mingled around with the women who were leaving one of the many different Bible study classes. I couldn't be more proud of the way I looked as I stood in the room with the other women. Over the years, my drug abuse had taken its toll on my appearance. There were countless times when I felt so ugly, and I was embarrassed to be around other women. But now I was clean and I was taking good care of myself, so I knew I looked as good as—or even better than—plenty of these women.

Most of the women from the Bible study class headed over to a table with all types of cookies, cakes, and a bowl of punch. I knew I was going out to eat with Thomas Kelly, but to curb my appetite, I walked over to the table and helped myself to a few cookies and a cup of punch. While I stood there, I listened to a loudmouthed, brown-skinned woman who looked like she could have played linebacker for the New York Giants. She was running her gum as if she were a candidate for a political office. Twenty women there were hanging on her every word.

"Now, y'all know I'm not one to run my mouth," the woman said. She looked each woman in the eye, including me, challenging anyone to speak the truth about just how much she did run her mouth. "But this church needs a first lady to keep these men in line and these hot-to-trot floozies' skirts below their knees."

"Mmm-hmm. You tell 'em, girl," a woman from the crowd shouted.

"Now, we all know that Bishop Wilson's a good man. I don't think any of us has a doubt about that. But no man, not even a man of God like the bishop, can stay strong with all this temptation running around. Y'all know who I'm talkin' about."

"We sure do! You tell 'em, Loretta," another woman said.

"And we all know there's only one woman who has experience dealing with this type of church matters, has dealt with the responsibility of being a first lady, and can keep the bishop happy, if you know what I mean. And that's my good friend, Lisa Mae Jones." Everyone applauded as the woman pointed at a tall, light-eyed, fair-skinned woman. Lisa Mae had a presence that mirrored the former first lady's. She stepped forward, and I'd be lying if I didn't admit her smile lit up the room.

Now, she could run for political office, I thought, *and she'd have my vote.* The way things were going, it did look like she was running for office. Her candidacy for first lady seemed to have been discussed prior to this meeting, and Loretta was simply giving a little nomination speech before the churchwomen's candidate spoke. When Lisa Mae Jones started to speak, she looked humble but not at all surprised by Loretta's suggestion that she should be the bishop's new wife. I had to suppress my urge to sneer at this woman who had suddenly become my competition for T.K.'s affections.

"Thank you, ladies," Lisa Mae said humbly. "As many of you know, my good friend, the former first lady, Charlene Wilson, wrote a letter asking me to take care of her husband, the bishop, and the church after her death."

I had to rest my hand on the table to keep from falling over when I saw what she held up. It was an envelope exactly like the one I'd found taped to my door. What the hell was going on? Charlene had written me a letter asking me to take care of her husband, and now here was another woman who had supposedly got the same message from the grave. I didn't yet know if I should be mad, but I was definitely confused.

"What you don't know," Lisa Mae continued, "is that Bishop Wilson and I have developed a very special friendship over the last year. One that I hope can blossom into a meaningful relationship." She pulled out a tissue and wiped her eyes. My stomach did a little flip. I felt like I was gonna be sick watching this woman's show. "You see, to be truly honest, I don't want the responsibility of being a first lady again, but if that's what it takes to spend the rest of my life with a man like Bishop T.K. Wilson, then I'll be the best first lady this church has ever seen."

I heard the last of her words and the applause they gave her as I walked out of the building. So, I was not the only one Charlene had given her blessing to, and this Lisa Mae seemed to have her shit together. She also had the support of the women of the church, which had to count for something. I'd never even considered that being with Thomas Kelly meant being the church's first lady.

Tears rolled down my cheeks. I'd never been so hurt and embarrassed in my entire life. Why was this woman playing with me from the grave? She knew I wasn't qualified to be the first lady. Well, I wasn't about to let her or anyone else make a fool of me. I began to walk home, thinking that Thomas Kelly and his high-and-mighty church were better off without me. Good luck to this Lisa Mae woman, and good riddance.

By the time I got to 109th and Guy Brewer Boulevard, the drug boys were out in full force, and I was so angry and humiliated that I actually contemplated getting high to pick up my mood. Thank God I didn't have any cash on me and the drug boys didn't take debit cards. I'd planned to ask Thomas Kelly to take me to an ATM machine so that I could pay for our dinner, although I'm sure he wouldn't have let me. Nonetheless, I took my lack of cash as a sign and started to walk down Guy Brewer Boulevard toward Rochdale Village, where I knew there was an NA meeting. It would be good to be around people who were supportive and knew what I was going through.

During the meeting, I actually got up and testified, something I'd rarely done since I graduated from the Apple drug program three years ago. Afterward, around eleven o'clock, I got a ride with a lady who lived on 110th Street. All I had to do was walk a few blocks to get home. I was feeling pretty good after the meeting. Matter of fact, I'd completely put the earlier events at the church out of my mind, at least until I stepped out of the woman's car and spotted Thomas Kelly's Cadillac standing at a traffic light. That light-skinned woman from the church was sitting in the front seat. Any good feelings from the NA meeting left me immediately as I watched the light turn green, and Thomas Kelly drove away with this woman who was sitting where I should have been. Don't ask me why, but that shit set me off. I was so mad, I could've spit fire. And the next person who approached me was gonna feel my wrath.

"Hey, Ma, whatchu need? Whatchu need?" Reggie shouted, running up on me like I was carrying a million dollars.

"Look, Reggie. I'm not in the best of moods, and I ain't got no money, so leave me the fuck alone," I snapped. "If I have to tell you one more time that I don't use that shit no more, then I—" My whole body tensed up. I just wanted to hit someone.

"Relax, Ma," Reggie said, putting his hands up and slightly backing away from me. "I was just running a special today is all. I got a two for one. I know you used to like a deal."

I didn't have to say a word. I'm sure Reggie could tell by the look in my eyes and my clenched fists that he had one second to get away from me. He took two steps back but still continued his sales routine. "I understand the no-money thing. And, seeing as how you used to be my best customer," Reggie said with a villainous smile, "I'd be willing to extend you some credit."

"I don't do drugs no more." I said it with as much strength as I could muster, to convince myself as much as him that drugs were not what I needed. I started to walk away, but he followed me step for step.

"You sure, Ma? I got this new shit they call Monster. My customers are saying it's the best shit they ever had. Each hit's like your first." Reggie stepped in front of me. "You remember your first hit, don't you, Ma?"

I did remember my first hit. It was the one thing in my life I wished I could forget, because it haunted me like the plague. That first hit was the one that turned my entire life upside down and landed me where I was now, a recovering addict who had lost the love of her life because of drugs, still struggling daily just to stay away from the poison. But as bad as things turned out because of that first smoke, a part of me recalled it fondly. It's hard to even describe how that first time makes you feel. Most addicts will tell you they spend the rest of their lives trying to relive that feeling, and I was no different. I was clean now, but something inside of me would always remember that first hit with longing. In a moment of weakness, it would be so easy to pick up another pipe to try again for that "first high" feeling. And the disappointment I'd suffered tonight was making me feel weak.

I started to roll my neck and swing my arms, motions that had become almost reflexes whenever I thought about getting high. The more Reggie talked, the weaker I became. I could almost feel the smoke filling my mouth and lungs. The only thing that was missing was the rush. I knew I had to get out of there, 'cause I was starting to jones.

"Excuse me, Reggie." I stepped around him and started to walk faster, but he must have known he'd gotten into my head because he kept pace with me once again. "Reggie, why are you following me? I told you I ain't got no money, and you know there ain't no such thing as credit."

"Yeah, I know, but you gotta try this shit. Look, Ma, you know you want this, and I want you to have it. So, I'll tell you what. You ain't even gotta use it now. I'll give you two for free." He stuck out his hand as we walked. "Here."

I looked down at the drugs in his hand and slowed my steps. I could feel the sweat forming on my brow as my conscience kicked into overdrive. I wanted to scream and run from the danger I knew I was in, yet part of me wanted to grab the drugs and take them with me. It was so much work resisting the temptation of crack every day, especially with people like Reggie constantly trying to get me started again.

I stared at Reggie for a long moment, wishing he would just disappear, before I finally sighed and said, "Okay, Reggie, you want me to take them from you? I'll take them, but I'm telling you now, I'm gonna take them upstairs and flush them down the toilet, so don't get your hopes up. I ain't gonna be a return customer this time." I took his packages and stuffed them into my purse, meaning every word I'd said. I was going to get rid of the drugs as soon as I got inside. Maybe then, the next time he saw me and I was still sober, this pain-in-the-ass dealer would know I meant what I said, and he'd stop trying to tempt me every time I stepped outside my damn door.

"Just remember, Ma, next time you pay!" he yelled, walking in the opposite direction. "Next time, you pay!"

As I entered my building, I felt like the drugs were burning a hole in my purse, sending out waves of desire to my brain. My hands shook as I put the key into my mailbox in the lobby. I could feel my resolve weakening, and now I wasn't so certain I'd be able to flush the crack down the toilet when I got upstairs. I cursed myself for being stupid enough to even put my hands on the drugs I now had in my possession. But my strength to resist returned to me when I pulled out my mail and saw a reminder of my biggest reason to stay clean and sober. There was an envelope from my baby Aubrey's school, containing his report card.

He didn't have straight A's, but there were three A's, and no C's, D's, or F's, which meant he made the honor roll. While Aubrey had always been a good student, this was the first time I could say that I had played some part in his success. Before, he managed to get good grades even though his momma was a crackhead. Now he was getting even more A's because his momma was a *recovered* crack addict, and I was able to help him with his schoolwork every night.

I was so proud of him—and of myself—that I felt like going to get him from his friend Jimmy's house so we could take the bus over to Green Acres Mall. We could go to the twenty-four-hour Wal-Mart and buy him that PlayStation 3 he wanted. But as I headed up to my apartment, I decided against it, because if I bought it now, what would he have to look forward to on his birthday next week? But I was going to get rid of these drugs for him and make him some of the chocolate chip cookies he liked.

I entered the apartment and put down the mail. Still clutching my purse, I headed to the bathroom to destroy the temptation I carried. But before I made it out of the living room, the phone rang. When I saw Tanisha's number on the caller ID, I stopped to answer it, eager to tell her about Aubrey's great report card.

"So, how did it go, Momma? Should I start planning a wedding?" Tanisha asked before I even had a chance to finish the word *hello*. Her enthusiasm just squashed any joy I was feeling. My mind had gotten past the date that never happened with T.K., but it was still in the forefront of Tanisha's thoughts. Her question brought me right back to where I started fifteen minutes ago, when I saw that woman in Thomas Kelly's car. I squeezed the purse in my hands, thinking about what lay inside.

"Momma, you still there?"

"Yeah, I'm here. Your brother got a real good report card. He made honor roll," I said, wishing I could have sounded as optimistic as I had just a few minutes ago.

"Oh, that's great, Momma, but we can talk about that later. How'd everything go on your date with the bishop?"

I wasn't really sure what to tell her. She'd been so excited about me and her father going out. The last thing she would want to hear was that my insecurity had gotten the best of me and that I'd left before the date even happened. But like I always said, if I owed her anything, I owed her the truth.

"I didn't go. I stood him up," I told her.

"What do you mean you stood him up? Momma, why would you stand the bishop up?"

"It's a long story, Tanisha. Let's just say we're not right for each other."

Sister Lisa Mae is a little more his style, I thought, feeling so stupid now. *I never should have let myself be fooled by some damn letter supposedly written by a woman who's been dead for half a year.*

"That's bull, Momma, and you know it. You told me you still love him." Tanisha was not willing to let this go easily.

"Love ain't got nothing to do with this, little girl. Your—"

She cut me off by raising her voice. "Love has everything to do with it, Momma. Jesus! How could you mess this up?"

Ignoring that she was speaking to me like I was the child, I tried to remain calm as I explained, "Things aren't like they used to be when me and your father were kids, Tanisha. Your father's a very complicated man with a very complicated job. The last thing he needs is my baggage."

"Momma, I don't understand. What baggage? You're not smoking again, are you?"

I looked down at my purse and felt my insides tighten. If only Tanisha knew how close I had come to using again. "No, I'm not smoking," I snapped, no longer calm. I knew I needed to get that shit down the toilet as quickly as possible. "And it's fucked up that you thought that."

"I'm sorry, Momma. I'm just having a hard time understanding why you stood up the bishop."

"Little girl, did you ever think that if me and your father got married I'd have to be the first lady of First Jamaica Ministries? Do you know how much responsibility that is? Your father's a very important man, Tanisha, and I do love him, but the only thing I could do is hold him back. Besides, he was just being polite when he told me he'd go out with me."

"No, he wasn't. When Dante talked to him, he said he was really looking forward to seeing you. And as far as that first lady stuff, the bishop doesn't care about that."

"I thought I told you not to tell your husband about this," I said, hoping to steer the conversation in a different direction.

"I didn't, but the bishop and Dante were talking and he brought it up. From what Dante said, he was very excited. And so was my husband."

"Oh really?" I was surprised to hear this, because Tanisha had said before that she didn't think Dante was ready for his father to move on. But even if I had Dante's blessing, it still didn't change a damn thing. Sister Lisa Mae was still the one in the front seat of his Cadillac tonight, not me. And hell, she probably belonged there a lot more than I did.

"You should call him and apologize, Momma. Maybe you two could go out tomorrow."

"I don't think so, Tanisha. Thomas Kelly and I are in the past. He needs a sophisticated woman, somebody who knows the politics of both the church and New York City. I'm sorry, but I'm not that woman."

Her tone softened as she said, "Momma, why are you always putting yourself down? You can be anything you want to be."

"A woman's gotta know her limitations, Tanisha. I know mine. I'm not cut out to be a preacher's wife."

"That's not true. I used to be a stripper, but now I'm married to a lawyer and going to school to be a nurse. If you really wanna be with Daddy, then you can do it. Nobody loves him like you do, Momma." Her optimism was starting to piss me off. Why couldn't she just let this go?

"I keep tellin' you that sometimes love isn't enough. Now, I'm not cut out to be no first lady. Them women in that church ain't making a fool outta me, and neither are you." I made no attempt to hide the anger in my voice, thinking that would put her in her place. But I was wrong. She came right back at me with her own anger and judgment.

"Always full of excuses, aren't you, Momma? You're never gonna get rid of that ghetto mentality, are you?"

"What's that supposed to mean?"

"It means I'm really disappointed in you, 'cause you're never gonna leave Forty Projects," Tanisha said just before hanging up.

"Fuck you, Tanisha!" I yelled into the receiver, then slammed it down. My purse fell out of my hands and tumbled to the floor. I was hot! That girl knew how to push my buttons like nobody else. As if it wasn't bad enough that those damn churchwomen made me feel less than little Miss Lisa Mae, now my own damn daughter felt she had the right to judge me.

I reached down to pick up my purse and the contents that had spilled onto the floor. I stared at the small plastic bags that I was supposed to have already flushed down the toilet. In my anger, it took only a few seconds for me to say, "Fuck it," pick them up, and head for the kitchen.

I quickly found aluminum foil to make a stem, and in no time I was sitting on my couch, staring at a picture of Tanisha, about to get high. "You know what, Tanisha?" I said to the picture just as I was about to inhale. "This is all your fault."

7

BISHOP

I was talking to James in the hallway of the church's administrative wing when Monique came walking down the corridor. She was wearing a tight red dress that left very little to the imagination. When James spotted her, his entire body tightened up, and his facial expression was one of disgust. He quickly pointed to my office as if to say, "If we hurry, we can hide in there." But Monique had seen us, and I was glad because she'd been on my mind a lot the past few days. We'd had several meetings about her bookstore proposal since our dinner two weeks ago. They were all very professional in the church conference room, with my secretary and/or James present at all times. But even in that setting, I couldn't stop myself from reliving that moment at her front door when she tried to kiss me. There was no denying that I was curious about what might have happened had I let that moment continue.

"Please, Bishop, this is not the time or the place to have Monique all up in your face." James's voice was low but stern. "Now, enough is enough. The women's Bible study class is about to get out, and that girl is dressed like a slut. I'm sorry, but we have to protect your reputation." I shot him an angry look, and he shook his head. "All right, I'll be quiet, but it's your funeral."

He put on a fake smile as Monique walked up and gave each of us a hug. "Hey, Trustee. Hey, Bishop."

When she released me, it took everything I had to concentrate on her face and not stare at the cleavage that was popping out of her dress. James, on the other hand, was staring at her chest so hard, it looked like his eyes were about to fall out of his head. For someone who just seconds ago was condemning her for the way she was dressed, he sure seemed to appreciate it now. I was just waiting for him to ask her something outlandish like, "Are those things real?" Thank the Lord, he remained quiet.

"So, to what do we owe the pleasure, Sister Monique?" I asked.

"We just finished up Bible study, and I wanted to know if you had some free time this week to talk some more about the bookstore, maybe over dinner?"

As if on cue, James doubled over and began coughing violently. This wasn't anything new for him, though. He'd used this ploy before when he didn't want me to answer someone, and I absolutely hated it.

Sister Monique fell for his little act and asked with genuine concern, "Oh, my goodness, Trustee. Are you all right?"

"He's all right. Aren't you, Trustee Black?" I placed my arm around his back, and as Monique stared at his face, I mashed right down on his foot with my size twelve-and-a-half shoe.

"Aaarrghh! Doggone it, Bishop, that's my toe!" James immediately stopped coughing as he jumped up in the air, then started hobbling around.

"Ah, I'm sorry, Trustee. My feet are so big, sometimes I don't know where they're gonna land. I sure am glad your cough is okay, though. Look, why don't you grab a seat in my office? You might wanna elevate that foot." James cut his eye at me as he limped into my office. When he was out of sight, I turned back toward Monique.

"Is he gonna be all right?" She stepped close enough that I could smell her perfume, and I inhaled deeply.

"Oh, he's going to be just fine. I step on his toes all the time. So, where were we?" I gave her a reassuring smile.

"I was asking if you wanted to get together tonight so we could talk more about . . . the bookstore, of course."

"I've got something planned tonight, but how about Saturday evening? I don't think I have anything scheduled." Even I couldn't believe what I'd just done. She was asking me to discuss church business, and I was suggesting that we do it on a Saturday night. I could have suggested any afternoon this week, but I chose a weekend night, which most unmarried people reserve for dates. This was the first time I had come remotely close to asking a woman out since my wife's death, and it took me by surprise. I guess that while my heart was still sorting out my feelings, my body had seen Monique in that red dress and decided it was ready to move on.

If I had any doubts about how my invitation would be received, Monique reassured me quickly that she was feeling the same way I was.

"That sounds good. Do you want to meet at my place again? I'll fix dinner."

I wanted to say yes, but after the way she kissed me at her place, I decided not to tempt fate. My body was ready, but my heart was still in turmoil. "How about we go out to dinner this time? My treat. We can go over the details of your plan in a little more depth."

A smirk crept across her face that made me think she had a little bit of the devil in her. "Are you sure you wanna take me out to dinner, Bishop? Folks might get the wrong idea."

"I'm not much for what people think, Sister Monique. Now that my wife has passed away, I don't have to answer to anyone but God."

Her smile widened. "Well, amen to that. I'll see you on Saturday. Let's say about seven?"

"Seven it is."

She leaned in like she was about to give me a kiss good-bye. This time I made sure her kiss landed on my cheek. Although I meant what I said about not having to answer to anyone, I instinctively glanced over her shoulder to see if anyone had witnessed the kiss. Then my eyes lowered and followed Monique's hips as they swayed back and forth down the hall. I wasn't sure if she knew I was watching and was doing it for my benefit, but she was putting on quite a show.

"Maaaaaan, now I know why you're so infatuated with that girl. Not only does baby got back, but she got one heck of walk too." I turned to see James standing in the doorway of my office, grinning.

I shot him a dirty look. "You know what, James?"

"What's that, Bishop?"

"You gon' make me step on your other toe in a second."

I stepped toward him, slamming my foot on the floor in front of his feet, and he jumped back.

"Stop playing, Bishop," James whined.

"Who's playing?" I stomped my foot near his again, then

laughed. "Look, I'm going to find Marlene in the common area. We've got dinner plans."

"Dinner plans with Marlene tonight? Dinner with Monique on Saturday, and didn't you have dinner with Savannah Dickens not too long ago? I don't know, Bishop. If I didn't know you so well, it would seem to me like you've become quite the Casanova lately." James chuckled.

I rolled my eyes at his not-so-humorous joke. If indeed I was getting back into dating, no one in the church was going to make it easy for me, including my good friend.

"I'll see you later, James, because you're making way too much of nothing."

"Am I, Bishop?"

As I headed away from James, I didn't answer him, but I did wonder if he was right. Dinner with three different women in the same week. Had I just allowed myself to become First Jamaica Ministries' most eligible bachelor without even noticing it happen?

I waited for Marlene for almost two hours before I got my briefcase from my office and decided to head home, figuring she'd forgotten about our dinner plans. Actually, I was *hoping* she'd just forgotten, because I'd called her house three times and got no answer, so I was a bit worried about her. I tried to reassure myself that everything was fine, but just in case, I'd stop by her place on my way home.

When I reached the church parking lot, I was surprised to see Lisa Mae Jones, the widow of my late friend, Pastor Lee Jones, standing in the parking lot next to her car with the hood up.

"Car troubles, Sister Lisa?"

"I don't know what's wrong with this thing, Bishop. I've never been good with cars. Lee used to always handle that." She sounded defeated.

"Well, I'm not that great with them, either, but let me have a look."

"I appreciate that. I probably should have just gotten a ride home with Sister Alison when she offered, but I was sure I could get this thing started," she said. "That'll teach me to be stubborn."

I smiled at her joke; then I got in her car and turned the key.

"Well, perhaps Sister Alison was right. The car won't start for me, either."

Even though the question was obvious, I still had to ask, "Do you have any gas?"

"I think I do." She didn't sound very confident, and I was fairly certain of what I would see when I looked down at the gas gauge. It was empty. I almost wanted to laugh at the thought of this woman trying to start her car, never once realizing the problem was simply an empty gas tank. But this was my friend's widow, and I couldn't do anything but feel sorry for her helplessness.

"Sister Lisa, I think you're out of gas."

"Oh, my goodness, I am so embarrassed. I feel like a fool. How in the world could I forget to put gas in the car?"

I was wondering the same thing myself, but I stepped out of the car, placed my arm around her shoulder, and said, "No reason to put yourself down, Sister. It happens to us all. I ran out of gas a few weeks ago myself. Thank goodness, I'd just pulled into a gas station. Listen, why don't I give you a ride to the gas station on Liberty, and then we'll get some? Do you have a gas can?"

She shook her head. "Like I told you before, Bishop, I don't know anything about cars other than I'm supposed to put gas in it. And as you can see, I'm not very good at that."

"Well, I've got a can at home in my other car. We could shoot over there and get it, or I could drop you off at home tonight, then have one of the brothers drop your car to you in the morning."

"Maybe we should do that. It's late, and I don't think either of us should be out here this time of night."

"Okay, but I'd like to have a bite to eat first. I'm famished. Do you mind if I stop by McDonald's or Popeye's first?"

"I certainly do mind. If you're dropping me at my house, you can finish off the pork chops I cooked before Bible study."

My mouth started to water. "You made pork chops?"

"I sure did. I thought Lee Jr. was coming over, so I made plenty."

"How is Lee? Is he still studying at St. John's Seminary?"

"Yes. He wants to be just like his father . . . and you."

"Well, he is a fine young man. We need more young men to come into the clergy."

"We sure do. Now, Bishop, what are we gonna do about those pork chops just sitting there at my house? I've got some homemade bread and some onions I could fry up. We could make some pork chop sandwiches."

My stomach started to grumble. "Well, Sister Lisa, who in the world could say no to some pork chop sandwiches?" I escorted her to my car, and we headed to her home in Rosedale.

8

LISA

I watched happily as the bishop ate my pork chops like they were going out of style. I had to give my girl Loretta credit. Our plan had worked even better than expected. Siphoning the gas from my car and waiting for the bishop to come out of the church was a brilliant idea. What man of God, especially a man the caliber of Bishop T.K. Wilson, would leave a woman stranded at night with a broken-down car? But offering him pork chops to get him to come over to my house was really just a stroke of genius. Charlene had told me years ago that pork chops were the bishop's favorite food, so I'd been perfecting mine since her death.

"Sister Lisa, I've gotta tell you like the kids would say—these pork chops are slammin'."

I watched the bishop finish off his third pork chop, cleaning the plate. "Why, thank you, Bishop. Would you like another one?"

Without hesitation, he nodded. "Don't mind if I do."

I placed two more pork chops on his plate and a small heap of fried onions. Watching him eat brought a warmth to my soul. Like my late husband Lee, Bishop T.K. Wilson could put away some food. He also knew how to conduct a conversation with a lady. We'd talked about so many things on the ride to my house and as I warmed up the pork chops and fried the onions. I was truly enjoying his company.

"So, Bishop, how's your family?" I asked.

"They're fine. Dante and Tanisha are still down in D.C. He's working for a big-time law firm while she goes to school and takes care of the baby. And as you know, Shorty and Donna are working for the church, running the youth ministry. Oh, and all three of my grandchildren are just a joy."

"That's good. So, how are you holding up after Charlene's death?" I hated to ask the question, afraid that it would ruin the mood of this enjoyable evening. But Charlene's death was like the eight-hundred-pound gorilla in the room; sooner or later the subject would have to come up. I would just have to try to use the conversation to my advantage, to show the bishop what a good, understanding listener I was.

"Sister Lisa, it's hard. It's real hard. Not a day goes by that I don't wish she was still here with me."

"I know how you feel. I think about Lee every day too. But it gets easier with time. Believe it or not, I've even gone on a few dates in the past six months," I lied. The only man I'd been interested in was the bishop, but I'd learned a long time ago that men love competition.

He looked up at me, surprised. "Really? I didn't think you dated."

I frowned. "Well, I'm not a spring chicken anymore, but I have my suitors."

I had a thought to be offended until I heard his reply. "I'm sure you do, Sister. You're a very attractive woman." There was an awkward silence for a moment before he asked, "So, are your suitors anybody I know?"

"Oh, one or two of them maybe, but like I said, they were just dates. Nothing serious. You see, Bishop, I won't settle. I need an intelligent, strong man, someone who's devoted himself to God but is worldly at the same time. It's very hard to accept any man less than the one I was married to. I just won't lower my standards for anyone. You'll see when you start dating . . . if you haven't already." I searched his face for any signs of an answer to my probing but saw none. "No one will compare to Charlene. Sure, you may find someone prettier or younger, but will they have her substance? Will they be able to stand next to you in the pulpit? Not every woman can be the first lady of her church. It takes a very special woman, like your Charlene. A very special woman, Bishop."

He finished off another pork chop and sat back in his chair like he was in deep thought. "You know, Sister, I never thought about it that way."

"That's because you had a strong first lady with you from the start."

"Truthfully, I hadn't given much thought at all to finding someone to fill the space left after my wife's death. It just seemed too soon. But now I hear there's grumbling among the women of the church. Why does everyone seem to think I need to get married anyway?"

"Well, speaking for myself, I don't think you should do anything until you're ready, Bishop. The grieving process is different for everyone. But at the same time, I do understand the position of the church. What you may seem to forget is that while you took care of the spiritual side of the church, your wife took care of the social aspect of it. While you may have kept things together in the pulpit, the social structure of our church has been crumbling."

"You think so?" He looked like this was news to him, and he was truly concerned.

I hesitated, thinking out my response before I continued. "Yes, I do. We haven't even started work on the Toys for Tots drive. Have we?"

"Not to my knowledge, but that's something Charlene . . ." His voice trailed off as he no doubt thought about his late wife and her role in the church. "It's one of the many things the first lady used to handle."

"Exactly. See what I mean? And what about this summer's revival? Do we even know where it's going to be?"

"Wow, that's something else I hadn't thought about."

I had planted the seed in the bishop's head, making him fully aware of how things had been slipping since the first lady's death. Now it was time to make him realize that I was the perfect woman to pull everything back together.

"I know how much you must miss her. We all do. I hadn't even thought about all these social things, either . . . until I got this." I reached over into my bag and pulled out the letter Charlene had written me. I handed it to the bishop.

He asked, "What's this?" but I could tell by his expression that he wasn't surprised I had it. It crossed my mind that he could possibly be the one who taped it to my door. Still, I had to operate under the assumption that he really didn't know what I had.

"It's a letter from your wife. I found it taped to my door a few days ago. I don't know how it got there. The only thing I could think of was that she had written it before her death, then left it with someone to deliver. It seems she thought that with both of us widowed, you and I would be perfect for each other."

"Really?" he asked with raised eyebrows, and this time I believed he really was surprised. I guess he wasn't the one who'd left it on my door. I watched as he read the letter, but his face did not reveal his thoughts.

He folded the letter and placed it back into the envelope, then handed it to me. He made eye contact briefly, and said, "Yes, it's from her." But he offered no explanation for how he was sure it was from Charlene and quickly looked toward the floor. I couldn't tell if the glistening in his eye was a tear or just a reflection.

We sat in silence for quite a long time before he took a deep breath, then spoke. "So, what do you think of this?" he asked.

I reached out and placed my hand on his, but he still wouldn't look up at me. "I think your wife loved you very much, Bishop. And I think she believed that if we tried, the two of us would make a great team." I watched him close his eyes tightly, perhaps trying to hold back tears. I asked gently, "What do you think?"

He didn't answer immediately. As much as I wanted him to make this easy, to just turn to me and say it was a great idea, I understood why he couldn't. I had been where he was now emotionally, in the first months after I lost my husband. It's not a simple thing to move on after losing a loved one. I was ready to do this, to become the next first lady as soon as possible, but I couldn't rush the bishop. I had to play this carefully so I didn't scare him away. It was important to be subtle as I guided his heart in my direction, but he had to feel like he was the one who decided he was ready. So I sat silently while he gathered his thoughts.

Finally, he looked up at me and said, "Frankly, I'm embarrassed and don't know what to say. I mean, she made a lot of good points in her letter. I did tell her I thought you were a very attractive woman. I also told her Lee was a very lucky man and that you were a great first lady."

Well, that was promising. I kept my composure, but I wanted to blush. It was one thing to read it from Charlene, but it was another to hear him say he thought I was attractive and was a great first lady. "Thank you, Bishop. I've always thought you were a very attractive man too." There was an awkward silence between us for a few more seconds. "And there's really no need for you to be embarrassed. Like I said, I think your wife loved you very much. It couldn't have been easy to write a letter like this."

"I'm sure it wasn't. And you're right, I shouldn't be embarrassed." What he said next sent a wave of adrenaline through me. "She sent me a letter too."

"She did?" I had to struggle to sit still because I was so eager to know what his wife wrote to him. "What did it say?" I asked as calmly as I could.

"Well, there was a lot of personal stuff in there, and she also said a lot of what she said in yours, except she didn't specifically name anyone. She just said it was time for me to move on and that the church and I needed a new first lady."

Well, she didn't name me specifically, which was a little disappointing, but at least I knew Charlene had told him it was time for him to start looking for a new wife. This would make my job a little easier. If he took her advice, at least I wouldn't have to do any more to help him see that it was time. Then I could get right to work on convincing him how perfect I would be for him and his church.

"So, do you agree with what she said?" I asked.

"I'm starting to. At least I think it's time that I started to date."

My heart started to beat fast. For a moment, I lost control and blurted out something much less subtle than I had planned. "So, would you consider me . . . I mean, to go on a date?"

He hesitated briefly, raising his hand to smooth out his salt-and-pepper beard. I was relieved when I actually saw a small smile cross his lips. "Yes, Sister Lisa, I would consider you. You just have to give me a little more time to figure this all out."

"Bishop, take all the time you need."

9

SAVANNAH

"I had no idea I would need to bring a box of Kleenex to a Yolanda Adams concert," I said as the bishop and I walked from Westbury Music Fair to the car in the parking lot. "I must look a mess with this mascara running down my face. I don't know why I let Daddy talk me into wearing makeup in the first place."

Daddy had claimed, when he brought home this bag full of cosmetics, that he was just supporting Sister Sophie's independent Avon business. But I knew better.

"Actually," the bishop said, "I thought you looked just fine. As a matter of fact, you still do."

"Oh, Bishop, you're just being nice," I said, fighting as hard as an angel trying to escape hell by not blushing. This was the second time this evening the bishop had made me blush. The other time was during the concert when he grabbed my hand and held it. Of course, Yolanda Adams had asked the entire audience to grab their neighbors' hands and repeat some song lyrics after her. But it didn't seem the bishop was holding my hand just because he had been instructed to do so. He made me feel like he genuinely wanted to.

"That's not it at all, Sister Savannah," the bishop corrected me. "You do look fine. Fine enough to stop for coffee if you're not too worn out." He looked down at his watch and said, "It's nine-thirty," then looked back up at me for my response.

"Well, I could stand a cup of coffee," I said with a smile as we approached the bishop's car.

"Then coffee it is." Like a gentleman, he opened the car door for me, and we were on our way.

It took us a good fifteen minutes just to get out of the crowded parking lot. By the time we arrived at a diner, it was close to ten o'clock, and I needed a cup of coffee just to stay awake. I generally stay out this late.

"I swear, I'd give anything to do what Yolanda Adams does—singing unto the Lord all over the world for a living," I said as we waited for the waitress to bring us our coffee. "Now that's living."

"Whew-wee, Sister Savannah! If you could have seen how your eyes just lit up," the bishop said to me. "You said that like it's truly your heart's desire."

"Well, it is, Bishop," I said sincerely.

"Then why haven't you done anything to pursue it?" he asked in an encouraging tone.

"I don't know." I shrugged my shoulders. "I don't know the first thing about that business. I wouldn't even know where to start, Bishop. Besides, I'm no Yolanda Adams."

"You sure aren't. You're Savannah Dickens," he said with authority. "You've got your own voice and style that you can't compare to Yolanda Adams's."

"You really think so, Bishop?" I asked, waiting for more confirmation and praise, something I heard so infrequently from my father and was so glad to get anywhere I could.

"I know so," he said as I beamed. "Why don't we look into starting off with maybe you and the church choir doing a CD? We'll find out about booking a studio or recording right there in the sanctuary if need be. You gotta start somewhere."

"Are you serious, Bishop?"

"The real question is, Savannah, Are *you* serious?"

Just then the waitress placed two cups of coffee down in front of us.

"Thank you," I said to the waitress as she walked away.

"I sure do hope your father is okay," the bishop said while he added creamer and sugar to his coffee. "I didn't think about him before suggesting we stop for coffee. Do you want to call and check on him?"

I was disappointed that he had changed the subject after all the praise he was heaping on me. I sighed as a shade of guilt flushed over me, both for my own vanity and for my father's deceit. "Bishop, I hate to say this, but I honestly don't think my father's sick at all."

His cup was halfway to his mouth when he stopped in midair. "What are you saying, Savannah?"

"You'll have to forgive my father, Bishop. I'm sure he means well, but I don't believe he fell ill at the last minute at all." It felt like a betrayal, revealing my father's lies this way, but after the bishop had been praising my singing in ways my own father never could, part of me felt like lashing out at Daddy. "I don't think he ever had any intentions of going to this concert with us in the first place."

"Well, why in the world would he pretend to be ill?" The bishop chuckled as if I were speaking nonsense.

"He deliberately wanted to get me alone with you." Still feeling guilty about my sudden lack of family loyalty, I immediately looked down into my cup of coffee, avoiding the bishop's eyes. I began guzzling the coffee as if it were a glass of refreshing water instead of the scalding hot beverage that it was.

"Pardon me?" Bishop said as he almost choked on the sip of coffee he had just swallowed.

"I could be wrong, Bishop, but I think Daddy feels that if you and I . . . you know, get together or something, it will help him politically, improve his chances of moving up in the church." There. I said it, and there was no turning back now.

The bishop looked a little disturbed by my comment. He took a sip of his coffee, swallowed hard, and then sat in thought for a few seconds before speaking.

"Savannah, if that is true, then I hate to say it," Bishop said with a serious look in his eyes, "but I think Deacon Dickens has some issues."

"More than you'll ever know," I said under my breath.

"What was that?"

I started to repeat myself, but then I just shook my head. "Oh, nothing, Bishop. Nothing I need to bother you with." I set down my cup and wrapped my hands around it as I stared at my reflection in the black liquid.

The next thing I knew, the bishop reached over and cupped his hands around mine. "Savannah, I know your father can be hard on you sometimes. I mean, we all have our way of raising our children, but you're a grown woman. I know the Bible says that we must obey our mother and father, but . . ." The bishop paused when he saw my eyes begin to water.

"Bishop, do you think there are exceptions to that scripture?" I asked him.

"Well, Savannah, there are no exceptions to God's word, but—"

"Never mind, Bishop," I interrupted him. "I didn't mean to put you in a position to contradict the Bible."

He stared at me for a moment, then released his hands from mine. "Look, Savannah, it's already late, maybe too late to get into certain things right now, but my spirit tells me that there is something heavy on your heart. Perhaps I can help you to allow God to lift it."

"What are you saying, Bishop?"

"I'm saying that I'd like to counsel with you, Savannah, find out what's going on in there." He pointed to my head. "But most importantly, what's going on in there." He pointed to my heart.

There was so much I could have told that man right then and there. I had more in my head and on my heart than anyone could have ever imagined. It was so easy to show up in church every Sunday and shout, "Holy, holy," all the while screaming bloody murder inside. But perhaps he was right. Maybe it was about time I allowed it all to be lifted from me.

"Bishop . . ." I paused. "I would like to take you up on that offer. You're right, there is so much that's gone on in my life, things that until now I never felt I could share. But I have to warn you, I think you are going to discover things that are going to make you think differently."

"Savannah." Once again, the bishop put his hands on mine. Just this little bit of contact, this connection to another human being, warmed me more than the coffee could have. "Don't worry. Nothing you share with me can make me think any differently about you."

Staring into the bishop's eyes, I knew he spoke with sincerity. I looked down at my hands, which were covered with his. His thumbs rubbed the backs of my hands. For a brief moment, this feeling arose from me out of nowhere. It was a feeling that made me want to lean across the table and actually kiss the bishop. And just for a moment, I wrestled with the thought of actually doing so. But what if I were wrong? What if the last thing the bishop expected was for me to lean in and slob him down? I couldn't dare embarrass myself in such a way. So, instead of allowing my lips to kiss his, I allowed them to say, "Thank you, Bishop."

"No need to thank me, Savannah." The bishop smiled and patted my hands. As we prepared to leave the restaurant, my heart already felt lighter, less burdened.

"Thank you for a lovely evening, Bishop," I said when we arrived at my house. He opened my door to help me out of the car. I took his hand and stepped out onto the sidewalk, wondering if he might try to kiss me good night. He didn't, and I was only momentarily disappointed. The kindness he had shown me that night did far more for my spirit than any kiss could have. Sure, Daddy was probably peeking out the window, watching the bishop give me a platonic pat on the shoulder and a handshake. He would berate me for not leaning in to at least attempt a kiss, but I was not going to let Daddy spoil my mood tonight.

"I'll call you later this week to set up a time for my first counsel with you," I said.

"I'm looking forward to it," he replied with reassurance.

"Oh, Bishop," I turned around and called as I made my way to the front door. "About what you said . . . I'm not worried that you'll change the way you think about *me*." I glanced toward the window where I was fairly certain my father was watching.

10

MARLENE

I left my apartment about four o'clock in the afternoon and walked down to Jamaica Avenue to get some money from the ATM. I hate to admit it, but this was my third trip that day. I knew my account was getting low, but I had no idea I'd totally wiped it out until the ATM spit out a piece of paper that read, CURRENT BALANCE $1.06. If I wasn't so concerned about getting high, I probably would have cried. Four hundred and sixty dollars, the entire amount I'd saved to buy Aubrey's PlayStation 3 for his birthday, was now down the drain, or should I say up in smoke. And I couldn't have cared less. Fuck Aubrey, and fuck his PlayStation 3. I worked for that money; he didn't. Besides, it wasn't like his sister wouldn't buy him one if I didn't. Anyway, now I had a much bigger dilemma—I was broke and I needed some money to get high.

I thought about collecting cans, but that shit took too long. I'd probably go out of my mind before I had enough money to buy one nickel. I walked back down to Guy Brewer Boulevard in search of Reggie. A couple of days ago he'd given me two nickels for free. I was sure I could talk him into giving me two more. Shit, like he said, I was his best customer, and I'd proven that in the past two days.

When I arrived on the boulevard, Reggie was standing next to two other dope boys who worked for him. He grinned, showing all of his gold teeth when he saw me. This time, though, he wasn't running up to me like he had done in the past. He waited for me to come to him.

"What's up, Ma? Whatchu need?" He no longer had that "I'm-trying-to-hook-you-up" sound to his voice. Now he had a matter-of-fact, let's-get-to-business tone.

"Hey, Reggie, remember when you told me you'd give me credit if I needed it? Well, you think I could get some credit now?"

Reggie burst out laughing like I'd just told the world's funniest joke. Not only was he laughing, but the two friends standing next to him were cracking up too. "Are you crazy? What you think this is, Baskin-Robbins? Ain't no free samples around here. I told you the other day. From now on, you pay."

I wasn't beneath begging at this point, but before I could get half a word out of my mouth, Reggie told me, "Look, get your ass outta here. You bad for business."

"C'mon, Reggie. I'm your best customer. You know how much money I've spent with you in the last two days? Over four hundred dollars. And I'm gonna spend more."

"Well, that's your problem, not mine." He gave his boys a slap on the hand. "Now, I told you to get your ass outta here. Nonpaying customers are bad for business."

"Don't do this to me, Reggie, please. I'm really hurting. You know I'ma pay you back."

"I don't know shit. Get your ass out of here." He balled up his fist as if he were about to punch me.

I started to walk away, thinking about what I could pawn, but before I got too far, Reggie called me back. "Yo, Ma, c'mere."

I had to suppress a smile before I turned to look at him. I was so relieved that he was going to reconsider giving me some credit. As desperate as I was to get high, the thought didn't even cross my mind that there would be strings attached.

"What's up?" I asked eagerly.

"My boy Tone over here thinks you got a phat little ass for a crackhead." He gestured toward his friend, a tall black boy in his early twenties who had to weigh more than three hundred and fifty pounds. "He said he'll give you a couple of nicks if you suck his dick." They all burst out laughing, but I couldn't see anything funny. A few days before, I would have been offended by this ugly young boy asking me to do that to him, but not now. As much as I wanted to get high, this wasn't funny to me. It was a serious business proposition.

"So, what's up? You gon' suck his dick or what?"

I scratched my arms, a telltale sign that my body was in need of some smoke. I stared at the large, acne-scarred young man in front of me. It wouldn't take me long to get him off. The question was, How bad did I want a hit? Truth is, I wanted it bad, real bad. And it wasn't like I'd never sucked a dick before to get some money or some crack. I just hadn't done it in a while. Back in the day, I'd turned hundreds of tricks for crack. But this wasn't back in the day, and I wasn't that far from remembering what it was like to be clean. I'd dodged the AIDS bullet for damn near twenty years. Was I willing to take a chance that I could dodge it another night? Because tomorrow, I was gonna get myself clean.

"Well?" the big man said, breaking his silence. He grabbed his dick and smiled, pointing at the alley with his free hand.

"Look, bitch, make up your mind. We ain't got all day," Reggie said.

"You ain't got to worry. I've made up my mind. I ain't sucking nobody's dick for no two nickels. I'll pawn everything in my house first."

I started to walk toward my apartment with a sense of pride, but goddamn Reggie couldn't just let me leave like that. He shouted at my back, "Yo, Ma, now you pissed me off. When you come back, you gon' suck all three of our dicks for two nicks of crack." I kept walking, trying to ignore the way my body seemed to be screaming for a hit.

When I got into my apartment, I went straight to my room and emptied out my jewelry box. I didn't have much, just a couple of thin gold chains and some costume jewelry, which were not enough to pawn for one nick, let alone two. I needed something I could sell quickly. Then it hit me: Aubrey's Xbox.

I went into the living room and stared at the game system. He didn't need it. I had already decided I was going to talk Tanisha into buying him a PlayStation 3 next week. Without another thought, I unhooked the Xbox and took all twenty of his games, thinking I could probably pawn the Xbox for fifty dollars and the games for at least five dollars each.

I checked the clock on the wall. It was 4:30. I had to get out of the house and to the pawnshop before Aubrey came home from basketball practice. I opened the window in his room. That way, when he came home and noticed his Xbox and games were missing, I could blame it on him by saying he must have left his window open and someone came in and stole them. I mean, why would he suspect me? I got a job . . . even if I hadn't been to work in two days.

I made it down the stairs and at least halfway out the door before my conscience finally kicked in. I couldn't do this to my baby. I couldn't blame him for something I did. He'd worked his ass off last summer at the YMCA job program to save the money to buy his Xbox and the games. And no matter how high I'd been the last two days, I hadn't forgotten the promise I'd made to Aubrey. His early childhood had been so messed up because of my addiction, and I swore I would make it up to him, that I would never let his life become like that again. If I took his games and pawned them now, I knew it would be only the first step down a long road that would put my baby right back in hell. Aubrey didn't deserve that. His momma was weak, not him. I turned around and went back upstairs, knowing there was only one way I was gonna get high without destroying my son in the process.

Ten minutes later, I'd returned the Xbox and was standing in front of Reggie and his two friends. "You know you gotta do all three of us now, don't you?" Reggie taunted.

If I had a gun, I would have shot him, but I didn't have one. I only had a monster craving for some smoke. So I simply nodded my head and walked toward the alley. "Yeah, I know what I gotta do. Come on, who's first? Y'all already said you ain't got all day, and neither do I. All I wanna do is get high."

11

MONIQUE

The bishop and I were at Umberto's seafood restaurant in Brooklyn having dinner. When I'd suggested a few days earlier that we get together, I used the guise that I wanted to talk further about my bookstore idea, but so far, he hadn't said a word about it. Not that I minded. His silence on that subject just confirmed my suspicion—oh, all right, my hope—that his invitation to dinner was more than a meeting, that it was a date. So, instead of talking business, we'd been enjoying our surf and turf, making the kind of small talk that people do when they're on their first or perhaps even second date.

As we joked and laughed together, I found myself liking him even more. The way he stole glances at my behind and my breasts made me feel beautiful and sexy, but plenty of men had admired me for my body. With the bishop, it was different. The way he spoke to me and the way he listened so intently to the things I said made me feel funny and smart. Don't get me wrong, I knew that, as with every other man I'd dated, in the end, this whole thing would come down to him getting some and liking it, but he still made me feel special for something other than my body.

Of course, I knew that my approach had to be subtle. Most of the men I'd dated made no qualms about what they wanted, and neither did I. But Bishop T.K. Wilson, despite his wants and needs, was determined to be respectable, even though my ultimate goal was to get him in my bed so we could consummate this relationship. After all, he, like no other man I'd ever met, deserved what I had planned for him—a night of lovemaking he'd never forget. Since I was pretty sure the man hadn't had sex since his wife died, and probably for months before that, he must be ready to jump out of his skin with desire. Well, I knew just what he needed, and

I was more than eager to show him my appreciation for this wonderful evening.

I thought that sharing a bottle of wine over dinner might loosen him up enough to get him over to my place, but he declined my offer. He admitted that he did drink socially from time to time, but not tonight. So, as I sat drinking my second glass of wine, I thought about other ways I might be able to get him to come home with me. My momma always said the way to a man's heart was straight between your legs. And I'd never met a man whose heart I couldn't win.

Although I was confident that it was just a matter of time before I got the bishop into my bed, I knew it was important that our lovemaking happen sooner rather than later. I wasn't sure if or when I would get another chance to be alone with him like this, so I had to seize the moment while it was right here in front of me. Rumors in the church led me to believe that I had serious competition for the bishop's heart, so I had to act fast, especially since I would be leaving for Mississippi soon to help my mother after she had her hip replacement operation.

Word among the women of the church, many of whom made no secret of their dislike for me, was that high-and-mighty Lisa Mae Jones had also set her sights on the bishop. And she had good reason to think she would get him. Not only did she have the support of most of the women in the church, but rumor had it that she also had the blessing of First Lady Charlene Wilson herself. Unlike the negative letter I'd found taped to my door, asking me to stay away from the bishop, the buzz around the church was that Lisa Mae had received a letter asking her to take care of him and his church. Now, if that wasn't some stiff competition, I don't know what was. Maybe I needed to try the alcohol plan one more time.

"Are you sure you won't have some of this wine, Bishop?" I asked, taking a sip from my glass and hoping I didn't sound as desperate as I was feeling. "It's delicious."

"No, Sister Monique. I have to drive. The Lord wants me to make sure I get you home safely tonight."

"You are so considerate. You always have my best interests at heart, don't you?"

"That's exactly the reason why I haven't had a glass of wine." He smiled as if he knew about my naughty plan.

"Thank you, Bishop." I shifted in my seat to sit up a little straighter, and the movement had the desired effect. Just the slightest backward movement of my shoulders and my cleavage stood out even more. And just as subtly as I had moved to display my best features, his eyes traveled to my chest for a quick glance. Then, ever the gentleman, he looked up into my eyes and gave me a seemingly innocent compliment.

"I must say, Sister Monique, you're looking exceptionally beautiful tonight. I absolutely love that dress."

"Thank you, Bishop," I said with a gracious smile. I knew it wasn't really the dress he wanted to comment on, but rather the package contained beneath it. After all, this dress was the plainest one in my whole wardrobe. The only skin it revealed was my cleavage. But it was okay. The way he'd been looking around the restaurant, always pausing to rest his eyes on my chest for a brief moment, said everything he was too polite to put into words. Just like every other man I'd ever been to dinner with, he was thinking about how he'd love to get a look at my beautiful breasts.

At least that's what I thought was going through his head, until he kept talking about the dress!

"Sister Monique, I know it's not my place, but may I make a suggestion?"

"Sure, Bishop. I'm open to any suggestion you may have."

"Now, this is a little personal, so if the conversation goes into a direction you're uncomfortable with, just let me know, and we'll drop it."

A little personal? Now that was what I liked to hear. I was hoping he was about to ask me to take him home and show him what I was working with beneath this conservative outfit. Oh, how wrong I was.

"No, Bishop, you just go ahead and say whatever is on your mind."

"Well, Sister . . . like I said before . . . I absolutely love your dress. And well . . . I wanted to know how come . . . how come you don't wear dresses like this more often."

Well, that wasn't what I was expecting to hear. He was the first man who ever wanted me to wear more clothes. My shoulders slumped ever so slightly. "You don't like the way I dress, Bishop?"

"No, no, it's not that I don't like the way you dress. I do like the way you dress, but—"

"But what?" I asked, trying not to become defensive.

"I think it takes away from who you really are."

Well, that was almost sort of sweet, I thought. At least he didn't tell me I looked like a whore, which I'd heard from jealous women and spurned lovers on more than one occasion. I remained quiet and let him explain himself.

"To be quite honest, people around the church find your choice of clothing to be distracting."

No kidding. It was supposed to be distracting. How else was I supposed to get a man's attention? But he was making it sound like a bad thing. As far as I was concerned, if those people in the church judged me because of my outfits, well, that was their problem, not mine. I was curious to know, however, if the bishop felt the same way as the other church members. I had hoped he was different.

"And you, Bishop? Do you find my clothes to be distracting?"

He couldn't look me in the eye when he answered. "Sometimes."

My feelings were a little hurt. "Well, I'm sorry to hear that, Bishop." I placed my napkin on the table and started to rise from my seat, but he placed a hand on mine and asked me to stay. I sat down again and leaned back in my chair, crossing my arms over my chest in a defensive posture as I waited for him to try and remove his foot from his mouth.

He leaned across the table and whispered, "Monique, I like you, and I think I can like you as more than just another parishioner, if you know what I mean."

This took me by surprise. Just a moment ago he had really hurt my feelings, but these words offered me more hope of a relationship than anything else he'd said the whole night. I was encouraged, but not yet ready to let him off the hook for his previous comment. I uncrossed my arms, leaned over, and kissed his cheek, then waited silently to hear what else he had to say.

"I'm the pastor of the church, Monique, and if the way you dress is less than admirable in the eyes of the church members, then anything we might share would be doomed from the start." He exhaled as if he'd just let the weight of the world off his shoulders.

"You know, Bishop, it's not like I haven't heard any of this before. I don't know if you know it, but women in the church have been saying things about my outfits to my face and behind my back for years."

It looked like my words made him uncomfortable. Of course they did, I thought. Knowing the way the first lady felt about me, he had probably heard her talk about me on plenty of occasions. But he didn't have to worry. I wasn't going to hold him responsible for what she said. The only thing that mattered to me now was that he didn't judge me the same way.

"I never understood why those women have such a problem with what I choose to wear. I always felt like God knows what's in my heart, so it shouldn't matter what I'm wearing. I pay my tithes, and I'm an active member of the church. As long as God knows my devotion to Him and the church, my clothes shouldn't matter to anyone but me. I mean, you've preached about tolerance on many occasions. I hope you're not telling me that you don't take your own words to heart, Bishop," I challenged.

"Sister Monique, I meant every word I ever preached about tolerance," he said, sounding a little sad now. "I know you're a special woman, a good woman, no matter what you're wearing. But that doesn't change the fact that others in the church will judge you differently because of what you wear. And while I wish I could just ignore their opinions, they are my congregation. Whether their opinions are fair or not, there would be no First Jamaica Ministries without its parishioners. They're like my extended family. And you have to know how important it is to get the approval of a man's family."

"I see," I said. "So, you're saying that you're choosing the opinions of a few jealous women over dating me?"

"No, I'm saying that I like you, and I want them to like you too. But your clothing sends the wrong message to them, so they don't want to even take the time to get to know you."

"That's so hypocritical," I complained.

"Perhaps it is," he answered.

"So, let me get this straight. You're saying I should change the way I dress so that those people will like me more?" This whole thing was pissing me off. I wasn't changing how I dressed, not even for the bishop, but suddenly an idea came to me, the perfect way to implement my original plan for our evening. Once I had him in bed, none of this would matter.

"You know, maybe it's not my whole wardrobe that needs to

be changed. I might have a few dresses in my closet that the ladies of the church wouldn't mind. If you'd like to come back to my place, I could show—"

"Oh, dear God," he said, cutting me off. He leaned away from me quickly, a look of concern knotting his brow.

"What is it, Bishop?"

He cut his eyes toward the door, and I turned my head in that direction. Now I knew why he looked so concerned. Two prominent elders of the church, Trustee Forrest, chairman of the church's finance committee, and his wife, Evelyn, had just walked through the door. She was one of the biggest gossips in the church, and he was without a doubt the most conservative trustee.

I turned back to the bishop. "What are they doing here?"

"My sentiments exactly." He looked like he wanted to run and hide.

"Did they see me kiss you?" Part of me hoped they did. I wanted the world to know how I felt about the bishop even if he didn't want the world to know.

"I'm not sure," he said nervously.

As big as Evelyn's mouth was, this little date might be front page news on the church bulletin unless we did something fast. Not too long ago, I might have said I didn't care what that old biddy thought of me, but now the stakes were higher. If I could show the bishop that I understood what he meant by keeping rumors at a minimum and keeping peace in the church, he would see just how right I was for him.

"Well, what do you wanna do? If you'd like, I could go to the bathroom and then sneak out the back door."

Did I really just say that? I wondered. If I was going to change my behavior to please these church women, this was going to take some getting used to. But as much as it went against my nature to give in to them, I was willing to try it if it meant proving to the bishop that I could make a good first lady.

He spoke in a whisper. "Too late. They just spotted us, and they're coming this way." His forehead was starting to perspire.

Within a few seconds, they stood beside our table. The bishop stood and smiled broadly, shaking the trustee's hand, then kissing his wife on the cheek. It was unbelievable. The man had just changed from a nervous wreck to happy, damn near gleeful, in a matter of seconds, like some type of chameleon.

"Trustee, Sister Evelyn, you know Sister Monique." Bishop gestured toward me.

The trustee greeted me warmly as his wife glared down at my cleavage, shaking her head ever so slightly. Instead of feeling anger at her obvious judgment, I felt sorry for the bishop, who was already running on protection mode and about to kick it into high gear.

"Yeah, well, it's good to see you two. Sister Monique and I were just going over her Christian bookstore proposal," the bishop said as he picked up the folder marked BOOKSTORE I'd brought with me, showing it to the trustee and his wife. He had no idea what was inside the folder, since we hadn't opened it once that night.

"Is that right?" the trustee replied. He glanced at his wife, and Sister Evelyn smirked, staring at the rose on the table, which Bishop had bought from the man who walked through the restaurant selling flowers.

"So, you two are working on a bookstore proposal?" she asked, her doubt evident.

"Yeah . . . yeah, Sister Monique's got some great ideas. We're thinking about opening it up in that vacant building directly across the street from the church." Thank God we had actually discussed some of these ideas at our first meeting, so the bishop had something to say now without having to make up lies.

"Oh, really? Well, since Trustee Forrest is on the finance committee, maybe we should sit down and discuss it with you," Sister Evelyn said. I wondered if anyone else could hear the hidden meaning behind her suggestion, or if a woman's hearing were like a dog's. Maybe I was the only one in the room who detected the true tone of this jealous bitch.

"You know, we'd really love to," the bishop said. "But as you can see, we're finished with dinner, and I was just about to ask for the check."

"We understand," Trustee Forrest told us. Once again, he glanced at his wife. "You folks have a nice evening. I'll see you at the finance meeting tomorrow night, Bishop. I'm sure we'll have much to talk about."

What the hell did he mean by that? For the first time, I started to think that maybe my reputation was worse than I thought. I watched them walk away, but as soon as they were far enough,

Evelyn started chewing a hole in her husband's ear. I glanced at the bishop, who had flagged down our waiter to pay the bill. I'd never seen him with so much worry on his face. It was going to be a long ride home, and from the look on his face, he was not coming in to see me model my "conservative" outfits.

12

BISHOP

I dropped Monique off, then came straight home, despite her repeated requests for me to come inside so that we could talk. We'd barely spoken during the entire ride to her place. It was not for her lack of effort, though. I just wasn't in the mood after running into Trustee Forrest and his gossiping wife, Sister Evelyn. Now there was no telling what type of nonsense was going to be running around the church. It's too bad, because I was just starting to feel I was making headway with Monique about her attire. I didn't want to change who she was; I just wanted to tone down her clothes so that I could get the church to accept her for the beautiful woman she really was.

I really liked Monique, and she was a good Christian, regardless of what others might think. To be honest, she reminded me of Charlene when she was younger. I guess that's why I liked her. My wife, God rest her soul, was a real spitfire back in her day. Most of the people in our church didn't even know it, but before Charlene and I got married, she had quite the reputation with the fellas. She truly lived up to the term *P.K.* Some might've even called her a slut, but with the proper help and God's love, she turned into the perfect first lady. I'd been thinking that Monique had the same kind of potential, but after tonight, I was worried that the wagging tongues of the church would put a stop to any relationship between us before it even had a chance to develop.

Once I got settled in the house, I walked into the kitchen and poured myself a glass of milk. I put it in the microwave to heat it up for a few seconds, thinking it could help settle my stomach. What I really wanted to calm my nerves was a good, stiff glass of that cognac James and I had finished off last week. I guess it's a good thing I don't keep alcohol in the house. Besides, the Lord probably wouldn't appreciate my drinking at a time like this anyway.

I picked up my glass of milk and headed for the living room. Sitting in the recliner, I downed half the glass, then picked up the phone and dialed James's number. I knew he'd still be awake, because he had mentioned he had a date with one of the sisters from the church. It was Saturday night, after all, and I hadn't known too many times that James didn't have a date on a weekend.

"Hello?" James answered.

"James? This is T.K. We've got a bit of a situation."

"Bishop, you've got the worst timing. Hold on a minute." I could hear some woman in the background. Her voice was muffled, but whoever she was, she didn't sound too happy about James answering the phone. I waited for him to calm her down; then he returned to the phone. "Okay, what happened this time, Bishop?"

"Remember that Armageddon you predicted?"

"Yeah?"

"Well, it'll be here tomorrow. Trust me."

"Oh, Lord. T.K., what have you done now?"

"Remember when I asked Monique out to dinner the other night?"

"Yeah . . ."

"Well, we were busted by some parishioners," I admitted. I had already resigned myself to the fact that I'd have to listen to James gloat about how he had been right from the start about my asking her out. Lord, why did these people hate her so much?

"Busted by some parishioners? You promised me you weren't gonna take her anywhere in Queens, T.K. How could you be so stupid?"

"I wasn't, and I didn't take her anywhere in Queens. I took her all the way to Brooklyn to Umberto's. Who would've thought Trustee Forrest and Evelyn would show up at Umberto's at ten o'clock at night?"

"Evelyn Forrest was there? Oh, Lord. That woman's got the biggest mouth in the church."

Now he understood the severity of the situation. He didn't even waste his time with "I told you so."

"T.K., you have a serious problem. That woman's gonna tell everyone in the church that you're sleeping with Monique."

That's what I was afraid of, but I had tried to convince myself that it wouldn't be so bad. I wanted to believe that even a gossipmonger like Sister Evelyn could take her pastor's word for it when I told her that I was just meeting with Monique to discuss the bookstore. But realistically I knew better. No one, not even the bishop, is immune from gossip. By tomorrow, the whole church would be talking about the things I was supposedly doing with Monique. If I were going to get through this, I needed at least one person to believe that the date was innocent. I needed my friend to believe me.

"We're not sleeping with each other, James," I snapped more forcefully than I had intended. "It was just dinner. We're just friends."

"Hey, T.K., you don't have to worry about me. I'm your friend. I believe you."

Was that sarcasm I detected in his voice? I wasn't sure if he did believe me, until he said, "But I'm not gonna lie. I kinda wish you *were* hitting it. At least then you'd be getting something out of it. 'Cause I can guarantee you that with Monique's reputation, most of the congregation is going to believe Evelyn. And a scandal like this could ruin *your* reputation. Perhaps your career."

"Tell me about it. Tomorrow night's the finance committee's review of my personal budget and salary. That meeting affects my income for the entire year." This was the issue I had worried about during most of my ride home that night. I may be the bishop of the largest church in Queens, but I still had bills, including a $250,000 refinance loan I used to pay for Dante's law school and Donna's college tuition. That's why I had barely spoken a word to Monique as I worried about the possible repercussions of our innocent night out.

"Can't you do something?" I asked James. "You're the chairman of the board of trustees."

"I'm sorry, buddy. I got a vote, but there's nothing I can do to direct things your way because Trustee Forrest chairs the meeting."

I dropped my head into my hands and rubbed my throbbing temples. "So, what are we gon' do?"

"What are *we* gonna do?" James said. "You mean what're *you* gonna do? I warned you about this whole thing. I told you to stay away from Monique. Look, T.K, I'm sorry, but I'm staying as far away from this as possible. I've got enough of my own problems with Evelyn Forrest's mouth. I hope seeing Monique was worth it."

I was a little taken aback by his words, having fully expected my friend to help me monitor this situation and keep things under control among the church members. It was then that I realized no one had ever had my back the way my wife had. I missed her so much. But since she wasn't here, I needed James, so I would have to ask him again.

"Don't do this, James. You're my best friend, and I need your help. I know I should've listened to you when you warned me about Monique, but you know I can be stubborn sometimes. C'mon, man, I need you to cover my rear. How many times have I covered yours?"

He hesitated momentarily, then said, "Okay, man. I'll help you, but if you're gonna get through this, you're gonna have to do everything I say."

I didn't necessarily like feeling I wasn't the one in control, but now was not the time to argue that point. "Just tell me what you want me to do."

He came up with his first plan of action remarkably quick. "Okay, first off, I want you to call up Lisa Mae Johnson and ask her out to lunch tomorrow."

"Are you kidding? This is how I'm gonna solve my problem—by asking another woman out?"

"Hey, look, you don't have to take my advice," he said with a touch of arrogance. "But you did ask for it. I was in the middle of something that I would like to get back to."

"Okay, James," I said resignedly.

"Now, if you wanna get out of this, you're gonna do exactly as I say. Understand?"

"Yeah, I understand."

"All right, then. Now, you're gonna pick up the phone, call Lisa Mae, apologize for how late it is, and then ask her to lunch tomorrow."

"Call Lisa Mae? That's the extent of your plan?"

"No." He sounded irritated. "That's the first part of my plan.

The second part of my plan is . . ." I could almost hear him thinking, which scared me. It was clear that he was making up this entire thing as he went along. "I want you to take her to the Olive Garden over by Starrett City. Do you know where that is?"

"Of course I know where it is. It's right next to Red Lobster, your favorite restaurant."

"Okay, good. Now, this is important, T.K. I want you to arrive at exactly 12:05, and when you walk into the place, I want you to take Lisa Mae's hand."

"Huh? Take her hand? James, this doesn't make any sense."

"It will when you get there. Now, call that woman, Bishop, and get her some flowers too. Your ol' buddy James has got everything else under control."

"I sure hope so."

I hung up, not really feeling any better than I had before I made the call. I still had no idea what James was up to. But he seemed awfully confident in whatever he had planned, so I guess I had to have some faith. One thing I had to admit about James was, despite his shortcoming with the ladies, he'd never let me down. Actually, it was his active dating life that had made him a master of rescue plans such as this one. Maybe he was making it up off the top of his head, but that didn't mean he didn't have a good plan. I quickly dialed Lisa Mae's number.

13

LISA

My girl Loretta was helping me get ready for my lunch date with the bishop. I'd already been to the hairdresser and the nail salon first thing that morning. I looked and felt gorgeous. I was still a little surprised that he had invited me out so soon after our conversation, when he told me that he needed more time before he was ready to start dating. But the fact that it happened sooner than I expected didn't make me any less eager to go out with him. That's why I spent so much time getting ready for lunch.

Even the rumor I'd heard that morning from Evelyn Forrest couldn't ruin my good mood. She had called me up, yapping about how the bishop had slept with that church floozy, Monique Johnson, the night before. Evelyn's gossip usually had some truth to it, but I knew this rumor wasn't true because I'd spoken to the bishop last night when he asked me out, so he couldn't have been with Monique Johnson. I would have to send Loretta and some of the women of the church to put a stop to that rumor.

When the doorbell rang, Loretta jumped straight up in the air, excited for me. I, on the other hand, tried my best to keep my composure, though I felt like I had an entire butterfly farm in my stomach. Loretta gave me a hug, then kissed me for good luck before she left to answer the front door. I waited in the bedroom, not wanting to appear overzealous. A few minutes later, I heard her call my name. I checked myself out in the mirror one last time, then made a very poised entrance into the living room.

When I entered, the bishop stood up. He was carrying a dozen roses.

"Are those for me?" I asked.

The bishop handed me the flowers. I in turn handed them to

Loretta, grinning from ear to ear. "Could you put these in some water for me, please?"

"I sure will," Loretta said as she disappeared into the kitchen.

"You look really nice, Sister Lisa. I love that dress," he complimented.

"Why, thank you, Bishop. This little ol' thing? I've had this for years," I lied. I'd bought the dress last week, and it had cost me a pretty penny. Even so, I'm sure the price tag couldn't compare to the Italian suit he wore. It had to have cost him at least a thousand dollars, and he was wearing the heck out of it. "You look rather handsome yourself."

"Now I have to thank you. Are you ready to go?"

"I sure am. Just let me tell Loretta that we're leaving." I walked back to my kitchen and said good-bye to my friend.

"You look happy, First Lady," Loretta said.

"I am happy, Loretta. For the first time since Lee died, I'm with a man I could spend the rest of my life with." She kissed me for luck one more time, and the bishop and I were off to the Olive Garden for lunch.

The ride from my home in Rosedale to the Olive Garden at Starrett City took about fifteen minutes, and the bishop and I chatted the entire way.

"So, I see you and Loretta spend a lot of time together, huh?" he asked.

"Yes, we've been friends for over twenty years. She moved in with me when I left First Hempstead Ministries, after Pastor Whitehead finally filled Lee's position. I guess you can kind of call us the female versions of Batman and Robin. She's like the sister I never had."

"Well, it's definitely good to have somebody you can trust. I feel the same way about Trustee Black."

"No, I doubt if our relationship is anything like yours and Trustee Black's."

He turned his head to look at me. "What do you mean by that?"

I really couldn't stand James Black, and I wasn't the only one in the church who felt that way. I knew Charlene had never really approved of James, either, but she hadn't pushed the issue with her husband. When I became first lady, I would have to end that friendship for good. For now, though, I tried to state my opinion subtly.

"From what I can tell of Trustee Black, it just seems you two are like night and day. Actually, you seem to have very little in common."

"Yeah, we are different in a lot of ways, but he's a good man and a good friend." The bishop didn't sound defensive, but for all I knew he was sugarcoating his true feelings just like I was.

"Well, yes, I've heard *quite a few* of the sisters say he's a good man." As soon as I said it, I realized I should have just kept my mouth shut. I knew better than to put a man's friend on blast, but I had done just that.

"Well, Sister Lisa Mae, I'm not quite sure what you're trying to say. Why don't you elaborate?" Now I was sure there was a defensive tone to his voice. I worried I might not be able to save myself now.

"Let's just say maybe we should find your friend a steady girlfriend and perhaps a wife before he's been with every single woman in the congregation."

Damn, Lisa Mae, I told myself, *you really need to learn some more self-control when it comes to your mouth.* I hoped I hadn't ruined the date before it even started.

"Every woman in the congregation? Really, I think that's quite an exaggeration." Yes, there was that tone again, and it seemed to be bordering on anger now. I was glad that we arrived at the restaurant so we could get off this touchy subject.

In spite of the tense discussion we'd just had, the bishop asked me to remain in the car as he trotted around and opened my door. I'd seen him do this a hundred times for his former wife, Charlene, and I'd always been a tad jealous. The man really knew how to treat a woman. A lesser man would have still been pouting about my comments concerning his friend.

I was just as impressed when he took my hand as we entered the restaurant. That simple gesture was kind, and to our surprise, it was also sort of the official "coming out" for us as a dating couple. The waiting area was filled with more than fifteen prominent members of our church. Ironically enough, the group included the subject of our previous discussion, the bishop's best friend, Trustee James Black.

"Bishop? I didn't think you were going to join us for the scholarship meeting," Trustee Black said.

"Well, to be completely honest, Trustee, I thought the meeting was being held at the church. When did this all happen?"

"You know, last night I was talking to Sister Maria here . . . on the phone . . . about having some Italian food. When I woke up, I decided it would be a nice treat if I took the committee out to lunch. So, here we are."

"That's wonderful, Trustee. Don't you think so, Sister Lisa?"

I nodded my head, but Trustee Black didn't give me a chance to speak. Typical. He continued, "You know, I would ask you two to join us, but you look like you want to be alone." He looked at our intertwined fingers, then placed a hand on the bishop's shoulder. "I don't know when this happened, but I'm really happy for you."

As the bishop turned to the hostess to ask for a table for two, Trustee Black gave me a hug. This took me by surprise, as we had obviously never been close friends, but I didn't mind. There was no better way to smooth over the friction I'd caused with my earlier comments to the bishop. I hugged him long enough for the bishop to turn around and see us. He smiled at me.

Trustee Black's hug started a deluge of hellos, handshakes, and congratulations from the remaining seven men and eight women who comprised the scholarship committee of our church. One of the women present was Sister Evelyn Forrest. Let her run back and spread this news to the congregation, I thought. Trustee James Black may have been a ladies' man, but I decided right then and there that I liked him. He may not have realized it, but he'd accidentally established me as the bishop's girlfriend, and the heir apparent to the first lady's chair. God, I couldn't wait to get home and tell Loretta.

I walked into the house and dropped to my knees. "Thank you, Lord. Thank you!" I shouted with excitement at the top of my lungs. Hopefully I had allowed the bishop, after he walked me to the door, to get far out of earshot. "Thank you for answering my prayers!" I yelled again.

"Lisa Mae!" Loretta said as she came charging out of the kitchen. "What in the world is wrong with you? You trying to wake the dead?"

"No, girl, I'm trying to praise the Lord!" I ran over to Loretta, grabbed her hands, and began jumping up and down as we spun in a circle. My eyes shone with tears of joy, and my smile felt as wide as the ocean. My emotions must have been contagious because the next thing I knew, Loretta was jumping up and down and smiling too.

"What is it, Lisa Mae?" Loretta asked. "Come with all the details. I want to know why I'm standing here jumping up and down like a damn fool."

I looked at her and opened my mouth to tell her the reason behind my excitement, but all I could do was scream again, and this time Loretta screamed right along with me.

After a few more seconds of acting like Laverne and Shirley, I was finally able to speak. "Now, you know I never did care all that much for that whore of a man, Trustee Black," I started as I released Loretta's hands and led her over to the couch where we sat down. "But I swear I could just kiss that man."

"With all the places that man's lips have been, this must be good. Keep talking," Loretta insisted.

"Well, thanks to Trustee Black, you are now looking at Bishop T.K. Wilson's girlfriend, which means eventually I'm going to be the next first lady."

This time Loretta screamed. "Ahhhhh!" She jumped up from the couch. "Okay, how did it happen? When did you see Trustee Black? Don't tell me he done talked the good bishop into double dating with him and one of his hussies." Loretta quickly sat down and started speaking again before I could answer any of her questions. "Who was it? I bet it was that Sister Maria, huh? I could tell by the way she dropped her offering in the basket he was holding last Sunday, you know, like she was slipping him her hotel room key or some—"

"Will you let me talk already?" I finally cut her off. "This is supposed to be my moment."

"Oh, I'm so sorry, sweetie," Loretta apologized. "I'm all ears."

I proceeded to run down the details of our date, how we'd showed up at the restaurant hand in hand, none the wiser that Trustee Black and the other members of the scholarship committee were dining there. Loretta couldn't have been happier for me, but no more happy than I was for myself.

Still, even though I was overwhelmed with joy, I became overwhelmed with worry. I wasn't exactly a shoo-in for first lady just yet. The congregation of First Jamaica Ministries was as hard to please as an audience at the Apollo, and although the women from the Bible study class had shown their approval when they heard I'd received a letter from Charlene, nothing was guaranteed. Those wenches could turn against me at the drop of a dime if they felt for one moment that I couldn't handle the responsibilities of being the wife of Bishop T.K. Wilson.

I knew that I could handle it, though, especially since I'd had experience as first lady of my late husband's church. There was not a situation I couldn't handle; I just had to prove that to the congregation, who would be watching like hawks. Then an idea came to me. With the monthly membership meeting coming up in two weeks, I couldn't think of a better time to start "interviewing" before the congregation. I turned to Loretta to get her help in formulating a plan.

14

MARLENE

The sun beamed directly on my face through the hole in the curtains over my bedroom window, finally waking me from my comatose sleep. I rubbed the sleep out of my eyes, then scratched my arm out of old habit and a need to get high. I didn't have a clue what time it was, but I was sure it wasn't morning, because of the hustle and bustle of the afternoon traffic under my apartment. I'd only been living here ten years off and on, but I guess I could call myself a true New Yorker, being able to distinguish morning traffic from afternoon.

As I lifted myself from the mattress, I grabbed my head, my fingers fighting their way through the weeks of unkempt naps. Wearing nothing but a cranberry-colored bra and some coffee-brown panties, I slowly attempted to get my tired body all the way out of bed. I turned to the edge, and before I could get either foot on the ground, my thirteen-year-old son, Aubrey, came through my bedroom door.

"Ma, you aw'ight?" he asked. It sounded more like a statement of surprise, like he wasn't sure if I had been asleep or dead.

"Yeah, baby," I said, putting my feet on the old hardwood floor and opening my arms wide. I saw a sense of relief in him, but at the same time, lurking behind Aubrey's eyes I could have sworn I saw disappointment and a little fear. Not regular old fear. It was a different kind, but an all-too-familiar look, the same one his sister used to have while growing up. The look was one I had promised myself my children would never have to wear again, yet here we were, and the fear was in his eyes.

Aubrey came over and gave me a hug, then planted a kiss on my cheek. "Ma," he whispered, then took a step back to make sure I acknowledged him. It took me a few seconds to look in his face, but when I did, he said, "You been smoking again, haven't you?"

I rolled my tongue around my dry mouth, then bit it as I stared at my son with contempt. "You better take your ass on, boy," I snapped, trying my best not to get mad. I wanted to smack him for asking me some shit like that, even if part of me knew he was just asking out of love.

"I will, soon as you answer my question." He folded his arms, looking like a little man, staring at me like he was the parent, same as his sister used to do. Damn, I hated to be in this position. I was suddenly amazed and proud of how much Aubrey had grown up, but at the same time I was wishing he would just go the hell away so I could go get high without his judgment.

Aubrey really loved me despite my shortcomings. I don't know why, with all the wrong I'd done to him over the years. Even when I nursed the crack pipe more than I nursed him, he still loved me. After I rented out our own apartment to dealers to use as a crack spot, he still loved me. I would even put my smoking buddies before him, allowing them to loiter, sleep over, and even eat the last crumb of food. By the time Aubrey would wake up for school, there was nothing in our cupboards, but he still loved me. And even after Child Protective Services took him away from me the time I was arrested, yes, he still loved me. When I didn't love me, my son did. And now here I was looking like the crackhead momma he hadn't seen during my three-year sobriety. I guess he did deserve an answer to his question.

I looked up at my son and half-smiled as I gestured for him to come closer. I held his chin in my hands so he could look directly in my eyes. "No, baby, momma's not smoking again," I assured him, stroking the side of his face. I could see the tension release from his shoulders. He had been carrying a heavy weight for someone still so young, and even if it was a lie, I was glad my words took some of that weight off him. As bad as I looked, I wasn't even sure if he believed me, but I knew my baby *wanted* to believe me, so he didn't push the issue any further.

"I made you pancakes for breakfast, but they're old now. You want some lunch?"

"Lunch? What time is it?" Although I had already guessed it was afternoon, I still wanted to know just how late it was.

"Two o'clock in the afternoon," Aubrey answered. "Do you want some lunch? You know I can make a mean PBJ."

I ran my hands over my matted hair again, slightly confused as to how so much time had come and gone without my even knowing it. I couldn't even remember when I laid down or why I laid down.

"Do you want some lunch?" he repeated.

"No, baby, I'm fine," I said, standing up slowly, once again being reminded that I had a splitting headache. "You go on and watch television while I get myself together."

I watched Aubrey head out of the doorway, pausing to look over his shoulder at me. There was that look again in his eyes. I smiled and he moved on. As I headed to the bathroom, I spotted my red polyester dress with the lace trim around the bottom, puddled on the floor. I couldn't even remember putting it on, much less taking it off.

I bent down to pick up the dress, and that's when I saw the letter. Lying next to the lamp on my nightstand was the second letter I'd received from Charlene Wilson. At that moment, everything came back to me like a yo-yo hitting me smack on the forehead. I slowly sat on the bed and looked over at the letter. I picked it up and reread those words:

Dear Marlene,

If you're reading this letter, then you've probably backslid into drugs again. I can't begin to explain how disappointed I am in you. Believe it or not, I actually thought you were going to be the front-runner in the race for T.K.'s heart. But then again, maybe you weren't the woman I thought you were. You still could prove me wrong, but time's running out. It's time to kick the habit, Marlene, because if you don't, someone else will be with T.K. and living the life that could be yours.

I'll be in touch.
Charlene

When I finished reading, I thought, *Who the fuck is she to say she's disappointed in me? Besides, bitch, you were the one who lived my life and fucked my man for over twenty years. Well, fuck you.* The letter said she'd be in touch, but what the hell could a dead woman say to make me change anyway? 'Cause I sure as hell didn't believe in ghosts.

I let the letter fall out of my hands onto the floor. I looked down and saw that my palms were sweating like a one-legged man trying to run a marathon in ninety-degree weather with a fur coat on. "Goddammit!" I cursed myself. "Why did I have to go and read that letter again?"

Now I felt the same way I had after reading it the first time—like I wanted to get high. It was all coming back to me now, everything. Now I knew exactly how I ended up passed out on my bed, letting an entire day get away from me.

I was so messed up after I got the letter that I decided to get my shit together and go to a meeting. But on my way there, I ran into this guy named Flapjack. Now, I liked Flapjack a lot; not only was he a trick, but he was the best kinda trick—the kind that liked to smoke. Fortunately for me, I caught him at the right time because he'd just cashed his SSI check at the liquor store. Two minutes after our initial conversation, we were on our way to the dope boys. Ten minutes after that, I'd sent Aubrey to his friend's house to spend the night, and Flapjack and I were alternating between fucking and smoking up his $800 Social Security check. Somewhere along the line, I passed out and didn't wake up until a few minutes ago. I couldn't remember when Flapjack left or when Aubrey came home.

"Ma." Aubrey snapped me out of my thoughts with his fatherly tone. When had my baby's voice started to sound so deep?

"Yeah, Aubrey?"

"You got company in the living room."

"Company?" Instantly, fear jolted my body. It could be anyone sitting in my front room, but whoever it was, chances were, it wasn't anyone I wanted to speak to. I scrambled to get my clothes on, trying to determine who it might be. Was it Flapjack back for some more? No, he'd spent all his money for the month. Was it the landlord looking for the rent? Nah, Aubrey wouldn't have let him in the house. Perhaps it was CPS? Jesus Lord, the lady across the hall did threaten to call them. If she did, I was gonna kill that bitch.

"Who is it, Aubrey?" I was starting to sweat.

He was hesitant.

"Just tell me," I demanded.

"It's the bishop."

"The bishop?"

What was he doing here? In all the years I'd been living here with Aubrey, he'd never just stopped by unannounced. And of all times for him to do it, why did it have to be now, when I was back on the pipe? Then it hit me. Tanisha! She probably had called him after I stood him up last week and convinced him to try again. That fucking little bitch. Why couldn't she ever mind her own business? Thomas Kelly and I were not meant to be together, and she needed to just accept that shit.

I looked over at Aubrey, who was still standing in the doorway. "Tell him I'm 'sleep, Aubrey."

"I can't. I already told him that you were awake." Aubrey was sounding a little too pleased with my discomfort, and he was about to make me pop him in the mouth.

I had no choice but to face the bishop now. "Aw'ight, tell him I'll be right there."

Once my dress was on, I walked over and stared into the mirror attached to my dresser. What looked back at me was more frightening than I could have ever imagined. I still had the weave Niecy put in my hair, but now it was all over my head like a bird's nest. My skin tone had become a couple of shades darker, and my skin was sagging so much, I looked like I'd lost about ten, fifteen pounds. I turned to the side and saw that my signature ass, which had attracted men from a distance, was a fraction of what it had been. There was no doubt in my mind that I'd officially fallen off.

Somehow, I had to keep it from Thomas Kelly. If he knew, he'd tell Tanisha and Dante, and they'd be up here from D.C. in a New York minute to lock me away in some drug program and take Aubrey away. I wasn't having that. Aubrey was my son, not theirs. He was all I had left.

I turned back toward the mirror and reached for my makeup and a hairbrush. Five minutes later, I'd done what I could do. I didn't look my best, but I looked better than I had. Maybe it would be enough to fool him.

I walked into the living room. Thomas Kelly was standing next to Aubrey, talking on his cell phone. He was probably talking to Tanisha and Dante, I thought, not that it mattered to me.

At least I didn't think it mattered until I saw what was on the floor next to Aubrey. By his feet was a suitcase and a small bin that held his Xbox and the games that go with it. That little piece of shit looked like he was moving out on me.

Shit, I shoulda pawned that Xbox when I had the chance, I thought, grabbing the arm of the couch to support my body since my knees had become suddenly weak.

"Aubrey, what the hell is going on here?"

15

BISHOP

I'd just dropped Sister Lisa off at her house after our date at the Olive Garden when I got a panicked call from Marlene's son, Aubrey, on my cell phone. He apologized for calling but said he didn't know who else to call. It appeared his mother had been in bed for almost two days, and he couldn't wake her. He also said he was sure she was using drugs again. I told him I'd be right there.

By the time I got to the apartment, he explained that Marlene was still in bed, but now she was awake. He proved his allegations about her drug use by handing me her stem. I sighed deeply, shaking my head. Even with evidence in my hand, it was hard for me to believe.

How the heck could she have gone back to this stuff? I asked myself. *She was doing so well.*

When I got over the initial shock of Marlene being back on drugs, I told Aubrey to pack his bags because I was sending him down to D.C. to live with his sister. That young man must have really been through a lot because he hurried off to his room to pack a bag without an argument. Not long after, he returned with his bag and a message that his mother was getting dressed and would be right out.

As I stood next to Aubrey, waiting for Marlene to get dressed, my mind wandered to my own problems and the events of the past twenty-four hours. James's plan to stop the rumors about Monique and me had worked like a charm. It didn't take the members of the scholarship committee long to spread the word that I had been spotted holding Sister Lisa Mae Jones's hand. I'd gotten two calls about that on my way over to Marlene's. Now my only dilemma was that every member of the church would believe that Lisa Mae Jones was my new girlfriend. I should have realized from the start that taking her out in public would become much more complicated than a simple diversion tactic, but I was desperate to prevent the rumors about me and Monique, so I'd accepted James's plan without truly considering it. Now, unless I wanted even more chaos from the members of my church, I had to at least try to make it work with Lisa for the time being. From the way she kept smiling and reaching after we'd left the restaurant, I was sure Lisa was happy about the turn of events.

Once again, it appeared my wife had gotten her way, even after her death. I just didn't understand why, with all the women in the church, she wanted me to be with Lisa. Not that I had a problem with Lisa. She was very attractive, social in groups, and she seemed to be very organized. However, all she wanted to talk about was how she could improve the church and help my career. Not once did we ever talk about us as a man and a woman dating. When we'd left the Olive Garden, I asked her if she wanted to take a ride to Long Beach. By then, I realized I would have to at least attempt a relationship with this woman, and I actually thought a walk on the beach would be romantic. But would you believe she said no, that she much preferred to go back to the church so we could go over my schedule for the rest of the month? I wanted to tell her that I had a secretary for that and this was a date, not a job interview, but I didn't have the heart to do that.

I liked my women a little more spontaneous than Lisa Mae appeared to be, and my deceased wife knew it. Most people weren't aware of it, but my wife had kept things very interesting in our marriage when she was alive. One time when we were in the Bahamas, she . . . well, that's another story. But the point was, I didn't see that in Lisa. Granted, maybe I didn't know her well enough yet, but I guess that was why I was so interested in Monique. She was easy to get to know and was very spontaneous.

Monique—I didn't even want to think about how she was going to feel once she found out about Lisa and me. I'd had such a good time with her the night before, until Trustee Forrest and Evelyn walked into the restaurant and spoiled it. If they hadn't showed up, things would be so different now. I would have gone over to her house that night, helped her pick out the right kind of dresses to be around these church folks. That was all but a dream now, although I did owe her an explanation.

As I waited for Marlene to get dressed, I unclipped my cell phone from my belt and dialed Monique's number.

"Hello." I liked the sound of her voice. It reminded me of Marlene's when we were kids, sweet and energized.

"Hello, Sister Monique. It's Bishop Wilson."

"Hey, Bishop." Her voice was now high-pitched and excited. "I was hoping you would call before I left town."

I raised an eyebrow. "Leave town? Are you going somewhere?"

"Yes," she sighed. "I'm going to Mississippi to look after my mother for a few weeks. She's having a hip replacement in a couple of days, and I'm going down to help. I thought I told you that last night."

"No, you didn't. I think I would remember something like that." I was worried that she had already heard something about Lisa Mae and me but I quickly dismissed that thought. If she had heard, she wouldn't sound so happy to get my call. "Are you sure you're going out of town because of your sister and nothing else?"

"Well, to be honest, with me gone, that rumor about us will die down faster and give you some peace." Now she sounded a little sad, but her words were so unselfish. "I'm not trying to get you in trouble, Bishop."

"Trust me, Sister Monique, I know you're not trying to hurt me or get me in trouble. And about that rumor . . . I wanted to talk to you about something that happened today. Something important." I hesitated, and before I could open my mouth again, she'd cut me off.

"My flight doesn't leave until seven tomorrow morning. Why don't you come over here so we can talk? Maybe you could take a look at those dresses we discussed last night before I leave. What do you say?" I thought I detected a bit of something suggestive in her voice, and it made me hesitate for a moment. Perhaps I should be making plans to meet her in a public place so there would be no risk of improper behavior.

Before I could answer, Marlene walked into the room, so I rushed off the phone, making a quick decision about our meeting place. "Look, I have to go, Sister Monique, but I'll try to stop by before you leave." If I made it a brief meeting, there was no danger of anything happening. I had already made up my mind about giving this thing with Lisa Mae a shot, so I was not going to bend to any desires that Monique might stir up in me. Besides, once Monique heard what I had to tell her, she might be rushing me out of her house anyway. "I can't stay long, but I really have something important to talk to you about."

"I'll be waiting." Her voice sounded like she was singing.

"Aubrey, what the hell is going on here?" Marlene demanded.

I hung up my phone, then clipped it to my belt buckle as I stared at Marlene. The way she was wearing her makeup was almost scary, and I could see the track marks from her weave. The woman looked absolutely horrible, and there was no doubt in my mind that she was back on drugs.

"I asked you a question, Aubrey. You planning on going somewhere?" Her voice grew louder with every word.

Before Aubrey could answer, I stepped in front of him, answering his mother's question. "He's going with me, Marlene. I'm taking him down to D.C. so he can be with his sister and Dante. The boy shouldn't have to live this way. He never asked for this."

"You're not taking my son any-fucking-where, Thomas Kelly."

"Momma, I'm going," Aubrey said sternly.

You could almost see the willpower draining from her when she heard his words. She shook her head, then flew into an angry tirade. "You're not going anywhere, boy." She stepped toward him with her arm raised high, and I took a step closer, making myself a barrier between them. If I hadn't been there, I'm sure she would have hit him. And from the look in his eyes, he might have hit her back.

"Marlene, he's going with me." The bass in my voice told her I was not fooling around. She froze for a second, then stepped toward the coffee table to pick up the phone. She confused me momentarily because I thought she was going to hit me with it.

"You're not taking him anywhere, and I want you out of my house right now. If he steps one foot out of this house with you, that's kidnapping. And I'll have your holy ass hauled off to jail." She started to push some buttons on the phone.

It was time to be tough with her. No amount of gentle coaxing was going to bring this woman back from the depths to which she had sunk.

"Go ahead, Marlene, call them. As a matter of fact, ask for Captain Jacobs, watch commander for the 113th precinct. He's a close personal friend. I'm sure he'll be interested in what I found here." I reached into my breast pocket and pulled out the stem that Aubrey had given to me when I first entered the apartment. "Go ahead, Marlene. Push the rest of the buttons and make your call."

She stared at me with contempt. "That's not mine. That could be anybody's."

I lowered my head, wishing she'd just admit to her problem so we could get her the help she needed. "Oh, really? Well, I'm pretty sure your probation officer will think it's yours. Last I checked, stems were considered paraphernalia, and he can violate you for paraphernalia, can't he? And we don't even want to talk about a urine test, do we, Marlene?" She put down the phone, but her eyes were still burning mad.

"You need help, Marlene," I told her. "Why don't you come to my house so I can help you? God has a plan. You can get clean."

"I don't need any help, and I especially don't need your type of help, Thomas Kelly, you two-faced bastard." She took a step toward me like she was about to do something, then stopped, looking defeated. "You're not taking my son. He loves me. Don't you, Aubrey?" She turned toward Aubrey, searching his face for some type of alliance, but he stood his ground.

"Yeah, I love you, Ma, but I can't sit here and watch you do this to yourself. I'm going to live with Tanisha and Dante." I was proud of him, but I felt his pain too. I know it must have been difficult to stand up to his mother like that.

"Baby, they can't do anything for you that I can't do." Her eyes were beginning to water as she approached him cautiously. "Don't you want us to be together?"

"Momma, only thing I want is for you to stop taking drugs."

"I told you I'm not taking drugs!" All signs of motherly tenderness were gone in an instant. Marlene flew off the handle and slapped Aubrey in the face. I could tell she wanted to take it back right away, but the damage had been done. I had to grab Aubrey to stop him from retaliating.

He looked up at me with tears in his eyes. "Bishop, can we go now?"

I nodded my head. "Sure, son. Why don't you take your bag downstairs? I'll carry the box. My car is open." He picked up the suitcase and headed for the door.

"Aubrey, please. Please, baby, don't go. Momma needs you. Please, Aubrey!" Marlene cried desperately, but her pleas fell on deaf ears. He walked out the door without a backward glance.

Marlene turned her attention to me. "This is all your fault, Thomas Kelly. This is all your fault."

She took a misguided swing at me, and I grabbed her shoulders, shaking her a few times as I shouted, "No, Marlene! This is your fault."

She crumbled in my arms. "He's all I've got, Thomas Kelly. He's all I got."

"No, Marlene. You've got me and everyone else. You've just got to get yourself together."

"But I don't have a problem."

It was like déjà vu. We'd had this same conversation about her addiction more than twenty-five years ago when I left her to come to New York. "Yes, you do have a problem, Marlene. And you know it, but nobody can help you until you're ready for us to help you." I guided her over to the sofa and picked up the box that Aubrey had filled with his video games. "When you're ready to get yourself together, I'll be here. Until then, I pray you keep yourself out of harm's way."

16

MONIQUE

It was around 10:30 P.M. when the bishop called me from the New Jersey Turnpike. When we'd spoken earlier, he said he wanted to stop by and talk to me, but I had just about given up on him by the time his call came in. He was a little more than an hour away from Queens, he explained, after dropping off someone's child in Washington, D.C. I didn't bother asking whose child it was, because he was always doing things like that, helping out friends and members of the church. Besides, I was more interested in the fact that he asked if it was too late to stop by and talk. With a smile so big, I was sure he could see it through the phone, I told him it was never too late.

He didn't go into any detail other than to repeat that he wanted to speak to me before I left for my sister's place in Mississippi, but I could tell from his voice that he was stressed and probably a little tired from the drive. No problem. I knew exactly how to fix that.

I hung up the phone and went down to the kitchen, taking out the pork chops I'd purchased earlier in the day just for this occasion. Him coming by much later than expected was actually a good thing. Despite everything that had happened the night before with Trustee Forrest and his wife, I had reason to believe he wasn't really coming over to talk. I hoped he was coming over to make love to me. Why else would he insist on coming over to my place so late? If he wanted to tell me he had to stop seeing me because of the church rumors, he could have done that over the phone. Calls at this time of night were usually only meant for one thing, a booty call, and I would be more than happy to oblige. Preacher or not, I knew he would come around sooner or later. I hadn't met a man yet who could resist me. We would just have to be a little more discreet.

Once I finished cooking the pork chops and fried some apples, I had about a half hour until the bishop's arrival. I went upstairs, took a shower, combed my hair, and made my face, then I slipped into my favorite black teddy and matching satin robe. When he showed up at my door, I planned on giving him something to look at—well, actually, I planned on giving him a lot more than something to look at, but that would come after my pork chops. No man should be forced to make love on an empty stomach.

When my doorbell rang, my heart was beating so fast, I thought it was going to come out of my chest. Something told me tonight was the night that I was finally going to make love to Bishop T.K. Wilson. I couldn't believe how excited I was, like a teenage girl about to lose her virginity with a cherished boyfriend. I couldn't wait to have him in my arms.

I opened the door, and the bishop glanced at my black teddy, swallowing hard. He was so mesmerized by my outfit that he did a double take, tripping over the threshold as he walked through the door. He was having such a hard time trying not to look at my satin-covered breasts that it took him a few seconds to gather his composure.

"Sor . . . sorry to be . . . stopping by so late, Sister Monique," he managed to say while he kept sneaking glances at my scantily clad body. "But I really needed to talk to you."

How cute. He was still trying to pretend that he was only here to talk. These churchpeople sure had him paranoid. "No problem, Bishop. You can stop by anytime you like. Why don't you have a seat in the living room?" I led the way, of course, to let him enjoy the view. He followed me into the living room.

"Have a seat. Can I get you a cold beer, Bishop?"

He shook his head as he sat down. "No. I'm not going to be here long. I know you have to catch a flight in the morning, and I just wanted to talk to you before you left."

"And I wanna talk to you, too, Bishop, but it's going to have to wait because I have a surprise for you."

He raised an eyebrow. "A surprise?"

I stood in front of him, just out of reach, and his eyes roamed over my body, stopping at my bare thighs. For the first time that

I could remember, he didn't even attempt to hide his gaze. The sexy way he looked me up and down made my nipples hard and my insides moist. I could tell he wanted me as much as I wanted him.

"Yes, a surprise." I teased him by closing the robe over my teddy to conceal my cleavage. "Have you eaten?"

"No, I was going to pick up something on the way home."

"Well, I knew you were going to be hungry when you got here, so I made you some dinner."

"That's very kind of you, Sister Monique, but I really think we should talk first." His eyes stayed on my face now. He was trying to get serious on me, and for a minute it cramped my style, but then I regained my confidence. He might try to pretend he didn't want me, but I wasn't having it. This was my last night in New York for a while, and things were going to go the way I had planned.

"We're going to talk, Bishop, but not until after you've eaten my pork chops and fried apples."

"Pork chops and fried apples?" His eyes lit up almost more than they had at the sight of my flesh. It was as if I'd just introduced him to Jesus Christ. There was something about that man and pork chops that was almost scary. "I thought I smelled something good when I walked in your house." Long gone was the serious face, replaced by a big grin.

"No, Bishop. That would be me that smells good." I chuckled.

"You always smell good, Sister Monique," he said coyly. "But I was talking about something edible."

So was I, I thought. *Something you could eat all night long.*

I stopped my little fantasy because I was getting off track. "So, are you hungry or am I going to have to throw those pork chops out?"

"Noooo, don't do that, Sister," he protested. "We don't want those pork chops to go to waste."

"Good. Then follow me."

He stood up and I turned slowly, walking toward the dining room, knowing his eyes were like laser beams on my swaying hips. I flicked on the light, revealing a platter of pork chops, fried apples, and a small ice bucket with three Heinekens in it. The table was set for one.

"Aren't you going to eat, Sister?"

"No, Bishop. I made this all for you. Now, make sure you drink that beer with your pork chops. Fried apples, pork chops, and ice-cold beer is a Mississippi delicacy." I pulled out his chair. "Now, you sit down and eat while I go get the second part to my surprise."

"A second part?" I couldn't tell from his expression if he was nervous or eager, but I chose to believe he was looking forward to more surprises from me.

"Trust me, Bishop. Just like the pork chops, you're going to love the second part of my surprise." I took the serving fork and placed two pork chops and some apples on his plate; then I popped opened one of the beers, pouring it into a glass. "Enjoy. I'll be back in a minute."

"How could I not?" He picked up his fork and knife and started to eat. I just hoped that when we made love, he would be just as enthusiastic, because he looked like he was in seventh heaven when he ate my pork chops.

About fifteen minutes later, I walked into the dining room and stood behind the bishop's chair, then began to massage his shoulders. His muscles were tight, a telltale sign that he was nervous about what I was doing, but you would have never known it from his words.

"Sister Monique, your hands are like magic. That feels so good. My wife used to massage my neck like this after a good meal."

I gave him an even deeper massage, and I could feel his body begin to relax. His muscles felt so good in my hands. "You'd be surprised at things I know how to do to make a man happy, Bishop."

He didn't respond, but he also didn't become tense at my obviously suggestive words. Well, that was a good start, I thought as I watched him swallow what was left in his glass. He'd finished off four pork chops, most of the apples, and drank two beers. "You know, I must say these pork chops were so good. And you're right, they do go good with a cold beer."

"Why, thank you, Bishop. Why don't you finish the last one?"

He reached for the last bottle, then pulled his hand back. "No, no, I better not. I still have to drive home. But before I leave, there's something we need to discuss." He reached up and stopped the massage, then cleared his throat like he had something important to say. "Sister Monique," he began, turning his head to look at me.

I walked to his side and posed to reveal my second surprise. The bishop stared at me in disbelief. While he was eating, I'd gone upstairs and changed into a pink dress. It was conservative enough to hide my cleavage but showed off enough of my figure to still attract a man's attention. I highlighted the whole ensemble with a pair of pink shoes and a pink-and-white hat. It may not have been my style, but you couldn't tell me I didn't look good.

"Well, what do you think? I told you I had a surprise. Could you take me to church if I wore this?"

He stood up, nodding his head. Aside from the appreciation in his gaze, I could tell from his eyes that the bishop had a little bit of a buzz. This was good, because as much as I knew he wanted me, he was the type of man who needed a little loosening up. He was also the type of man who needed to protect his reputation, so I would have to make the first move.

"The way you look right now, I would take you anywhere. You look beautiful." He said it so sincerely, it made me feel warm inside, and if I'd had any reservations before about my next move, I no longer did. I stepped up and kissed him gently on the lips.

"I just wanted you to know that I heard you loud and clear last night. I understand that if I wanna be with you, I have to at least *appear* to play their game. I'm willing to do that, but I want you to know that I'm still me underneath." I reached back, unzipping the dress until it fell forward, revealing my black teddy, this time without the robe.

The bishop took a deep breath, knowing it was time to make a decision. He was either going to walk out the door or take me to my room and make love to me. And I was going to do everything in my power to entice him to stay. I stepped forward and reached up, placing my hand behind his head and pulling him toward me. Neither of us said a word, and before long, our lips met. I slid my tongue into his mouth, and he met it eagerly with his own. When our kiss broke, I was out of breath, but somehow I was able to mumble, "I want you, Bishop."

I waited a moment for him to give me an answer. God only

knows what was going through his mind, but I was actually getting a little impatient. I wanted him, but even more, I wanted him to want me. He just wasn't moving fast enough. Too many people think that love is about friendship, communication, and respect, but my momma didn't raise no fool. No man can truly love a woman unless he's sleeping with her, and I wanted him to love me, so I said it again. "I want you, Bishop."

"I want you too," he finally whispered. "God forgive me, but I want you too."

He lifted me up, and I melted into his strong arms. He carried me into the bedroom, our lips still locked together, then gently laid me down on my bed and began to undress.

17

BISHOP

Have you ever had a dream that was so good, you wanted to just close your eyes and go back to it? Well, that's how I felt as I clutched my pillow with my eyes shut tight. I just wanted to get back to my dream of making love to Monique. I knew it was lustful and wrong, but it was so doggone good and felt so real that I wanted it to continue forever. I lay with my eyes closed for a moment, mulling over the idea of being with Monique for real. If she were anywhere close to being as good in bed as she was in my dream, it just might be worth losing my church over.

Okay, that was the devil talking, not me. I would never risk my church, no matter how tempting she might have been.

I took a long whiff into my pillow, savoring Monique's scent. The dream had been so vivid I could actually still imagine her perfume as if it were real. I inhaled again, and as my mind entered full consciousness, I froze in shock. My eyes flew open, and a chill ran through me, reality hitting me head-on like a Mack truck. The scent I'd been savoring was real. My dream was not a dream at all, but reality.

I turned over cautiously and looked around the room, and my fears were confirmed. Not only had I slept with Monique, but I also was still in her bed. A wave of panic overtook me.

"Father, what have I done?" I asked out loud, trying to ignore the lustful memories of Monique and me making love that were flooding my head one after the other. My mind and body knew exactly what I had done, and they were trying to overrule my heart, which was burning with guilt and shame now. I placed my hands over my eyes and dropped my head, hoping to will away the visions.

Eventually, I lifted my head and glanced about the room nervously, my gaze finally resting on the empty space where Monique had lain naked in my arms when we drifted to sleep. She was no longer there, and I was glad. I wouldn't have known what to say to her if she were. On her pillow was a note. I picked it up and read it:

Dear Bishop,

I know you said to call you T.K. from now on, but it's going to take a while to get used to. To me, you'll always be the bishop, even though you're my man. I would have loved for you to awaken to a plate of my hotcakes and hand-rolled sausage, but as you know, I had to be at the airport early in order to catch my plane to Mississippi. You were sleeping so peacefully that I didn't want to wake you. But not to worry, I'll make it up to you. I'm sure we'll have plenty more chances for me to make you breakfast in bed.

If you couldn't tell from my screams of pleasure, last night was the most wonderful night of my life. I've never had a man make me feel the way you did. I didn't think it was possible. I just hope in some way I made you feel just as good as you made me feel. I realize it's going to be a while before we can show others our true feelings for each other, but I'm willing to be patient because this is something I truly want. When I return, the church is going to see an entirely different me, but when I'm with you, I'll always be myself. (Wink, wink.)

Keep me in your prayers because you'll be in mine. I'll see you in a couple of weeks.

Love,
Monique

I put down the letter with a guilty sigh. Monique was already making plans for our future, but I couldn't imagine myself ever moving beyond the incredible turmoil I felt right now. I tried again to push the thoughts of our lovemaking out of my mind, but my manhood wouldn't allow me. I could still feel the effects Monique's body had on me. My heart was stuck on the idea that I was a man of God who had given in to the temptation of the devil and committed a sinful act, while my body was stuck on the idea that I was indeed a man of the flesh who had wants, needs, and desires, all of which Monique had fulfilled like they'd never been fulfilled before.

I jumped out of bed and got down on my knees and began to repent in prayer: "Oh, Lord, my Savior, for the first time ever, I'm at a loss for words while speaking to You. For years I have prayed on the behalf of others that they would be forgiven for giving in to the sins of lust and fornication, instead of being obedient to the Word . . ." I tried to continue, but my voice cracked and shameful tears began to fall.

"Please, Lord, forgive me. And forgive Sister Monique for her transgression. It is I who am responsible for her loss of virtue. She's a good woman, Lord, and I led her astray."

I stood up and sat on the bed. I didn't even feel worthy of being on my knees, begging for God's mercy. Too ashamed to talk to God, I decided to reach out to the one other being to whom I could confess my sins. I picked up the phone and dialed.

"Hello," James answered.

"James, it's me." I was trying to keep it together, but the thoughts of me and Monique last night, with her on top of me . . . and me on top of her . . . Lord! I just couldn't get those images out of my head.

"Bishop, is that you?"

"Yeah, it's me, T.K." I didn't feel worthy of being greeted as Bishop. "I failed Him, James. I failed God like I've never failed Him before."

"What are you talking about? Matter of fact, where are you? This isn't your number . . ." James's voice trailed off. I knew he was checking his caller ID. In a moment, he was going to realize I was calling from Monique's house. "Bishop! You're . . . you're at—"

"Yes, James, I'm at Sister Monique's," I confessed.

"But it's not even eight o'clock in the morning yet. What in God's name are—" His voice stopped abruptly. If I knew my friend, and I'm sure I did, he'd just sat up straight as a board in his bed. His eyes were now as large as silver dollars.

"Oh, no, you didn't! Not after everything I did to set you and Lisa Mae up to kill that rumor. T.K., please tell me you didn't."

"I'm sorry, James. I did. I slept with Monique." I choked back tears, waiting for him to reply. "James, you still there?"

"I'm here, T.K. I'm just a little surprised is all."

"Not as surprised as I am. I failed Him, James. I failed God. I'm no better than Jim Baker, Jimmy Swaggart, or Jesse Jackson, for that matter. I tried, but when the true test was in front of me, I just couldn't keep it in my pants." I broke down, crying and sobbing like a child. I'd never felt so lost in my entire life.

James tried to comfort me. "Come on, now, T.K. Just calm down. I mean, it's not the end of the world."

I wasn't too sure anymore that James was the man I should have called on. Don't get me wrong, he was my best friend and I loved him to death, but with the number of indiscretions he had committed, this was pretty much the norm for him. Would he truly be able to understand my internal suffering and turmoil?

"Where's Monique now?" James inquired. "She's not ready to tell the world about this situation, is she?"

"She had to go out of town for a few weeks to visit her mother in Mississippi."

"What! And who said God wasn't on your side? This is perfect."

"Perfect? Are you crazy? I slept with that woman, James. What if she thinks I took advantage of her? This is not perfect."

"Ha!" James blurted out. "If anything, I'm sure she's the one who took advantage of you, T.K. You're a man who's been without relations with a woman for almost a year. You were at your weakest point. No man is going to hold that against you. Maybe some women, but not a man. Hey, you're just like everyone else. You're just a man."

"I'm not just a man, James. People look up to me. I'm their bishop."

"Bishop, minister, reverend, priest, pastor, call it what it is, T.K. You can't hide from the fact that you're a man. Jesus was just a man."

"A perfect man."

"And God knew that He would be the only perfect man to ever walk this earth, so God expects us to make mistakes. You of all people know that, T.K. You just taught it in the men's Bible study class last month," James reminded me. I felt like a babe in Christ, like everything I had lived by was foreign. "That's why God is a forgiving God. But you can't keep making the same mistakes. At least not with the same person," James said in a lower tone.

"Anyway, listen to me, friend. Monique would be a logical

first pick for you to sleep with, but as you can see now, she's loose. She's no first lady. Your first pick for that should be Lisa Mae or maybe Savannah. I mean, Lisa Mae didn't spread her legs for you, did she?"

"Of course not," I said quickly. Did he honestly think I could have had relations with Monique if I had also just been with Lisa? Maybe James's morals were a little more lax than even I suspected.

"T.K., don't you see? You can still put this little transgression behind you and do what you're supposed to. You said it yourself—even your wife wanted you to be with Lisa Mae."

As I let my best friend's words sink in, I looked over at a picture of Monique at the church's summer picnic. I had to admit, Daisy Dukes weren't the ideal outfit for a church function and weren't something a first lady would dream of wearing. It was also an outfit Lisa Mae wouldn't be caught dead wearing in public. There was just no way around it. Monique was a beautiful and genuine woman. What you saw was what you got with her, and I think that's what I was so attracted to, but so much more had to be figured into the equation. I thought about the positive and negative, her reputation versus my reputation, the advantages and disadvantages, but when it all came down to it, being with her was wrong, and the consequences were great.

"You there?" James asked after a few moments.

"I'm here."

"Look, take Monique being gone as a sign. It's not meant to be between you two, and when she comes back, you can make her understand that. In the meantime, take this time as a chance to get to know Lisa Mae. I'm not asking you to sleep with her. Just get to know her."

I thought about the afternoon I'd spent with Lisa Mae, and I knew it would be no easy task to get to know her as a woman, aside from her ambitions to help me better the church.

"Anyway," James continued, "a woman like Monique is surely going to find someone to keep her entertained while away. She'll have forgotten all about you and her little rendezvous by the time she returns. I'm gonna tell you the same thing you always say to me. Pray on it, and fast, T.K., and you'll see I'm right. I mean, what's done is done. Now you just have to move on," he said with finality. "I'll see you later at services."

After ending my call with James, I'd like to say that I felt better, but in actuality, I only felt worse. It wasn't just because I had given in to the desires of my flesh. Now that I had done so, I was mostly afraid that this wouldn't be the last time. Maybe Lisa Mae was wrong. Maybe I was a lot more like James than she thought.

I returned to my knees and started to pray again, asking God to forgive me, to grant me renewed strength, and to give me a sign about who should be the next first lady. And as I realized that I would soon have to make some hard decisions about the women vying for that title, I wondered how I could proceed without having the entire church fall on top of my head.

Alison and the First Lady

From half a block away, I watched the bishop's Cadillac pull out of Monique's driveway; then I drove straight to the cemetery. It was time to update the first lady on the turn of events and decide which letters to deliver to the candidates next.

When I reached the gravesite, I said, "Good morning," then got right to the point. There was no reason to dilly-dally when I had so much to say and so little time to say it. I had to get home and dress for church before my husband realized how long I'd been gone. After all, I had been spending a lot of weird hours away from home, and I didn't want him to think I was having an affair.

"Well, Charlene, it looks like the poop has hit the fan a little sooner than we expected, but things are still going according to plan. I have some good news and a lot of bad news, depending on how you take it. Which would you like to hear first?" I stared at the headstone as if expecting an answer; then I replied as if I'd received it. "Okay, good news it is.

"It appears that Lisa Mae and the bishop are definitely dating. They showed up yesterday at the Olive Garden while we were having the scholarship meeting, holding hands. They make such a cute couple. And you were right. Everyone thinks she's going to make the perfect first lady." I couldn't help but smile, although it soon faded when I realized it was time to get to the bad news.

"I'm sorry to tell you this, but one of the candidates has dropped out." I hated to continue because I knew Charlene had felt that more competition would make the women get catty, and the bishop would see their true colors. "I know how much you wanted Marlene to be a part of this because of her connection to your family, but I don't think she's got a chance. She's back using drugs, Charlene. The bishop told me that he had to take her son down to Tanisha because she's on the stuff so bad." I bent over and picked up a few scattered weeds. "I know . . . she was clean for so long. I wonder if the first letter we left her put too much pressure on her instead of helping her. I gave her another one telling her to get her act together, but I don't know if that's gonna help." I threw the weeds to the side. "I'm thinking about leaving her one of the letters of encouragement that we wrote. Perhaps that'll persuade her to get help. What do you think?" Like a messenger from above, a bird began to sing nearby, and I knew exactly what I had to do.

"There is a bit more bad news." I frowned, staring at the ground instead of the headstone because I knew what I was about to say was not welcome news. "I just saw the bishop leaving Monique Johnson's house. He was putting on his suit jacket as he walked to the car. I don't quite know how to tell you this, but . . . well, here goes. I'm pretty sure he slept there last night." I held my breath for a moment, hating to be the bearer of such bad news. I knew that somewhere in the heavens my best friend was weeping. "If it's any consolation, from the look on his face, I think he regrets it now." I finally got the courage to look up at the headstone. "I'm sorry I have to tell you this, Charlene, but you knew this was going to happen, that Bishop is only a man. He might be a good man, but he's still only a man. I guess now we find out if he's really a man of God who learns from his mistakes and continues to follow the Lord or a man of lust who continues down the road to hell." I smiled at my friend one last time. "I'm betting he's a man of God."

18

LISA

By the evening of the church's monthly membership meeting, I was well prepared to show everyone in the congregation my suitability for becoming first lady. And there was no better time than at the members' meeting. Unlike the deacons' meeting or the board of trustees meeting, it was open to the entire congregation. It was also the meeting where members started the most drama, which is why it was usually more crowded than some of the early Sunday morning church services. Negroes love drama, and trust me, there's no better drama than church drama. When my husband was alive, I'd seen deacons fight in the aisles over things as trivial as what color the men's choir robes were going to be. I'd also heard of pastors losing their jobs because of unruly membership meetings. Thankfully, the bishop ran a tight ship, so very seldom did things get out of hand at First Jamaica. And if I had my way, this particular membership meeting would be totally drama-free as I made my presence known as a candidate—the perfect candidate, really—to become the woman by the bishop's side at the head of the church.

As Loretta and I were putting the finishing touches on the refreshment table, Sister Savannah, followed by her power-hungry father, Deacon Joe Dickens, called themselves bringing some tired old peach cobbler to the table. Now, I knew Savannah heard me the week before when I told the sisters that I would supply all the food for this meeting. Besides, there was barely any room on the table for the cobbler by the time Loretta and I finished laying out my spread. Why those two couldn't get the hint was beyond me. Everyone in the church knew the bishop and I were an item, but Savannah always seemed to be in the bishop's face, and so was her father;

although I don't know why, because there was no way the bishop could ever be interested in someone like Savannah.

If you ask me, something was not right about that woman. She was in her mid-thirties, and her daddy followed behind her like she was thirteen. And he must have thought his daughter was dipped in platinum or something, because he sure as heck thought Savannah was going to catch the bishop's eye sooner or later. I had it on good authority that her father had said, "Until I see a ring on Sister Lisa Mae's finger, the bishop's still a single man." Well, he and his daughter were in for a surprise because after today, I don't care how much peach cobbler, or pork chops, for that matter, they brought to the table. This meeting was like my coming-out party, and it would be only a matter of time before the bishop slipped a ring on my finger.

"You can set it in the back over there," Loretta told Savannah when she brought the cobbler over to the table, playing that coy role she always did. "If we end up needing it, I'll set it out. If not, no need in it going to waste. You can take it back home. I'm sure you and the deacon will enjoy it."

Savannah stood silent and still, frowning at Loretta, while holding the pan of cobbler in front of her. Her eyes finally traveled past Loretta, then landed on the table as if still looking for a spot to rest her pan. Loretta shifted her weight to one side, then propped her hand on her hip, preparing to tell Savannah where else she could take her cobbler. Still determined to make this night drama-free, I stepped over to intervene.

"Savannah, honey, how about giving the cobbler to me?" I asked, reaching for the pan. "I'll take it to the back for you."

Nobody asked Deacon Dickens for his two cents, but of course he spoke it anyway. "Why don't we just put it here?" the deacon suggested, making it sound more like a demand. He moved two of the sweet potato pies I'd brought to the back, where no one could see them. "Ain't no need in having four sweet potato pies sitting on the table at one time anyway. I'll just get these two out of the way; then Savannah can put her cobbler right here. You ladies got an issue with that?" He turned to face Loretta and me, obviously displeased with us for trying to block Savannah's dowry.

"You think this spot will do?" He frowned as he pointed to the empty space he'd made on the table.

Loretta looked at me and twisted her lips. I grabbed her hand

and squeezed it before she could say something. "Sure, Deacon," I said in the most pleasant voice I could find. "I think that'll work."

"Good. We wouldn't want the bishop to miss out on his favorite treat, now, would we? He's very fond of Savannah's cobbler, you know." He looked me dead in the face when he said that.

Loretta nodded, then gave Savannah a fake smile, which she kept plastered on her face until the deacon and his daughter walked away. When they had both taken a seat, Loretta picked up the cobbler and placed it under the table.

From here on out, the only treats the bishop is going to be sinking his teeth into are mine, I thought.

"All right, men and women of God, I'd like to get this meeting started." The bishop stood. He was looking tired and had lost some weight in the past two weeks because of a fast he was coming off of today. That was why Loretta and I went so crazy with the refreshments. I wanted to make sure my man had some good food after his long fast. "As always, I'd like to open this evening's meeting with prayer."

Everyone bowed their heads as the bishop blessed the meeting. Then the different committees gave their reports, and finally, the question-and-answer session began. Right off the bat, the congregation started hitting Bishop with all types of queries. When would the summer revivals start? With all the money our church raises, why did we only give out ten scholarships and not fifteen? And were we going to have an Easter egg hunt for the kids? The demands seemed endless, but he was holding his own until about fifty of the women got started on him about the women's month being canceled.

Women's month was the one month out of the year when the women of the church ran everything, from church services to Bingo. It had always been the first lady's baby, but since she'd passed, it was put on the back burner. No one had stepped up to take Charlene's place as the chairperson of the committee that planned the events for women's month, so the committee had pretty much disbanded, and the month was canceled. Interestingly, none of these women who were questioning the bishop now would have even cared about the cancellation if Loretta hadn't brought it to their attention a couple of days ago at women's

Bible study. She also suggested that they come to the meeting to get it reinstated.

"Why'd you cancel our month? It's bad enough this church is run mostly by men. You didn't cancel the men's—"

"Well, uh, as far as women's month . . . ," the bishop stammered. I don't think he had even realized it was canceled. The poor man was obviously having a hard time keeping everything together since his right-hand *woman* was gone. But I was just the woman he needed to pull things back together, and I was about to prove this to everyone present.

I let them cut him to shreds for about two minutes before I decided to jump in. After all, he was my future husband—and coming to his rescue was well planned in advance by me and Loretta.

"Excuse me, Bishop," I said, stepping from behind the refreshment table, "but I think the ladies are misinformed. I have the notes on everything we discussed as far as the women's month is concerned."

Ooooh, if I could have bottled up that precious look on the bishop's face when he shot me a glance. He looked momentarily perplexed, but then his features flooded with an expression of pure relief. He knew I had his back. I would've winked at him, but at this point, all eyes were on me.

I caught a glimpse of Savannah when she snapped her neck around to check me out. Both her father's and her facial expressions were priceless, a mixture of confusion and envy. Though I didn't have a ring on my finger, the deacon was about to find out that what I had with the bishop was a lot more than he'd ever expected. We needed no symbolic ring to show our dedication to each other.

"Do you mind if I address the congregation?" I asked the bishop, "or would you like to do the honors?" I stuck out my hand to present to him the yellow folder I had brought for this little "demonstration."

"By all means, Sister Lisa Mae," he said with a nod, then moved to the side.

I looked out among the faces in the crowd and saw that I had the members' undivided attention. Perhaps some of them were hoping for some drama to jump off, but I was prepared to handle this little misunderstanding about women's month with such grace and tact that no one in that room would be left with any doubt about who should be the next first lady. My eyes caught Loretta's briefly; just long enough for her to give me a little wink.

I stood in front of everyone and began to read from my notes. "The women will be handling the morning services on the following Sundays," I started, then proceeded to run down the dates. "We have speakers for each Saturday, with the exception of the seventh, so if any members can suggest someone who might be able to share a word from God with us on that day, please see either myself or the bishop."

I looked over at the bishop, who gave me an encouraging smile and a nod. In all actuality, I could have very easily booked a speaker for each Saturday, but I knew that if I didn't leave an opportunity for church member participation, they'd swear up and down that I was trying to take over the entire women's month.

"This year, the bishop and I decided that with all the gifts and talents the women of First Jamaica Ministries have, you should take a greater role in women's month."

The women's eyes just lit up as I began to ask for volunteers to assign them to different functions and duties. I ended up with a volunteer co-chairperson, a welcoming committee, a hospitality committee, and several women members to do the scripture readings, announcements, offerings, and altar call.

Before it was all over, the first women's month since the death of the former first lady was under way, and who better else to organize it than the next first lady? The bishop closed the meeting with prayer and grace; then everyone split up to go in separate directions. Some members went straight to the refreshment table, and others stood around chattering. All the ladies seemed pleased with the outcome. Several of them came over to shake my hand and tell me what a fabulous job the bishop and I had done with the plans.

I looked over at the bishop, and he was shaking hands and thanking the members for coming out to share with us at the meeting. Just when I saw Savannah about to step up to him, I excused myself from a conversation with Sister Alison in order to break up Savannah's little happy moment. She couldn't have said more than three or four words to Bishop by the time I walked up, interrupting her in midsentence.

"Well, Bishop, the member's meeting went pretty well this go-round, don't you think?" I asked, cupping my arm under his. I totally dismissed Savannah's presence.

He smiled, then hugged me with his free arm. I seized the opportunity to snuggle my head on his chest. "The best meeting in a long time, Sister Lisa. Simply the best." Although it was a brief hug, his timing couldn't have been more perfect—just the thing I needed Savannah to see.

She seemed pretty choked up. "Well . . . um, Bishop . . . um . . . I won't hold you up. I just came over to make you aware of the cobbler I made."

"Really? You made cobbler? Did you bring some here tonight?" The bishop sounded excited.

Savannah's face lit up as Bishop inquired about her dessert. "I sure did. If it hasn't somehow jumped off the table and walked under it again, there should still be nearly a full pan over there," she responded, glancing at me. The bishop looked lost. I just kept smiling. "Would you like for me to fix you some?" she offered.

"No!" I abruptly interrupted. The bishop looked at me with surprise, and I wanted to kick myself for losing control for that brief moment. After my triumph at the meeting, I didn't want to ruin it now by embarrassing myself over some tasteless dessert this nobody had brought. I tried to clean it up as much as possible. "I mean, um . . . not right now, Savannah. I need to speak to the bishop for a minute. I'm sure once we finish talking, he'll fix his own, and if not, I'll be happy to take care of it for him."

Savannah looked as if she didn't know how to accept my reply and leave us alone. Either she was trying my patience, or she was simply clueless. I didn't want things to get ugly, especially not in front of the bishop, so I attempted to beg her pardon. But before I had a chance to, the bishop came to my rescue.

"Sister Savannah, you know I always appreciate your baking skills. As soon as I finish having a word with Sister Lisa, I'll be sure to reward my belly with a helping of your fine cobbler."

Savannah nodded at the bishop, then rolled her eyes at me before walking away. Bishop grabbed my hand, then pulled me out into the hall. I was expecting him to ask me why I had planned the women's month without him, so I was prepared to make him understand my intentions were all in his favor. I had rehearsed this moment in my head, so I was ready to lay on the charm pretty thick.

Once we were in the hall, I took Bishop's other hand.

"Bishop, I—"

He stopped me before I could complete my sentence. His lips were pressed against mine before I could tell what was happening. "Lisa, I can't thank you enough," he said immediately upon unlocking our lips. I was stunned. "I don't know what made you do it or even when you had the time to do it, but you really stepped up to the plate this time. I actually felt like I had a partner out there."

"Thank you, T.K. I figured you could use a hand. Besides, isn't that what the pastor's woman is supposed to do?" I purposely left out the words *first lady,* but I'm sure he knew what I meant. "I saw you needed help, so I used my experience and contacts to pull things off. I've worked with a few of the speakers before, and they were more than willing to be participants."

Bishop just kept shaking his head and smiling. "When I tell you God moves in mysterious ways, I really do mean it."

"I believe that, Bishop. But tell me why you're saying that now."

"You know I had been fasting lately, right?"

"Yes, I know, Bishop."

"Well, my fasting ended this evening. And, well, I can't share with you why I was fasting and praying . . ." He grabbed my hands and pulled me close. "But what I will say is that it appears God has given me an answer." He embraced me, squeezing me tightly. "Thank you again, Lisa. Thank you for everything."

I squeezed him back, smiling inside and out as he kissed me again. "You're welcome, Bishop. You're quite welcome," I said, and returned his kiss.

19

MONIQUE

For days I'd been trying to get in touch with the bishop to let him know I was back in town after three and a half weeks with my mother. I had missed him quite a bit and couldn't wait to see him, but I was having no luck so far. The only number I had was his cell, which he never seemed to answer, even before I'd left town. And after everything that had happened before my trip, I didn't want to take any chances by calling the church and leaving my name. When he introduced me to the congregation as his woman, I wanted it to be timed correctly, not forced on him because the rumor mill started churning after some nosy person started checking his personal phone messages. We'd have time for my formal introduction to the church later. So, since there didn't seem to be any other way to reach him, I decided to go to my favorite Saturday night church activity, Bingo, in hopes that we might "bump" into each other. He'd know what to do when he saw me. After what I put on him, he was going to be breaking down my door to get some more. Besides, I loved some Bingo, and I was good at it—usually.

By the time we were on the last round of Bingo, I still hadn't won anything, and I had yet to see the bishop, so it was not a good night. I was playing eight cards at a time and had wasted somewhere in the neighborhood of $120. I'd never come to Bingo without winning at least one game to get my money back. Usually I was one of the luckiest people in the room. People were always getting mad because I'd win so often at Bingo and the church raffles. Over the last three years, I'd won three TVs and a computer. So I wasn't used to losing. What made it even worse was that the bishop's secretary, Sister Alison, and her overly handsome, wheelchair-bound husband, Trustee Brent, sitting next to me, had won five Bingos between them, and they were using only one card each.

"You and the trustee sure got the Lord on your side today, Sister Alison," I said enviously when she returned to the table from a trip to the ladies' room.

"Yes, ma'am, Sister Monique. He sure has blessed us today."

"He sure has."

"Where have you been, Sister Monique? I haven't seen you in a few weeks."

"I was out of town. My mom had an operation, and I went down to Mississippi to help her out. Truth is, Sister Alison, I needed to get away and recharge my battery, if you know what I mean."

"I sure do." She glanced at her husband. He may have been in a wheelchair, but you could tell she sure did love him.

I looked around, as I had been doing all night, hoping to spot the bishop. He usually stopped by Bingo if only just to say hello to the congregation. I decided to leave a note on his car when this card was finished. It was time to make sure he understood that Sister Monique was back in town and that our last time in bed wasn't just a fluke. If I had my way, it would become an everyday occurrence.

"Have you seen the bishop this evening, Sister Alison?"

"No, I haven't, but he's probably somewhere around here with Sister Lisa Mae."

I whipped my head around toward her. She noticed the severity of my action, so I tried to tone it down by asking nonchalantly, "Why would he be with her?"

"Oh, you haven't heard?"

"Heard what? I've been out of town for a couple of weeks, remember."

Sister Alison looked around, then leaned her large frame close to me so her husband couldn't hear her gossiping. "Girl, the bishop and Sister Lisa Mae are an item."

"Shut up. No, they're not." My voice was low so as to not attract attention, but I was fuming. Either Sister Alison was a damn liar, or Sister Lisa Mae had swooped in and picked up my prize while I was away. Now that would put me in the middle of the biggest losing streak of my life. I was not used to setting my sights on a man and *not* getting him, especially after I'd already shown him my considerable talents in the bedroom.

"No, I'm not lying. Them two been walking around here holding hands like they Luke and Laura from the stories. I think we done found the new first lady."

I wanted to slap her for saying that with a smile on her face. My stomach felt as if a lead ball had been dropped in it. The bishop and Sister Lisa Mae? This couldn't be happening. The bishop wanted me. He said it that night. He told me he cared. And the way he made love to me before I left . . . A man doesn't make love to a woman like that unless he wants to be with her.

I was about to get up to see if the bishop was in his office when Alison jumped up in the air. "Bingo!" she yelled. Not only was she the deliverer of bad news, but that woman had just hit the five-hundred-dollar jackpot that I was only one number away from winning. As Alison ran to the front to collect her winnings, I packed up my stuff and headed for the door.

"Sister Monique . . . Sister Monique," Michael, the young man who'd sold us the Bingo cards, called. "Somebody left this at my table for you." He handed me an envelope that looked exactly like the one that had been taped to my door.

"Who left this for me?" I asked, looking around to see if anyone in the room was watching us. Someone in the room had to be delivering the first lady's letters. But if it were, that person wasn't giving himself away. Not a soul was looking in my direction.

"I don't know who left it. I went to the bathroom, and when I came back, there was a note that said to give this to you."

"All right. Thank you, Michael." I stuffed the letter into my purse and continued out of the church. I was anxious to know what the first lady had to say this time, but I'd be damned if I would read it in front of whoever left it for me.

20

MARLENE

I woke up one morning a little more than a month after Aubrey left and decided this was the day I would get clean—but after I find ten dollars to get one last blast to start my day off right. But when I looked around my apartment, I realized I'd already sold everything of value. Other than my bed, the only thing I had left was my phone, and I couldn't get anything for that. So, there were only two possibilities: I could go out and do a few tricks, or I could call Tanisha and see if she'd lend me a few dollars.

I picked up the phone and dialed *67 to block my number, since I suspected she might not answer if she saw it was me. The call didn't connect right away, so I said a quick prayer that I still had long-distance service. I relaxed just a bit when I heard the call go through.

"Hello?"

"Hey, Tanisha, what's up? It's Momma."

"Momma, whatchu want?" That girl had some real attitude in her voice.

"What do you mean what I want? I called to see what you were doing and to check up on my son. He is still my son, isn't he?"

"Yes, Momma, he's still your son. But Aubrey's at school right now. And I'm about to go to class myself."

"So he's doing good?"

"Yeah, Momma, he's doing fine." Her voice was flat. "Look, Momma, I've gotta go."

"Hold up, Tanisha. I wanna ask you something."

"Oh, Lord. What?"

"Can you send me some money? I just need about fifty dollars. I ain't got no food, girl."

She was quiet for a while. I listened to her breathing, but I didn't say anything. Best not to piss her off when I needed her right now. When she answered, though, it was clear I had already made her mad.

"You know I'm not sending you any money. Are you crazy? What happened to that fifty dollars I sent you two weeks ago? I bet you smoked it up."

"I didn't smoke nothing. I'm clean now," I pleaded.

"Oh, my gosh. Stop lying, Momma. You know what? I gotta go. Bye."

"Tanisha, please, baby, don't hang up. I really am trying to get clean. I just need a little help."

"Momma, we've been down this road too many times before. You know I can't help you. The only person who can help you is yourself. Now why don't you go take yourself down to detox? If you can stay down there for a week, then I'll come get you. Me and Dante will pay to help put you in a program."

"I ain't going to no damn detox! I told you I'm clean. I just need fifty dollars to get some food!" I screamed, no longer worried about what Tanisha thought. "Now stop playing games and send me some damn money."

My daughter's answer was a dial tone. And when I tried to call back, I got her machine. At that point, I knew there was no reason to leave a message, so I hung up the phone.

I walked into the bathroom to splash some cold water on my face, but when I looked in the mirror, I had to turn away. I looked so bad, it made me cry. And when I say bad, I mean real bad. My hair hadn't been combed in at least two weeks. My skin was breaking out, and I'd lost at least thirty pounds in the past two months.

Still, I had to do what I had to do to get some money. I dried my tears and went into my bedroom to find what was left of my makeup. I tried to fix myself up, but to be honest, when I finished, I looked something like a sick clown.

"Ah, what the fuck? Those dumb tricks will probably think I look good." I headed out the door and down the block, then stood at the corner of Guy Brewer Boulevard and 111th, trying to look cute so someone would pick me up. Attracting tricks was always harder in the daytime than at night. After dark, the dirty old men drove around, looking for the blow jobs their wives wouldn't give them.

After an hour and a half of standing on that damn corner, and after practically scratching my skin off, I finally gave up. Time to try another angle. I walked up to 109th, where Reggie was standing with his friends.

"What's up, Reggie?" I started to pace around in a circle, continually scratching my arms.

"What the fuck do you want?"

"I was hoping big man might want me to suck his dick for 'im," I said, trying to sound enticing. "You know, kinda start his day off right."

The big man looked me up and down with pure disgust. "You really fell off, you know that? I used to think you was kinda fine for a crackhead," he said. "But now I wouldn't let you suck my dog's dick."

Everybody on the block started to laugh. There was a time I would've been embarrassed by something like that, but right now all I wanted was a hit. I didn't have time to be embarrassed.

"Hold up, Black. That's a good idea," Reggie said with a laugh. "Yo, go get Big Al for me."

The big man looked at him for a second, then a big smile spread across his fat face. "Yeeaahhhh," he said, and headed for the car.

"Don't worry, Ma. We gon' hook you up in a second," Reggie said.

A few minutes later, the big man came back with a tan-and-white pit bull that looked to be on steroids. Reggie patted the dog's head, and it started to pant and wag its tail. Then Big Al rolled over on his back so Reggie could rub his belly.

"Hey, y'all, check this out. I read this shit in a book," Reggie announced to the small crowd. Then he looked up at me, stuck his hand in his pocket, and came out with two nickel bags. I started sweating in anticipation of the rush I'd soon be feeling.

"You want this shit?"

"Hell yeah." I nodded my head.

"Aw'ight, then," Reggie said with an evil glint in his eyes. "You can get it, but you got to take care of my dog."

I heard what he was saying, but I didn't move. My stomach

jumped. I almost vomited at the thought. I should have turned and ran, but the damn craving for some rock was much stronger than my dignity at that point. I convinced myself that Reggie was just showing off for his boys. He wouldn't actually make me do anything with his dog . . . would he?

"You joking, right? You don't want me to do that, Reggie. Come on, Re—"

Reggie cut his eyes at me angrily. "Do I look like I'm joking, bitch? You wanna get high, don't you?"

By now we were surrounded by at least ten people, and they were all laughing. All the attention was just hyping Reggie up. "So, what's up? I ain't got all day, and neither does he." He pointed at the dog. "Now, get on your knees and suck my dog's dick."

I've done a lot of fucked-up things in my life—stole from my kids, stole from friends, and allowed men to disrespect me in so many different ways, I don't even want to think about it. But I'd never done anything like this to an animal. Had I really sunk so low that I might go through with it? Did I need the hit that bad?

Somebody pushed me from the back. "C'mon, bitch. Suck it." I looked up at Reggie, who was smoking a blunt and waving the two nickels near my face, taunting me.

I had a momentary vision of me snatching the nickels out of his hand and running down the street. It almost seemed like a good idea, until I realized there was no way I could outrun this crowd of Reggie's boys. No, that would only amount to a beat down. But what was worse—getting a beat down or degrading myself in front of all these people by sucking a dog's dick? Shit, I thought, at least if I suck off the dog, I'll get the drugs. If I get a beat down, all I'll get is a bruised-up body and no crack to make the pain go away.

Slowly, I lowered myself to my knees, cringing as I listened to the crowd's growing excitement. The dog was so calm, I thought he might know what I was about to do. Maybe I wasn't the first addict Reggie and his boys had done this to. I reached out cautiously, rubbing the dog's belly the same way Reggie had. To my surprise, the dog wagged his tail as if he liked it.

Well, at least he's friendly, I thought, trying to prepare myself mentally to go through with this. *Come on, Marlene, you can do it. It's only a dick. You've sucked plenty of dicks in your day.*

I took a deep breath and lowered my head, staring at the dog's penis. By now, half the block was surrounding us, and there was a chorus chanting, "Suck, suck it, suck it!"

Suddenly, something inside me just snapped. I had talked so many times before about wanting to get clean. I had lied to my kids, to Thomas Kelly, and to myself, promising that each time I smoked would be the last. But here on my knees in front of half the neighborhood, listening to them practically beg me to degrade myself as low as humanly possible, I finally realized that getting high just wasn't worth it. I was done disrespecting myself.

I stood up and dusted off my knees.

"What the fuck are you doing?" Reggie sounded frantic. I had fucked up his show, I suppose. He waved the two nickels in my face, still thinking he was in control. "You want this shit, don't you?"

I shook my head. "Naw, I don't. Not anymore." I threw my shoulders back and walked away, holding on to whatever shred of dignity I had managed to save during my two-month crack binge. The spectators' disappointed groans meant nothing to me. I was ready to start my life over again.

21

MONIQUE

It took a lot of makeup for me to cover the puffiness around my eyes from all the crying I'd been doing lately. As if reading the first lady's letter after Bingo wasn't hurtful enough, I had spoken to three different church members over the past week who confirmed Sister Alison's story that the bishop and Lisa Mae were seeing each other romantically. I felt like such a fool. The bishop still wasn't returning my calls. But as I walked into the church forty-five minutes early for the eleven o'clock service, I knew I wasn't the only one who was going to feel like a fool when this day was over. Ignoring the people who still lingered from the early morning service, I walked to the front of the church and placed a small shoulder bag on the first pew, directly in front of the pulpit. Then I stomped out of the church and went home to change my clothes.

I returned exactly one hour later. As always, the eleven o'clock service was standing-room only, because this was the only sermon of the day that the bishop preached himself. Ignoring the usher who tried to hand me a program, I swung my hips and strutted my stuff right down the center aisle. I was looking good, and all eyes were on me, including the bishop's. I was showing off my legs in stilettos and wearing a tight, short, off-white skirt-suit that showed everything the men desired and the women wished they had.

I was sure everyone in the church was wondering what the hell I was doing when I paused in front of the pulpit and glared at the bishop as if I were about to accuse him of murder. I practically heard the collective sigh of relief when I stepped away, lifted the shoulder bag I'd used to reserve a seat, and sat in the pew. I glanced over at Lisa Mae, who was sitting three seats down from me. She looked down at my short skirt, and her high-yellow face screwed up into a frown. It did nothing for her looks, I thought with satisfaction.

I sat up a little straighter so my cleavage was displayed front and center, and then I settled in to hear the bishop's sermon. Although my grand entrance hadn't stopped him completely, it took him a while to get back into the rhythm of his sermon. I wondered if the other members of the congregation noticed his discomfort; but even if they didn't, I know I was enjoying it. He seemed to be watching me from the corner of his eye. Oh, he probably thought people believed he was gazing at his beloved Lisa Mae, but I knew better. He was looking at me, and only me. I shifted and moved in my seat throughout the entire service, allowing my short skirt to ride up even higher, just to make him more uncomfortable.

When the service was over, I planned to wait a few seconds to let the crowd disperse a bit before I got out of my seat to confront the bishop. I pretended to fumble with the shoulder bag on the floor by my feet. When I lifted my head, I saw dark trousers. Someone was standing beside me. For a moment I thought maybe my conversation with the bishop would happen sooner than I'd expected, but then my eyes traveled up to see that it was his errand boy, Trustee Black. I sucked my teeth at him as he stood there looking all somber with his suit jacket buttoned up and both hands in his pants pockets. This was clearly not a friendly Sunday morning greeting.

"Sister Monique, can I speak to you for a second?"

I rolled my eyes at him and shook my head. "Not right now, Trustee. I have something much more important to speak with Bishop about."

"But this is important," he said, taking hold of my arm. To an observer, it would look like a casual gesture, but the way his fingers gripped my elbow, I knew he meant to send me a message.

I swung my head toward him. "If you don't let go of me right now . . . ," I hissed.

He released my arm and took a step back, still with a fake-ass smile on his face for anyone who might be watching. "Sister, I hope you're not planning on starting any trouble in the church today. Especially not on the Lord's day."

"Trustee Black, I'm not here for any trouble. What I'm here for is answers. And the only one who can answer my questions is your friend, the bishop. Now, you'd best keep your hands to yourself." I walked away from him, toward the back of the church, where the bishop was thanking members of the congregation for coming to the service.

I waited in line for almost twenty minutes, watching the bishop shake the hands of the men and kiss the women on their cheeks. I hated to admit it, but Bishop Wilson looked good. As angry as I was, the man still made my knees weak. A vision of our passionate night flashed through my mind, but I wasn't about to let my desire for him stop me from demanding the answers I deserved.

When it was finally my turn to be greeted, I didn't give the bishop a chance to say a word. I just pointed my finger in his face and said, "We need to talk." I didn't give a damn who heard me, and trust me, a lot of people heard.

From the way his eyes darted around to see who was witnessing this, it was obvious he was embarrassed. "That's fine . . . uh . . . Sister Johnson. Uh . . . why don't we . . . uh . . . Why don't we meet in my office after I thank these kind folks for coming to the service?"

I smirked, knowing that the words he left unspoken were, "Please don't make a scene in front of my church." Good. Let him sweat.

"That's fine, Bishop. I'll be right over here." I sashayed to a spot about five feet away and folded my arms. I didn't take my eyes off him once while he greeted the remaining people in line. He had plastered the smile back on his face, but it was definitely much less bright than it was before.

When the line finally ended, the bishop gestured wordlessly for me to follow him. I did, noticing that Lisa Mae was just a few paces behind me. The bishop didn't turn around, so he didn't even realize she was with us until we were in front of his office. In the hallway, he turned to say something to me but stopped when he saw that we weren't alone.

"Uh, Lisa, is it possible that Sister Monique and I can meet in my office in private?"

I would have expected some attitude from her, but instead, her face lost all emotion. "Why?" she practically whispered.

Ah-ha, I thought, *looks like someone is still a little insecure about her relationship with the bishop. Well, Sister Lisa, you just better watch your back, because if there's any weakness at all between you, I'll be there to break y'all apart. Can I hear an amen?*

The bishop cleared his throat and spoke patiently to Lisa Mae. "Because what Sister Monique and I have to talk about is personal, and it's best kept between the two of us."

"You got that right," I said, placing my hands on my hips and twisting my lips. If she wasn't going to show any backbone about the whole situation, I'd show enough for both of us.

She must have taken my attitude as a direct challenge, because the real Lisa Mae suddenly stepped back into that emotionless person who had stood before me a minute ago. Her eyes became small with anger, and I could see the muscles in her jaw tightening. I'm sure if Bishop wasn't there, we would've had a physical confrontation. But he was there, and when he placed a hand on her shoulder, it jolted her out of warrior mode and back into that fake-ass submissive role she was playing for him.

"Okay, T.K.," she said sweetly. "Whatever this is, please make it fast. We're supposed to have brunch with Reverends Thompson and Simmons at one o'clock, and we wouldn't want to be late." She looked at me to be sure I got the message. Yeah, I got it. She was the bishop's woman, and she was being included in his brunch plans with some very important members of the church. I rolled my eyes to tell her I really didn't give a damn. I was still going to meet with her man privately in his office, and I knew that every second I was in there with him would be eating her alive.

The bishop said, "I understand. We're going to make this as quick as possible. Aren't we, Sister Monique?"

"If you say so, Bishop," I told him. "But you've got a lot of explaining to do."

I glanced at Lisa Mae, and the look on her face said my last statement had struck a deep nerve. Bishop Wilson would definitely be doing some explaining today, to me *and* to her.

He turned away from both of us as he sensed the tension building. I know he didn't want a catfight in the hallway. I smirked at Lisa Mae and followed him into his office. This time, Lisa didn't follow, but I knew she stood there watching us, so I placed a hand on my hip and strutted even more than usual. Take that, bitch.

Once inside his office, the bishop shut the door behind us. "Have a seat, Sister Monique," he said in his authority-figure voice. He had some nerve, this man who not long ago had shared my bed like we were newlyweds, talking to me now like I was just some anonymous church member.

"That's all right. I'll stand." The bitterness was obvious in my voice, and I truly didn't care. Was it possible to love someone and hate him at the same time?

"Well, I hope you don't mind if I sit."

"This is your office."

He sat on the edge of his desk. "That was quite an entrance you made today during the service."

That brought a wicked smile to my face. "I thought it might get your attention. I've been calling you for the last three weeks. It seems you don't want to answer my calls or return my messages."

"Calls? Did you call me? I never got any messages." He glanced at the phone on his desk.

I rolled my eyes. "You know, Bishop, you are not a very good liar." He opened his mouth to protest, but I wasn't interested in hearing it. "You don't have to lie, Bishop. All I want is the truth."

He reached for a bottle of water on his desk and took a long drink before he could finally look me in the eyes again. He said, "You're right. I'm not a good liar. I guess that's because I hate to lie. So, you want an explanation?"

I nodded. "That would be nice."

He ignored my sarcasm and continued. "Okay, remember the day before you left for Mississippi?"

"You mean the night we made love?" Of course I remembered. I would never forget that night. It was like a dream come true. The way we made love was like music.

Oh, God, I should never have gotten on that stupid plane. He'd still be mine if I didn't. I just know he would.

I pinched the back of my hand to stop myself from reminiscing about the last tender moment I'd shared with the bishop. I was determined to stay mad at him for his betrayal.

"Yes, I remember," I said coldly. "I think that's part of the problem, wouldn't you say?"

He ignored my comment and plowed ahead. "Well, remember I kept telling you I had something to tell you?"

"Mmm-hmm." My heart was in my stomach. When I had woken up that morning, I rushed out of there so fast that he never did tell me what it was he came to say. Could he have been preparing to tell me then about Lisa Mae? And if he was, then that just made matters worse. He should have told me before we made love, not after he allowed me to feel his passion. My feelings might have been hurt, but at least I wouldn't have spent all that time in Mississippi fantasizing about the relationship we would start when I returned to New York. I crossed my arms and cocked my head to the side, waiting for him to say whatever it was he "forgot" to tell me the first time.

"Well, I was supposed to tell you about Lisa Mae and me." He looked very uncomfortable, but that was fine with me. I was not about to say anything to ease his trials right now. "Uh . . . well . . ." When he did finally get himself together enough to speak, it came out as one long, fast sentence. "It's a long story, but somehow I got trapped into dating her, and I didn't want things to turn out this way, and I'm really sorry they did, Monique, and I wanted to tell you myself, but this whole thing just got out of hand."

I interrupted his never-ending sentence. "You got trapped? Let me see if I got this right. You're seeing Lisa Mae because of church politics? You listened to those people who think that I'm less worthy of you just because my clothes don't meet their standards? Oh, my God. I thought you were a man. You let them choose your woman for you." If I weren't so offended, I might have laughed at how crazy that sounded. Some man of God he was, preaching about accepting all of God's children, then rejecting me—not because I had an evil soul, but because my dresses showed a little cleavage. And God forbid, his precious church members ever found out just how much that cleavage tempted him. He was just pitiful.

He didn't even try to defend his weakness. "I'm sorry, Monique. I wish things could have worked out differently."

"You wish they could have worked out differently?" I asked. "And why is that? You got what you wanted, didn't you? You got a piece of this." I gestured to the region below my waist, "and you still get to keep your pristine image for the church."

He tried to protest, but I wasn't finished yet.

"I really thought you were a different type of man, Bishop. But as it turns out, you're just like all the others. I should have never let you make a fool out of me."

"I'm sorry," he said, and suddenly I was no longer angry.

I found myself on the verge of tears, but I couldn't quite identify their source. Was I crying because I had been taken advantage of, or was it just the realization that I wasn't going to be with the bishop again? As much as I hated to admit it, the latter seemed to be what was upsetting me the most. I guess somewhere in the recesses of my heart, I had hoped that if we had this little private conversation, he would see his error and we could still be together. Yes, he had done me wrong, but deep in my heart I still knew he was a good man, and I still wanted him. Perhaps that's why his simple apology was enough to completely change the path of my emotions.

"I thought you felt something for me." My voice shook as I struggled to keep my tears at bay. "Are you saying there's no chance for us now? I can be discreet."

"I can't live like that." He lowered his head. "Besides, I promised Lisa I'd give this a try. No matter how we became a couple, she's proven herself to be a good woman, and she deserves a chance. These circumstances are not her fault; they're mine."

"I just can't believe you're letting the congregation make your decisions for you," I said sadly, then took a step closer to him. If my words couldn't make him understand how much I cared, maybe my actions would. I leaned in and gently kissed his lips. When he didn't resist, I slipped my tongue into his mouth, but before I could even enjoy the kiss, he pulled away, frowning.

"I can't do this, Monique. I just can't. It wouldn't be right to you or Lisa. I made one mistake. I'm not about to make another."

He stepped away from me to put some distance between our

bodies. As the first few tears spilled out of my eyes and ran down my cheeks, I asked, "Well, can you do me one favor, Bishop?"

"Sure. What do you need?"

"I need you to recommend another church for me."

"Sister Monique, you don't need another church."

"Yes, Bishop, I think I do."

22

BISHOP

As I watched Monique turn and walk out of my office, I sensed that it was more than an exit from a room. I felt as though she were walking out of my life. The man inside me wanted to run after her and stop her, to grab her and kiss her again, then carry her into my office so we could make love on my desk.

So, what's stopping you? I asked myself right before I walked out of my office behind her.

Lust, that's what was stopping me. I had to resist my lustful urges and examine my conscience. But that wasn't the only thing that stopped me from following Monique.

As I turned the corner, I saw Lisa standing there, chatting away with two other female members of the congregation. I should have known she would find a reason to stall and hang around. Seeing her there was like a cold shower of reality, reminding me of just the kind of man I am—a man of God. I slowed my pace.

Lisa looked up and smiled when she noticed me.

Good, she's not angry, I thought. At least she didn't look angry. Then again, that could have been a front for the two women she was talking to. I wondered briefly if they had noticed Monique exiting the hallway near my office, but as I watched them wrap up their conversation, no one's face betrayed any sort of indignation. They seemed to be having a perfectly innocent conversation, which ended with quick hugs and a good-bye from Lisa as she left them and approached me.

I looked over Lisa Mae's shoulder and I saw Monique making her way through the church doors. My heart fluttered briefly, but I stayed in my spot, hoping I wouldn't regret letting her walk out. I plastered a big smile on my face as I reached out my hand to Lisa.

"So, did you two get your little talk out of the way?" Lisa Mae asked, trying her best to hide the underlying sarcasm that laced her tone. It didn't go unnoticed, but I chose not to respond to it.

"As a matter of fact, we did," I answered, taking her hand in mine. "And trust me, there won't be any more talks needed between Sister Monique and myself," I said, watching a slight smile creep across Lisa's lips. She had such an angelic smile, I thought, a smile that any person who walked into the sanctuary would love to be greeted by. Yes, that right there was the smile of a first lady.

Just as quickly as that thought entered my mind, the angelic smile disappeared. It was as if someone had tapped her on the shoulder and reminded her of the situation.

"And just why should I believe that, T.K.? Why should I believe that there will be no more *private talks* with sisters like Monique and Savannah Dickens? Every time I look up, there's a woman in your face. It'd be nice if everyone knew what direction our relationship was going in. It would be nice if *I* knew what direction it was going in."

Her statement made me freeze for a moment. Was she hinting that she wanted a ring? Yes, I think she was. The question was, Was I ready to give her one?

"I can understand where you're coming from, Lisa, and why you might feel a little insecure about things, but you have to remember, I'm the pastor of the church," I said, grabbing her soft, delicate hands and looking into her eyes. "I have to listen to the women's problems as well as the men. But believe me when I say that you are the woman I want to be with. I made that very clear to Sister Monique. Besides, everybody sees it, Lisa. Everybody but you."

"Bishop . . . ," she said as she put her head down. I suspected she was trying to blink away the tears that had formed in the corners of her eyes.

"I mean it, Lisa," I continued. "Sister Monique is not a threat to you."

"What about Sister Savannah?"

"She's not a threat, either. From everything I can see, you're the one for me. I don't believe in long engagements, so I just need a little more time to get to know you."

Almost forgetting where I was, I leaned in to kiss Lisa, but before our lips could touch, a voice interrupted the moment.

"Well, look at you two lovebirds." My secretary, Alison, seemed to appear out of nowhere. "But you two better be careful." She lowered her voice to a dramatic whisper. "Everybody pretty much knows that you two are an item, but you still don't want to give folks something to talk about by making out in the church lobby," she said, chuckling.

"You're right, Sister Alison," Lisa said coyly. "We won't do it again."

"No problem," Alison replied. "Just glad I showed up when I did before you two kids got out of hand." Alison laughed at her own joke, then turned toward me, looking at my mouth. "Although, it looks like I might have been a little too late, after all."

She took a tissue from her purse and wiped the side of my mouth. "Nice color," she said to Lisa with a wink, referring to the lipstick that was smeared on the tissue.

I closed my eyes and listened as Alison's footsteps faded, afraid to look at Lisa Mae. I wasn't sure if when I opened them I'd see a hand coming at me, or even worse, Lisa would be gone. But when I did open my eyes, neither of my fears came to pass. Lisa was standing there with arms folded and bottom lip trembling.

"Yes, Bishop, it is a nice color," Lisa pouted icily. "Too bad it's not mine."

23

MONIQUE

I was dreaming about Bishop Wilson making love to me when the aggravating buzz from my alarm clock woke me out of a deep sleep. I still couldn't get my mind off him, and dreaming about our lovemaking had become a nightly occurrence. I missed him so much. I just couldn't find it within myself to face him. This was the third Sunday in a row I'd set my alarm clock for church, only to hit the OFF button after deciding not to go to church after all. Lord knows if I walked in there and saw the bishop and that Lisa Mae all hugged up or something, I was liable to show my—well, I think you know what I mean.

On that thought, I decided not to lie in bed all day wondering what was going on over at First Jamaica Ministries or what word God had put in Bishop T.K. Wilson's heart to deliver. Instead, I was going to get up, read my Bible, go to Curves, and maybe take a walk in the park or go see a movie. If the bishop wasn't man enough to stand up for what he wanted—and everything in that man's eyes told me that he wanted me—then so be it. I damn sure wasn't going to waste my time waiting for him. Sooner or later his dick would get hard, and when it did, he'd beg me to give him some, just like every other man who'd ever had a taste of this. Then we'd see whose foot the shoe was on.

I threw the covers off and headed for the bathroom, where I opened up my medicine cabinet to grab the bottle of vitamin C. As I reached for it, I knocked over the box next to it, and down came my tampons, tumbling into the sink.

"Damn it!" I shouted as I began to gather them. Just as I was putting the last one into the box, a horrifying thought came to mind. Immediately, I dropped the box and ran into the kitchen, scanning over the calendar attached to the refrigerator by a magnet that had the church's mission statement on it.

"Oh, no," I softly whispered. "Oh, no." I closed my eyes, praying I'd wake up from what could only be called a nightmare. My hand covered my mouth, but still I repeated the only phrase my brain seemed to be able to communicate. "Oh, no."

I made my way trancelike back to my bedroom and sat down on the bed. "Oh, my God, no. I'm three weeks late. No. This can't be right."

Refusing to believe that my monthly cycle was almost a month late, I ran back into the kitchen to recheck the dates. Sure enough, I hadn't had a period since a week before that night with the bishop. I began to fight back the tears of fear that swelled up in my eyes.

"It's just the stress is all," I tried to convince myself as I paced back and forth. "It's just me putting my body through all this mess worrying about that man. I'm not pregnant. I'm too old to be pregnant."

The last thing I needed was to be pregnant with the bishop's baby. Those wenches at that church would stone me for sure. They already thought that just because every man in the church couldn't keep his eyes off me, including some of their husbands, I wanted to sleep or had slept with each and every one of them. To turn up pregnant with the bishop's baby would be the final nail in the coffins—mine and his.

Frantically, I ran back into my bedroom and picked up the phone to dial my mother's number in Mississippi. As the phone rang three times with no answer, I prayed that I hadn't missed her before she had left for church. My momma, like me, was a big churchwoman.

"Hello," she finally answered, out of breath, like she had run to the phone.

Although I tried to hide my despair, my voice quivered slightly as I spoke into the receiver. "Hey, Ma, it's me."

"Monique? Is everything all right? You sound like you been cryin'." I opened my mouth but nothing came out. "Monique? You there?"

Finally I spoke, if you want to call it speaking. But technically it was a bunch of jibber-jabber as my eyes flooded with tears and a wailing sound rose from the back of my throat. I was able, though, to get the last sentence out clearly. "And I don't know what I'm going to do," I cried.

"First off, just calm down. Secondly, I didn't hear a word you just said. All I could make out was, *Bishop, late,* and *baby.*" And then it must have hit my mother like a ton of bricks almost as hard as it had hit me. "Oh Lord, Monique. You're not . . . not pregnant, are you?"

"Oh, Momma, what am I going to do?" I wiped away my tears, finally able to form an intelligible sentence.

"Well, the first thing you're going to do is stop worrying about it. Worry is the thief of joy. And besides, what good is sitting around worrying about something that very well may be nothing at all? It could just be your nerves or something. You're going to be forty-one in a few months, so you could even be experiencing signs of early menopause. I started getting hot flashes in my early forties," she said with certainty. I don't know if she was really so sure or if she was just pretending to be, because that was easier than facing the reality that I could be in a whole heap of trouble.

"You really think so, Momma?" I asked, wanting her to be right.

"Who knows? It's possible." Her voice was not convincing. She changed her tune a little to allow for the possibility that I might be pregnant. "Besides, you said you wanted to be first lady of that church, didn't you? Well, if you're pregnant, it looks like you gonna get your wish. He's going to have to marry you. I always knew you were going to amount to something."

"But, Momma, I didn't wanna become first lady this way. I wanted him to fall in love with me." I started to cry.

"Girl, how many times I gotta tell you? The only thing a man loves about a woman is between her legs. Now, this is not for you to cry and carry on about. If you're pregnant, that man has a responsibility to marry you, just like Reverend Johnson, God rest his soul, had a responsibility to marry me. Hopefully your Bishop Wilson is more of a man than Reverend Johnson was. Only thing I got from that man was $200 and a train ticket from Atlanta to Jackson, Mississippi."

"Momma, he was already married at the time."

"He sure didn't act like it when he was pulling down my britches. No, then he was as sweet as sugarcane in the summertime. Just like all the rest of 'em."

My momma had a lot of issues when it came to my daddy, and to men in general. I guess that's what happens when you have six kids by four different men.

"Now, I was on my way out the door to church, but I want you to promise me that you'll try to relax and get some rest. You can call the doctor first thing in the morning and see if you can't get in for an appointment to get checked out. But like I said, it's probably nothing."

I think my mother really believed she was reassuring me, but all she was really doing was making me nervous. I wanted to tell her that, but you don't tell my mother anything. She's the type of woman who tells you.

I took a deep breath to calm myself before I spoke. "Okay, I'll try to keep myself busy and not think about it. I'll call the doctor first thing in the morning," I promised before ending the call. I then rested the phone in the cradle and stared at it for a moment, replaying my mother's words in my head.

Relax and get some rest . . . call the doctor first thing in the morning. . . . It's probably nothing.

"The hell it ain't nothing," I said as I jumped out of my bed, threw on some clothes, and darted out my front door. This was something. My period was never late.

Once I arrived at the drugstore, I was overwhelmed by all the different types of pregnancy tests filling two rows of shelves. Piss on that, stick that here and poke that in there—sounded like having sex all over again. Freaky sex anyway. After about ten minutes of reading the instructions on the different boxes, I decided to purchase an EPT, which was one I had seen in commercials and magazine ads. Supposedly it gave the most accurate results and could detect pregnancy in its most early stages. Grabbing it off the shelf, I made a beeline to the checkout counter.

There were three people in front of me, including one who wanted to argue with the clerk about the price he was ringing up for the laundry detergent she was purchasing. Once the clerk finally got her squared away, he was able to wait on the next person, who couldn't remember whether she was supposed to be picking up a pack of lights or menthol for her aunt. So, she had to pull out her cell phone to call her and ask. After determining that it was menthol, she made her purchase, and the last gentleman in front of me was able to quickly complete his transaction.

"Sister Monique?" I heard a voice just as I laid the pregnancy test down on the counter.

This really can't be happening, I thought, but once I heard my name a second time, I knew it was real. I wanted to grab the pregnancy test and hide it, but the clerk had already scanned it. There was nothing left to do but turn around, smile, and try to act nonchalant.

"Hey . . . Sister Alison . . ." I said, hoping my smile didn't look as insincere as it felt. "How you doing? Didn't expect to see you here."

"I've been standing behind you in line the entire time and didn't even know it was you." She then held up a bottle of cold tablets. "My husband believes he's coming down with a bug or something, and I told him I'd pick him up a little something for it before we went to church." She eyeballed me up and down, examining my gray-hooded sweat suit. It was something I worked out in but never would have been caught wearing in public before now.

"You're not dressed for church, Sister Monique. And come to think of it, I haven't seen you in church for a couple Sundays or so. Is everything—"

"Excuse me, ma'am," the clerk interrupted, "but this box is damaged. Would you like to exchange it for another?" He was waving the pregnancy test in front of me like a flag. The damn thing might as well have been a neon sign for Alison that read, SISTER MONIQUE THINKS SHE'S PREGNANT!

I stood there momentarily frozen as I looked at Alison. To my surprise, I saw concern in her eyes. In all my years attending First Jamaica Ministries, no woman of the congregation had even tried to fake concern for me.

"Ma'am, do you want this one?" the clerk asked.

"I'll take that one," I told the clerk. I was so embarrassed.

"Your total is $23.58," the clerk said, but I barely heard him.

My mind was racing, trying to come up with anything at all that I could say to Sister Alison at this point.

"Miss, your total is $23.58," the clerk repeated.

"Oh yes, I'm sorry." I turned to the clerk and pulled two twenty-dollar bills out of my purse. I handed the money to the clerk and grabbed the pregnancy test. I wanted to rush out of the store without another word, but I managed to offer a quick "Good-bye" to Alison so as not to appear too rude as I stepped away from the counter.

I had just made it to my car and was unlocking the door when I heard that familiar call once again. "Sister Monique? Sister Monique?" Alison called.

Why was this woman following me? Did she just not have a life? Maybe what I had imagined to be a look of concern on her face was really amusement. I just wanted to get out of there, so I ignored her as I nervously tried to unlock my door. When I fumbled and dropped my keys, I could feel tears welling up in my eyes.

"Sister Monique, you left your change in there." She wasn't going away, so I turned to face her. Alison held out my change in her hand. Her face wore that same look again, and despite my momentary doubts, I still believed it was concern she was feeling for me.

Keeping my head down, I scooped the money from her hand. "Oh, thank you, Sister Alison. Hope you enjoy church."

"Wait a minute, Sister Monique." I tried to put my key in the door, but Alison reached out. "You left your receipt too." She held the paper out to me, the words HOME PREGNANCY TEST clearly printed on the itemized slip. I knew she had to have seen the words as she handed me the paper. "I saw what the clerk was holding. I also saw you put the box down on the counter," she confirmed.

At that point, the flood gates opened and the tears just began pouring out. I took the receipt from her with trembling hands. I was scared. Scared of being pregnant and scared of what Alison might go back and tell the people in the church. Although I hadn't been back in a few weeks and wasn't sure if I'd ever be able to return, I wanted it to be on my terms. This news might be enough to make some of those women bar the doors if they ever saw me approaching the church again. Then Alison did something that made me think she wouldn't be running back to the women of the church to share my heartache.

"Now, now, it's gonna be all right." She wrapped her arms around me, and the anointing in her started to comfort me.

Even as I was feeling the relief of her kindness, I couldn't help but think, *If only these were the bishop's arms around me.* I wanted to smack myself for being so unrealistic.

"You wanna talk about it? Why don't you get in my car and I'll drive us down to that coffee shop on Farmers Boulevard? That way we can talk about things, okay?"

I didn't know what I wanted at that moment, but I knew I didn't want to be alone, so I nodded my head in agreement.

"But what about church?" I asked her. "I don't want you to miss church. And your husband's sick."

"He's a grown man. He'll be all right. And some things are worth missing church for," Alison assured me as she took my arm and began leading me to her car. "And you being pregnant is one of them."

Ten minutes later, we were sitting down in the coffee shop, discussing my situation over a cup of coffee.

"What makes you think you're pregnant?" Alison asked.

"I'm three weeks late. My period is never late." My eyes were starting to fill up again. I couldn't believe I was sharing this information with someone I didn't know very well, but I was too emotional to care at the moment. Besides, Sister Alison had never given me any indication that she was as cruel and catty as some of those other women. She basically kept to herself and took care of her child and her husband, who was paralyzed after a vicious mugging.

"Oh, wow. That's not good. Not good at all." She shook her head and frowned, but her expression seemed void of any judgment about the fact that I was unmarried and possibly pregnant.

"Tell me about it. I'm forty years old. The last thing I need to be is pregnant." I wiped my face as tears began to roll down my cheeks again.

"So, do you know who the father is if you're pregnant?" Her

question was like an unexpected slap across my face. Maybe she was judging me after all. It almost sounded like the father's identity was of personal concern to her. Did she know who the father might be? I wondered.

"Of course I know who the father is! And before you ask, he's not married, okay?" I did not appreciate her question or her sudden attitude, so I gave her some attitude back. "Don't tell me that you're one of them too."

"One of who?" Her voice had picked up a defensive edge.

"One of them gossiping women at the church who thinks they know me and everything I do and who I do it with," I snapped. "Or even worse, you're one of them women who just listen to the gossiping women at the church. Not that it matters, because one's no worse than the other."

Alison was briefly silent, and her face softened. "You're absolutely right, Sister Monique, and I'm sorry," she apologized. "And, no, I'm not one of them, but yes, I guess I did allow the devil to use me as a listening ear instead of rebuking their words. Again, I'm sorry."

Everything about Alison seemed genuine, so it was easy to accept her apology. "But anyway," I continued with a less aggressive tone, "I know exactly who the father is *if* it turns out that I am pregnant."

I know she wanted to ask me who he was, but she probably didn't want to risk looking nosy. Then we'd be right back to where we were a few minutes ago. I wondered if she had any idea but decided she couldn't. If she thought it was the bishop, she wouldn't be sitting there so calmly. After all, she was his secretary and the former first lady's best friend. Come to think of it, since she was Charlene Wilson's friend, I was surprised she hadn't already prejudged me . . . or maybe she had. Hell, I didn't know who I could trust among those churchwomen, but I decided to take a chance on Sister Alison for the time being.

"Well, have you told this man that you might be pregnant? He does have some say in this, doesn't he? Maybe he'll want to get married."

I shook my head vigorously. Up until Alison asked, I'd forgotten about what telling the bishop would mean, what it would do to him, what it would do to his life. It would possibly mean destroying him as a man of God, perhaps even destroying the church. But raising the baby on my own would be hard. Was I willing to sacrifice my way of life, and a child's right to its father, just to save the bishop's career?

"So, are you going to tell him?" Alison pushed.

"I don't know," I told her after considering it for a short time. "I just don't know. He's a pretty important man and I love him. I just don't wanna ruin his life."

ALISON AND THE FIRST LADY

I dropped off Monique at her car and headed straight for the cemetery. But when I got there, it took me a while to get out of my car. I sat behind the steering wheel, wondering how I could break this news to her. Of all the possible scenarios she and I had discussed before her death, a pregnancy never even entered our minds.

When I finally stepped out and walked to the first lady's gravesite, I paced around for a good five minutes without saying a word. Suddenly, a vision of Charlene seemed to appear out of nowhere. She wasn't wearing the same beige-colored dress she always wore. She was wearing red—the devil's colors. And I have to admit, it scared me. Did she already know? Lord knows I would do anything for Charlene, but what I'd heard from Monique was something I did not want to tell her.

"I guess you're wondering why I'm so quiet. Well, I've got some bad news . . . really bad news, and I just don't know how to tell you."

I paced around for a few more seconds. All the while, I could hear her pleading with me to tell her what was going on. I tried to open my mouth, but the words wouldn't come out, at least not at first.

When I could finally form the words, I said, "I was on my way to the church this morning to open up the Sunday school when I saw Sister Monique pull into the pharmacy. I hadn't seen her at Sunday services or around the church in a while, and I figured it would be good to get an update. She seemed to have dropped out of the race for the bishop's heart, but you never know what a woman like her is doing behind the scenes."

I sat on the grass next to Charlene's headstone and continued, plucking blades of grass nervously as I spoke. "I sat in my car in the parking lot for a while before I went into the pharmacy. I figured I'd casually bump into her and strike up a conversation, but I was totally unprepared for what I saw, Charlene." I paused, pulling up larger clumps of grass as I tried to stir up the courage to finally drop the bomb. "Lord have mercy, Charlene. You'd never believe what that woman had in her hands. A pregnancy test!"

I could just see the first lady's face now. She would be angry, yes, probably fuming. But she'd be hurt too.

"Well, you know from that point on, I had to find out whether the pregnancy test was hers or not, so I became Alison the church mother. I took her over to that little coffee shop over on Farmers Boulevard and listened to her spill her guts for close to two hours. That woman is so warped that she actually tried to convince me she's not a tramp and hasn't messed around with any of those men she's rumored to have slept with. But you know I know the truth. You're the one who told me about all those men she'd been with."

I stood up, brushed the blades of grass off my dress, and began pacing again. In the pharmacy when I first saw the pregnancy test, I had tried to convince myself that Monique and the bishop hadn't really slept together and that Monique's child was fathered by someone else. Unfortunately, by the time I finished talking to Monique that morning, I was pretty well convinced that Bishop T.K. Wilson was the man she believed was the father. And if Charlene were holding out any hope that the bishop hadn't really been with Sister Monique, I would sadly have to burst that bubble now.

"I'll tell you something, Charlene. Sister Monique has brought one scenario into this whole thing that we never planned for, and that's a baby. 'Cause I'm telling you, that girl is pregnant." I stared at her tombstone and heaved an apologetic sigh. "Not only is she pregnant, but I'm also sure she's pregnant by the bishop."

I hated being the one to bring this terrible news to Charlene, but I had promised before her death that I would help orchestrate her husband's courtships from behind the scenes and make sure he married the right woman. Even though we'd hit a serious bump in the road, I wasn't about to step out of the driver's seat now.

"Charlene, what I need to know now is what you wanna do about it. We never wrote a letter for this." I sat down again and waited for an answer that I knew would, realistically, never come from my friend. For the first time, we'd just have to let things take their natural course.

24

BISHOP

It had been a very busy day, with a christening and a wedding ceremony to perform. Now I was at home, changing out of my suit and into a tuxedo for the awards ceremony hosted by the civic group 100 Black Men. I was supposed to be getting an award, but I'd much rather have stayed home to watch the big fight on HBO with James. Of course, I couldn't admit that in front of my date.

Lisa Mae was waiting for me downstairs, eager to get to the elegant affair. She looked beautiful in her evening gown, and I would be proud to have her by my side that night. We'd been dating a little more than three months, and this would be our first affair together outside of the church. At the church, however, she'd already been taking over some of the duties of a first lady. Not that I minded. She'd actually taken a lot of weight off my shoulders.

The thing that bothered me, though, was that after all that time, we still hadn't really gotten to know each other on a personal level. Oh, it was nice to have someone to accompany me to parties and events, and she was skilled at the art of public life. She knew just what to say to make people like her and feel good about themselves at the same time. This trait would serve her well if she did become the next first lady of First Jamaica Ministries—something I'd been giving a lot of thought to and something she seemed to be hinting at more often the past few weeks. But if we were really going to be together, it would be nice to spend an evening together, just the two of us. We hadn't eaten a meal alone since our first date, when we went to the Olive Garden, and even then we'd had the scholarship committee playing chaperones, one or more of them passing by our table every few minutes under the pretense of heading to the restroom. It always seemed like someone from the church was hovering over us, or even more often, her friend Loretta. This was an issue I would have to discuss with her at some point soon, but tonight would once again have to be about our public courtship, not a private relationship.

I slipped on my tie and jacket, then headed downstairs. Lisa Mae was sitting on the couch, talking to somebody on her cell phone. She hung up when I entered the room.

"I just confirmed you to be on Channel Five's *Positively Black* next Saturday at two o'clock. They're going to be talking about church and the black family." She beamed with pride, as if her announcement were as earth-shattering as perhaps discovering the cure for cancer.

"Lisa, what did I tell you about scheduling things without me looking at my calendar first? I know I have things scheduled for Saturday." It wasn't that I didn't want to be on the show; it was just that she was making a habit out of scheduling my days.

"Okay, T.K., calm down. I've already checked your calendar. You have only one christening on Saturday morning, and then you're free to do the show that afternoon." She placed a hand on her hip and gave me a look that said I shouldn't have questioned her.

It was moments like this that made me rethink my decision to start dating again so soon after my wife's death.

"Where're you going?" she asked as I turned to walk away.

"To the kitchen to get some aspirin."

"Well, don't take too long. We wouldn't want to be late."

"Yes, dear," I said under my breath.

I filled a glass with water, then swallowed the aspirin, hoping I'd taken it soon enough to avoid the headache that could surely ruin my night. Little did I know that the little spat I'd just had with Lisa was nothing compared to the stress I was about to endure. As I stood at the sink rubbing my temples, I heard a knock on the back door. I flipped on the outside light and peered out the window. I was shocked to see a frail semblance to Marlene.

"Dear Lord." I cracked the door. "Marlene? Is that you?"

"Mmm-hmm. It's me, Thomas Kelly. Can I come in?"

I opened the door, stepping aside so she could enter. She looked so bad, I was almost afraid for her. And she smelled like she hadn't bathed in weeks. The first thing I thought was that I wasn't giving her any money. She could have something to eat, but I was not about to support the habit that was slowly destroying this once-beautiful woman.

"Sit down at the table," I said, trying to sound more concerned than disgusted. "Are you hungry?" I asked as she settled into a chair at the table. She nodded, and I went to the refrigerator to get the plate I had brought home from the wedding reception that afternoon. I removed the foil from the plate, and before I could even offer to heat it up, she said a quick "Thanks" and dug in. I went to get her a fork so she would stop eating with her hands. It bothered me to see her devouring the food like some sort of animal. The Marlene I once knew had too much dignity to act this way. She'd truly hit rock bottom.

I watched her shovel in the food for a moment, then asked, "Why are you here, Marlene?"

Without putting down the fork, she said, "Because I need your help, Thomas Kelly."

"I'm not giving you any money, Marlene, so you can just get that out of your mind right now."

"I don't want any money, Thomas Kelly." She finally stopped eating and looked at me. "I want you to help me get clean. The same way you got clean." She sounded sincere, but I knew from past personal experience that crack addicts were some of the world's best liars.

"Are you for real? You want to get clean?"

"Yes. I'm tired, Thomas Kelly. I can't live like this anymore." Tears rolled down her face, leaving streaks in the makeup and dirt on her cheeks.

It had been decades since we were a couple, but I still felt protective of this woman who, at one time, was the love of my life. Ignoring her odor, I wrapped my arms around her and pulled her in close. I kissed the top of her head. "It's okay, Marlene. I'll help you. It's gonna be all right. Everything's gonna be all right."

"T.K., what's taking so—" Lisa Mae stopped in midsentence,

her mouth still hanging open in shock when she walked in and saw me at the table with Marlene. "What's going on in here? Who is that? And what is that smell?" She took a few steps back, fanning her nose with her hand.

I released Marlene and stood up. "Lisa Mae, this is Marlene, the mother of my daughter, Tanisha." I looked down at Marlene, almost wanting to apologize for what I was about to reveal. But Marlene's appearance was so bad that her addiction couldn't have been a secret anyway. "Marlene needs our help, Lisa. She's been on crack, but she wants to get clean. I told her we'd help her."

A momentary look of disgust passed over Lisa's face, but then she turned to Marlene and put on that smile she was so good at producing on demand. It might have been enough to fool the average person, but I had seen it often enough to know that beneath that smile she was seething.

"Of course we can help her, T.K.," she said a little too sweetly, "but not just now. We've got a dinner engagement. This is the 100 Black Men awards ceremony. They're giving you the Preacher of the Year award. We can't miss this."

She might have thought she was fooling me, but from the way she looked at Marlene, I could tell she really wanted to say, "We can't miss this for some damn crackhead."

"I'm sorry, Thomas Kelly. I didn't know you had plans." Marlene shoved some food in her mouth, then stood and spoke with her mouth full. "I'll come back another time."

"No, Marlene," I insisted. If I let her out that door now, she might never come back again. I couldn't miss this moment, this opportunity to help her get clean. "You don't have to be sorry about anything. I can call my friend and have him accept my award. He'll know what to tell them."

"You can't do this, T.K.," Lisa protested. "Not for a—"

I knew it! She almost let her true feelings slip, but I cut her off before she could insult Marlene.

"Lisa, this woman is my daughter's mother. She's family—unlike some other people in this room." Part of me regretted hurting Lisa Mae with these words, but her lack of respect for Marlene made me angry. Crack addict or not, Marlene was still one of God's children, still worthy of human compassion. No award on Earth could make me neglect my obligation as a man of God.

Lisa Mae's face turned crimson, and she took a step back, obviously shocked by my words. "I'm sorry, T.K. I . . . didn't mean any harm. I was just trying to look out for you." Unlike her fake smile from before, this apology was sincere.

"I understand that, and I'm sorry for my harsh words, but Marlene needs help. I won't turn my back on her, especially not at this critical point in her recovery."

"Look, why don't we drop her off at Jamaica Hospital on our way to the ceremony?" she suggested. "They've got a detox program over there. Let the professionals handle this."

"Look, Lisa, I am a professional when it comes to this drug. I've helped people through this same situation dozens of times. Detox won't help. If it could, then she could have detoxed at home. Getting clean is about *wanting* to be clean and putting God first. Now, Marlene and I have a lot of praying to do, so why don't you take her upstairs and give her a bath? I'll go find her some clean clothes and some Scriptures for her to read. It's going to be a long night."

Lisa Mae grabbed my arm and pulled me out of the kitchen. In the hall outside the kitchen door, she protested, "I'm not going to give that woman a bath, T.K. That woman is disgusting. She might have AIDS or something. I can't believe you even let her in your house."

Lisa Mae's voice was loud enough for Marlene to hear every hurtful word. She was disgusted by Marlene, but personally, I found Lisa Mae's uncharitable behavior to be far more offensive than Marlene's appearance or her odor. I don't know how I kept my composure when I spoke, but I did.

"Maybe it's best if you just take my car and go to the awards ceremony alone. We'll talk in the morning."

"But . . . I can't go alone." She looked confused. Obviously she hadn't expected any resistance from me. Well, it was time for Lisa Mae to get to know the real me. I was a man who took care of his family, who had devoted his life to taking care of God's family.

"I'm sorry, but God brought Marlene here to seek my help, Lisa Mae, and I will not turn my back when God calls. I can't go with you, and you don't seem to want to be here. My car keys are on the table next to the front door if you'd like to drive yourself to the ceremony. I'll call James and ask him to take care of accepting the award." I turned to go back into the kitchen, and moments later, I heard Lisa Mae slam the front door.

25

LISA

I pulled into my driveway after the awards ceremony, still fire-funky hot. I couldn't believe that T.K. would choose to stay with that damn crackhead instead of coming to the awards ceremony with me. I'd never been so humiliated in my entire life. Everyone there was asking about him, including his little male-whore friend James. I couldn't believe I had to watch him accept the award for T.K. All week I had been looking forward to T.K. getting up there to accept the award and acknowledging me so that everyone inside and outside the church would know that I was his woman.

Loretta greeted me at the door with a smile. "Well? Does the entire world know that you are the future first lady of First Jamaica Ministries?" But her face fell quickly after the angry look I gave her. "What? What happened? What's the matter?"

"I don't even want to talk about it," I said angrily, slumping on the couch and punching the throw pillow next to me.

"Lisa Mae, honey, what's the matter? Don't tell me he broke up with you." Loretta sat next to me and placed a hand gently on my knee.

I released a long, frustrated sigh. "No, he didn't break up with me, but he didn't go to the awards ceremony with me, either. All because of some stupid crackhead he had a baby with over twenty years ago."

Loretta stopped stroking her hand over my knee and stood up in front of me, arms folded and head cocked to the side. "Crackhead? Baby? What in the world are you talking about? Just get to the point."

"T.K.'s crackhead baby momma showed up at his house right before we were supposed to leave for the awards ceremony. Loretta, you should've seen her." I shook my head as I recalled the image of this frightening woman sitting at *my man's* kitchen table. "She was a hot mess. The woman was skin and bones, and she smelled so bad, I wanted to take a bath for her."

"Ugh!" Loretta's face crinkled, and her nostrils flared as if she knew the smell I was talking about. "So, what was she doing there?"

"She said she wanted T.K.'s help, but I think she wanted to help herself to some of T.K.'s money so she could get more drugs."

"Did you tell him this?"

"Yes, I told him in so many words." I folded my arms and exhaled. "Would you believe that man had the nerve to tell me that this was a family matter and that I wasn't part of his family? Who the hell does he think he is? I'm gonna be his future wife!"

"Calm down, Lisa," Loretta said gently. "He didn't mean it. Sounds to me like things were just getting a little emotional. You know what kind of man he is. After all, that is his child's mother. But the bishop knows on what side his bread is buttered and so does the church."

Loretta was going to piss me off if she kept trying to defend his actions like that. "That doesn't mean he had to embarrass me by not going to the awards ceremony with me. Loretta, I looked like a fool sitting at that table by myself. And all because of that crackhead." I folded my arms and pouted like a child.

"Listen. You need to relax." She wasn't giving up. "I'm sure the bishop's gonna call you and apologize soon. Or maybe you should call him."

"Call him! I'm not calling him. What kind of lady calls a man after he disrespects her like this?"

"I'm not saying call him now. Like I said, you need to relax."

About an hour later, I was lying on the sofa, still trying to cool my emotions. Loretta had left me alone for a while and went to take a shower when she realized she wasn't going to be able to talk me down so easily. When the phone rang, I glanced at the caller ID. My face broke out in a grin, and *poof!,* like magic, my bad mood vanished. Loretta was right when she said the bishop would call.

I picked up the phone. "Hello?"

"Hey, Lisa. It's T.K."

I counted to three before I spoke because I didn't want him to know how excited I was to hear from him. As angry as he had made me, I was still determined to stay the course until he was ready to take our relationship to the next level. And by showing him forgiveness after his cruel words, I would make him see yet again how perfect I was. Now all I had to do was give him the chance to apologize.

"Oh hi, T.K. How are you?" I asked nonchalantly.

"I'm all right. I just wanted to apologize for what happened at the house and for not going to the ceremony."

I knew he would apologize! I thought with satisfaction. *But remember, girl, control your temper. Control your mouth. Tell him everything you know he wants to hear for now. You can always set him straight about this whole thing later, after you get your ring.*

"Oh, I understand. Like you said, it was a family matter. Truth is, I'm the one who should apologize. I guess I took it a little personally that you didn't want to go to the event with me, and I completely forgot that you are a pastor and these are the type of things pastors should do."

"Well, I appreciate that, Lisa Mae. You're a much bigger woman than I gave you credit for. I just hope you can be a big woman about what I have to tell you."

That didn't sound good. I was banking on the fact that he had handled things with the crackhead and that she was now long gone so we could get back to living our lives after this small distraction. Now I wasn't so sure that things were as status quo as I thought.

I held my breath. Was T.K. about to break up with me? Had I gone too far and shown him a side of me that I didn't want him to see? If he broke up with me, I swear I was gonna hunt that junkie down and . . .

"Ah, what do you have to tell me?" I asked sweetly.

"I talked to Marlene, and I really think she wants to get herself clean."

"I see," I responded. So the crackhead wasn't gone after all. "Well, I'll be praying for her," I lied.

"I appreciate that, Lisa Mae. But I want you to understand that I'm committed to helping her fight this terrible addiction."

"Of course, T.K." I reassured him. Where was this going?

"So . . . she's going stay with me for a while. This way I can help her, be there to pray with her at any hour of the night when she has to fight through her body's cravings. I've been through what she's going through. It's not easy. You need all the support you can get."

I wanted to cry, but I was so angry, the tears wouldn't come. What the hell did he mean, she was staying with him for a while? He couldn't do that. Didn't he know how that would look?

"But T.K. . . ." I was about to argue but then just gave up. I heard Loretta come into the room, and I turned to look at her. I'm sure my face revealed my inner turmoil, and hers reflected sympathy for my pain. I needed some of her comforting. Maybe she could help me see a light at the end of this dark tunnel my relationship with the bishop had entered. I needed to get off the phone and talk to her.

"Whatever you think is best, T.K.," I said, feeling defeated. "Look. I'll see you in the morning when I bring your car. I'm lying down, and I'm a little tired."

"Okay. I'll see you in the morning. Good night, Lisa Mae." He sounded as anxious as I was to end this uncomfortable conversation. I wondered if he'd be willing to listen to me should I need him in the middle of the night, the way he'd be helping Marlene now that she was living in his house.

"Good night, T.K." I was so mad that the second I heard a dial tone, I threw the phone across the room.

"What is the matter with you?" Loretta asked as she ducked out of the way of the flying phones.

"That was T.K. on the phone. Do you know he moved that crackhead junkie woman into his house?"

Loretta straightened up and took a deep breath. "Well," she started as she ran her hands down her yellow-and-pink rose-printed bathrobe, "the bishop's only going to allow her to stay with him so long before he realizes she's a lost cause."

"Hmph," I grunted. "I really don't see how. She's going to be living with Bishop, for Christ's sake! Next thing I know, she'll be sitting in the front pew during worship with her hair all done up, singing and clapping like she done already been delivered from her habit or like she ain't but one prayer from it."

Loretta laughed until she doubled over. "She might be one prayer away from delivery, but at the same time, she ain't but a rock away from being a fiend."

I loosened up and was able to chuckle myself. "Yeah, but I'm sure T.K. will keep her far away from that stuff. Ain't no way she's going out to get no crack while he's around."

"Yeah, you're right, but just because she can't go to the crack don't mean the crack can't come to her." A mischievous grin covered Loretta's face. I knew the way her mind worked, and I was pretty certain of where this conversation was going, but I had to test it. I refused to be the one to suggest out loud what I knew Loretta was leading up to.

"And just how do you suppose the crack comes to her?" I asked as I stood up and folded my arms.

It was as if Loretta couldn't wait for me to ask that question. She raced over to me and started running down the plan. "We take it to her," she said easily.

"What?" I frowned to keep myself from smiling right along with her. What she was suggesting was wrong, very wrong, and I knew it. I didn't want to believe I would go along with the plan, but I also knew as well as Loretta did that she wouldn't have to work very hard to convince me. Still, as someone who viewed myself as a good Christian, I had to at least try to resist the temptation to play so downright dirty.

"Come on, now you're talking like you're on crack, Loretta. I'm going to make me some tea. You want a cup?"

"Sure," Loretta said, following me into the kitchen.

"So, we take it to her, huh?" I questioned, trying to make the question sound casual as I prepared our tea.

"I'm serious, Lisa." Loretta sat down at the small kitchen table.

"Even if I were to think twice about this twisted little plan of yours, just where on earth would we get it?"

Loretta shrugged her shoulders. Just as I had suspected, she hadn't thought that far in advance. Nevertheless, she was willing to try to come up with a solution. "Well, hell, I'm sure we could go right over there to one of those corners near Forty Projects and cop something."

"Cop something," I repeated, using Loretta's street lingo with a little laugh. "Loretta, you been watching *New Jack City* again?"

Loretta giggled. "Something wrong with that?"

As crazy as it was, I actually began to contemplate her plan as I poured each of us a cup of tea. Could I really go through with it? I mean, was it really so important to me to become the first lady of First Jamaica Ministries that I was willing to compromise another person's life? Well, yes, I decided, it really was. Not only did I have my heart and soul set on being by the bishop's side, but there was no denying that I would be the best woman for the job. That church needed me. After all, who else could fill Charlene Wilson's shoes as well as I could? Certainly not Marlene, drug addict or not. And if I let her stay in T.K.'s house long enough to get clean, she might have her own scheme up her sleeve—one that would have her still living in his house, in the perfect position to take my prize. No, I couldn't let that happen. We would have to be careful not to supply her with enough crack that she could overdose, but the more I thought about it, the more I liked Loretta's idea. All we needed to do was give her enough to make it clear to T.K. that this junkie was a lost cause.

"You really think she's just one rock away from losing it again, huh?" I questioned.

"Mmm-hmm," Loretta said, blowing on the cup to cool her steaming tea.

"Let's say we did take the crack to her. How in the world would we get her to smoke it?"

"Here's what I know of recovering addicts: give 'em any type of mood-altering substance, and it will lead them straight back to their drug of choice." Loretta looked inside her teacup. "Suppose we put brandy in some tea and then offer it to her? She'll be too high to know what hit her."

I nodded. "Okay . . . okay . . . I see where you're going with this."

"Before we go, we could somehow leave the crack there for her to discover. Someplace she'd be sure to find it, though, like the bathroom, perhaps."

I don't know how Loretta thought of that scheme so quickly, but she had me excited. "Loretta, as strange as it sounds, your plan could actually work. We just have to make sure T.K. is out of the house on some kind of church business. We could pay a visit to Marlene then."

"Sounds good to me." Loretta grinned slyly.

"All right, then, Operation Crackhead is officially a go."

"I'll drink to that," Loretta said. She raised her glass, and we clinked our cups together.

"Cheers," we said in unison.

I have to admit, I felt ten times better after talking to Loretta. She'd never let me down during my times of need—a true friend indeed. Knowing Loretta and I would be off to complete the first part of our mission in the next few days put my mind at ease. Given our plan, it would be only a matter of time before that crackhead would be out of my man's house. There was a light at the end of the tunnel, I thought with satisfaction.

26

BISHOP

I hung up the phone with Lisa and released a heavy sigh. She'd been a real trooper, but I knew she wasn't happy with the idea of Marlene staying at my house. I would have felt the same way if I were in her shoes. But with Tanisha and Dante down in D.C. taking care of their baby and Aubrey, somebody from the family had to help Marlene, and that person was me.

I checked in on Marlene, who was sound asleep in the guestroom, and a single tear traced a path down my cheek. At one time, Marlene was the prettiest woman I'd ever seen. Now, even after a long bubble bath and wearing a clean nightgown I took from Charlene's closet, Marlene still looked like a vagrant. I touched her matted hair. The three braids looked like dreadlocks.

"Marlene, girl, what have you done to yourself?" I whispered, shaking my head. "You were so beautiful."

I closed my eyes, letting my imagination travel into the past, and I remembered who Marlene was when I fell in love with her, before the drugs took over.

Lord, how could You let this happen to her? She's a good person.

I pulled the covers up over her shoulders, tucking her in, then turned out the lights and left the bedroom. "Sweet dreams, Marlene," I said. "May tomorrow be a better day for all of us."

I walked downstairs to my study. Stooping in front of the closet, I rummaged through the boxes piled on the floor until I finally found what I was searching for. Picking up the old shoe box, I carried it to my recliner and sat down. When I removed the top of the box, I looked at the photos piled inside, taking them out one at a time. Each picture contained a memory from my teen years. I saw pictures taken at King's Dominion, Virginia Beach, football games, basketball games, the prom, and my first day at college. Marlene seemed to be in every one. I still considered myself lucky that she even wanted to date me back in high school. Every boy in the school wanted to be with Marlene Hernandez, the fly half-black, half-Dominican girl with the dynamite figure.

I paused when I came across the picture of Marlene and me at our high school prom. Our Jheri-curl hairstyles made me laugh out loud, especially when I noticed the Jheri-curl juice on the shoulders of my powder-blue tuxedo and on her light-blue prom dress. We thought we were hot stuff back then. And I guess we were. You couldn't tell us nothin'.

I loved Marlene so much back then, I would've killed somebody over her. She was the first woman I ever slept with, and you know what they say about a man and his first—he'll never forget her. And I never forgot Marlene. Even after Charlene and I were married, I prayed to God every night that Marlene would be safe. I had no way of knowing for sure if she was doing okay, because once I left Virginia, we lost contact. But no matter how much distance was between us or how much time had passed, I always held a special place in my heart for Marlene Hernandez. Even now, I would do just about anything to have the woman I fell in love with become herself again and be drug-free for good. She was such an important part of my life, and with Charlene gone, I couldn't afford to lose much more. I still really didn't understand how things turned out the way they did. Then again, who was I to understand God's will?

I closed my eyes and shook my head. God knew my heart; I would spend an eternity trying to help Marlene if I had to. But I knew I might not be able to do it alone, so I went over to the desk to retrieve the phone.

"Deacon, how are you?" I asked when Deacon Dickens answered.

"I can't complain, Bishop. How about you? To what honor do I owe this call?"

"I was hoping I could speak to Savannah. Is she there?"

"No, Bishop. I thought she was with you." He sounded alarmed.

I was at a loss for words. I knew that Savannah had chosen not to tell her father about her musical aspirations, but she never told me she was using me as her alibi. I didn't want to lie to Deacon Dickens, but neither did I want to reveal the truth and ruin things for Savannah. So, feeling like a dummy, all I could do was stutter, "Oh . . . um . . . well . . . um . . . I just . . . um . . ."

I guess he sensed my discomfort, because the deacon actually offered an explanation for me. I don't know if he believed his own words, but at least the awkward moment was ended. "Oh, so she must've just left, huh? Well, she isn't in right yet, but I'll be sure to have her give you a call. Or better yet, Bishop, you should give her a shout on her cell. Do you have the number?"

"No, I don't," I answered, wondering if this small admission would somehow compromise Savannah's plans.

Deacon Dickens recited the number, seemingly unfazed by the fact that I didn't already have it; then he bid me a good day. "Now, Bishop, I suggest you keep that number handy. You may need it again sometime."

"You're right, Deacon. I will." And if Savannah could help me the way I thought she might be able to, then he was right, I would probably be dialing her number frequently. Just not for the reasons that Deacon Dickens hoped.

As soon as I disconnected the call with the deacon, I dialed Savannah's cell phone.

"Hello," she answered tentatively. She probably didn't recognize my phone number, and since she was out of the house under false pretenses, her nerves were probably on edge.

"Savannah, it's Bishop. Your father gave me your number." I heard her gasp and realized that I probably hadn't helped her nervousness one bit. "It's okay. I know what you told him, and I didn't give him any reason to believe anything different." I didn't scold her for the lies she had obviously been telling, but I couldn't let her think I approved. "I want you to understand, though, that I did not lie to him, and I will not lie to him in the future."

"Oh, okay," she said quietly. Poor girl would probably be a wreck when she went home. I would say a prayer for her to be forgiven for the string of lies she would surely have to tell her father that night.

"Do you have a minute to talk to me?" I asked.

"Um, yes, I can talk. Is everything okay? You don't sound like yourself." Her own worry about the predicament with her father vanished quickly, and now she was concerned for my feelings. Savannah was a sweet girl. Her selflessness made me think she was just the person I needed to help Marlene.

"Well, to be honest, it was quite uncomfortable talking to your father after he said he thought you were with me."

She sighed. "I'm sorry, Bishop. I've been at the studio. Is he angry that I lied?"

"I don't know that he's figured it out yet. But I don't want to get into that now. I called to ask a favor of you."

"A favor. What kind of favor?"

"My very good friend, Marlene, who is also the mother of my daughter, Tanisha, is living with me now. She's relapsed on crack cocaine, and I need some help. I couldn't think of anyone else to call except you."

"Say no more, Bishop. I'm on my way. Just give me a minute, though. I need to tell someone I'm leaving."

"Well, that's okay, Savannah. I hate to interrupt what you're doing. I actually need you tomorrow anyway. Are you available in the morning? I have a meeting I need to make, and I don't want to leave Marlene here by herself."

"Sure. I can be there as early as you need. How about eight o'clock?"

"Eight o'clock will be fine. Thank you, Savannah."

"You're welcome. And, Bishop, if you don't mind, let's keep the fact that I wasn't with you today between you and me."

I wasn't exactly happy about it, but I needed her help, so I couldn't very well refuse. "Savannah, I don't know what you're up to, but just be careful," I cautioned. Then, to lighten the mood a bit, I added, "And since you're coming to my house for real tomorrow morning, you can tell your father the truth."

We laughed together, then said our good-byes.

I went over to where I'd left the pictures scattered, stuffed them back into the box, put on the lid, and then placed it on the table next to my chair. Then I went to the bathroom to retrieve Marlene's dirty clothes. As I walked toward the laundry room, I had to hold them at arm's length because of the smell.

I dumped the clothes into the washing machine and was just about to add some soap when I decided to check her pockets. I doubted she had any money, but there was always the possibility she might be carrying some ID.

I went into one pocket and found only a glass stem. That would go straight into the trash. In the other pocket I found a folded piece of paper that was so tattered, she had obviously been carrying it for weeks. But as worn as it was, something about the lavender paper seemed familiar. Suddenly, a thought struck me. I remembered where else I had seen this shade of paper. Was it possible? Could it be? Nah, it couldn't be, I decided, yet my curiosity compelled me to open the paper. As I unfolded it, my hands began to tremble. I struggled to comprehend what I had just discovered. The paper was the same stationery on which my deceased wife had written to me and to Lisa Mae. Marlene, it seemed, had also received a message from the grave.

After reading the note, which basically scolded Marlene for slipping back into drug use, I was surprised but also a bit ashamed. I loved my wife with all my heart, but this note reminded me of the qualities she possessed of which I was least proud. When she wanted, my wife could be a very kind, caring person. But just as often, she lacked compassion and was quite demanding of others. I had told Charlene many times the story of my own struggle with drug addiction, which I might never have survived if it weren't for the encouragement of Reverend Jackson, Charlene's father. So, my wife knew as well as I did that an addict needs love and understanding to rise above the drugs. What Marlene needed most right now was some genuine kindness, but this letter seemed to condemn her more than support her. Could this letter have pushed Marlene into an even deeper despair? I would never be sure, but of one thing I was certain: now I was even more convinced that Marlene's recovery from addiction was my responsibility.

With the letter in hand, I walked down the hall and into my living room, where I stood glaring at a large portrait of my deceased wife. "How many of these damn things did you send out?" I yelled in anger at the picture. "Is this what sent Marlene over the edge? Do you have any idea what type of pressure you put on her? I can't believe you. Have you been trying to drive her crazy from the grave?"

In my mind I ran through the list of people who might be sending these letters—or perhaps even writing them. Was it a friend or an enemy? Each letter I had read seemed to be written in words and phrases that came from my wife. Could someone have stolen her stationery and imitated her style? I doubted that was possible, nor could I imagine what reason anyone would have to do such a thing. No, I concluded, this was Charlene's doing.

"You have no right to play God with these people's lives, Charlene. You have no right to play God with my life. And I'm not going to have it. I'm going to figure out who you've got delivering letters."

27

MONIQUE

It was a few weeks from the day I bought the pregnancy test. Things had been difficult for me since I took the test and confirmed that I was indeed pregnant with Bishop T.K. Wilson's child. I spent a few days in utter shock, not even calling my mother to tell her the news. I don't know, maybe I thought that if I didn't acknowledge it, it wouldn't actually be true. But of course it was true, and once the numbness wore off, I knew I had some serious decisions to make.

Could I be a single mother? I had done it before with my other two boys, but look how that turned out. They didn't even live with me now. Yes, I was a good mother, but when it came right down to it, those boys hit their teenage years with a vengeance and I didn't feel equipped to deal with them, so they went to live with their father. What if this baby I was carrying was another boy? Would he have to go live with his father too?

And that, of course, brought me to the biggest question of all: Was I going to tell the bishop that I was pregnant? There was always the option of abortion, I suppose. I could terminate the pregnancy, and the bishop would never even have to know I had been carrying his child. But no, I was a Christian woman, so it really wasn't even something I would consider. This child was coming into the world whether or not I was prepared.

The next idea that entered my mind was adoption. I could have the child easily enough. I had already stopped going to church, so it wouldn't be that hard to conceal my pregnancy from the bishop. It wasn't like he was dying to get in contact with me or anything. Shoot, I hadn't even heard from him since our last conversation, when he told me about him and Lisa Mae. As long as I didn't run into anyone from the church while my belly was swollen, word would never get back to him. Then I could have the baby and give it away, and he would be none the wiser.

I spent a few days and even more sleepless nights thinking about this option. For a while, it seemed to be the best choice. That way, I could get on with my life once the nine months were over, as if nothing had ever happened. I might even be able to forget about how close I came to being the bishop's woman, after enough time had passed.

Of course, in order to forget about him, I would never again be able to attend Bishop T.K. Wilson's church, never again set eyes on him. That was when I decided to visit some other area churches, to find a new spiritual home. One of those other churches, though, was the place where I realized I couldn't just have this baby without at least telling the bishop. The pastor at this church had just finished speaking about the need for positive black male role models for our children. He urged all the men in the church to stay active in the lives of not only their own children, but also those of their friends, family, and neighbors.

I started thinking about Bishop Wilson and his family. He had raised two children who became happy, successful adults. He was also a powerful role model in the lives of so many other children. Could I really deny this child the right to get to know this great man, its father? He might have wronged me and hurt me deeply, but Bishop T.K. Wilson was still a good man, and any child would be lucky to have him for a father.

When I went home that day and called my mother to finally tell her about it, she supported my decision, although her perspective was a little different from mine. She thought that he should be involved with the child and that I should convince him to kick Lisa Mae to the curb so I could marry him. I tried to tell her that wasn't happening, but my mother doesn't give up that easily. So, I said whatever she wanted to hear to get her off the phone, but in my heart I knew I wouldn't be trying to win him back. I did not want to humiliate myself by trying to force a relationship on a man who had made it clear I wasn't good enough to be by his side. No, I would just tell him the news, then leave the ball in his court.

The problem, of course, was that I had no way of knowing how he would react to the news. He had already proven that he was heavily influenced by the opinions of his church members. Would this weakness also guide his decisions when it came to an unborn child? I worried that I might tell him about this child only to get a rude awakening about the bishop's true character. Regardless of his possible reactions, though, I knew I had to tell him. It was the right thing to do. And if he rejected me and the child, I told myself, I could easily go back to my plan of finding a suitable family to adopt the child.

When I gathered my courage, I put on a loose-fitting dress to hide the first signs of a bulge in my abdomen, and headed for the church. It was probably the most conservative dress I had ever worn to church, and the irony was painful. If only they knew what had made me finally put on a dress that they would deem appropriate. Some of the most judgmental women might just keel over on the spot. But I didn't care. No matter how hard it would be, now that I was back, I would not let anyone chase me from my church home.

Yes, First Jamaica Ministries still felt like home. As I took the first steps into the church after what I thought had been a permanent exit, I was surprised by how good it felt to be there. I felt more at peace than I had in weeks. I got down on my knees in the quiet sanctuary and prayed to God, asking Him to watch over me and this unborn child, to forgive me for my past mistakes and to help me move forward into happiness and renewed devotion to Him.

When I finished my prayers, I got up from the pews and walked toward the administrative wing. The bishop and I were way overdue for a talk. I was nervous but determined, certain that in the end, God would work things out.

When I reached the door to the bishop's office, I saw that it was closed. I turned toward the door marked SECRETARY, wishing there were some other way I could do this. Sister Alison was the only person in the church who even had an inkling about why I had been away from church for so long. She was probably the last person I wanted to face now, especially since she'd spot the loose-fitting dress and guess the rest. But I couldn't worry about that. I had gathered the confidence to do this, and if I left now, I might never have the nerve to come back. I turned the doorknob slowly, took a deep breath, pasted a fake smile on my face, and walked in.

"Hey, Sister Alison," I said casually, as if the last time we spoke I hadn't spilled my guts to her.

Alison's head snapped back like she'd just seen a ghost. There was a flicker of something in her eyes that made me pause for a moment and wonder if I was making a mistake by being in there with her. But it passed quickly as she greeted me with what sounded like sincere enthusiasm.

"Sister Monique, where've you been? I been worried sick about you." She got up from behind her desk and gave me a huge hug and kiss. "I've been trying to get in touch with you for two weeks now. I thought you said you were going to start coming to church again."

She had been calling me ever since our conversation at the coffee shop. As a matter of fact, she'd left quite a few messages, and her concern was touching. She was a much sweeter person than I ever could have imagined. Still, while I was fretting over the decisions I had to make, I couldn't bring myself to return her calls. It was days before I could even speak to my own mother about it, so although I had poured my heart out to Alison once in the coffee shop, I just couldn't bring myself to confide in her again. I erased each of her messages as she left them.

"I'm sorry, Sister Alison. As you already know, I've had a lot on my mind lately. I kinda lost my way from God for a little while. But I think I've found my way back to Him now."

"Well, I'm sure He's glad to have you back. Has everything been confirmed?"

I wasn't quite sure what she meant at first, until she peeked around the corner like someone could be listening, then rubbed her belly.

"Has everything been confirmed?" she asked again.

"Oh, confirmed." I nodded my understanding as I gently touched my stomach. "Yes, everything's been confirmed." If she honestly didn't know, I guess I was wrong about my dress being a dead giveaway. This thought was actually comforting, because it meant that I wasn't showing yet. I might have a few weeks to attend services without the stares I would get once my belly popped out. Oh, who was I kidding? Those heifers had been giving me ugly looks forever, and that wasn't about to change.

"Have you decided what's best for you? You know, about um . . ." She scratched her head as she peeked out the door again.

There must be a lot of nosy people in this building because Sister Alison seemed pretty paranoid.

"I'm still praying on it, Sister Alison. I know God is helping me with the situation right now."

"Good . . . good. As long as you're okay. And just so you know, Monique, I'm keeping you lifted in my prayers also."

"Thanks, Alison. I really appreciate that. It's good to know somebody in my church family cares." As nice as that was, I was still eager to change the subject. "Have you seen the bishop?"

No sooner had the words left my mouth than Trustee Black appeared as if from thin air. Now I understood Sister Alison's concern about who might be listening. I was grateful that she hadn't spoken the word *pregnancy* out loud. I shot her a glance, hoping she understood how much I appreciated her discretion.

"Sister Monique," Trustee Black said in a very condescending tone. "The bishop's not in right now. He's been handling some personal business. Can I help you?"

I did my best to keep my tone civil. "No, I really need to see him. Do you know when he'll be back?" For all I knew, the bishop was behind his closed office door, and Trustee Black was just running interference to keep me away from him.

"Like I said, it's personal, so I'm not sure. But I'm glad you came by. I've wanted to talk to you for a while."

"Trustee, I really just came by to talk to the bishop." I felt like adding, "And I really don't want to talk to you." What in the world could he want to talk to me about?

"Please, Sister Monique, this will take only a moment." He glanced at Sister Alison, and a funny look passed over her face. Oh, my goodness, I thought, maybe she was thinking that Trustee Black was the father of my baby. After all, I did tell her the father was an important man. But depending on how my meeting with the bishop went, it might not be a bad thing for her to believe it was Trustee Black's child. That way, if the bishop and I came to some sort of amicable understanding and I was willing to keep his secret for a while, there would be no danger of Alison revealing anything. If she did decide to gossip, it would be Trustee Black's name she used.

"Okay." I gave him a friendly nod and waved good-bye to Sister Alison, then followed the trustee into his office.

He motioned for me to have a seat, then got straight to the

point. "Sister Monique, I just wanted to make sure everything between you and the bishop was all right."

I sat with my arms folded tightly and legs crossed, feeling ambushed. The way he asked the question made it obvious that he knew something, if not everything, about what had happened between me and the bishop. Well, he probably knew that we had slept together, but he had only heard the bishop's side of the story, so I'm sure he didn't know that his best friend had broken my heart. For all I knew, the two of them had a good laugh together about good old Sister Monique, who opened her legs so fast, a man could get whiplash. This wouldn't be the first time a man had disregarded my feelings. I decided that if he knew what had happened, there was no sense in beating around the bush.

"No, Trustee. I don't think everything between me and the bishop will ever be all right. . . . And I think you already knew that too."

His eyebrows rose to meet his hairline. "Really? And why is that, Sister Monique?"

I shook my head. "Don't let my large breast size fool you, Trustee. I'm not stupid. I know the bishop told you about our relationship, or friendship, whichever you prefer to call it. So, do me a favor and don't insult my intelligence, okay? Now, what do you want?"

"Fair enough, Sister Monique. I'll get right to the point. It was my understanding that the bishop said everything he needed to say to you. Do you feel there's more that needs to be said?"

"On the subject of him being weak and choosing a woman with his head and not his heart, I think he knows how I feel. But I do have something else to tell him. Something I think he needs to hear from me."

"Mind if I ask what?"

I had entered the church that day with such a sense of calm and really hadn't intended on unleashing my attitude, but this man was starting to piss me off. "Actually, I do mind, Trustee Black."

"Well, I'm sorry to hear that, because there's no telling how long the bishop's going to be taking care of his personal matter."

I rolled my eyes. "So what are you," I asked sarcastically, "his cleanup crew while he's away?"

He smirked at me. "If that's what you want to call me, then

fine, that's what I am. I helped him clean up his mistake with you by giving him a little nudge in Sister Lisa Mae's direction. You can hate me all you want, Sister Monique, but I'm telling you now that the bishop has made up his mind concerning his personal relationships. There is no chance of anything between the two of you."

Did he just call what happened between me and the bishop a mistake? My heart shattered as I imagined the bishop describing it to his friend as just that. Now I was pissed off.

"All right, Trustee," I began slowly, trying to control the angry tremor in my voice. "You're his best friend, and since you seem to think you should handle all of his personal matters, I guess you can give him a message for me."

"Okay, and what's that?"

I made sure he was looking me directly in the eyes. "Tell him I missed my period, and he's going to be a daddy." I folded my hands over my knee, then challenged the trustee with a look that said, "Now what?"

I'd never seen it before, but the man literally looked like he was choking on his words. "Huh?" he exploded. "What did you say?"

Enjoying his distress, I spoke louder and enunciated each word as if it were a dagger plunging repeatedly into his heart. "I. Said. Tell. Him. He's. Going. To. Be. A. Daddy."

The trustee lowered his head and tapped his forehead repeatedly against his desk. "Oh, dear Lord," he muttered before lifting his head to look at me. "Are you sure about this, Sister Monique?" His condescending attitude had vanished, and he sounded scared. You would have thought he was the one who got me pregnant. I relished the moment.

"Yes, I'm sure. I know when I have my period and when I don't. What, do you wanna see the plus sign on the home pregnancy test?"

"No, no, I believe you." His brow was creased with worry. "You realize this could get very complicated, don't you? Everyone in church knows he's seeing Lisa Mae Jones." He actually said it as if we were both part of some team whose only purpose in life was to preserve the bishop's reputation. The pathetic thing was that after everything that had happened, I was still harboring a soft place in my heart for the bishop and just might be willing to join that team.

"No, Trustee." I sighed, feeling disappointed in myself. As much as I wanted to hate the bishop, to feel indignation about the way I was treated, I couldn't bring myself to stop caring about him. "It's not going to get complicated. I care about the bishop, and I know he cares about me."

I had foolishly hoped, I suppose, that Trustee Black would confirm what I'd said, that the bishop did in fact care about me. My ego could have used that boost. But no, he was still stuck on the same note—his precious bishop's reputation. Trustee Black couldn't care less about me.

"And just how do you expect the bishop to react to such news?"

"Trustee, he can react any way he wants to. I have the final call on what happens with me and this baby. I just came to inform him because I thought a man of God would want to know he fathered a child."

"Well, what do you plan on doing? You're not going to keep the baby, are you?" Again, he wasn't concerned about the fact that the bishop had committed a sin, only that his precious congregation wouldn't view the indiscretion too kindly. He was making me sick.

"Keeping the child is an option," I told him, though I had pretty much decided that I couldn't do that. I was enjoying his worried expression.

"Sister Monique, you can't have a child by the bishop. You'd ruin his career. The man would never be able to preach again."

Suddenly, it dawned on me how serious this whole thing was. While I was enjoying watching Trustee Black squirm, the reality of the situation was not so easy to accept. The trustee was right. A scandal this big could cost the bishop his church, and I did not want to be the cause of that. In spite of how deeply he had hurt me, Bishop Wilson was a great leader, and First Jamaica Ministries was a great church. It would be in chaos without Bishop Wilson in charge. People needed—their spirits deserved—to be able to hear his message from the pulpit every Sunday. I didn't know if I could live with myself if I deprived so many people of God's word.

Tears rolled down my face. "Don't you think I know that? I don't want to hurt him, Trustee."

"Well, we've got to come up with some other options." His tone had softened just a bit, but I wasn't fooled. I knew that was only because he was starting to believe he could maybe convince me to come over to his side.

"Yes, we need options. That's why I'm here. I didn't want to take matters into my hands without at least talking to him. I know I have the final say, but I also have a conscience. The bishop has a right to know about the pregnancy as well as about what I decide to do with the baby. But that doesn't mean I plan on hurting him." Tears flowed freely as I thought about how he had hurt me.

"Well, what do you plan on doing?"

"I was thinking maybe adoption. We could find a good Christian home. There are plenty of people who'd want a newborn baby right here at First Jamaica." The idea to search for a suitable family within the church had just come to me, and I felt like maybe it was some sort of divine inspiration, the best solution for everyone involved. At least I felt that way until Trustee Black shut me down.

"Now, Sister Monique, let's be for real here for a second. You said you didn't want this to get complicated, and you didn't want to ruin the bishop's career, didn't you?" I nodded. "Now, do you really think that man would let someone else raise his child? A member of his church nonetheless?"

I remained silent as my mind turned around his words. He was telling me that the bishop would not support the idea of adoption for a child he conceived. But he'd already made it clear that the bishop wouldn't risk his career by accepting the child and raising it as his own. So, if he weren't going to raise it and he wouldn't let anyone else raise it, there seemed to be only one more option, one I had long ago decided was not a choice I could ever make. The trustee's voice was sinister as he confirmed what I was afraid he was trying to say.

"I think we both know there's a better solution . . . a more permanent solution. A solution that a woman who truly loves the bishop would choose under these circumstances."

Trustee Black wanted me to have an abortion! Would the

bishop really support the murder of this baby just to protect his reputation? "I think I should talk to him first," I sobbed.

"Well, don't worry about that," Trustee Black soothed. "I'll talk to him. What's important right now is that we take care of the situation." He pulled out his checkbook without waiting for my response. "Now, if I'm not mistaken, a procedure like that costs around five hundred dollars, correct?"

I looked at him wide-eyed and shrugged my shoulders, only slightly surprised that he expected me to know the answer to that question. My reputation was that bad, even if the rumors were incorrect. Contrary to popular belief, I'd never had an abortion.

He wrote out a check and handed it to me. "Here . . . this should cover it."

I took several long, deep breaths before I looked down at the check. It was written to cash in the amount of fifteen hundred dollars.

"This is too much," I said stupidly. I was so numb, I didn't even have the wherewithal to just hand the check back to him and storm from the office. I had let this man railroad me into a conversation about something I thought I could never even consider, and all I could do was tell him he'd given me too much money. When would I ever believe I deserved better from the men in my life?

"No, it's just enough for you to have your procedure and take a nice vacation. Jamaica is nice this time of the year. Have you ever been?"

"No," I answered, my voice sounding as vacant as my soul felt.

He smiled triumphantly and patted my shoulder. "Well, enjoy yourself."

28

BISHOP

"Bishop, when I'm in that studio, I feel like an entirely different person," Savannah said as she sat in my office during one of her counseling sessions with me. Her eyes were lit up. She stared off as if she were describing a dream instead of reality. "I mean, there's nothing that compares to the way I feel when I croon over a mike and even when I make my voice dance with full-hearted, strong notes in that sound booth. My music is important to me. That's what God put me on this earth to do. If I didn't know it before, then I know it now."

"Sister Savannah, I believe you're right. You and music are an undeniable pair," I said. "You definitely have talent. I know I hear you sing every Sunday at church, but when you were in that studio, it was like a special anointing was all over you. I don't remember the last time someone's singing moved me the way yours did in the studio."

She smiled. "Thank you, Bishop. And your support means a lot to me. I can't explain how much I really appreciate you."

"Well, I'm glad to know you're so passionate about singing. Your voice is an inspiration to many. I know when your father hears that demo, he won't be able to fight the tears back." As I had expected, Savannah's smile quickly vanished from her face. "Is something wrong, Sister Savannah?"

She dropped her head. "No, Bishop."

I hated to put rain over the cloud she was floating on, but after all, this was a counseling session. Considering that Deacon Dickens was one of the proudest fathers at First Jamaica Ministries, I knew he wouldn't keep Savannah's accomplishments from everyone, so she obviously hadn't let him in on her newfound career. If telling her father about her desire to make music was one of her biggest apprehensions, then it was my job as counselor to address the issue. Savannah had been trying to skate over the subject of her father since our session began.

"Sister Savannah, you suddenly went from glee to gloom. Was it something I said?"

"Well, uh, actually, Bishop," she stammered, "I haven't told my father about my song recordings yet." She looked in my face, apparently awaiting my reaction.

"I'm not gonna lie. I kind of felt that must have been the case. Your father and I communicate quite a bit. He would never keep something like this from me. Why on earth are you hesitant about telling him of your passion for singing?"

Savannah folded her arms across her chest, then started pouting. "A couple years ago, when I merely mentioned it, he hit the roof—ranting and raving about hoochie videos and bootie shaking." She shook her head. "But, Bishop, that's not me at all."

"Hmm . . . Deacon Dickens is a man of God. He has to understand that you won't be singing for the world but that you'll be singing for the Lord. I'm sure he has to know you wouldn't be gyrating while singing the Lord's praises."

"I don't know, Bishop. He must have thought something along that line. Plus, he said that many of his gospel favorites left singing praises for the Lord to sing secular music. He thinks if I record gospel, the right scout will come along with the right price to convince me into the ways of the world."

I certainly believed everything Savannah said. For as long as I'd known Deacon Joe, he'd been grounded in the Lord. But, as a parent, I knew we can't live our children's lives for them. After raising them right, prayer and trust are all we can do to keep from going crazy over some of the decisions they make. What I couldn't believe was that the deacon had no confidence in the way he'd brought up Savannah.

"Have you ever asked your father to just have some faith in you?" I asked.

"Yes, but nothing alters the way he thinks."

"And how do you feel about what he thinks?"

"Nothing pleases me more than praising the Lord. Secular music isn't for me. My heart is with writing and singing gospel. My voice belongs to Him."

"Then maybe you should try talking to your father about it

again, and tell him the same thing you just told me. I'm convinced your heart is where it belongs."

"No, Bishop. I just don't see trying to have that conversation with him again."

"Well, Sister, he can't be kept in the dark forever. You're his daughter. I know how I would feel if my children kept something so important from me. You need his love and support. At some point or another he'd have to come around."

Savannah sat back in her chair. "I can't do it. Maybe you should try telling him I need him," she said. "As a matter of fact, Bishop, that might not be a bad idea."

"Oh, no, Savannah," I said quickly, shaking my head. "That's not my battle."

She paused for a moment. "Bishop, I don't know if the battle is mine, either. It's the Lord's. I sing for Him, so maybe I ought to just let Him tell my father."

"Oh, Sister Savannah." I laughed. "I don't think that's quite the interpretation the Lord had in mind."

She had to laugh herself. "I know, Bishop, and I'm going to tell my father, I promise," she said as she stood up. "But not tonight. I've got a song in my head that I need to get home to put on paper."

"Well," I said, standing, "in our next session, I can't wait to hear about your father's response to finding out about your future successful singing career," I hinted.

"Oh, Bishop," she said, reaching out and grabbing my hand. I looked down in time to watch her other hand stroke the back of my hand.

When I looked up at her, our eyes locked. In order to brush over the somewhat awkward moment, I said, "But in the meantime, if there's anything else I can help you with—"

"As a matter of fact, Bishop," she said quickly, cutting me off. She looked down at her hands caressing mine, then dropped them to her sides. "There is something you can help me with. Well, not actually me, but a friend of mine."

"A friend," I said with a raised eyebrow and peculiar look on my face.

"Yes, Bishop," she said, taking a seat again. "You see, there's this friend of mine and she sort of has a crush on this man." She looked embarrassed, then stopped herself. "Maybe I shouldn't call it a crush. I mean, she's much too old for a crush." Savannah blushed. "But my friend really likes this man, and she *thinks* that he likes her too."

"Thinks? So you're, uh, I mean your *friend*, hasn't told this person how she feels about him?"

"No, because she doesn't want to embarrass herself." She looked down. "She's never approached a man about such feelings before, and the fact that he's someone she admires makes things more difficult for her. She really looks up to him."

"I guess I can understand her being reluctant. No one likes embarrassment. But maybe there's nothing to be embarrassed about. Are you sure he's never expressed stronger feelings for her?"

She continued to look down as she shook her head. "No, their relationship started off with him being someone she could get advice from. But now she thinks she's fallen in love with this man. She's pretty sure he likes her, but I believe she'll do anything to have him love her as much as she loves him."

Talk about the covers being pulled off someone. But here it felt like Savannah was pulling the covers off herself and that she was sitting before me butt naked in that chair. I mean, it was more than obvious who this so-called friend was and who the man she admired was. I believe Savannah even sensed I knew what she was trying to say. She clearly was looking for a positive reaction from me, but she'd caught me by surprise. I tried to think of a quick response, but I was stumped.

"Well, uh," I finally said, loosening my tie. I tried not to look uncomfortable with the conversation, but I know I failed. The only thing that helped me was, Savannah didn't have the courage to look me in the eye for an extended period of time. "Is this man that your friend is in love with . . . is he a man of God—assuming that your friend is a woman of God."

"Oh, he's definitely a man of God, one of the Lord's servants indeed. He doesn't know it, but she's extremely attracted to this side of him too. She loves everything he represents and all that he's about."

Lord have mercy. I was at a loss for words, but fortunately I was able to scrape a few up. "Well, I think you should pray on it . . . for your friend, that is. Pray for your friend. God knows all of our hearts, and I'm sure He has someone in store for her. You know He always delivers on time."

"But, Bishop, isn't it kind of unfair for her to hide her feelings from this man? Shouldn't she at least try to talk to him? Who knows? Maybe God wants them to be together. They won't know until an effort has been made. This man is very caring. If she stresses how she feels, he might be willing to give them a try."

For some reason, my tie didn't feel loose enough at that moment. I pulled on it some more, clearing my throat and mentally pleading for God's help. "You're right, Sister Savannah. Who knows? But hold off on talking to your friend about her developing more than a platonic relationship with this man. If it's meant to be, God will lead their hearts together. In the meantime, I still think you should just pray for your friend. That's the best thing you can do for her right now."

"You're right, Bishop," she said, standing again and throwing her arms up like she felt silly. "Prayer is always the answer." Looking into Savannah's face, I could see she was embarrassed. She began to hurry toward the door. "Well, I better go. And thank you for everything, Bishop."

"Uh, you're quite welcome," I said, standing to see her out, still a little stumped by the subject of our last conversation. "See you later."

"Yes, Bishop. And tell Marlene I asked about her," she said as she exited my office.

"Whew," I said as I walked back over to my desk and sat down in my chair. "Oh, boy, I sure wasn't expecting that one."

29

LISA

After stopping by a liquor store, Loretta and I sat parked down the street from the bishop's house, opposite the direction in which T.K. would have to travel to reach the church for the deacons' board meeting. We were waiting so long that I was starting to think he was skipping the meeting to be with his crackhead baby momma like he'd done so many other times during the past few weeks. I was getting tired of her real quick, and it was taking all my self-control not to just jump out of my car and bang on his door and demand that he kick her out. Fortunately, Loretta was there to cool me down enough that I could wait with my anger on a low simmer rather than a full boil.

"Lisa, I know you're mad, but remember who you are. You do not want your man witnessing you showing your ass. He needs to believe you support what he's doing for that crackhead. Then when he catches her using drugs again, she's the one showing her ass, and you can be the concerned girlfriend there to soothe his disappointment. So keep your ass in this car. He'll be coming out any minute now."

Loretta was right too. At the last minute, his garage door opened and he pulled out into the street. We watched him drive in the direction of the church; then both of us knew it was time to put Operation Crackhead into motion. I was determined to show my beloved T.K. Marlene's true colors.

"You ready?" Loretta started the engine and put the car in drive.

"Ready to take my man back from that crackhead? Loretta, I've never been more ready for anything in my entire life," I told her as she drove slowly up to his house.

We glanced at each other quickly, then got out of the car and headed up the walkway. Marlene answered the door a few seconds after we knocked. She looked much better than the last time I saw her. No more rat's nest on top of her head; her hair looked smooth and shiny. Her face had filled out, as had her hips, and she wore clean, well-fitting clothes. None of this made me very happy. She'd risen so far in such a short time; maybe it wouldn't be so easy to get her back on crack.

Marlene greeted us cheerfully. "Well, hello, Sister Lisa Mae, Sister Loretta. I'm sorry, but Thomas Kelly isn't in right now." Lord, I hated it when she called him that. Why couldn't she recognize that he wasn't the same man she knew when they were kids in Virginia? He was Bishop T.K. Wilson, for goodness sake!

I smiled at her while I imagined putting my hands around her neck, but when I spoke, I was sure not to give away my true feelings. "That's okay, Marlene. We're not here to see T.K.," I said sweetly. "We're here to see you." I extended my hands and held out a medium-sized box with a pink bow on top. Marlene looked down at the box but didn't reach for it. I saw the hesitation in her eyes. This definitely wasn't going to be as easy as I thought.

"Go ahead, Marlene," Loretta urged her. "It's a gift from Lisa Mae and me. Nothing special, but I'm sure you'll enjoy it nonetheless."

Marlene stared at the box as she took it from my hands. I really couldn't blame her for being a little suspicious about me bringing her a gift. After all, the last time I stopped by, I'm sure she could tell that I was not happy. Not only did T.K. have Marlene living with him, but he also had Savannah Dickens supposedly helping him with her recovery. T.K. seemed oblivious to my feelings, but women sense these things about other women, so I know that Savannah and Marlene knew how I really felt.

"Well, thank you, but I—"

"No need to thank us, Marlene," I interrupted. I was not about to let her refuse now that I'd set my plan in motion. "Besides, you're family . . . church family, so we just want you to know that you have our support."

"Go ahead and open it," Loretta insisted.

Marlene lifted the lid off the box and pulled out the package inside. The muscles in her jaw relaxed a bit. I guess she'd been expecting to find a poisonous snake or something. Come to think of it, that wouldn't be a bad way to see her go . . .

"This is nice, ladies. Thank you." Marlene interrupted my morbid fantasy.

"T.K. told me how much you like tea," I said.

"Yeah, I really do. Will you ladies join me for some?" And just like that, we were in. I would have to thank Loretta later for the great idea of bearing gifts when we came to set our trap.

Marlene led us into the kitchen. I liked the wench better when she didn't have any manners. I couldn't stand the idea that she was escorting us through T.K.'s house like she owned it. God, I couldn't wait to get rid of her junkie behind.

"The bishop has such a lovely house," Loretta said as she took a seat at the kitchen table. "And it was so nice of him to open it up to you during a bad time."

"Yes, it was." Marlene stared off into space for a minute as if she were daydreaming about my man, whose heart was too big for his own good. T.K. had a heart so big that he couldn't see this crack whore for what she really was. But all that was about to change.

"I appreciate the two of you taking your time to bring me all these different teas," Marlene said as she pulled out the pot. "I mean, I drink regular ol' Lipton mostly, but when I got a few extra dollars, I like to splurge a little."

Thank God her back was turned to Loretta and me so that she couldn't see us laughing our asses off at her. The woman had no class. I was starting to wonder why I ever saw her as a threat in the first place, but then I reminded myself that she was T.K.'s first love. Whether or not she had class, a man's first love always holds a special place in his heart.

Loretta nodded to let me know it was time for my show. "Um, Marlene, dear," I said politely, "why don't you sit down at the table and let me take over? Loretta has a brother who has struggled with a crack addiction for years, and she'd like to talk with you, if you don't mind. Maybe you could offer some insight for her and her family, since you seem to be doing so well now."

Marlene set the pot on the stove, then walked over to the table. "Well, I don't know how much help I could be, but okay. At least I can start off by listening." She took a seat while I took over preparing the tea.

Loretta began to go into a fictitious spiel about how her brother had been smoking crack cocaine on and off again and how she just didn't know what she could do to help him. When the water came to a boil, I took the pot off the stove. Marlene was so engrossed in Loretta's tale that she didn't even seem to notice the kettle whistling. That was good. Then she wouldn't be watching me as I lifted up my long, loose shirt, removed a tiny bottle of brandy from each front pants pocket, and poured them into an oversized coffee mug. The smell was strong, so I had to think of something quick.

"Excuse me, ladies. I don't mean to interrupt, but I was wondering, Marlene," I rambled. "Do you mind if I mix the cherry flavor with the chamomile? There's only one sample of each flavor, but the packets are only strong enough for two servings. Two packets should be enough for all three of us."

"Cherry and chamomile?" Marlene asked, wrinkling her nose at the sound of the awful combination.

"Oh, it will be fine," I said. "I've done it many times before."

"Well, since you know what you're doing, go ahead."

Loretta continued chattering to distract Marlene as I finished the tea. "Here you ladies go," I said, setting three cups on the table in front of them. "Marlene, you go ahead and take the larger mug."

"Oh, no, that would be rude of me. One of you ladies take it, please," Marlene said. Oh, so not only was she clean, but the heifer also had some manners now, too, huh? Ooh, I couldn't wait to get her out of here.

"Don't be silly, Marlene. The tea was supposed to be for you to enjoy, so you should have the larger cup."

"You didn't have to do that, but thank you," she said as she lifted the large mug and took a sip. I held my breath, waiting for her response. If she tasted the brandy, our plan would fail, and I might be in big trouble with T.K. She swallowed, then frowned slightly, but at least she didn't spit it out.

"Oh, Marlene, I forgot to mention, you shouldn't let the superior taste fool you. The two flavors mixed together will shock the taste buds at first, but keep drinking. You'll fall in love with it," I said to reassure her.

By the time I had taken my first sip, Marlene was humming. "Mmm, you're right. This mixture is good."

Well, that was even easier than I could have hoped, I thought with satisfaction.

We made plenty of small talk while we watched Marlene finish her special tea.

"Marlene, do you ever jones?" Loretta asked.

She looked surprised when the conversation abruptly returned to drugs. "What do you mean?" she asked. Oh, please, I thought, she knew exactly what Loretta meant.

"I mean for crack," Loretta explained, although it was obvious Marlene was just acting. "I understand you're clean and all, but my brother has explained why he's relapsed so many times. He says he can't seem to get rid of that jones feeling he often gets." Loretta began to describe her brother's cravings—or at least what he might have told her if she really had a brother who was an addict. She made the high sound so enticing that it was as if she were a paid advertiser for the crack industry. "He says all he can think of is experiencing the ultimate high that comes in less than ten seconds of taking in that smoke. Then for ten minutes, he's on cloud nine, but ready to get the next hit after that. He says if he can't get that next hit immediately, he's restless, irritable, and will stop at nothing to get the next taste in his system."

Shoot, by the time Loretta finished talking, even my throat was dry. Loretta's description had obviously affected Marlene, too, because she started taking even bigger sips from her laced tea, apparently unable to respond. Loretta finished her cup, then asked if she could be excused to use the bathroom.

"Sure. I'll show you where it is." Marlene set her glass down and stood.

Loretta stopped her. "No, no, you can just point me in the right direction. I'll find it from here. Sit back down and finish your tea with Lisa." She winked at me.

"Okay. Go out the kitchen to your right. It's the first door on your left."

"Thank you," Loretta said as she disappeared around the corner.

Marlene returned to her seat and immediately picked up her mug again. She was quiet, probably busy thinking about that ultimate high Loretta had reminded her of. I let her reminisce for a few minutes, then figured I better make some idle conversation with her to end the awkward silence.

"Marlene, we just want you to know that you are a sister of

the church, and we are here for you," I said. "And I hope you will take Loretta and me up on attending Bible study with us tomorrow evening."

"Well, I'll have to get back to you on that. Thomas Kelly, Sister Savannah, and I have Bible study here." Marlene stared off again. "I swear I don't know what I would do without that man in my life."

I imagined jumping across the table and tearing her apart, one limb at a time, but as I looked at her eyes and noticed they were becoming slightly glazed, I knew I could afford to just sit back and watch. It was only a matter of time before Marlene would do herself in.

From her silence, it was clear she had a lot on her mind. So, I made certain to add to her troubles. "Would you look at this," I said, pointing on the floor. "How'd this *crack* get down here?"

Marlene jumped to my side of the table. "Huh? Where?"

"See. Right here." I traced my finger over a broken piece of tile. "It's *cracked*. I wonder how this happened. I'll have to mention it to T.K. when I see him."

I looked up at Marlene and felt satisfied. When I saw how uncomfortable she appeared just from having heard the word *crack*, I knew that Loretta's plan would work. Once she found the other little gift that Loretta had just left for her in the bathroom, Marlene would be on a fast trip right back into the gutter—and out of my man's house.

Loretta stepped into the kitchen, relieving me of the responsibility to further entertain the pathetic little being. "Well, Lisa Mae, are you about ready to go?" she asked.

"I'm ready when you are," I replied.

"Fine, then I'm all set."

"Well, Marlene," I said, rising, "it's been an absolute pleasure."

"Same here," she said as she escorted us to the door, her steps a little less steady than they were when we'd arrived. "We'll have to do this again sometime."

"Yes, but hopefully next time it will be in your own apartment," I said, then quickly softened my tone. "I mean, because you'll be drug-free and strong and independent."

"God willing," Marlene said.

"You take care," Loretta told her. "And you keep on keepin'

on. We're so proud of you, Marlene. We know how hard recovery can be for a drug addict."

"We'll be praying for you," I said right before Marlene said her final farewell to us, then closed the door.

"So, did you leave it in the bathroom?" I asked anxiously as we walked to the car.

"I left it right there on the sink," Loretta answered, pulling out her keys.

"How can we be so sure she's going to go in the bathroom and find it?"

"Oh, don't worry," Loretta assured me as she unlocked the car and opened the driver's side door. "We fed her so much tea, I'm sure she's in the bathroom this very moment, fixin' to cook up her real surprise. And you can damn sure bet it ain't no chamomile tea!"

30

MARLENE

I closed the door behind Lisa Mae and Loretta, then made my way back into the kitchen, glad to be rid of them. I know I was supposed to be trying to be a churchwoman now, so God forgive me, but I couldn't stand either one of them. My instincts told me to steer clear of certain women, and Lisa Mae and Loretta were at the top of the list. I didn't have a clue what Thomas Kelly saw in that uppity Lisa Mae. And I didn't know who Loretta thought she was fooling with that "I've got a brother who's on crack" crap, but it sure as hell wasn't me. I got ten dollars right now that says she didn't even have a brother. As far as I was concerned, I knew they were both phonies since the day I saw them campaigning for Thomas Kelly's love like it was some kind of political prize.

In spite of their visit, I was feeling pretty good when I got back to the kitchen table. I reached for my Bible and began to read. Thomas Kelly said his meeting would be short and that he would be home early, and I was looking forward to his return. I couldn't wait to tell him about the positive things that were happening to me with his and Savannah's help. I had to give them credit, I thought as I reread an inspiring passage. This whole God and Jesus thing was really intoxicating. As I sat there and read, I actually felt like I had a little buzz.

I enjoyed a few more passages, then realized I had to pee. That fancy tea those two phonies had brought me would probably have me in the bathroom all night. Lisa Mae might as well have given me the entire pot with that sixteen-ounce cup she gave me. Who ever heard of mixing chamomile and cherry together anyway? Give me some plain old Lipton any day.

I relieved myself in the bathroom, then went to the sink to

wash my hands. Looking in the mirror, my reflection made me smile. I had only been in recovery a couple of weeks, and already I looked healthier. My cheeks didn't look so hollow, and my skin was returning to its natural tone. But then I ran my hand through my coarse hair and my smile disappeared. My hair was the one feature that still reminded me of how far I had fallen. At one time it was manageable, but after months of smoking crack and not taking care of it, the texture had changed into something fierce—something I dreaded and despised putting a comb through.

If only I could do something with my hair, I thought. Tanisha had promised to send Thomas Kelly some money so that I could get it done. Her friend, Niecy, could probably hook it up with little to no problem. That girl was good. As soon as Tanisha sent the money, I would call Niecy for an appointment. It was time for my outside appearance—all of it—to reflect the positive changes I was making inside. Thomas Kelly would be proud of me when I sat in the front pews at First Jamaica Ministries.

I reached down to shut off the water and dry my hands, and that's when my heart almost stopped. I blinked several times, thinking my vision wasn't clear as I gazed at the object lying on the counter beside the sink. Were my eyes playing tricks on me? It couldn't be what I thought it was—ten nickels of crack. Maybe I was hallucinating, I thought, but as I leaned in closer to focus on what lay before me, I saw that my eyes hadn't been lying to me at all. What lay before me was definitely crack. But how had it gotten there?

I tried to look away but found it impossible to stop my gaze from wandering back there again and again, as though the crack might disappear if I didn't keep an eye on it. And that's what worried me. I didn't know how the stuff had come into Thomas Kelly's house, but I didn't want it gone. Suddenly, all the sensations that came along with my urge to get high were starting to overwhelm me: the sweat on my brow, the telltale itch in my arms that I could never quite scratch away. With a shaking hand, I reached for the crack. Only when my fingertips reached the plastic bag did I pull back.

Maybe this was some sort of test. Maybe Thomas Kelly had left the crack there to test my strength. Or what about Savannah? Would she do something like this? Perhaps it was even God Himself who put this ultimate temptation in front of me. I turned toward the door, expecting to see Thomas Kelly or Savannah standing there, but the doorway was empty.

My soul knew I was supposed to run from that bathroom without looking back, get as far away from that poison as I could. But my body wasn't ready to let go just yet. I turned back to the sink, staring longingly at the small plastic bags. My thoughts traveled through the series of events that might come to pass. What would happen if I picked up that bag and just took one hit? Maybe I had come far enough in my recovery that I could just take a hit and then be strong enough to get rid of the rest. You know, just one hit for old times' sake. Or maybe not. Maybe I would take that first hit, and just like all the other times, that first hit would only leave me wanting that feeling again, and I'd keep going until I'd smoked up the very last bag.

I cursed myself for my weakness. When I sat at the table reading Bible verses just a few minutes before, I'd felt a little buzz. Why couldn't that be enough for me? I wanted to be able to just march back into the kitchen and sit down with God's word as my comfort, the desire for drugs totally gone. That was probably what God wished for me, too, but first I had to pass this test He'd put in front of me. I wasn't feeling too confident about resisting this temptation.

As I wondered why God would test me this way, I had a sudden sickening realization about how this had all come to pass. And I had let the devils into the house! Considering ten nickels had just happened to land in Thomas Kelly's bathroom, ten nickels that weren't there just an hour before, I now understood that God had allowed Lisa Mae and Loretta to step into His work. There was no longer a doubt in my mind about where the drugs came from.

I screamed toward the ceiling, "Lord, You know I'm weak! Why? Why, Lord? You know me better than I know myself. Why would You put this burden on me when You know I can't handle it?" I was near tears, but I was also angry, bitter about the test God was putting me through. "I guess if this is my cross to bear, then I better carry it, huh?" The tears began to rapidly flow.

Somewhere in the deep recesses of my soul, I knew God would give me strength, but it was as if my body weren't ready to accept his blessing. Those plastic bags were calling me louder than God's love. I could hear God telling me to turn and walk away, that He would never forsake me, but my body was pleading with me to answer the call of the drugs. It was a spiritual warfare, and I felt my resolve weakening. Through a steady stream of tears, I looked up one last time.

"If You're half of everything I've learned of You, I'll still be Your child, and You'll still love me."

I wiped my tears and reached out to pick up one of the bags, staring at the dried-up, soapy-looking substance that to me was more beautiful than a handful of pearls. I scooped up all the bags, barely able to breathe. Every inch of my body was telling me I needed a hit. Words can't truly describe the ecstasy of what I was expecting from this first hit, but it's like the best orgasm you've ever had, with the intensity and pleasure multiplied by ten. It's just an unbelievable experience, and I couldn't wait to feel it again. My mouth felt like a desert, and my hands shook wildly. Fuck it. If this had been some kind of a test, then I'd just failed.

Quickly moving to the kitchen, I tore the place up looking for some foil and a match. I found the aluminum foil in the cupboard and a box of ten-inch wooden matches in the drawer next to the stove. The wooden spoon was in the sink. I sat down at the table. I pushed my Bible and all the religious papers I'd been reading to the floor to make room for my paraphernalia.

I wrapped a piece of foil around the wooden spoon's handle, shaping it to my liking, then slid it off and looked through the tube I'd created. It wasn't the most ideal stem, but it was good enough to get me high. I opened one of the nickel bags and removed the largest rock, placing it at the tip of the tinfoil, then struck a match. I hadn't touched the flame to the rock yet, but just that familiar sulfur smell from a lit match had me excited. I could already feel how good it was going to be. I leaned over, bringing the stem closer to the flame. The anticipation was intense, but before I could inhale that first glorious hit, Thomas Kelly's voice boomed in my ear, making me drop the match.

"What the hell are you doing? Dear Father God, I know this woman is not smoking that stuff in my house!"

I immediately dropped the stem. My first instinct was to protect the crack, so I reached for the bags, pulling them close.

Thomas Kelly didn't waste a second. "Give it to me!" He rushed toward the table, his hand outstretched with palm up, expecting me to give him the drugs just like that.

I was shaking with fear. Thomas Kelly had always been a big man, but right now he looked like a giant, with a voice to match. I could see the anger burning behind his eyes and the tension straining to be released through his bulging neck muscles. Right now he was not a man to be played with.

"It's not what it looks like," I protested weakly. My mind raced as I tried to come up with a way out of this situation with the crack still in my possession. I gripped the plastic bags tightly in one hand and the tinfoil stem in the other as I watched Thomas Kelly to see what his next move would be.

He took a step closer. "Then what is it? 'Cause it sure looks like you're in my house about to get high."

I glanced at the stem in my hand, then put it behind my back as if Thomas Kelly hadn't already seen it. "Naw, I wasn't," I lied hopelessly, though I couldn't think of any other explanation to offer. "I told you it's not what it looks like."

"Don't lie to me, Marlene. Not after everything I've done for you." He stepped closer and grabbed my wrist. Although I kept my fist closed, parts of the plastic bags peeped through my fingers. "Why did you bring this stuff into my house?"

"I didn't bring it in here. Lisa Mae and her friend Loretta brought it in here."

He grabbed my shoulders, and for a brief moment, I really thought he might rear back and hit me if he loosened his vicelike grip. "You know what?" he began in a voice that expressed both fury and disgust. "I want you out of my house. If you're going to make up lies like that, you can't stay here. Get out."

"I ain't lying," I protested as the reality of my situation sunk in. I was about to be homeless if I couldn't convince Thomas Kelly to give me another chance. "They came over just after you left. Please, Thomas Kelly, you think I had time to go to the other side of town to get crack, then be back before you got here? I swear to you that Lisa Mae and Loretta brought it here."

"So, they just brought it here for you to get high, right? Just handed it to you like they were bringing over a cake or something, right? They didn't want to get high with you; they just wanted to bring you some crack. Do you realize how that sounds? Just admit that you called one of your old dealers to bring it to you."

"Thomas Kelly, I've been broke since I got here. Where do you think I would get money to buy drugs?"

"I don't know where you got it from. Maybe you didn't even pay with money," he said with a small shudder, "but Lord knows I'm not trying to figure it out. I just know you said you wanted help, but it's obvious to me you just came here for a place to stay. You're not going to lay up in my house and smoke that stuff, Marlene."

"Thomas Kelly, that's not my intention. You've got to believe me."

He ignored my pleas as he pulled me roughly out of the chair.

"Please, Thomas Kelly. Look at me. Can't you see how much I've changed since I've been here? If I was still using that stuff, I would still look like it."

His eyes went straight to my hair, the dry, unhealthy tangles a reminder of my addiction. Then he changed his focus to the drugs I was still clutching. "You know what? It doesn't matter how they got here. What matters is that you're clutching them in your hand when you should be holding the Bible." With one strong hand he pushed me toward the kitchen door, and with the other he reached for the bags in my hand. "Get out, Marlene."

Something came over me, sending me into a mad fit. I wrestled with Thomas Kelly, trying to retrieve the plastic bags he now held. A few of them fell to the floor. We scrambled vigorously, each trying to keep the other from getting the bags first. Although I managed to collect two of the bags, Thomas Kelly's strength was too much for me. I gave up on the others.

He stood up, panting vigorously from our struggle. "Get out!" he screamed ferociously.

"Thomas Kelly, please! I swear to God I didn't bring that stuff into your house."

"Don't swear to my God and lie."

"Thomas Kelly, please don't kick me out. I wanna get clean."

"Yeah, right. You wanna get clean, but I walk in here less than two hours after leaving you alone to find you with a ready-made stem, about to destroy whatever brain cells you have left."

By now I was sobbing. "Thomas Kelly, I don't have to remind you how hard it is for a recovering addict to resist temptation. I know it's been years, but you have firsthand knowledge. You remember . . ." I brought my tears under control and pleaded with him to recall what it was like, to understand how difficult this was for me. "I know you remember. I'm not trying to defend what you saw when you walked in here. I only want you to believe what's in my heart. I'm an addict—a struggling one. But, please, whatever you do, don't put me out like this. Thomas Kelly, you gotta help me."

He grabbed my shoulders harshly again. "Ever since the day you knocked on my back door asking for help, I've wanted nothing more than to see you get clean. Today, I've been made to feel I was a fool for letting you in here." He squeezed tighter, as if he were trying to crush bone. "Look me in the eyes and tell me you don't wanna get high."

I stared at him, knowing I couldn't deny how much I wanted a hit. If I admitted my weakness, he might just give me one final shove out the door, but I had no choice. He would see right through my lies anyway. And besides, I felt like I owed him the truth after all he had done for me and my kids.

"I won't lie anymore, Thomas Kelly. I do wanna get high . . ." When he didn't make an immediate move toward the door, I continued. "But I want to get clean even more."

He was unmoved by my words and replied harshly as he took a step closer to the door. "That sounds real good, Marlene, but actions speak louder than words."

He was right. Thomas Kelly had every reason to distrust me after what he had just witnessed. But I knew that just as the devil had sent Lisa Mae and Loretta into my path to test me, God had sent Thomas Kelly and Savannah to me, to guide me back onto the right track. I couldn't let Lisa Mae and Loretta win. It was up to me to accept God's gift, and there was only one way to prove myself to Thomas Kelly.

"You're right, Thomas Kelly, actions do speak louder than words." I reached over and dropped the drugs into his waiting hands, and he wrapped his strong arms around me, holding me as I cried.

31

MONIQUE

Sitting nervously now in the abortion clinic, I couldn't shake the feeling that I was in a butcher shop, waiting for my turn to get slaughtered on the chopping board. My fingernails dug into the padding on the chair arms as I willed myself to stay seated, to not run screaming out the door. It had not been easy to reach the decision that brought me to this place, and now it was even harder to make myself stay put.

After my conversation with Trustee Black, I had left the church an emotional mess. I had raced home and thrown myself across the bed, where I lay for hours, unable to comprehend how my life had spiraled so out of control. Not too long ago, I had been pretty content with my life. Sure, I was single and didn't necessarily want to be, but at least my life was uncomplicated. I went to church every Sunday, where I had perfected the art of ignoring the women's jealous stares and enjoyed the attention of the many men who admired my good looks. Now I was carrying the bishop's child, wondering if I would ever be able to show my face at the church again. Even worse, I worried that I was actually leaning toward the solution that Trustee Black had suggested, endangering my soul for eternity.

Before I'd spoken to Trustee Black, I thought that I would never consider abortion. Taking the life of an unborn child was just not right for a Christian woman. But Trustee Black had convinced me that there were really no other options. The bishop didn't want me, and from what his friend James had said, he wouldn't really want our child, either. When it came right down to it, I had to make a choice between myself and the bishop. I could either have the child, then sit back and watch the ensuing controversy destroy the bishop and First Jamaica Ministries, or I could make the ultimate sacrifice. In the end, I decided I would rather condemn my soul to burn in hell for eternity than to hurt Bishop T.K. Wilson.

As I reached this heartbreaking conclusion, I lay crying, soaking my bedcovers with salty tears until I drifted into a fitful sleep. When I awoke a while later, the room was dark and evening had arrived. A knock at my door forced me to finally lift my body off the bed.

I was shocked to see Sister Alison at the door, but my heart ached so badly that I didn't even stop to think before I invited her in and began to unload my painful story. Only when she asked me again who the child's father was did I hold back. If I were having an abortion to protect the bishop, then I would have to take his identity to the grave with me.

"I'm sorry, Sister Alison. You've been such a good listener, and I appreciate how kind you've been to me through all of this, but I just can't tell you who he is. I know it might sound crazy to protect a man who doesn't even want me, but then you'll just have to call me crazy. I can't reveal his name because I don't want to do anything to hurt this man."

To my relief, Sister Alison did not push me any harder. I don't know if she agreed with my determination to protect him, but she respected the decision as mine to make. Even more amazing to me, she refused to pass judgment even when I tearfully admitted that I was planning to have an abortion. Her eyes grew wide, and I don't know, maybe she had to work hard to bite her tongue, but I appreciated the fact that she did so. She didn't utter one word to try to convince me to change my mind. She just held my hand and listened, and when I was done, she said quietly, "I'll come with you if you want."

So now we were sitting together in the abortion clinic in Long Island City, where the chances of running into anyone from the church were slim. Although Sister Alison had made the journey with me and occasionally reached out to pat my hand, I still felt alone. I scanned the waiting room, where nearly two dozen women sat in silence. One couple looked like they were barely out of diapers themselves. Some appeared to be grandmothers who had come to their senses and realized that it was ridiculous to be pregnant at the same time as their daughters. There was even one woman who was visibly pregnant and would definitely be going under general anesthesia for her termination, if they allowed her to have one at all. She was so far along that if they didn't hurry up and call her number, she'd spit that baby out right there in the waiting room.

"Are you okay?" Sister Alison asked me as she took my hand in hers.

I had come to consider her a true friend. She'd been there with me every step of the way, consistently offering support, even when I didn't think I wanted it or needed it. During the ten days since I'd made the decision to have an abortion, she'd comforted me, listened to me, and even cried with me. She knew that I had decided this was the best choice, so even when I'd waffled a bit and considered backing out, she helped me stay strong. If this was the decision I had reached after careful thought, she said, then it was probably the best decision for me. "Don't second-guess yourself," she said. I considered this to be pretty amazing, since many others would have tried talking me out of abortion. Sister Alison kept her judgments to herself and supported me, and I appreciated her for that.

"Yeah, I'm okay," I said listlessly. "But no, I guess . . ." I sighed. "I don't know. How am I supposed to feel?"

"Maybe it's just the picketers out there carrying those signs with the disgusting pictures of aborted babies that got to you. I know they got to me."

"Yeah, maybe that's it," I half-heartedly agreed.

Or maybe, I thought, it was the fact that I really didn't want to be having an abortion. What I really wanted was to be with T.K. right now, joyously anticipating the birth of our first child and making plans for many happy years together. But those things were fantasies, no longer options, and they hadn't been since that day in T.K.'s office when he told me about Lisa Mae.

"How I feel right now doesn't really matter, Sister Alison," I informed her. "It's just something I have to do." I held back the tears that were threatening to escape.

"Well, what has the father said about all this? I wish you would just go ahead and tell me who he is."

"Sister Alison, please," I said, irritated that she would choose now to start badgering me for that information. I thought I had already made it clear why I couldn't tell her his name.

"I'm sorry, Sister Monique, but I just want to make sure that you have really thought this thing through, because you know once you're in there," she said, pointing toward the examination rooms, "there's no turning back."

I was taken aback by her statement. Not once in the days leading up to this office visit had she advised me to rethink my decision, but now when I needed support the most, she wasn't offering it so freely. Maybe those abortion posters outside really had *her* shaken up. I was glad I had looked the other way when we passed by them.

She's right, I thought sadly, *I can't do this. I can't do this.* But I had to do it. Keeping this baby would mean destroying T.K.'s life. I loved him too much to ever hurt him like that.

Then a thought entered my mind. It wasn't the first time I'd considered it, but I had rejected the idea long ago. Maybe I could find a way to keep the baby without T.K. ever knowing. Trustee Black was the only person in the church who knew, and he would certainly keep it a secret from the bishop if he could. Yeah, I could come up with a way to keep the news from spreading throughout First Jamaica Ministries. I could get up right now and run out of this place. I could go home, pack my things, and use the money Trustee Black had given me to move to the West Coast or something.

I bolted from my seat, invigorated by my new plan, but then the nurse's voice came like a bucket of ice water dousing my enthusiasm.

"Monique Johnson," she said, entering the waiting area with a yellow folder in her hands. It was probably my medical record, where she would ask me to sign on the dotted line, like an executioner signing a death warrant for her own child.

I looked down at Sister Alison with tears in my eyes. Hers were also glistening and wet.

"Oh, sweetheart," Sister Alison said as she stood up and hugged me.

"Ms. Johnson, come right this way, please," the nurse said as if she sensed that if I spent five more seconds standing in the lobby weeping with Sister Alison, I'd change my mind and they wouldn't get their $500. "If you could just follow me this way." I imagined the desperation behind her voice, as if she wanted to tell me, "Come on, keep it moving."

"Yes, I'm coming," I said, pulling away from Sister Alison.

"I'll be waiting right here when you get finished. Right here," Sister Alison said, and emphasized her point by planting herself firmly back in her seat.

I nodded grimly and followed the nurse into one of three examination rooms.

"Hello, Ms. Johnson," the nurse said after she closed the door behind us. "Before we perform the actual procedure, just like we discussed in the briefing, we need to run a couple of tests just to determine how far along you are. As you know, you have to be at least six weeks pregnant in order to get the procedure; otherwise there is a chance that the abortion won't be successful and the fetus could remain, continue to grow, and you'd have to come back."

"Yes, I understand. Please, if we could just move on," I said. I was eager to get this over with, as I was becoming sick to my stomach.

"Yes, certainly, Ms. Johnson," she said as she picked up a paper gown and handed it to me. "Just put this on and I'll be back in a few minutes. We need to get some blood and perform an ultrasound."

"Will I have to see it?" I said in a panic. "Will I have to see the baby?" There was no way I could see my baby on a monitor and hear its little heartbeat and still go through with the abortion.

"No," she assured me with a smile, though I swore I could see dollar signs in her eyes. She patted my hand in an attempt to calm me, once again making sure I didn't run up out of there without leaving my $500. "I'll be back in a few."

I proceeded to undress, removing the bulky gray sweat suit I had worn per their instructions. They suggested that I wear something warm because the recovery room would be chilly. I put on the paper gown, then hopped up on the examining table, feeling numb. A few minutes later, the nurse returned with another woman, who took a blood sample from my arm. She left the room; then the nurse asked me to lie back so she could perform an ultrasound. As she ran the cold instrument over my belly, I turned my head away from the monitor, not wanting even a glimpse of the life forming inside of me.

The ultrasound was only a few minutes long, but the nurse didn't speak a word. The room was completely silent. I thought about the tiny child that must be displayed on the screen, agonizing as I wondered what it would look like. Would it have T.K.'s eyes, my curls? These were questions a woman shouldn't want answered as she's lying on a table, preparing to abort her child, I thought. I felt my heart splitting in two.

"Please keep the gown on, Ms. Johnson," the nurse advised when she was finished and had covered my stomach again with the paper gown. "I'll be right back after the doctor gets a look at the test."

"Okay," I said, staring up at the ceiling to avoid looking at her. By the time I heard the door close, a puddle of tears had formed on the table.

It's not too late, I told myself. *I can still get up and run out of here right now.*

I rose slowly to a sitting position, clutching the flimsy gown around me. Before I could swing my legs off the table and onto the floor to make a run for it, the door opened.

"Ms. Johnson?" the nurse said, entering the room with a most puzzled look on her face. Gone were the dollar-sign eyes as she stared down into the open yellow folder. "I have some good news for you, I suppose."

"Excuse me?" I was as confused as she looked. What could possibly be considered good news in this chamber of death and broken promises?

"Well, we've run the blood test, and we've read the ultrasound, and, Ms. Johnson, you're not pregnant at all."

"What?" I jumped off the table, unable to contain myself. Elation at the thought that I didn't need an abortion was mixed with a strange sense of loss that I was not carrying T.K.'s baby. "I'm not pregnant?"

"That's right, Ms. Johnson."

"But the pregnancy test, my periods, the morning sickness . . . I don't understand." I was bewildered.

"Ms. Johnson, have you ever heard of what is called a false pregnancy?"

"No," I answered, unable to form a sentence.

"Well, with a false pregnancy, your body thinks it's pregnant. It goes through the motions and sometimes performs as if it's pregnant, but in actuality, you're not pregnant at all." I stood frozen in silent shock, so the nurse continued. "Now, the doctor has written you a prescription for a medication that will shrink your uterus, which, we noticed on the ultrasound, has expanded just slightly. You might feel some cramping, and there will be some bleeding, but after a couple of weeks, you should be back to normal."

Still, I stood there silently. It was hard to process her instructions when I still couldn't get my mind around the words *you're not pregnant.*

"Well, you can get dressed now, Ms. Johnson," the nurse said, starting to look a little uncomfortable with my silence. "And there's no charge today, but the fifty-dollar deposit is nonrefundable, as explained before, as it covers the cost of the test. You take care of yourself, Ms. Johnson, and have a good day." She left without waiting for a reply, which was fine, because I was still mute.

Even after she exited the room, I stood frozen for some time, allowing her words to really sink in. When they finally did, I quickly got dressed. I think I even put my panties on inside out trying to rush out of there. I darted from the examination room and into the waiting room, where Sister Alison sat reading one of the pamphlets an abortion protestor had handed her on the way in.

"Sister Alison! Sister Alison!" I shouted, not caring that every woman in the place was staring at me.

"Monique, you changed your mind?" she questioned. "You're going to keep the baby?"

"No, Sister Alison. No. There is no baby," I said with unbridled joy.

"What?" The blank expression on her face was probably the same one I wore when the nurse gave me the news.

"Something about a false pregnancy," I said quickly as I grabbed her arm, unwilling to stay in that place a moment longer. "I'll explain it to you on the way home. Let's get out of here."

She scooped up her purse, and we headed out of the clinic. As I thought about this miraculous turn of events, all I could say to myself was that there definitely is a God. I was able to walk away without destroying T.K.'s life or condemning my own soul. And short of a $50 deposit, I still had the money that Trustee Black had given to me. Maybe I would go take that vacation in

Jamaica after all, I thought, my heart feeling free. Who knows, now that I'm not pregnant, maybe I can talk the bishop into taking a trip to Jamaica with me. One thing's for sure—Lisa Mae Jones better hold on to her man because Monique Johnson is about to make it her business to reclaim what's hers.

Alison and the First Lady

I got out of my car and practically skipped over to Charlene's gravesite. I was so happy, I was sure Charlene could feel the joy in my spirit the moment I set foot onto the grass. I couldn't wait to share the good news with her.

"Charlene, guess what? Girl, I don't know what you and God been doing up there, but y'all certainly pulled off a miracle today." I began to happily tell her of the turn of events. "I went down to that abortion clinic with Monique, and, girl, you not gonna believe this, but she didn't have an abortion. Matter of fact, she wasn't even pregnant." I could feel my best friend's smile. "Go 'head on, girl. Pat yourself on the back, click your heels, and sing hallelujah one more time."

I knew Charlene was dancing. I could feel her energy, and the image created in my mind made me smile. "And, Charlene, get this. I ain't never heard of this before, but the doctor said she had a false pregnancy." I chuckled. "Seems she was so in love with the bishop that she talked her body into thinking she was having his baby." The whole idea of a false pregnancy was so crazy that it made me laugh all over again.

"I'm not gonna lie, though," I said, becoming serious. "I am so relieved that she didn't need an abortion. I know how you feel about protecting the bishop, but I have to tell you, it was weighing heavy on my soul to be telling that woman that abortion was a good choice. She might not be the right woman for your husband, in my opinion, but it was still hard to do."

I wasn't sure what Charlene would have said in reply if she were able to talk to me. If she were in my shoes, I wonder if she would have stood strong and taken the woman to get an abortion? It had been almost impossible for me not to back down. A few times, I had almost gone to the cemetery to apologize to Charlene and tell her I was no longer able to help her find the right woman for the bishop. Then, in the waiting room with Monique, my conscience had almost got the best of me. If they hadn't called her name when they did, I might have just dragged her out of there myself and told her everything. It was only after she'd gone into the examining room with the nurse that I regained my strength to continue fulfilling the promises I'd made to Charlene.

Shoot, I concluded, I had done worse things in my life than take someone to get an abortion, and I hadn't been struck by lightning yet. People will do plenty of things that are out of character when it's in the name of love. I loved my best friend, Charlene, enough to do what had to be done.

"Now, I haven't had a chance to tell you about everything else that's been going on because I was so wrapped up in Monique being pregnant, but you'll never believe what I'm about to tell you. Guess who's drug-free these days? Mmm-hmm, you guessed it. Marlene. She's looking real good, too, Charlene. She hasn't made a total turnaround, but from what I can see, she's well on her way. If she keeps on the path the bishop is laying for her, she'll be fine. I'm sure of it. Bishop has Savannah helping him out with her, and Marlene's staying at your house with the bishop." I could sense Charlene's uneasiness, so I waited quietly for my words to sink in.

When I felt that Charlene would be receptive to hearing more, I continued. "Listen, Charlene. There's no need to get your panties in a bunch. I don't think there's any hanky-panky going on, especially with Lisa Mae and Loretta creeping around in the shadows. Even if Lisa Mae thought the bishop and Marlene were getting close, she'd find a way to run interference.

"I have to say, though, that Lisa Mae might have her hands full now that Monique is not pregnant. I think the only reason Monique didn't put up a fight to get the bishop back was because of the pregnancy. But I can tell she still loves him, and now that she's not worried about ruining his reputation with a baby, her claws just might come out. I'm sure she's going to be putting a lot of pressure on the bishop in the weeks to come.

"I think it's time we step things up a bit with Lisa Mae. She might be able to handle Marlene and Savannah, but Monique is an entirely different situation." I leaned over and touched the headstone. "I guess we're going to have to give Lisa Mae the 'by any means necessary' lesson on 'How to Keep a Man 101.' I'll make sure she gets the appropriate letter right away."

32

BISHOP

Savannah arrived at the house precisely at 8:00 A.M. and would stay with Marlene until around dinnertime, just as she'd been doing several times a week for the past few weeks. One night she had even stayed until nearly midnight so that I could go to dinner with Lisa Mae and a few of the deacons from the church. She made the offer after Lisa stopped by once while Savannah was there. Lisa tried hard to conceal her feelings, but I knew she wasn't happy that there was not one woman, but two women, in my house. Savannah sensed it, too, which was why she offered to stay with Marlene so I could have dinner with Lisa.

I hadn't seen much of Lisa Mae lately, because I was so busy juggling my duties at the church and my responsibilities to Marlene. But Lisa Mae told me she understood and was happy with the few moments we were able to spend together on the days I saw her at the church. I promised to make it up to her once Marlene was back on her feet, though there was no way to be sure when that might be. I did know, though, that her chances of recovery were even better now that Savannah was helping.

A former drug addict myself, I knew how hard it was to resist your urges those first few weeks, and I also knew the steps Marlene needed to take toward recovery. While Savannah had no personal experience in the area, she brought to the table a warm spirit and a kind of connection with Marlene that only a woman could have, and it was genuine. Because Marlene had spent so many years on the streets, she knew a fake when she saw one, so it took someone as genuine and sincere as Savannah to be able to communicate with her. Savannah treated Marlene with respect and because of that, Marlene opened up to her without hesitation, giving Savannah a deeper insight into what she needed for a successful recovery. Not only had Savannah been helping me get Marlene through the beginning stages of her recovery, but she also was helping me to bring the word of God front and center into Marlene's life during the process.

This day, I returned home a little later than usual. The women had already eaten dinner and were now together in the living room. I watched appreciatively as Savannah and Marlene sat side by side, an open Bible between them.

"Even though Psalms 23 is read at funerals," Savannah said to Marlene after reciting the Scripture, "I think it should be read and believed by a person while that individual is alive on earth."

"Why?" Marlene asked curiously. "I mean, if he's gonna lead me to 'lie down in green pastures,' I'd rather it be while I'm dead. To lie down, in that particular Scripture, doesn't that mean death?"

I was waiting for Savannah to look to me for assistance in explaining the verse to Marlene, but she didn't. She just went right on to explain it as if she were teaching Wednesday evening Bible study. As a pastor, I must admit I was proud of my sheep. As a man, I was impressed.

"You need to know that you don't have to want for anything; God will provide all of your needs," Savannah explained as she took Marlene's hands into hers. "You don't need crack." She shook her hands for emphasis. "God is your rock."

Marlene nodded her head in agreement as she fought back tears. "Yes, I know that now."

"But I want you to believe it, Marlene." I decided to jump in. "Believe that God will deliver you from this. He delivered me."

Savannah looked up and smiled at me as a single teardrop fell from Marlene's eye. We made a wonderful team.

"Well, Marlene," Savannah said, looking up at the clock on the kitchen wall. "It's almost nine o'clock. I better get ready to head out. But before doing so, let's close in prayer. Pastor, do you mind if I close?"

"I don't mind at all," I stated. "Shall we join hands and bow our heads?" Savannah proceeded to say a nice little prayer that sealed our accomplishments with Marlene for the evening. It allowed us to touch on and agree on a successful and permanent recovery for Marlene.

"Well, Sister Marlene," Savannah said, rising, "you just keep on keeping on, and trust in God."

"I will, Sister Savannah," Marlene said, rising and giving Savannah a hug. "I'm going to turn in too. I never knew how much all this praying could wear folks out." We all chuckled. "But on a more serious note, it works. Prayer really works, and I'm living proof because I'm getter better and stronger each day," Marlene said with conviction and pride.

"Amen, my sister," Savannah said, giving Marlene a high five. "Amen."

"Well, you drive home safely," Marlene said before she exited the kitchen and went to her room to prepare for bed.

"Sister Savannah, let me walk you to the door," I said, leading the way.

"Marlene really is making progress, isn't she, Bishop?" Savannah asked as we walked to the door.

"She certainly is, and you are a big part of that," I said.

"Oh, Bishop," she said modestly, shooing her hand at me.

"Seriously, Sister Savannah," I said, looking into her eyes so that she'd know I was sincere. "You have a powerful anointing. It's as though your every word is guided by God Himself."

"Well, Bishop, I do ask God to give me the proper words to speak, so my words are, in fact, guided by God. But I'm not in there working with Marlene alone, Bishop. The way you open up and your honesty . . . I mean, you are such a humble man, and I admire you so much for that."

As Savannah spoke, she looked up at me wondrously, and her eyes reflected her feelings. And for the first time, I noticed just how beautiful she was, not just on the inside, but on the outside too. I bet if she'd let down that bun she always wore, her hair would flow like Samson's. I bet she was hiding a lot of things—things she would hopefully reveal through her own counseling with me—things that, once she could let go of them, would allow her to be an even more beautiful woman, if that were at all possible.

Just look at her. If I weren't seeing Lisa Mae, I swear I would consider—

Before I could finish my thoughts, I felt Savannah's lips press against mine. It was almost as if she were reading my mind and decided to thank me with a kiss for all of the wonderful compliments I had just given her in my head. Before I could even let the first kiss sink in, she immediately gave me a second peck on the cheek, then told me good night and slipped out the front door.

I wiped my lips, still a little shocked. It was a nice, soft kiss. It was a good kiss; nothing like the passionate kisses that Monique and I had shared, or even the occasional kiss Lisa and I shared, for that matter, but nice nonetheless.

The thought of Monique and the way she had kissed me, the way she had touched me, only made me miss her even more than I had. For the past few Sundays, I had been hoping to walk out and spot her somewhere in the church pews, but that never happened. Part of me regretted the decisions I'd made. I knew I had hurt Monique deeply when I started seeing Lisa Mae, and I had also hurt myself. I was enjoying the time I spent with Lisa Mae, and there was no doubt she was good for the church, but in the back of my mind—or maybe it was my heart—I had a nagging sense that I was missing something. I thought perhaps seeing Monique return to Sunday services would ease that feeling. Maybe it was just guilt over allowing one of my flock to believe she was unwelcome in my church. Or, if I was completely honest with myself, maybe I was second-guessing my decision to let Monique go. Perhaps I should have given our relationship a chance. It hurt to think I might never see her again, especially since she was still so often on my mind.

As I turned around to shut off the lights and get ready for bed, the phone on the end table caught my eye. I thought about calling Monique. Part of me just wanted to hear her voice—a big part of me. But there was another part of me that just wanted to check up on her as the pastor of the church, to make sure she was okay both mentally and spiritually. Just because she was mad at me, it didn't mean she had to be mad at God. I picked up the phone and dialed Monique's number.

What am I thinking? I asked myself, hanging up before it could even ring once. I broke her heart. If I weren't calling to tell her I'd split with Lisa Mae, there was probably nothing I could say that Monique would want to hear. It would be best for me to just leave her alone and let her get on with her life.

Shaking the thought of Monique out of my head, I went into the kitchen, where Marlene was in her robe and slippers, fixing a cup of tea. It was really good to see her doing so much better.

She had regained some of her weight; not a whole lot where she was fat or anything like that, but enough so that her ribs didn't show through her blouse anymore. Her face looked less sunken, and her skin had regained some of its brightness.

"Did Sister Savannah make it out okay?" Marlene asked when she spotted me.

"Yes, she did." I smiled, allowing my mind to linger back to the kiss Savannah had given me before she left.

Observing my smile, Marlene said, "Yeah, she's worth smiling about, all right."

"Excuse me?" I asked.

"Sister Savannah. She'd put a smile on any man's face. Matter of fact, I don't know why that girl ain't married yet. Maybe if she'd do something different with that hair of hers. But you have to admit, she's kind, genuine, and loves the Lord. What more could a man ask for?" Marlene hinted. "Especially a man who loves the Lord just as much."

I knew what Marlene was getting at, and she was right. Savannah was a sweet woman, and her strong Christian values would be a great asset to the church. But just as I had no choice when I ended things with Monique, I couldn't even dream of starting something with Savannah. Lisa Mae and I were an item, a couple accepted by the church, and Lisa Mae was also a fine candidate for the position of first lady. Sure, I knew there was still no real spark between us, but I had to give those feelings a chance to develop. Lisa Mae had done nothing wrong, so what kind of man would I look like if I broke up with her now to start dating another woman? No, I had made my bed, and now there was no unmaking it.

"It's okay, Thomas Kelly," Marlene said when I didn't respond to her comments about Savannah. "You don't have to admit that you like her, but don't worry, I won't be jealous if you do."

Things were just getting stranger and stranger. Now Marlene was throwing in her two cents about my love life. Everything had been much easier before people decided I was the church's most eligible bachelor. "Marlene, I—"

She interrupted me quickly. "You don't have to explain yourself, Thomas Kelly. I'll admit that for a short while I thought about us getting back together, but now I see what's real. You need a woman who can help you lead that church, and with my problems, I sure don't need that kind of pressure."

Her words left me speechless. I had no idea that Marlene had given thought to us being together again, and it was almost more than I could handle right now. Lisa Mae, Monique, Savannah, and now Marlene; these women swirled around in my head, making me wonder how I had ended up in this situation, less than a year after my wife's death. Then I thought of Charlene and those letters.

"Marlene, I . . ." When I couldn't express a complete thought, I just gave up. "I think I need to go to bed. Good night." I headed for my bedroom, hoping I could quiet my troubled mind and get some rest.

33

SAVANNAH

"Marlene?" I questioned, still uncertain of the identity of the person standing before me.

"Savannah, you're right on time," Marlene said as she stepped aside so that I could enter the house. Speechless, I stepped in, staring at Marlene with my mouth open. Dressed in her Sunday finest, she certainly didn't look like the same sickly, drug-addicted woman I had met not long ago.

"Now, where I'm from, you better not leave your mouth open wide for that long. No telling what might end up in it, especially if you're trying to get high."

I laughed at her sassy words. "Marlene, you look . . . you look . . ." My eyes welled up with tears. I couldn't find the words to tell her just how much healthier she looked, so I just threw my arms around her. "I'm so proud of you, girl." I pulled away from her, holding on to her arms and admiring the beautiful, sharply dressed woman who stood before me.

"You like?" she asked with a playful twirl, modeling her outfit for me.

It was a blue two-piece suit with a long skirt that had a slight slit up the back. She wore matching blue pumps with a blue-and-white flower on the ankle strap, which matched the blue-and-white flower on the blue hat she was wearing. The strap of a blue purse dangled from her forearm, which she had covered with long white gloves.

"Oh, Marlene," I said, hugging her again as I began to sniffle.

"Well, I must not look as good as I thought if you're crying," she said as we separated.

"Oh, no, Marlene, you look absolutely beautiful. You stand

before me looking like a true woman of God. Now this is the Marlene I know you were meant to be."

"Thank you, Sister Savannah, but you know I have to give you some credit for all of this. If it weren't for you and the bishop praying me through my addiction for the past four weeks, then I don't know where I'd be right now."

"All glory to God, Sister Marlene. All glory to God. He's working through me to help you. It's all Him."

"Well, you and God can fight over who wants to take credit for my successful recovery thus far," she said with a smile, "because as you know, I have to take it one day at a time. This is only the beginning. But you know what, Sister Savannah? I think I'm going to make it."

"I know you are," I said, amazed at God's power to change even the worst circumstances.

"Well, we better head on out to church. Thanks for picking me up. That way I didn't have to go early with the bishop. It gave me more time to get myself together."

"It's no problem at all."

The mention of the bishop made me feel a small twinge of embarrassment as I recalled how I had boldly kissed him the last time I was at his house. I'd left that night feeling like a fool. God had brought us together for a much higher purpose than becoming a couple. He'd brought us into a partnership to help save Marlene's soul, and I felt childish having let that greater goal become confused with my crush. I felt even worse about what I'd done because it was well known that he was involved with Sister Lisa Mae. I was not usually the kind of woman who would try to steal someone else's man, but that was exactly what it looked like I was trying to do. I hoped my brazen behavior hadn't offended the bishop. I didn't want him to think badly of me, especially since, if he and Lisa Mae ever broke up, I still wouldn't mind having a chance at love with him.

"I know this is a big day for you, Marlene," I said, struggling to divert my thoughts back to more sensible things. "You're going back to church a changed woman. But let's take a moment for prayer before we head out," I suggested.

We joined hands and bowed our heads, and I began to pray. "Dear, Lord—"

"Uh, pardon me, Sister Savannah," Marlene interrupted, "but I'd like to say the prayer this time if you don't mind."

I smiled. "Of course I don't mind."

"Lord," Marlene began, "I have been through some dark times. I have abused my body with drugs, neglected the needs of my children, and strayed from your Word. But I know now, Lord, that through it all, even when I was at my lowest, You were by my side. I know You love me, Lord, because You sent Thomas Kelly and Sister Savannah to save me. They pulled me out of the darkness, Lord, so that I might see Your light and experience the fullness of Your love. For that, I am forever grateful. Amen."

Her prayer was short, but moving. Marlene's progress had touched me deeply, and I was grateful that God had put me in a position to be a part of it. My father's meddling matchmaker ways might have been a nuisance, but in the end, he brought me closer to the bishop. If it weren't for that, I never would have been asked to help Marlene, and I would have missed out on this powerful food for my soul.

She squeezed my hand and said, "Now let's go to church. I want to make my entrance as a new woman and let everyone see the power of God's love."

Marlene was right about the impact her improved appearance would have on the congregation at Sunday services. From the moment she stepped out of my car, it was as if all eyes were on her.

"Sister Marlene, is that you?" a woman asked as we made our way up the steps and into the church.

"Well, Sister Marlene. We sure are glad you've come back to visit us, and you are looking very well," Brother Rodney said, tipping his brim.

When we entered the sanctuary, the ushers dang near fell over themselves trying to seat Sister Marlene. "We got a seat up front that we reserved just for you," one young man said, taking Sister Marlene by the arm.

"Sister Marlene, I'm going back to join the choir now, so I'll see you at the end of service," I told her. She nodded, then gave me a wave as she allowed the usher to lead her down the center aisle. I'm not sure if the seat had really been reserved for her, but it didn't seem to matter to Marlene as she strutted like a proud peacock down to the front pew.

During the service, the choir performed our usual schedule of praise and worship songs: two upbeat tunes giving praise, and two slower tunes to go into worship. Then I stepped toward the microphone for a special surprise, a solo that God put on my heart.

"Praise the Lord, Saints," I started.

"Praise the Lord," the congregation repeated.

"I know this morning we've been singing for the Lord."

"Amen," a couple of the choir members stated.

"And every time I use my voice, it's for the Lord."

"That's right," someone shouted. "Give praise."

I turned my attention to the front pew and said, "Well, this solo I'm about to perform is dedicated to an individual. But God is still using my voice to let this person know just how much He loves her, just how much He believes in her, and how, through Jesus, He will keep her."

"Well, all right," I heard a man exclaim.

Many members of the church were also looking toward the front pew, where I kept my eyes focused. I was sure they could guess the meaning of my dedication, but I wanted to speak the words out loud to Marlene.

"Sister Marlene, God is good. He has held you up through your most difficult times, and He has brought you here today so that all of us may witness the power of His love through your amazing transformation. Thank You, Lord, for Your eternal love and devotion to us all."

"Amen!" could be heard throughout the church, and several people raised their hands up in praise. I noticed Marlene wiping a tear from her cheek, but she sat tall and proud and wore a beautiful smile on her face.

"So, Sister Marlene," I said, looking right at her, "this is for you."

By the time I finished singing "Amazing Grace," there wasn't a dry eye in the house, mine included. The church filled with applause, but it wasn't for my singing. Folks were clapping to give praise to God, showing thanks for the miracle he had allowed us to witness in Sister Marlene's salvation. Gradually, though, the applause turned into something else. Several folks stood up and shifted their attention to Marlene. Their clapping became directed at her, a way of congratulating Marlene for pulling herself out of despair and finding a way back to the Lord.

The applause reached a crescendo when, in a move that surprised everyone, the bishop stepped down from the pulpit and approached the pews. He reached out his arms to Marlene, and she leaned against him in an embrace that spoke volumes about their history and the love that they shared for each other.

Only one person in the church seemed unmoved by the outpouring of love in the room. Sister Lisa Mae sat at the other end of the front pew, arms crossed angrily over her chest, watching as Marlene held the bishop as he shouted, "Praise God!" It didn't look like she was even making an attempt to hide her disapproval.

On the one hand, I suppose I could understand her reaction. No woman is supposed to enjoy watching her man hug another woman. But on the other hand, it would take a cold heart not to feel the joy of the Spirit in this church and respond to it. I wondered if the bishop noticed how Lisa Mae was reacting, and if he did, how he felt about it. But when I turned my attention back to him, I was sure that Lisa Mae was the furthest thing from his mind. He was too caught up in the moment, celebrating how far Marlene had come.

And Marlene was clearly enjoying herself too. I could tell she felt honored by all of the well-deserved VIP treatment she was receiving. I hadn't seen the members of this church shower one person with so much love since . . . well, since they surrounded the first lady on the last day she was well enough to attend services before her death. And then it hit me. Now I knew why Lisa Mae was frowning so hard. Maybe she saw what I did: maybe the new, sober Marlene had a better chance at becoming the next first lady than anyone ever dreamed she would.

34

MONIQUE

"Dear, Lord," I prayed as I kneeled alone in the empty sanctuary, "I am here in Your house, asking for Your help."

This was the first Sunday I had been back at First Jamaica Ministries since learning that I wasn't really pregnant. You might think that I would have rushed back to church to praise God for sending me a solution to my problem, but it wasn't that easy. I still had so many mixed emotions about the whole thing, and I needed some time alone to sort through my feelings. Luckily, Sister Alison must have understood this, because unlike before, when she was calling me constantly, she hadn't called at all since we left the abortion clinic that day.

I felt conflicted about the fact that I wasn't carrying T.K.'s baby. Right before the nurse had come in and informed me about the false pregnancy, I'd had a momentary vision of leaving the abortion clinic and raising the bishop's child, with or without him. Some small part of me had felt robbed of that opportunity when I found out the pregnancy wasn't real. So, while the false pregnancy had solved some of my problems, it hurt me deeply in other ways.

I struggled with the idea that my body had actually mimicked a pregnancy. What did that say about me? T.K. had broken my heart. Did I really love him so much that in spite of the pain, my subconscious wished I could have his child? I wanted to hate him for rejecting me the way he did, for choosing Lisa Mae over me, but as hard as I tried, I couldn't make myself do it. Instead, I found it easy to come up with excuses for his behavior. Maybe he hadn't called me because he felt guilty about what he'd done. Or maybe, as Trustee Black had said, he really was busy with some personal matters and just hadn't found the time to contact me yet. Whatever the reason, it didn't take me long to realize that I would be willing to forgive him once he explained his silence. In fact, now that there was no pregnancy to complicate matters and threaten his career, I began to entertain the idea that we might still be able to work things out and have a relationship. Yes, I admitted to myself, what I really wanted was to have the bishop back in my life.

I knew the first step in getting T.K. back was making him see what a mistake it was to choose Lisa Mae. I knew the woman was a phony from the moment I met her, but sometimes men aren't as quick to read people, especially women. Some people call it the power of the pussy. I didn't know if Lisa Mae had actually given some up to him, but I did know that the bishop was just like most other men: As long as a woman is giving him some attention, satisfying his male ego, it's impossible for him to look beyond that to see the woman's true motives.

Even if T.K. couldn't see it, I knew what Lisa Mae's intentions were. She was all about becoming the first lady. And even if she did have some feelings for him, she couldn't possibly love him as much as I did. I just needed to figure out a way to make the bishop see that. So, as I stayed at home, taking the medicine they'd given me to shrink my uterus, I tried to come up with a plan.

Since Sister Alison hadn't been keeping in touch with me, I realized I had no way to know what was happening at the church. For all I knew, the bishop and Lisa Mae could be getting ready to announce an engagement. That's when I decided that it was foolish for me to be staying away from First Jamaica Ministries. If I wanted to win T.K. back, he had to be reminded of what he was missing. And if I wanted to compete with Lisa Mae, then I needed to be watching her, ready to make a move the moment I saw her slipping.

So, on Sunday morning, I woke up early and put on the same conservative pink ensemble that I'd shown to T.K. the night we made love. With my body back to its pre-pregnancy—or should I say pre-*false*-pregnancy—shape, all eyes would be on me. That was nothing new, of course, but the only eyes that I cared about on this morning were the bishop's. Once he got a look at me in this dress, he would remember that night. I had a vision of T.K.

losing control when he saw me, jumping down from the pulpit to pull me into his arms right there in front of the entire congregation.

"Sister Lisa Mae who?" I said with a laugh to my reflection.

T.K.'s reaction to me at services wasn't quite as dramatic as my fantasy, but it was enough to give me some hope. I decided to sit in the back of the church rather than taking my usual place near the front, thinking it would be wise not to stir things up just yet. This tactic seemed to be the right choice, too, because I actually got a few approving nods from some people sitting nearby. One woman even complimented my outfit—a first for me at church. Maybe it wouldn't be so bad to tone things down once in a while, I thought, if this were the kind of reception it would get me from the women who usually threw daggers my way.

T.K. announced that it was time for the altar call. Members were invited to the front to leave their burdens and heartaches there, and I decided it was time to make my presence known. I stood up and smoothed the front of my dress, preparing to walk down the aisle. T.K.'s eyes met mine, and a brief smile passed over his face. It was nothing earth-shattering, but it was enough to encourage me. At least now I knew that his silence didn't mean he had forgotten about me.

His smile was also enough to bring me to my senses and make me sit down. What was I thinking? I couldn't very well go to the front for altar call and announce my burdens to everyone. What would I say? "Please pray for me, because I just went through a very difficult false pregnancy." No, I had just received a smile from the bishop and some friendly gestures from a few members of the church. I was not about to ruin that progress by going up there and sharing my business with everyone for their gossip fodder. I had made a good first step, so I sat myself back down and listened to other people unburden themselves at the altar. T.K.'s smile had already done more for me than any altar call ever could.

When services ended, I stayed in my seat while the church cleared out so I could talk to God one-on-one. With everything that had been going on, I had stayed away from church for too long, and I wanted to set things right with Him. I kneeled down, my hands clasped tightly and my head bowed.

"I have been through so much, Lord, and it has caused me to stay away from Your house when I needed You most. Please, Lord, forgive me for my absence and help me to understand the trials You have sent my way. You know my heart, and You know that what I desire most is the love of a good man. But if that is not what You have planned for me, then please give me the strength to move on." I paused for a moment, considering the idea that maybe, no matter how much I wanted T.K., it wasn't in God's plans to bring us together. That would be painful for me to get through, but somehow I would manage. I always did, every time some man broke my heart. But this time, I didn't want things to end that way. I decided to cling to hope.

"But if by chance my heart's desires are part of Your plan for me, I ask for a sign, God, so that I will be able to recognize the way in which You are ordering my steps. In Jesus' name I pray. Amen."

I stood up and made the sign of the cross on my chest.

"Um, excuse me, Sister Monique . . ."

I heard the voice coming from behind me, and I closed my eyes to say a quick thank you to God. I turned around and looked into the eyes of the man I loved.

"Hello, Bishop," I said warmly. He gave me that smile again, and I had to fight the urge to run to him and jump in his arms.

"I'm sorry, Sister Monique," he said, "but I'm getting ready to lock up the church."

Well, I might have preferred it if he'd said something a little more romantic, but at least he was here with me. God had given me the sign I prayed for, and now the rest would be up to me.

"I'm sorry, Bishop," I said. "I was just in here praying, and I didn't know what time it was."

"I understand, Sister. I'm just glad to see you back at church."

"It's nice to see you too," I told him, wishing I could tell him just how I felt. We were both a little awkward, so many things still left unresolved between us. But I couldn't just blurt it all out, and I knew he wouldn't speak his mind, especially not here in the sanctuary, where anyone could walk in.

"So, how have you been?" he asked.

"Okay . . . I guess." I wondered if Trustee Black had told him anything about our conversation, but I doubted it. If T.K.

thought I had been pregnant, it would have been written all over his face right now.

"Well, I'm glad that you've come back to church. I've missed seeing you here."

"And I've missed being here."

His eyes traveled over my body, and I knew that my pink dress had the desired effect on his memory. I watched his face as he fought unsuccessfully to suppress a smile. He cleared his throat and looked away from my body, but it was too late. I knew exactly what he was thinking about, and it encouraged me.

"So, Bishop, how have you been?" I asked. "And how is Sister Lisa Mae?" I asked boldly to test the waters. The mention of her name might put a damper on this whole reunion. Or, if I were right about his true feelings, she wouldn't have much of an effect at all, and then I would know that I had a green light to reenter the competition for his heart.

"Oh, Lisa Mae . . . ," he started, but his voice trailed off momentarily, as if he were quite sure what to say about her. He definitely wasn't gushing forth with praise for her, and that made me a very happy woman. There was some kind of weakness in their relationship, and once I found out what it was, I would be there to tear things down. "She's fine. Thanks for asking, Sister Monique."

"Of course, Bishop." I turned to exit the pew. "Well, it really was nice to see you again. I'll see you next Sunday at services. I look forward to another one of your inspiring sermons." I headed down the aisle, my hips performing their trademark sway for his benefit. There was no doubt that his eyes were glued to my perfect behind. Lisa Mae was probably being crowded out of his heart with every single swish of my hips.

That's right, I thought. *Push her to the side and make room for me, T.K.*

"Um, Sister Monique," he called out before I made it to the doors. I turned around to look at him, and he asked, "I was just about to head out to get a bite to eat. Would you like to join me?"

Bingo! Bye-bye, Lisa Mae. Things were happening even faster than I expected.

"That's nice of you to offer, Bishop. Will Lisa Mae be joining us?" I asked, trying to make the question sound innocent.

"No, she won't," he answered. "She made plans to have lunch with her friend Loretta today."

"Oh, that's too bad. It might be good for Lisa Mae and I to get to know each other a little better, don't you think? I mean, if you and I are going to be friends, right?"

I had obviously made him uncomfortable, but I didn't regret the question. His answer would tell me everything I needed to know about my chances. If he agreed that it would be good for Lisa Mae and me to become friends, then I'd know to give up immediately. If a man is interested in you romantically, he does not want you to get to know his current woman.

"Friends . . . yes, friends. Maybe someday you and Lisa Mae will get to know each other." Ah-ha! The best he could do was, "Maybe someday." He didn't want me to spend time with Lisa Mae any more than I wanted to.

"So, as my *friend*," T.K. said, "will you join me for lunch?"

"I would love to," I answered happily. I waited for him to meet me by the doors, where he placed his hand on the small of my back and guided me outside. The gentle pressure of his touch sent a small shiver through my body. I couldn't wait to feel his hands on my skin again, and I hoped it was only a matter of time.

At the restaurant, we made small talk for a while after we placed our orders. We skirted around the major issues and unspoken words that hung in the air between us. I wished I could tell him about the false pregnancy, about how frightened and guilty I had felt in the abortion clinic. But it was too soon to talk about those things, for both of us. A few times I caught him looking at me like he wanted to say something, but then he would quickly look away when I met his gaze. Finally, when we were halfway through our meals, T.K. broached the subject of our sudden breakup—or rather the relationship that never really had a chance to get off the ground.

"Monique," he said solemnly, "I want you to know how sorry I am for the way things happened between us. I never meant for you to get hurt. I hope you believe me when I say that."

I looked into his eyes and felt my heart softening. How could

I not forgive a man with eyes like those, eyes that seemed to look right into my soul? "I accept your apology, T.K. I'm not going to lie, it hurt like hell, but I forgive you."

"I appreciate that, Monique. I spent many nights feeling guilty about the way I ended things with you. I hadn't planned for things to happen this way, you know. It's just that the members of the church—"

I held up my hand to stop him. "Please, Bishop. Don't explain. We've been through this all before. I don't think I need to be told again how the church feels about me. I don't know if my self-esteem could handle it."

He dropped his head, then raised it again and looked into my eyes. "You're right. I apologize. I just don't want you to be hurt, Monique."

"I'll be fine, Bishop," I assured him, hoping it was true. I would be fine, as long as he was mine in the end.

"I'm glad to hear that," he said. "Does that mean you'll be coming to church regularly again?"

"I think so. I can only stay away from First Jamaica Ministries for so long, you know."

Besides, I thought, *how can I get Lisa Mae out of the picture unless I'm always around, like a thorn in her side, my beautiful body reminding you every Sunday of what you're missing with that dried-up old woman?*

Just as I thought of her, Lisa Mae appeared before us at the table, with Loretta at her side. Was this woman some kind of witch or something?

"T.K.," she said. I think she was trying to sound pleased to see him, but she couldn't hide the truth from me. She was pissed! When he turned his head to look at her, I smirked at Lisa Mae. "I didn't know you were going to be here, dear. And I certainly didn't know you would be having lunch with Sister Monique." She tried to force a smile onto her face, but it came out more like an ugly grimace. Not the most flattering expression, I thought with satisfaction.

"Well, Sister Monique just happened to be at the church as I was getting ready to leave," he explained innocently, "so I asked her if she'd like to come along. She hasn't been to church in a while, you know, and—"

"Yes," Lisa Mae said arrogantly, "I had noticed your absence, Sister Monique. I do hope everything is all right with you."

"Everything is fine, Sister Lisa. Thank you for asking." *Everything is fine,* I thought, *especially since I'm sitting here with your man, you fake bitch. Ha!*

"T.K.," Lisa Mae said, turning her back to me as if she wished I would just disappear, "I'd like to speak to you about the interview I'm trying to set up with the *Amsterdam News.* Can we step outside for a minute?"

I looked at T.K., and he squirmed ever so slightly in his seat. I tried to will him to stay put. *No, T.K., don't do it. Don't give in to her demands. Please!*

"Well, Lisa, I thought we had already discussed the particulars of that interview, but if there's more you'd like to tell me, we could discuss it later. Sister Monique and I are just finishing up our meal, and then I'll come join you and Loretta at your table. How does that sound?"

I had to actually bite the inside of my cheek to stop myself from laughing out loud. Lisa looked like she was about ready to bust, the way he had just brushed her off.

"No, T.K." Her voice was suddenly several decibels louder than before. Oh, she was getting ready to show out, I could tell. "I really think that now would—"

"Um, Sister Lisa Mae," Loretta interrupted, grabbing Lisa's arm hard. She was obviously trying to stop her girl from letting her claws out in front of T.K. I wondered how many times before now Loretta had been there to save the day for Lisa Mae. "I'm really getting hungry, Lisa. You can talk to the bishop later, okay?"

The muscles in Lisa Mae's shoulders visibly relaxed as Loretta's calm words pulled her back from the edge of a tantrum. "Fine. We can go sit down, but I think I've lost my appetite." She cut her eyes at me, then glared at the bishop. "T.K., we'll talk later," she said, then walked stiffly away from our table.

"I'm sorry, T.K. Maybe I should just leave so you can go talk to her," I suggested when they were gone, though of course I had no intention of leaving anytime soon. And just like the gentleman he was, T.K. politely declined my offer.

"Don't be silly, Monique. Lisa Mae will be fine. She's a trooper."

A trooper, huh? That sure didn't sound like the way a man describes a woman he feels passionate about. Oh, yeah, there was definitely a chance for me and T.K. I would battle Lisa Mae as hard as I had to, and round one had just been decided in my favor.

35

LISA

"Can you believe what just happened?" I asked Loretta, slamming my fist down on the table. A few patrons' heads turned my way. They were probably going to report me again, but I didn't care. I was good and pissed off. I had remained a lady long enough, but now there was just something about that Monique that brought the ghetto up out of me.

"Yes, I can believe it, but what you have to do is get over it," she responded.

"And just whose side are you on here?"

"I'm on your side. But what everyone seems to keep forgetting, including you, is, Bishop is a man. I'm not saying he was here with Monique on other business than to just have a cordial meal. I'm just saying men love attention just as we women do. You told him you were having lunch with me today. What? Did you expect him to call Trustee Black and go out with him?"

"Why not? Anybody except that slut Monique. You can say what you want to, Loretta, but if that was your man over there having dinner with a tramp, you'd be pissed too." Loretta shrugged, then continued eating. "How do you think I feel sitting over here while they're on the other side of the restaurant, laughing and talking like they're in love? I'm his girlfriend, not her."

"Oh, Lisa Mae, you're making way too much out of this." I noticed Loretta glance toward the door. I turned to see what she was looking at. "Well, they're leaving now," she continued, "but even if they were laughing and talking, that's what you should be doing. Bishop ain't going nowhere. Considering who Bishop is and what he means to the community, do you really think he'd slide you off his arm for someone like Monique—a female with no class?"

"I hear you, but I just can't help the way I feel right now. Monique Johnson—the nerve of him."

"Well, don't look now, but *him* is on his way over to the table."

"You mean he came back?" I whispered to Loretta, but before she could reply, T.K. walked up to the table.

"Excuse me, Loretta, but do you mind if I borrow your lunch date for a moment?" he said, nodding toward me. "Lisa Mae, could you join me outside for a moment?"

"I guess so, considering how I've lost my appetite anyway," I said with attitude, sliding from the booth and storming right past T.K. and out the door.

"Lisa Mae, can you wait, please?" T.K. asked as he exited the door behind me.

"Damn it, I'm tired of waiting," I said as I spun around to stand face-to-face with him. "Pardon my French, but I'm mad. As a matter of fact, I'm not mad, I'm hurt." I stood there staring into T.K.'s eyes. I quickly folded my arms and turned my back to him. Looking into those gorgeous eyes was just too much. How could I stay mad at him gazing into those eyes of his? And I wanted to stay mad for at least ten more minutes. That much he deserved.

"I never meant to hurt you, Lisa Mae," T.K. said, reaching out and touching my arm.

I took a step forward so that I would no longer be within his reach. He still had a good nine minutes coming. "It's too late; I'm already hurt. I gave you the courtesy of knowing who I'd be having lunch with, and I didn't even choose a man."

"Monique's a friend. I never saw the rule in the date book that says friends shouldn't have lunch when involved in a relationship with someone else."

I turned around with my hands on my hips and managed to give him a stern look. "It's only okay for friends to have dinner when neither of them wants to get the other one into bed."

T.K. looked shocked. "What?"

"C'mon, T.K., don't give me that 'what' stuff. You know Monique Johnson would love to have you. And if the shoe were on the other foot, you might not be so accepting of me going out with a man who obviously has feelings for me, especially if I didn't tell you in advance about the meal."

T.K. scanned the parking lot, seemingly thinking. He looked at me, then reached for my hands. "You're probably right. Perhaps I should've told you. I apologize. But, if you ever plan on being my wife, then you need to have some faith."

T.K.'s last comment threw me off. I was flattered by the fact that he all but confirmed that he's going to ask me to marry him. But at the same time, I wanted to be mad that he was also calling me weak.

Eight minutes left. "Don't you think I've had enough faith?" I snatched my hands from him, then spun around, my purse almost hitting the couple walking past us.

"Come on, Lisa Mae, let's go to my car and discuss this," T.K. said, showing a little embarrassment.

We walked to his car. T.K. opened the passenger door for me and I slid in. He walked around to the driver's side and got into the car. Once settled, he turned to face me.

"Like I was saying, Lisa Mae, God comes first in my life, so being a bishop takes priority, and before I'm anything, I'm the bishop. I have a herd of sheep that I must lead to heaven."

"Well, you need to open your eyes, because some of those sheep don't want to be led anywhere but to your bedroom."

"Lisa Mae, I take offense for the women you are referring to."

"You mean you take offense for Monique. Yeah, I said it, T.K. Do you think I'm blind? How much more of this do you expect me to take? Do you really think I'm going to put up with Marlene, the woman you have a child with, living with you? Savannah in and out of your house every other day? And now meals with Monique? Do you really think I'm going to put up with that, T.K.?"

"Well, you don't have a choice," T.K. said sternly. "Those women, and countless others, are my friends. I'm not going to give up my friendship with those women any more than I'd give up my friendship with you if the tables were turned."

I took in T.K.'s words before speaking. "Sounds like your mind is made up about your relationship with these women."

"Lisa Mae, *these women* are your so-called sisters of the church," he reminded me, "and Charlene never seemed to have a problem with it."

Oh, that comment right there did it. Not the comparison to the previous wife. Oh these next seven minutes of being mad at him were going to be a breeze. "T.K., I think maybe you better take me home right now."

T.K. just sat there glaring at my profile for a minute. Finally, he sighed and tried to place his hand on mine, but I pulled it away before he could do so. No way was he going to make these next six minutes difficult.

Eventually he started the car engine. "Do you want to go back inside and tell Loretta that I'm taking you home?"

"She'll figure it out," I said, too upset to even get out of the car and go inside. On that note, T.K. pulled out of the lot and headed toward my home. For the next five minutes we drove in silence until he pulled up in front of my house. I hurriedly opened my door so that he couldn't get out to open it for me and walk me to my door like he usually did.

"Wait and I'll—"

"Like I said, T.K., I'm tired of waiting. And since you were so quick to jump to Monique's defense earlier, then maybe you should be with Monique." Before I knew it, I had slammed the door shut and began my journey up the walkway.

The walk seemed so long as I thought about my last words to T.K. I couldn't believe I had just said that to him. I said words that might practically drive him straight into Monique's arms, or even worse, her bed. *God, I hope that comment doesn't backfire on me. Maybe I should take it back.* As I turned around to head back to T.K.'s car, not wanting to end things on that note, he was looking over his shoulder, backing out of the driveway. The ten minutes were up, but yet my time was up, so I turned back around and headed up the walkway. When I opened the screen door, an envelope fell to my feet. I bent over to pick it up and realized that my good friend Charlene had sent me another note. Receiving another letter sure felt strange. I always thought once a person was deceased, physical communication would end too. I noticed my name was written on it with the same handwriting as before.

"But how could this be?" I said to myself. I even looked over my shoulder, expecting to see Charlene standing there. *You're pissed off but not crazy*, I had to tell myself as I opened the envelope and began reading the letter:

Dear Lisa Mae,

First allow me to say that I am very proud of your efforts toward T.K. By now I'm sure you've already figured it out for yourself, but just in case you've been too caught up in your pursuit to become my husband's new wife, I thought it might be a good time for me to bring it to your attention. Lisa Mae, you are a beautiful and kind woman, a woman deserving of a man like T.K., but there are outside elements that exist that may hinder you from becoming the next first lady.

T.K. is a wonderful man of God, but there is one important thing that you must remember, my dear—he is a man no less, and men have needs. Without being too explicit, I have to warn you that if you don't tend to these needs, and soon, someone else will.

Charlene

I looked over my shoulder again as I tucked the letter into my purse. I fumbled with my keys until my shaking hands were finally able to unlock the door. I opened it up and then quickly closed it behind me as if a ghost were chasing me. And if I didn't know any better, I'd think that one was. The timing of this letter was scary, but it explained what I was once again too blind to see: this outside element did exist and it had a name—Monique.

It was plain and clear what Charlene was suggesting that I do. But how could my trying to get T.K. into bed make me a better candidate for the first lady? If anything, T.K. might start looking at me as if I were the kind of woman like Monique. But, as I gave the situation more thought, I realized if I showed Bishop I could satisfy him in bed as well as possess the leadership qualities that it takes to be a first lady, then he'd see I had more of an advantage over Monique. Direction was just something Monique would never have. The one and only thing that she had going for her, fortunately for me, I had too.

The clicking sound of the lock on the front door snapped me

out of my thoughts. Just then, Loretta came through the door carrying a doggie bag.

"Hey, Lisa," Loretta said as she walked over, set the bag on the coffee table, and sighed as she flopped down on the couch. "I'm so stuffed, I feel like I'm going to explode." She began rubbing her stomach. "I knew I shouldn't have gone for that dessert, but you know I can't resist chocolate cake."

I heard Loretta's words, but my thoughts were still on my dilemma of getting T.K. into bed, and I couldn't allow my mind to focus on anything else. "Loretta?" I asked.

"Yeah?" she replied.

"Would you agree that all men, even men of the cloth, have needs?"

"Do they all have dicks?" Loretta said bluntly. "Then there's your answer. Why do you ask?"

"Uh . . . well . . . uhh," I stammered.

After a few seconds of staring at me, waiting to see if I were going to get the words out, Loretta's eyes grew to the size of saucers. It was evident that she had figured out on her own why I was asking.

"Lisa Mae, you hoe you," she said as she sat upright, putting her hands on her hips. "So you finally figured out where the real power lies?"

"Oh, Loretta, please," I said, blushing and shooing my hand at her and rolling my eyes. "It's nothing like that at all."

"Who are you kidding? Besides, even if it wasn't T.K.'s needs you were worrying about, I wouldn't blame you if you only had your own in mind."

"Now that's enough already," I said, standing up, flushed with embarrassment from Loretta's foul talk.

"Oh, please, you might as well take out stock in Duracell batteries. You think I don't hear all that moaning and groaning coming from your bedroom at night?"

My first instinct was to curse Loretta for eavesdropping during my intimate moments, but that wouldn't have changed the fact that she knew about my acts of touching myself. I'd just have to make a mental note to be less vocal. "So you hear me in there, huh?" I asked her after swallowing my clumpy pride.

"No need to be embarrassed. We're Christians, but we ain't dead," Loretta stated. "You think you feel bad? How do you think I felt when I found out that Denzel was cheating on me with you?" Loretta laughed. "And from the sound of it, he makes you feel a hell of a lot better than he ever made me feel."

"Loretta." I laughed along with her, picking up one of the decorative pillows from the couch and throwing it at her. "But seriously, how do you think T.K. would react to me . . . well . . . you know . . . pushing up on him?"

"Oh, my dear friend, Lisa Mae," Loretta said as she rose from the couch. "Didn't you hear a word I said? He'll do what any other man would do. He'll pull that condom out that he carries around in his wallet for such an occasion and take you up on your offer, girl."

"T.K. doesn't carry a condom around in his wallet," I rebutted.

"His wife might be dead, but he ain't," Loretta said. And before she disappeared into her bedroom, she stated, "And neither is that thing in his pants."

First Charlene and now my best friend agreed that if I wanted to stay ahead of the race, I had to fulfill T.K.'s every possible need. On that thought, I picked up the phone, hoping I could still catch T.K. in his office at the church before he made plans. I could only hope he'd accept my attempt to make up with him by inviting him to dinner the next night. And everybody knows that makeup sex comes along with making up. When T.K. picked up his office phone after the third ring, I was relieved. When he agreed to allow me to cook dinner for him the next night, I was ecstatic.

Loretta helped me whip up some baked chicken, green cabbage, and cornbread, and rice pudding for dessert. She then conveniently just happened to be heading out when the bishop arrived.

"Smells delicious," the bishop said as he stood in the living room. I was so nervous that I had forgotten to offer him a seat, so we both just stood there in the middle of the living room, looking and smiling at each other. Finally, T.K. broke the silence. "Look, Lisa, about yesterday—" he started.

"Shhh," I said, cutting him off. I instinctively placed my index finger on his lips. Oh, his soft thick lips felt like cotton under my fingertip. Before I knew it, I gently ran my finger across his lips.

T.K. closed his eyes, taking in my touch. I think I even heard a slight moan, and without thinking, I replaced my finger with my tongue as I smothered him with a passionate kiss. "Oh, Lisa," he softly spoke, almost in lustfully. I could tell by his tone he was ready for his need to be fulfilled. "I'm sorry for—"

"T.K., I'm the one who's sorry. I'm sorry that it's taken me this long to know that I want to give myself to you; all of me."

Just then a blank look covered T.K.'s face. "Lisa Mae? Are you saying what I think you're saying?" I thought I saw excitement in his eyes. If I had to guess, I would've said he was getting wet in his pants.

"Yes, T.K., you heard me right," I said, not allowing yet another moment to pass before giving him what I knew I should, something I should've known to give him without his former wife having to tell me from the grave. "I know you came for dinner, but we can skip right to dessert."

Boldly I took T.K. by the hands in order to lead him to my bedroom. But he didn't budge. It was as if he wore cement boots. "Lisa Mae," T.K. said. "We can't do this."

I studied his face and then realized why he was saying what he was saying. "Oh, T.K., you're right. Wait right here," I said as I dashed off to my bedroom to retrieve a condom from my dresser drawer. I had gone out and picked up a box of condoms from the drugstore, just in case Loretta was wrong about T.K. carrying one in his wallet. I returned pretty quickly.

"Listen, Lisa Mae. I can't do this," he said with concern.

"Now you can," I said with a mischievous grin while waving the condom.

"No, Lisa, I'm sorry if I've given you the wrong idea, but I don't want to go to bed with you." He might as well have taken a huge red rubber stamp that read, REJECT and stamped my forehead with it. I had never felt so humiliated in my life. "You're a beautiful woman of God, and I know you have needs, but I can't be an accomplice to you sinning against God through fornication."

I felt so embarrassed. "What? Me have needs? What about your needs? How do you handle those?"

Bishop grabbed my hands, then said confidently, "I open my Bible to read; then I pray."

I couldn't wait for Loretta to get home so I could slap the shit out of her, and if Charlene wasn't already dead, I'd put her six feet under too. Because of them, I had it all wrong and now I had ruined any and all chances of becoming the first lady. There was only one thing to do now, and that was to let T.K. off the hook by ending our dinner date.

"I understand your wanting to leave now," I said, praying to God that He'd allow me to hold back my tears long enough for me to close the door behind T.K. and retreat to my bedroom and cry my eyes swollen.

"Lisa Mae, I came here to have dinner with you, and that's just what I'm going to do. Why in the world would I want to leave?"

"I don't know, T.K. . . . maybe because now that I've made a fool of myself, you might find me a little less desirable."

"Lisa, you're a good woman." He squeezed my hands as he spoke. "And I'm going to make sure that you stay a good woman," T.K. said. I guess this was his meager attempt to make me feel better, and it worked somewhat. It worked enough that we were able to sit down to have dinner.

Not much talking went on over dinner. I still couldn't believe T.K. had declined my offer to lay me down. He seemed to be enjoying supper with nothing on his mind at all. Since he came here only to eat, I was expecting him to leave shortly after he was done—totally against my original plans, but considering how humiliated I was, he needed to leave. I wanted to sulk without him knowing it.

T.K. sat back in his chair, rubbing his stomach. "Mighty fine feast, Lisa Mae. Mighty fine."

"Thanks," was all I managed to mumble.

"I haven't tasted pork chops this good since Charlene used to cook them. I hope you'll invite me to dinner again soon."

I shrugged. "That depends, T.K."

He sipped his water before speaking. "Depends on what?"

"You . . . because you seem to have issues with respecting our relationship, T.K."

"Lisa Mae, what are you talking about? Your behavior this evening—not to mention yesterday at the restaurant—is way out of character for you. Help me understand what's going on with you."

"Oh, my fault, T.K. I guess I'm just not used to being in a relationship with a man who doesn't know how to put his lady first. Frankly, I think you're confused, and now you've got me confused. Who do you want, T.K.? Is it Marlene . . . is it Savannah . . . is it Monique . . . or do you want me?" T.K. sat quietly, unable to respond. I threw my napkin on the table. "You don't know, do you?"

I was shocked to see T.K. stand up, heading for his suit jacket. I followed him. "Lisa Mae, I need some time alone. Thanks again for dinner. I'll call you later."

I put my arms around his waist and pulled him to me. "T.K., I've been thinking I was your woman for a while now. What happened?"

He held me back. "Nothing happened. Everyone knows I'm dating you."

"Then why was my question so difficult for you?" I asked. He stared at me with those sexy eyes, but he seemed to be at a loss for words. "I love you, T.K. Can you say the same to me?" Again silence. I dropped my arms from his waist. "T.K., you have to make a choice."

He sighed. "You're right, Lisa Mae. I do need to make a choice. And I plan to do so soon. If not for my sake, then for the church's." He kissed my forehead. "Have a blessed night, Lisa Mae." And just like that, he was gone.

Alison and the First Lady

I was feeling a little depressed as I carried an arrangement of Charlene's favorite flowers to her gravesite. The orchids and lilies were an attempt to pick up her spirits and mine, maybe soften the blow before I told her about what I considered to be an absolutely horrible morning. Things had occurred at the church that could quite possibly change everything we'd worked so hard to set into motion in the last six months.

"Hey, Charlene," I said, bending over to place the flowers in front of her headstone. I fussed with the arrangement for a few seconds, thinking about the best way to break the news. "I been trying to figure out a way to tell you this, but I guess the best way is just to say it, so here goes." I took a deep breath to gather my courage. "I . . . well, we've been busted." I felt extremely uncomfortable having to tell her this. It meant I'd messed up and that we'd have to prematurely stop handing out the letters, which would surely disappoint Charlene.

I reluctantly continued the explanation. "When I got to the church for work this morning, the bishop was sitting at his desk, waiting for me. In his hands were two of the letters you dictated to me—his and Marlene's—and the handwritten draft of a letter he'd dictated to me a week ago. I think you get the picture." I cringed as I remembered the look on his face. I don't think I'd ever seen someone so disappointed in me before. "Let's put it this way: He matched up the handwriting; he knows I'm the one who wrote the letters, and he's not happy about it."

I paced back and forth in front of her headstone as I continued to ramble. "At first he thought I had written the letters by myself, without any help from you. Like I just stole your stationery and started writing. I mean, come on. What reason would I have to do that if it weren't for you? He thought about that question for a few minutes, and I finally convinced him that the letters were actually your words. I thought maybe he'd calm down a little then, but I was wrong. I mean, Charlene, he's really upset with me—a lot more upset than I thought he would be.

"He said something like we were trying to play God, and it wasn't fair to the people we were sending the letters to. Charlene, I never looked at it that way. I mean, we were only trying to provide some guidance for his benefit, right?" I quietly thought about my own answer to that question. "Or is that the lie I convinced myself of?"

I stopped pacing and stood directly in front of Charlene's headstone. "It's over, Charlene. The bishop knows what we've done, and it's time to stop it. I won't deliver any more letters to these women."

I couldn't begin to imagine what Charlene was thinking now, but I felt good about the decision I'd made. Still, she was my best friend, and I didn't want her to feel betrayed, so I made her one final promise.

"The only letter I will deliver is the last one that you dictated for the bishop. I won't be orchestrating anything from behind the scenes anymore, but at least your husband will know how you felt at the time of your death, and then he can make his own decision."

I waited to feel Charlene's spirit comfort me, to let me know that she was okay with this change of plans, but that comfort never came. I said my good-byes to my friend, then told her I'd be back to chat with her soon. I returned to my car feeling like I had let down my best friend, but somehow I still knew I was doing the right thing.

36

BISHOP

I'd been tossing and turning in my bed from the moment I lay down. As I rolled over onto my side, I looked at the clock. It was only 11:00 P.M., though it felt like 3:00 in the morning. My mind was still spinning, as it had been ever since I read the letter Alison had given me, the last one my wife dictated before her death. Charlene made no apologies for trying to orchestrate my love life from the grave, but that was to be expected. I loved my wife unconditionally; still, there was no denying that she liked things to run according to her plans and no one else's. As I read the letter, I wondered if I could grant her final wish. Was I really ready to choose a new wife and let go of the past? Of all the women I had been considering for the last six months, I knew who I was leaning toward, but I didn't know if I were ready to make a final decision and if I should choose the woman she wanted me to.

So, my mind was already working on overdrive as I tried to sort through my conflicted emotions. And then, just to complicate matters, I saw Marlene in a way I hadn't seen her for years. She had taken a shower and was headed down the hallway to her bedroom, wrapped in a towel. Just as she passed my bedroom door, the towel slipped, and I got a full view of her rather nice backside. Since she'd stopped using drugs and started eating regularly again, Ms. Hernandez had developed quite the derriere. I tried to purge the image from my mind, but it only served to dredge up memories of the days when Marlene and I were a couple, in those early years, when I lost my virginity and her body became my playground. She was my first love, and those early sexual experiences are something a man can never forget.

For a preacher, this is a hard thing to confess, but I'd been lying in bed, aroused, ever since Marlene dropped the towel.

I said a quick prayer to ask God's forgiveness for my lustful thoughts, over which I seemed to have no control. Mercifully, I drifted off to sleep not long after I said, "Amen."

I soon felt something rubbing against my leg. *What the—?* I turned over, and the sight of Marlene lying there made me bolt upright, immediately wide awake. Marlene lay on her side, facing the wall, giving me the same view of her naked behind that I'd seen earlier.

"Thomas Kelly?" she murmured in a sleepy voice as she turned over to face me, a smile glazing her lips.

"Marlene? What are you doing in my bed?"

"Shhh." She placed an index finger against my lips, and in one smooth motion, she grabbed me by the shoulders and pulled me on top of her. Even if I had words to speak, she didn't give them a chance to come out of my mouth as her lips connected with mine.

"Mmm," Marlene moaned, reaching her hand down between us. I knew this was wrong, but my body was responding just the way she wanted. She took hold of my solid manhood and placed it inside of her.

"Marlene . . ." I heard a moan escape from my throat. "We can't do this."

"Don't stop, Thomas Kelly. Please don't stop," Marlene pleaded, though I didn't need much convincing. I thrust my hips and she returned the motion. "Ohhhh, this feels so good. Thomas Kelly, you've taken the drugs away. Now I need you to be my drug."

Once again, her tongue entered my mouth and we shared a wonderful, passionate kiss. I lifted my head to gaze into her eyes while we made love, but the vision before me was so startling that I felt my body freeze in midthrust.

"Huh? Monique?" I squeezed my eyes shut as if that could erase the vision, but when I opened them slowly, it was still Monique smiling up at me.

"Yes, T.K., it's me." Monique stroked her hands down my back. I reached out to touch her. "Who'd you think it was, Lisa Mae?"

"No, I thought it was—"

She pulled my head toward her. When I felt her soft lips against mine, it sent a spark of recognition to my midsection and I was instantly hard again. There was no way I could forget the fervent kisses Monique and I had shared the first time we made love and no way my body could not respond.

"I love you, T.K.," she said, her voice cracking with emotion. "It feels so good that I could cry." She pushed me gently off of her, then rolled on top.

I enjoyed the view of her hair, loose and flowing, brushing against my chest as she lowered her head and rode me passionately. After a long, deep stroke, she threw her head back and sat up, still straddling my hips.

This can't be happening, I told myself as I stared in disbelief at the woman before me. "Lisa Mae?"

"Yes, T.K.," she said, slowly gyrating her hips. "That's it. Now say my name."

Before I knew it, my hands were entwined in her beautiful curls. "You're wearing your hair down," I said in awe. I had never seen Lisa Mae looking so relaxed. She flung her head back down and allowed her strands to tickle my face and shoulders, then in a sensual rhythm, she lifted her head again.

"Savannah!" I shouted as I watched her rocking on top of me. "Savannah!" I called out once again, pushing her off me. "I can't do this with you."

The room started spinning and everything became a blur. I rubbed my eyes, and when I opened them to try to focus, that's when I saw all four of them: Savannah, Monique, Lisa Mae, and Marlene. They were sitting on my bed, each wearing a wedding dress and staring at me with pleading eyes.

I looked to Savannah first.

"Bishop," Savannah spoke, "you've been my mentor. You've believed in me even when I didn't. I love you, Bishop. Can't you see that?"

"But T.K.," Monique said as I turned to her. "You've shown me for the first time in my life what real love is. You accepted me just for me, for what I was and for what I wasn't. I love you, T.K. I love you."

Next it was Lisa Mae whose lips parted to speak. "You are the most perfect bishop. I appreciate that about you more than anybody. And with my appreciation comes an understanding and desire to serve God alongside you. T.K., I've shown you that I am the perfect first lady. Together we make the perfect team. Will you marry me?"

Knowing Marlene would have something to say next, I allowed my eyes to rest on her. "T.K.," she said, "we share a child. We share a grandchild. We have a history. You've accepted me into your present life. It's only natural that we should share our futures."

"What are you all doing here? Why are you here?"

"You know why we're here, Bishop," Savannah stated.

"Yes, T.K.," Monique said. "You know why."

They all sat quietly, a desperate desire heavy in the air. I felt as though a clock were ticking and a bomb was designated to go off any minute now.

"No," I said to them. "I can't do this." I turned toward the door, wanting to run away, but my muscles wouldn't move. As I sat helplessly immobile, the door opened.

"T.K., you can't run from this," Charlene said when she appeared in the doorway. "You know what you have to do, T.K."

"Honey?" I looked at the vision of my dead wife, feeling like some sort of Ebenezer Scrooge surrounded by ghostly apparitions. "Is that you? Are you really there?"

"Yes, T.K., it's me, and I'm here to tell you that you have to make your choice. You have to make your choice now. These four women need to go on with their lives, one of them spending the rest of her life with you. T.K., one of those four is the woman you should be with."

"But, Charlene, I love them all," I told her. "Each one has something that makes her special, and it's that something special that makes me love each of them."

"You have a big heart, T.K. That's what I loved about you so much. You can find something to love about everybody."

"That's what makes this so hard," I said. "I don't want to hurt anyone. I'm afraid of making the wrong choice."

"You're not afraid of making the wrong choice; you're afraid of making *any* choice. Remember, T.K., I was your wife for a long time. I know your heart. You're having a hard time choosing someone because you're afraid to let go of me. But I know Alison gave you my last letter, and you've read it. You know how I feel. I love you with all my heart, and I have faith that we will be together again someday, but now, First Jamaica Ministries needs a new first lady, and you need someone to take care of you. It's time for you to move on with your life. Choose one of these women to be your wife."

Charlene came closer to me and held out her closed fist. Instinctively, I knew she was coming to give me something, so I put out my hand to receive it. Her fingers uncurled, and I saw in her palm the wedding ring I had given her so many years before. She dropped the ring into my hand and said, "It's time to make a choice." Then she bent down, and our lips met in one last kiss that was so familiar and comforting.

The next thing I knew, I was sitting up in my bed in a cold sweat, my heart racing uncontrollably. My eyes quickly darted around the room, half expecting to see the women still sitting there. The dream had seemed so real.

The bed was soaked with sweat. I threw the covers off me, then turned and placed my feet on the ground. I looked up at the clock, which read 1:00 A.M. It had only been two short hours since I fell asleep, but it felt as if I had relived my whole lifetime with Charlene. My love for her was stronger than ever, but I felt a peace come over me as I realized I should move on, and even more importantly, that I could move on.

With a shaking hand, I picked up the phone on the nightstand and dialed James's phone number.

"Hello," he answered groggily.

"James," I said without apologizing for the lateness of the call. "I think I've made my decision."

"Decision about what?" he asked.

"The decision about who I'm going to spend the rest of my life with. I know the woman I want to marry. I want you to meet me tomorrow morning to go shopping for a ring. I know who's going to be the next first lady."

37

THE PROPOSAL

The monthly membership meeting was more crowded than usual. Bishop T.K. Wilson made sure of that when he personally called every prominent member of First Jamaica Ministries to make sure they'd be in attendance. They, in turn, called their closest friends to urge them to be there as well. This type of fanfare before a meeting was rare, and speculation ran rampant throughout the congregation about what the bishop had planned. Among those Bishop Wilson had personally requested to be at the meeting were Marlene, Monique, Savannah, and Lisa Mae, all of whom now sat anxiously, awaiting the bishop's arrival.

Each woman sat whispering to her loved ones—well, all of them except Monique. She didn't have friends or family who attended First Jamaica Ministries. Sure, she had been receiving a warmer welcome at Sunday services now that she was dressing more conservatively and trying harder to blend in with the crowd, but she hadn't yet made the leap to any true friendship. So, she sat in the front row, flipping through a pocket calendar, trying to distract herself from her loneliness. She wondered what was so important that the bishop had phoned her to ensure she didn't miss this meeting.

Perhaps he wants to announce to the members the upcoming grand opening of my new Christian bookstore, she thought hopefully. *That would be so like T.K. to want the congregation to support me.* They had been speaking quite frequently ever since their reunion at lunch, and T.K. was one hundred percent behind her decision to open the store. Monique was eager to get the business up and running so she could spend even more time with the bishop.

Deacon Joe Dickens rambled in Savannah's ear about his speculations. Of course, he hoped that whatever the bishop had in store would mean good things for the deacon's own standing in the church, perhaps the powerful alliance he had wanted from the beginning. He talked to Savannah about how happy he was that she seemed to be visiting the bishop's office pretty regularly now, but Savannah just sat quietly. She wondered how her father would react if he knew that the bishop had never once made any romantic overtures toward her, even after all this time. Would he see it as a failure on her part? Probably, she decided, for that always seemed to be the case when things didn't go the way he wanted. But Savannah had grown stronger in recent months and knew she could weather her father's disappointment if the bishop announced something Deacon Dickens didn't like.

Aubrey, who had returned from his sister's house in D.C. and spent a couple of nights with Marlene at the bishop's house, had his arm around his mother. She was thrilled to have him with her at the meeting because she was sure the bishop was about to publicly recognize her great strides toward recovery. She had come so far that she was ready for the next phase; she would be moving into her own place again soon.

Lisa Mae and Loretta also felt certain they knew what the bishop was ready to announce to this large crowd. This was it—the big day when Bishop would finally propose. With Loretta's help, Lisa Mae had successfully weathered the latest storm and controlled her anger over his recently repaired friendship with Sister Monique. Oh, she had her suspicions about why the friendship had ceased for a while, and she knew she would have to keep an eye on Sister Monique now that she was buzzing around again, but Loretta convinced her that it was best to be patient. The bishop was close to a proposal, they felt, and once she became first lady, Lisa Mae could do whatever she had to do to get rid of Sister Monique.

Loretta was relieved that Lisa Mae would soon be wearing an engagement ring. She was getting tired of being her friend's conscience whenever her temper threatened to get the best of her. In the meantime, Lisa Mae believed she well deserved the upcoming proposal. Not only had she been the model girlfriend, but she had also repeatedly exemplified the makings of the first lady that the church members were hoping for. This would be a day of celebration for everyone, Lisa Mae thought. Then she caught sight of the women who had been her competition.

Well, maybe not everyone will be celebrating, but I sure will.

Bishop Wilson walked in, and the room hushed in an instant. He stood on the platform in front of the microphone and looked out over the crowd. The place was standing room only, just as he had hoped. Still, the fact that all eyes were on him as he prepared to make this monumental announcement made him even more nervous than he'd been. He gathered his thoughts, steadying his hands on the podium to stop their trembling, then cleared his throat and broke the silence.

"I'm glad everybody came out this evening," he said. "It seems all those whom I stressed to be in attendance have made it, and this is good. I have a lot of important things to say—personal things, in fact. And I want to share them with you all."

Bishop waited a few moments as he listened to the murmuring that passed over the crowd. No doubt, the members in the audience were again discussing their speculation, even more energized now that he had admitted his announcement was of a personal nature. He looked around the room, then set eyes on Savannah. A big grin appeared on Deacon Dickens's face, but Savannah avoided the bishop's gaze, staring straight ahead, afraid to even wonder what might be about to happen.

Bishop Wilson began. "First, brothers and sisters, I'd like to take this opportunity to bring something to your attention. We've got a star among us." He directed his smile at Savannah and said, "Sister Dickens, please stand up." She was embarrassed by the attention and was confused, but did as the bishop asked.

"How many of you knew Sister Dickens dreamed of becoming a gospel recording star?" The room was silent. People looked around at one another, raising eyebrows and shrugging shoulders. Savannah imagined that her father, sitting beside her, would be rolling his eyes right about now. "I feel we, as brothers and sisters in Christ, need to care more about one another. Fellowship. That's what I'm trying to say. It only takes a few minutes after Sunday service or Bible study to shake a few hands and find out what's going on in some of our members' lives."

He reached into his jacket pocket and pulled out a CD. Savannah's eyes grew big. "What I hold in my hand is an outstanding gospel CD, recorded by none other than our very own Sister Savannah Dickens." Oohs and ahs filled the room, and a few members began to clap.

"Hold on now," Bishop said, holding up his hand. "I think you should applaud, but before you do, let me add that I feel we should acknowledge her wonderful father, Deacon Joe Dickens. He's done a fine job with Savannah, and I imagine it would've been difficult for her to live out her dream without him around. Deacon, you should be proud. Not many of our children dare to dream, but Savannah did. And not only did she dream, but she also set out for achievement. And here is the end result. Move over, Yolanda Adams, because Savannah Dickens is about to give you some serious competition when her CD is released under the United Gospel Recording label." Bishop shook the CD in the air. "Deacon, stand proudly next to your daughter so we can all give you a hand."

The room burst with enthusiastic applause. Deacon Joe stood and hugged Savannah tightly as the members jumped to their feet, and the applause reached a crescendo. Deacon had a new sense of pride as he sat down next to his daughter. Several members reached from behind him to pat him on the back. This was truly a time for him to sit up straight and square his shoulders. Savannah held on to her father's arm, then gave the bishop a wink. Bishop smiled back at the woman whom he had come to love with a fatherly affection.

When the crowd settled down, Bishop continued. "Next, I'd like to address my best friend of over thirty years—Marlene Hernandez." Bishop looked directly at Marlene as he spoke. She sat tall and proud in her chair, her son's hand clasped lovingly in hers. "I don't think I know a stronger woman. Talk about trials and tribulations . . . mmm, mmm, mmm. Sister Hernandez has had many. She endured them all, shaping herself into the highly favored woman she is today."

He shifted his gaze to look out at the crowd. "Brothers and sisters, if you don't know that God has a plan when it comes to your life, I think you better ask Sister Hernandez, because I believe she knows it better than any of us. Some of us can't relate to the pain and the struggle Sister Hernandez has gone through. But for those who can, God has fixed it so she can be an instrument to guide them back on the right path." A few amens were thrown around as Bishop continued to speak.

He turned his attention back to Marlene. "Sister Hernandez, I love you . . . and you know I love you. In fact, you know now that God loves you." Marlene nodded and stroked Aubrey's arm as she listened. "Thank you for your request to start and head a drug intervention program here at First Jamaica Ministries. When I took the idea to the board of trustees, the decision was unanimous to go forth with it. We can't think of a better person than you. God bless you." Everyone applauded while Marlene shed a few tears of joy.

The crowd settled quickly. The bishop had already treated them to such uplifting news, but they all knew he had yet to get to the personal things he had promised to address. And his words assured them there was more to come.

"Just so you know, I'm not done yet."

"Take your time, Bishop," a woman yelled out.

"Thank you, Sister Boyd. Next, I want to address a woman who's meant so much to me over these last months since my wife passed away. She's been everything to me—an assistant, a sister, and a friend. I just don't think there's a more valuable woman to this church than Sister Lisa Mae Jones." Loretta patted Lisa Mae on the back. Lisa Mae flashed a Miss America smile to the crowd, who turned to look at her.

"Sister Jones, will you step up here with me for a moment?"

Though she had been anticipating his proposal for some time now, Lisa Mae was still nervous about the sudden spotlight. She approached the bishop on shaky legs. He took her hand and helped her onto the platform. Lisa looked over the crowd and sought out Loretta, her biggest supporter. When their eyes met, she relaxed, feeling a sense of accomplishment for having made it to this point with the bishop. She felt like a winner.

"Sister Jones, you are extremely wise. And not only that, you're a faithful servant of the Lord too. After careful consideration with the board, we all agree you should be the first female member of the board of trustees." The audience roared with applause, and Loretta led the crowd in a standing ovation.

Lisa Mae stood shocked. She was surprised at the announcement, practically taken off her feet. There had never been a female member of the board of trustees, so this was indeed quite an honor.

Lisa Mae heard the cheers and clapping, and knew she was clearly loved by the members of the church. She was extremely proud of this recognition and appreciated the warm feelings and well wishes. But, she suddenly realized as the shock subsided, this was not the recognition she expected to be receiving at this moment.

She turned to the bishop, who held his hands high as he clapped, and she waited for him to say something else. Perhaps he would pull a ring out of his pocket just as he had done with Savannah's CD. That would be the greatest proposal, she thought, offering her the position of trustee first, then asking her to take the highest position of all—first lady of First Jamaica Ministries.

The bishop took Lisa Mae's hand and gestured for the crowd to settle down. Her heart skipped a beat as she anticipated his next move. But then, when instead of asking her to marry him, he simply asked, "Would you like to say something, Trustee?" her heart felt as if it might stop beating.

Lisa Mae was at a loss for words. In fact, that's exactly what she managed to say to the onlookers: "Wow! I'm at a loss for words." She wished she could have Loretta by her side to advise her now, as Loretta had done so faithfully for the last six months. As she looked at her friend in the audience, she could almost hear Loretta telling her, "It's okay, Lisa Mae. Just take this honor gracefully. When the time is right, he will ask you, and until then, you just put on that perfect face like only the future first lady can do."

And Lisa Mae did just that. She smiled graciously at the bishop, then addressed the audience, her voice concealing any trace of disappointment she was feeling. "This honor is something I certainly didn't see coming; however, I gladly accept it. To the board and to the rest of the congregation, you can count on me. I won't let you down. Thank you."

Lisa stepped down off the platform as the applause started again. Back in her seat, Loretta squeezed her hand and nodded proudly. "Who knows?" Loretta whispered. "Maybe he isn't finished yet."

Lisa Mae perked up. "Yeah, you're right," she replied. Loretta could always restore her hope. "Besides, I'm now a trustee. He thinks a lot more of me than I really knew."

"The next announcement," Bishop said, "has to do with my deceased wife, Charlene." Everyone became silent immediately. With the mention of the former first lady, they suspected he had arrived at the portion of the meeting when he would address the matters of a personal nature. "As some of you know, a series of letters have been circulating over the last months." Several people nodded, confirming what the bishop had always suspected: nothing traveled faster than church gossip.

Upon mention of the letters, Savannah stole a glance at her father. Loretta and Lisa Mae looked at each other wide-eyed. Marlene and Monique just continued to stare at the bishop, awaiting his next statements.

"Well, I want you to know I recently discovered who was responsible for assisting Charlene with those letters, but that's not important right now." The grumbling among some of the more ardent gossipers made it clear that they did think the person's identity was important. The bishop, however, was not going to satisfy their curiosity. And they were so busy mumbling to each other that they failed to notice Sister Alison suddenly looking slightly uncomfortable.

"I've been able to confirm that not only was the stationery Charlene's, but every one of those letters contained words from her heart. To those who received letters, I thank you for understanding. I know that sometimes what you read could not have been easy for you. I want you to know that no matter what you read, I hold each of you dear in my heart.

"Now I come to the most important reason for bringing you all here today." He held up a sheet of stationery. "I have one last letter here, and I ask for your patience as I share a portion of it with you."

A buzz of excitement passed through the crowd. There had been no need for the bishop to ask for their patience, because they were all quite eager to hear what the first lady had set down on paper before her death.

Bishop cleared his throat. "Now, I won't read the whole letter, because some words should stay between a husband and wife. I will read the end to you. I felt it was important for you to know the final words I read, which helped me reach the decision I came here to share with you all."

He held up the paper and spoke into the microphone, reading the letter's final paragraph aloud. "'And so, T.K., I know you are probably surprised by my change of heart. I was surprised myself when I came to this conclusion. But when it comes right down to it, this woman has the fire in her belly to handle anything that might come her way as first lady of First Jamaica Ministries. And even more importantly, I believe she would love you with the total devotion that you deserve. You might encounter some resistance from certain factions within the church, but you and I both know you've withstood your share of trials in the past, and with her by your side, you two could get through this one too. So, with my love and blessings, go with your heart.'"

Not a sound was heard in the room as the bishop concluded the letter.

"I'm sure you're all wondering," he said, "who this woman is my wife was referring to."

A few people were bold enough to nod in agreement, while others sat back, pretending they hadn't been gossiping for months about the bishop's love life. Lisa Mae, of course, was not wondering, because she was so certain that the person Charlene wrote about was her. She shuffled her feet nervously, waiting for the moment she knew was coming, when T.K. would call her to the front of the room and propose to her.

"Brothers and sisters, I want you to know that my wife is right: I am in love. The woman I'm in love with loves me, but she loves the Lord more. She's been a faithful member of this congregation—in fact, I don't know of a time when she's missed a church function."

Loretta patted Lisa Mae on the back. She smiled, showing all of her pearly whites.

"Sister Monique Johnson, I'd like for you to come up here," Bishop requested. The audience, including Monique, erupted in one collective gasp. Monique looked around the room, then raised her eyebrows and pointed to her chest. "Yes, you," he confirmed.

Bishop reached for Monique's hand as she stepped tentatively onto the platform. She wondered if the audience could see her heart pounding through the fabric of her dress. She was glad she had chosen another conservative outfit to wear this night, especially when the bishop said, "A lot of you folks have had negative things to say about the way Sister Johnson dresses. But none of you ever tried to see past her attire." He gazed into Monique's eyes. In the audience, Lisa Mae felt like she was about to faint. " 'Cause if only you had looked further than her clothes, you'd know Monique is a good woman, a God-fearing woman who wants to be loved and respected and who also has First Jamaica Ministries at heart.

"The rumors about the way Sister Johnson carries herself have got to stop. Truth be told, my beloved Charlene started many of those rumors. But I'm sure if she could speak to you all today, she'd take those unkind words back. I know this to be true, because the woman Charlene was referring to in that letter was Sister Monique Johnson. Charlene's told me to follow my heart, and that's what I intend to do. Some of you may want me to leave First Jamaica Ministries after this, but for the record, I ain't going nowhere."

Bishop reached into his jacket pocket for the second time that night and pulled out a small box. He kneeled on one knee in front of Monique and opened the box, flashing a two-and-a-half-carat princess-cut-diamond ring. Monique's tears began to flow fast and steadily, but they were tears of joy. Lisa Mae's eyes were also wet, but for another reason entirely. She sat on the edge of her seat with her eyes and mouth open, frozen solid—"stunned" would be an understatement.

"Monique Johnson, it took me a while to come around, but at least I did. Better than not coming around at all, right?" He smiled. "I realize now that I was letting Man decide how I should live my life instead of letting God do His business of further wedging you into my heart. And Lord knows best, 'cause I've learned that in my heart is exactly where you belong. All I wanna know is will you allow me to love you always and forever? Will you become my wife?"

Monique was so excited, she couldn't even speak for a second. She had to blurt her response in order to get it out. "Yes! I will," she cried.

Lisa Mae tried to stand up and protest, but her knees turned to jelly as she watched the scene unfolding before her. She turned to Loretta, then looked back at Bishop embracing Monique. Loretta hardly had time to catch Lisa Mae as she fainted.

Bishop placed the ring on Monique's finger, then pulled her into a tight embrace. Again, the members of the church jumped to their feet and roared with cheers and applause. Even those people who had judged Monique most harshly through the years were moved by the depth of love that the bishop displayed for this woman. God works in mysterious ways. They had all heard the saying before, and this night they were witness to the truth in those words.

Epilogue: Alison and the First Lady

From the graveyard, I could hear the church bells ringing, signifying that the bishop had just been married; now Monique Johnson was the new first lady of First Jamaica Ministries. The flowers I'd left last time I visited Charlene's grave were wilted, and I made a mental note to bring some new ones back in a couple of days. I removed the flowers, then knelt down, placing a lavender box at the foot of the headstone. I began to pull up the few weeds that had sprouted, and when the gravesite was weed-free, I stood up and read the inscription written on my best friend's headstone:

HERE LIES CHARLENE WILSON, WIFE, MOTHER, AND FIRST LADY OF FIRST JAMAICA MINISTRIES. EVEN IN DEATH HER PRESENCE WILL ALWAYS BE FELT.
1962–2006.

As always, when I read the inscription, a few tears sprang to my eyes. I took out a handkerchief, wiped the tears away, then began to clean off Charlene's headstone. It really wasn't that dirty, but I needed something to keep me busy as I tried my best to avoid the conversation I knew was inevitable.

Eventually, I just said, "Charlene, they're married now. The bishop and Monique are married now, so it's over. You can let go. You can rest in peace, girl."

A strong wind blew by, giving me a chill. I believed it to be a sign from my friend, and she was not happy. Not happy at all.

"I know you're mad at me." Tears began anew. "I know you're mad at me, and I'm sorry. But I just couldn't do it. I just couldn't give him that letter suggesting that he marry Lisa Mae."

I glanced down at the lavender box. There were still more than fifty undelivered letters in it, each one written to encourage or discourage Bishop Wilson's suitors. For the last six months, I'd been handing out those damn letters, following and spying on people to be sure that the correct letter was left so that we would get the final result Charlene had desired. And it was working too. We plotted and planned, and even when things looked like they weren't going our way, we had another letter that I would deliver to set things right.

But after I left the bishop's office the day he busted me, I did some serious thinking about everything that had happened since I started handing out letters. While I was observing the "competition," I did feel twinges of guilt from time to time, but I managed to put them out of my mind and continued to deliver letters in order to stay loyal to Charlene's dying wishes. Then, when Bishop suggested we were playing God, I realized he was right. These were human beings we were playing with. Every letter we wrote, we tried to predict how it would affect the bishop's love life, but we failed to even think about how it would affect the emotions of all people involved.

We never stopped to think that Marlene, already fragile from years of drug abuse, might be pushed over the edge if she started to feel pressured. Lisa Mae, who was once an outgoing and likable person, now seemed always stressed, like it was impossible for her to relax once she started to feel the competition. It seemed she was paranoid of everyone except Loretta. And Monique . . . I knew Charlene never liked her, and I never cared much for her, either, but sitting with her as she suffered through her guilt in that abortion clinic, I realized she was a human being with feelings, and I couldn't help but think that we'd been unfair to her. Maybe she wasn't the right woman to be first lady of the church, but that wasn't my decision and didn't mean she deserved the cruel letters I delivered to her.

The only person who seemed to derive any benefit from our letter-writing campaign was Savannah. At least her interactions with the bishop had caused her to loosen the chains her father had her in. She was getting out more often, and even her singing voice in the choir on Sundays sounded more brilliant than ever. But still, I wondered, was it right to even suggest to her that she should compete for the bishop's affection? The more I watched her, the more I realized that Savannah had a lot of growing up to do. She needed to branch out on her own, spread her wings outside of her father's house before she allowed herself to become involved with a man. And I think the bishop realized this, too, because any time I'd seen him speaking with her, he behaved more like a mentor, or even a father figure, than someone with romantic interests. Savannah should never have been included in our list of potential candidates. Charlene and I had been way off base with this one.

In fact, now that I saw the human side of what we had done, I realized that we might have been way off base with all of it from the start. I know she loved her husband dearly, but maybe Charlene should have just let him make his own decisions. After all, he was a kind and thoughtful man. He would never do anything to intentionally hurt his church or any member. I couldn't really say the same thing about me or my best friend.

In the end, I could tell that just because it was right for us, it didn't mean it was right for Bishop Wilson. So, just when he seemed to be ready to ask Lisa Mae to marry him, when I was supposed to give him the final letter Charlene wrote, suggesting how happy she would be to have Lisa Mae as the next first lady, I wrote a new letter and gave it to him. That was the letter he read to the congregation. He didn't know that Charlene had nothing to do with that particular letter, but it was the one that helped Monique Johnson become the first lady.

I kicked the box, and the letters began to flop away in the wind, bouncing off tombstones and grass with the heavy wind. "This was wrong, Charlene. We shouldn't have ever done this. No, you should have never done this, and I shouldn't have ever allowed it. It wasn't your choice to decide who the bishop was going to marry. It was his choice, and I'm starting to think he made a damn good choice."

A READING GROUP GUIDE

THE FIRST LADY

CARL WEBER

ABOUT THIS GUIDE

The following questions are designed to facilitate discussion in and among reader groups.

DISCUSSION QUESTIONS

1. Who did you think was going to marry the bishop when the book started?
2. Would you marry the bishop or a man like him?
3. What did you think of Lisa Mae?
4. Did you think he would sleep with anyone else?
5. What did you think of Alison? And would you have done what she did for the First Lady?
6. Did you feel sorry for Marlene?
7. Who was your favorite character in the book?
8. Were you turned off when the bishop slept with Monique?
9. Would you want to choose your spouse's next relationship if you were terminally ill?
10. Did the bishop make the right choice?

Turn the page for a preview of Carl Weber's next book,
SOMETHING ON THE SIDE!

1

Kim

I could feel myself getting excited when my twin sister Karen's car turned down my block. I was excited because I'd spotted a light on in my apartment and my boyfriend Tony's SUV parked on the corner. With any luck he was in my bed naked waiting for me. Trust me, I needed him to be there after discussing Mary B. Morrison's new book with my book club. Lord, talk about a sexually charged conversation. I don't think one of us walked out of that meeting without the need of a panty liner and some good old-fashioned male companionship, if you know what I mean. I swear I don't think I've ever been so horny in my entire life. Even Mrs. Turner, the seventy-year-old mother of my sister's best friend Tammy, who hosted the meeting, said she was going home to wake her husband up.

"Well, at least one of us is going to get some," Karen mumbled jealously as she pulled up behind Tony's truck to let me out. I felt sorry for my sister but it wasn't my fault she didn't have a man. Karen's standards were so damn high she wanted someone with Russell Simmons's money and Terrance Howard's looks. The fact that she couldn't find him made her bitter.

"Why don't you call Greg? I'm sure he'd be willing to stop by for a booty call."

Karen raised her finger as if to chastise me, then hesitated for a second, giving it some thought. She shook her head. "Nah, if I give Greg some I'll never be able to get rid of him. The boy's got some good *dick*, but he can't keep a job."

I shrugged my shoulders, then leaned over to kiss her. "You mean he can't keep a six-figure job."

She changed the subject 'cause she knew where I was going. "Hey, Kim, speaking of dick, you'll never guess what Tammy asked me." She was right, I would never guess. Tammy was always up to something.

"Girl, I ain't got no time to be guessing nothing. My man is upstairs, and I need to get to him before he falls asleep."

"My God, will you calm down a second. You act like that man's dick is made of gold. Damn, it's only gonna take a second."

"Whatever." I stepped out of the car, then leaned my head into the window.

"Well, you know Tammy always gives Rashad a birthday party every year, right?"

"Uh-huh."

"Well, she's not having a party this year. Guess what she wants to do this year."

"C'mon, Karen, get to the point. I told you I ain't got a whole bunch of time."

"Okay . . . okay . . . She decided to give him something a little more special; she' taking him to hedonism, in Jamaica."

"Hedonism, isn't that the place where everyone walks around nude?"

"Mmm-hmm. And check this out sis: she wants me to go with them.

"What?" I raised an eyebrow. "Go with them for what?"

She wants to give Rashad a threesome for his birthday. And she asked me to be the third person. Can you believe that shit? Now is that the ultimate birthday present or what?"

"Stop lying, Karen. That woman does not want you to fuck her husband."

"I'm not, girl. She even gave me the brochure, look." She reached in her bag and pulled out a pamphlet that looked like a page out of a porn magazine. "For real, Karen, she wants me to go with her and her husband to the hedonism so the three of us can get our groove on."

I stared at my sisters in silence for a few seconds. "Please tell me you told that woman no."

Her face became very serious. "Do I look like a fool? That's my best friend, and the best way to lose your best friend is to sleep with her man, even if she's going to be in the room. I'm just shocked that she would even ask me some shit like that. I can't even imagine sharing my man like that."

"I know, that's right. Just the thought of Tony being with another woman makes my stomach turn. Speaking of Tony, I've gotta get upstairs, girl." I blew my sister a kiss, then waved as I made my way to my front door. When I got into the apartment Tony was sitting on the living room sofa fully dressed with a beer in his hand. From the empty bottles on the coffee table I was sure it wasn't his first. I didn't mind, though, because when Tony drank, Tony was aggressive in bed, and that was exactly what I needed.

"Hey, daddy," I purred affectionately as I walked over and sat in his lap. We kissed and I could taste the beer on his tongue as he held me tightly. "Daddy, momma's been thinkin' about you all day."

"I've been thinking about you, too, boo. We really need to talk."

I kissed him. "Well, we can talk later. Right now, I need you, baby. I need you inside of me." I reached down and caressed the part of him I needed most. He grinned showing me the slight gap in his teeth, which, in some strange way, I found very sexy.

"You just can't get enough of me, can you?"

"No, baby. I sure can't. Now give me what I need, daddy."

Tony stood up, lifting me in the air as I held on to his strong broad shoulders. As he started to walk toward the bedroom, I could feel myself getting even more moist. The thought of him laying on top of me, pounding me or riding it from the back, was all I could think about on the way home.

I'd met Tony about two years ago at the Q Club. We'd taken it slow at first to get to know each other. As a matter of fact, we'd taken almost six months before we even had sex. But, once we'd committed the act, it had been on. It seemed like every time we saw each other we'd have sex. And, I'd done things with Tony that I never even dreamed about doing with other men. Matter of fact, I expected an engagement ring toward the end of the month, perhaps around my birthday. God, I couldn't wait to marry that man.

Tony had wanted to have at least three kids. And, although I was thirty-two, I planned on giving him exactly what he wanted. I loved that man's dirty drawers, and that was nothing that would make me leave my man. Sometimes, I sit back and think about how my friends and sister would talk about how men don't wanna help out and don't wanna work, and the ones that did wanna work were never around to romance you. But, my Tony was like a magician. Not only did he work one job, but he had two. And, although he didn't live with me, he still helped me pay half the rent. And when it came to romance, what he couldn't do as far as quantity of time, he sure made up for it in quality, because my beau romanced me every chance he got—flowers, candy, shopping, candlelit dinners, and every six months we took a trip to a different island. Yeah, I had the perfect man, and in the next five minutes, the perfect man was about to give me some of that perfect dick.

Tony kicked the unlocked door to my bedroom open, then lay me down on the bed, slowly unbuttoning his shirt. I looked up at him. He was a good six feet four inches tall with an extremely athletic build. His golden-brown complexion was framed by solid, chiseled features, and a clean-shaven face. "Rough, Tony. Rough. I want it hard and rough. I don't want that gentle shit tonight. I want my Mandingo warrior."

"Is that what you want?" He grinned holding his manhood like it was a sausage. "You want it rough, huh? Well, get your shit off. 'Cause I'm about to break your back and two of your ribs."

"You can try." I teased as I hurried to get out of my clothes off.